Winner of Grand Prize at the London Book Festival, 2013

Honorable mention at the New England Book Festival, 2013

"*Beyond is written with panache from start to finish, and is almost certain to engage all manner of readers...*

...The recent availability of well-documented, clearly writeen histories and biographies has prepared the way for a finer grade of fiction...

...This is a volume to simply enjoy...

...Beyond takes us to a Popham that may well have existed, a fort and land peopled with Indian town on the brink of tumuluous changes. It is beautifully handled."

—Willim David Barry, *Portland Press Herald*

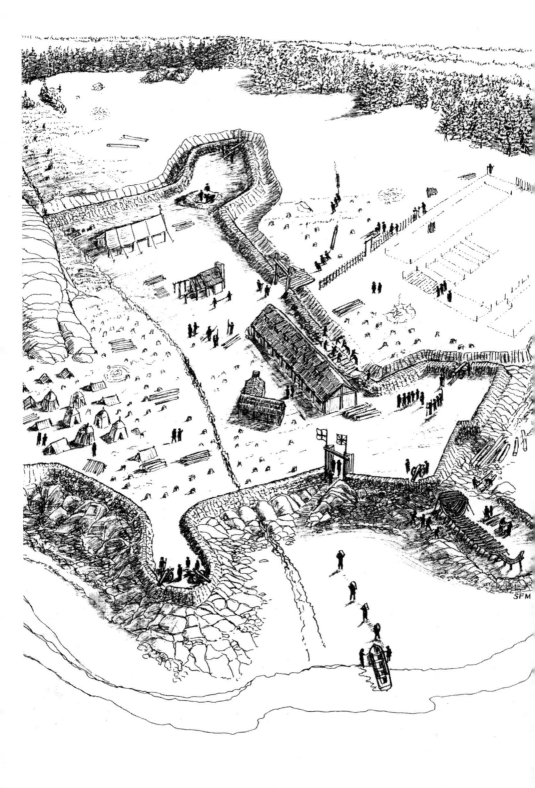

BEYOND

Popham Colony: The first English settlement in New England

∽ a novel ∽

R. deVillers Seymour

BEYOND
Popham Colony: The first English settlement in New England

Copyright © 2013 by R. deVillers Seymour

ISBN: 978-1-938883-51-4

CREDITS:
Cover Photo of Popham Beach   Courtesy Sandra Skibinski
Frontispiece   Courtesy Sam Manning and *Maine's First Ship*
(p. vi) *Sir John Popham*   Courtesy Liz Elwell
(p. 452) *The ship* Virginia   Courtesy of Ken Hendricksen
(p. 455) *Draught of Georges Fort*   Courtesy Jeffry Brain and *Maine's First Ship*

Designed and Produced by
Maine Authors Publishing
558 Main Street, Rockland, Maine 04841
www.maineauthorspublishing.com

Printed in the United States of America

To Ro.

Sir John Popham

ACKNOWLEDGEMENTS

In the notes section, I mention more than once Douglas Rice, author of *The Life and Achievements of Sir John Popham, 1531–1607* as well as Bruce Bourque, author of *Twelve Thousand Years: American Indians in Maine*. Both offered me information and enthusiasm.

I'd also like to thank Bud Warren and John Bradford, two men who know as much about the Popham Colony as anybody. They, too, gave me reading matter and names of people to contact.

My friend, Linda Letendre, my wife, Rosie Armstrong, and my brother, Jim Seymour, a professor of dramatic literature, all read an early draft. They were able to overlook the messiness and give me the impetus to continue.

Finally I'd like to thank Maine Authors Publishing and specifically my editor Jennifer Caven.

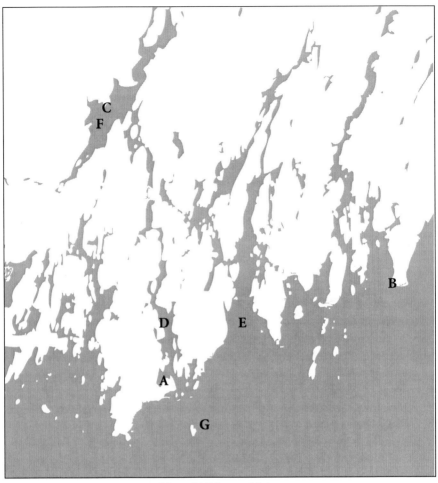

Map of Midcoast Maine

KEY

A Fort St. George

B Village of Skidwarres and Nahanada

C Sabenoa's village

D Sagadahoc River (now Kennebec)

E Aponeg River (now Sheepscot)

F Quabacook Bay (now Merrymeeting Bay)

G Seguin Island

What is truth that is bounded by these mountains,
and is falsehood to the world that lives beyond?

—Michel de Montaigne 1533–1592

INTRODUCTION

Get out of the car. Beyond the vacant parking lot, two lectern-like historical markers stick out of the lawn that slopes to shallow Atkins Bay, Maine. You can't help but stare at the majestic Kennebec River. Behind you lie Popham Beach and the Atlantic.

You're standing on the site of the first English colony in New England. In 1607, thirteen years before the Mayflower, the Virginia Company established both Jamestown to the south and Fort St. George to the north. You are standing squarely in the middle of Fort St. George. One of the markers provides a rendering of the fort. It has a medieval look: a dry moat, earth and rock walls, and nine cannon, much more substantial than Jamestown's wooden-walled fort. You can count over sixteen structures: a chapel, a seventy-foot-long storehouse, a kitchen, a munitions building, the admiral's quarters, and houses for a hundred and twenty men: soldiers, sailors, artisans, trappers, fishermen, and gentlemen.

Jamestown, Virginia is a multi-million-dollar tourist attraction. Fort St. George offers an empty parking lot, two historical markers, and a bronze plaque on a boulder. Touch the relief of a fifty-foot sailing craft, the pinnace, Virginia. She's the first ship built in the English New World, there, just a few feet away on the rock and mud shore.

Fort St. George survived for fourteen months. After the first two, no firsthand records exist. Even its exact location couldn't be confirmed until 1994, when archaeologists found the charred remains of the storehouse's wooden underpinnings, as well as numerous artifacts now displayed at the Maine State Museum.

Fort St. George vanished. A colonist, Robert Davies, kept a journal. But he left two months after he arrived. We know of Sir John Popham, the initiator and energy behind the project, but he remained in England. Sir Ferdinando Gorges dedicated himself to colonizing Northern Virginia (now Maine) but wrote little about Fort St. George. Presumably, other written evidence was lost, destroyed, or never existed.

Because we don't know much, a novelist is given a good deal of open field in which to run. In the following pages, I try to stick with the facts. When I can't, I look to historical probability—then possibility. Often I have no choice. I must jump into the "who knows?" branch of history.

The end notes are my attempt to help the reader sort out fact from fiction. I'm not sure which I prefer. Inevitably, I think, history becomes an intriguing mix of fact and fancy.

I first read about the Popham colony in 1974. At the time I was teaching Maine history on North Haven Island in Penobscot Bay. My namesake, the chaplain at the fort, Richard Seymour, struck my imagination. I learned that nineteen Richard Seymours had lived in England at the beginning of the seventeenth century, when there was a population of less than four million. The Richard Seymour, chaplain from Hanford, Dorset County, and I, who live fifteen miles from the Fort St. George site, meet somewhere in the Seymour genealogy.

My own ancestry can be traced to another Richard Seymour, a poor Puritan who landed in Cambridge, Massachusetts in 1632. Chaplain Richard Seymour's family tree grew closer to the ducal Seymours—that is, relatives of Queen Jane Seymour, the third wife of King Henry VIII and mother to young King Edward VI. I'd guess most Seymours might consider themselves as part of that royal branch. But, as historical record shows in Chapter 3, one might have second thoughts about being in bed with royalty—if you appreciate having your head connected to your neck!

Since teaching on North Haven Island, I've become a clinical psychologist. This vantage point provides me with a privileged opportunity to witness the motivations, hopes, and, fears of others. Perhaps my actual life might support my fictional one.

—Dick Seymour
Brunswick, Maine 2013

Principal Characters

Gentlemen of Quality:

Sir John Popham, prime mover of the Northern Virginia Company, Chief Justice during later part of Queen Elizabeth's reign and the early years of King James

George Popham, nephew to Sir John and president of Fort St. George

Admiral Raleigh Gilbert, nephew to Sir Walter Raleigh and second-in-command at Fort St. George

Sir Ferdinando Gorges, supporter of colonization efforts, colleague of Sir John Popham

Sir Robert Cecil, member of both Queen Elizabeth's and King James's Privy Council

Sir Francis Bacon, eminent scientist, philosopher, and Seymour's instructor at Middle Temple

Sir Walter Raleigh, adventurer, historian, supporter of colonization of New World, prisoner at the Tower of London

Gentlemen and Gentlewomen:

Richard Seymour, chaplain

John and **Agnes Seymour**, Richard Seymour's parents

Sir Robert Seymour, Richard Seymour's elder brother

Margaret Throckmorton, Richard's friend

Emily, Margaret's friend

Notable English:

Captain Robert Davies, sergeant major of Fort St. George; captain of the *Gift of God*, the *Mary and John*, and later the *Virginia*

Captain James Davis, captain of Fort St. George

Captain John Elliott, captain of the *Gift of God*

Master Digby, shipwright

John Fletcher, highwayman and sailor

Lance Roberts, fifteen-year-old crew member

Jimmy Smith and **Paul Meeks**, also young members of the crew

Native Americans:

Skidwarres, a Mawooshen (the people between the Sagadahoc and Penobscot Rivers), captured and later tutored by Richard Seymour

Nahanada, the sagamore (leader) of the Mawooshen village at Pemaquid

Bessabez, highly respected sagamore of the Maswooshen

Mikowa, a Micmac boy of fourteen

Sabenoa, Lord of the Sagadahoc and sagamore of the village at Merrymeeting Bay where the Sagadahoc and Androscoggin Rivers meet

Nolka (deer), Nahanada's eldest wife

Sipsis (bird), member of Nahanada's village, granddaughter of a French trapper

Sokw (cloud), wife of Skidwarres

Nahnibssat (moon), daughter of Skidwarres

Moskwas (muskrat), member of Nahanada's village and friend of Lance

Woboz (Elk), member of Nahanada's village and anti-English

Kasko (heron), elder of Nahanada's village and father of Woboz

English and Native Names for Rivers and Bays on the Northern Coast of Virginia, now the State of Maine

Sagadahoc River (Kennebec River)

Aponeg (Sheepscot River)

Quabacook (Merrymeeting Bay where the Kennebec meets the Androscoggin)

Sakohki (Saco River)

Segohquet (St. George River)

Aucocisco (Casco Bay)

CHAPTER 1

April 15, 1607, Exeter, England
Lord Chief Justice, Sir John Popham Presides

Shafts of dusty morning light illuminate the fourteenth century Mercantile Court. Recently installed Elizabethan windows feature small diamond-shaped panes, some colored, others clear. The rising sun leaves a kaleidoscope of red, green, yellow, and blue patches inching across plaster walls and worn stone floor. For one young gentleman observer, the display appears festive in an otherwise portentous morning. Today the ancient structure hosts judicial proceedings.

One shaft of light spotlights three dispirited men who are chained together. The tallest wears a grimy bandage around his head with a brown stain of dried blood across his forehead, accentuating his abysmal condition. The other two show red and purple bruises from the beatings they'd received from the guards, who are only moderately better off than the expanding prison population of paupers and petty criminals. The men's filthy clothing smells of urine and excrement. Their stench carries to the four judges a few yards away, elevated three steps up in the manner of a church nave. Their noses twitch with disdain.

The aroma mars the otherwise sweet, warm, early spring air drifting in through the open windows. A small group of rueful men and women stand to the side awaiting trial. Within arm's reach, guards hold erect lances. Some thirty observers, both gentlemen and common townspeople, sit on long wooden benches.

The chained men all appear under age thirty. Their charges: robbery and treason. Under duress, the youngest had confessed to being a member of a ragtag group of Catholics who some years ago attempted to poison Queen Elizabeth, and according to the prosecutor, have similar plans for the King James.

Chief Justice Sir John Popham sits at the head of the table, bathed in bluish light from one of the windows. His crimson robe shines. Ornate gold lace hangs around his roast-beef neck and obdurate septuagenarian jowls. A large medallion, presented by the Queen some years before for his services, rests on his broad chest. Sir John appears as he is: a success at business, the law, an advisor to Her Highness and now His Majesty. Popham has presided at many trials over the years. At one, Sir Walter Raleigh was found guilty of treason and thereby sentenced to death—then commuted by King James, leaving to this day Sir Walter at his apartment in the Tower of London. Popham and Raleigh, two prominent men of the West Country, their lives intertwined and at odds.

In Exeter everyone knows Popham's reputation as a "hanging judge." In the Mercantile Court, no light shines on the other three judges. They remain in the shadows, inanimate, their heads resting in circular white ruffled collars, their faces adorned with well-cropped pointed beards. A young gentleman in the third row, who has watched the kaleidoscopic light, now whispers to the swarthy friend sitting next to him, "They look like identical alien flowers, cut and dried."

Excessive attention to dress, so prevalent during the middle of Elizabeth's reign, is slowly giving way to plainer wardrobes. The Privy Council, the sovereign's top advisors, became alarmed by the expense and time devoted to style by the aristocracy. Additional sumptuary laws discouraged what had become for men a flamboyant and rather feminine look. Reformers of the Church of England have also begun preaching modesty and austerity, a sentiment held in the extreme by the Puritans. None of the three other judges, who still hold to the old ornate dress habits, utter a word during the proceedings. They appear under the Chief Justice's spell.

Popham had invited the two men in the third row: Richard Seymour, age twenty-three, a young gentleman, and his companion, Skidwarres, age twenty-four and a kidnapped native from the New World. The two are dressed in the less ostentatious fashion of the English gentry: white hosiery, dark green breeches ending just below the knee, boots rising a few inches above the knee. Over sober brown shirts, both wear black doublets. Because Skidwarres daily plucks his thin facial hair, Richard has shaved his beard in support. They differ only in Richard's fair skin and light brown, wavy hair juxtaposed with Skidwarres' tawny skin and straight, raven black hair, though both wear it wrapped in the back by a velvet red band. Otherwise they might be brothers, so similar are they, and so easy together.

During the summers, Skidwarres' people had become accustomed to foreign sails appearing on the horizon. Mythical stories handed down by many generations told of blond haired men in serpentine boats arriving, settling briefly and then disappearing—gods of sorts. Now on the coast of what used to be called Norumbega, the whites typically stayed offshore, fished, and dried and salted their catch on the outer islands. Then they'd sail over the horizon before the snow flew. Some ships journeyed up rivers and parlayed with the natives, though the English showed much less interest and patience than the French. Skidwarres' people were known as the Mawooshen.

Interaction between the Mawooshen and the English was infrequent. When Captain George Weymouth arrived under orders from Popham in 1605 to explore the region near the Sagadahoc River, Weymouth invited five braves on ship, including their sagamore or leader, Nahanada. The natives had little reason to take precautions. After the initial pleasantries, including the sharing of tobacco and some words spoken in French, the English crew fell upon the natives. They later complained how difficult it had been to subdue the "naked slippery savages." It had been summer, and the natives wore only leather loincloths. It became necessary to grab Skidwarres' long hair and slam him to the deck, knocking him into semi-consciousness. The other four experienced similar fates. Before other tribe members became aware of the abduction, the English hauled the braves' two canoes on deck, weighed anchor, and sailed away

Chief Justice Popham from the West Country, along with business associates in London, planned to create two colonies, one at the mouth of the Sagadahoc, the other way to the south that would be known as Jamestown in honor of the King. The southern operation would be supported by a council out of London. Another council in Plymouth would support the northern outpost. Except for the failed Roanoke settlement, inspired by Sir Walter Raleigh some twenty years before, these would be the first English settlements in the New World. The Virginia Company would lay claim to most of the East Coast of the New World. From Popham's perspective, it was a race against the Spanish and French, a matter of Protestant against Catholic. The savages, especially Skidwarres and Nahanada, would be returned and act as interpreters and diplomats. Popham placed high value on developing good relations with the inhabitants. In this regard, Roanoke was a perfect example of English stupidity, given its ignorant treatment of the natives. Besides, the expansion of English interests, colonizing, and trade promised to be extraordinarily profitable. Richard Seymour, by Popham's bequest, became Skidwarres' instructor in all things English: its language, social mores, government, and religion.

Sir John Popham, Chief Justice, one of Queen Elizabeth's trusted advisors, especially on the law and trade, held a colorful reputation. The years of Elizabeth's rule, 1558–1603, involved incessant struggles for power. When Elizabeth began her reign, England rated much poorer and less influential than France, Spain, and Portugal. By her death, England dominated the seas and had increased her coffers, much thanks to English privateers, sometimes referred to as "adventurers"—a polite term for pirates. Popham had maintained his wits during the turbulent Elizabethan era, when torture, hanging, and burning at the stake constituted royal punishment and intimidation. Poverty ran rampant, especially after the fading of Spanish hegemony, following the defeat of their Armada, thereby lessening the need for large armies and navies. Men roamed the countryside looking for work. The decades-long religious strife between Catholics and the breakaway Church of England and other reformers made for all sorts of treachery. The potential for war with Spain and France remained in the air, as did plots to murder Elizabeth or to marry her to this or that prince or king for the purpose of international advancement. Elizabeth became adept at negotiating with the ever-powerful aristocracy. Because of his deftness, Popham remained her ally. Many others lost their heads.

While a student at Oxford, Popham boasted he had taken part in highway robberies. "Good sport. No one got hurt," he explained later. The thefts involved small sums. Popham insisted he was always polite and traveled in large enough bands that resistance was futile. He took lightly his legal training at Middle Temple in London, but not his life afterwards. As with many men of modest means who became wealthy, Popham invested in real estate.

Landed families in the counties of Somerset, Devon, Dorset, and Cornwall financed the adventurers, the pirates—the most well-known being Francis Drake and John Hawkins. Popham and others backed the more legitimate exploration of the New World. Most infamously, Popham helped fund the failed, bloody colonization of Ireland, sowing seeds for centuries of strife.

By 1607 Popham had reached the age of seventy, and his disdain for the growing social disorder had hardened. For over a century, the

Enclosure Acts had denied peasants land that used to be available to them, their source of food and fuel. Land previously hayed, cut for timber, grazing, cultivation, hunting, and fishing became private. If it weren't for Popham's advocacy for vagrancy laws that he had a hand in creating—essentially making unemployment a crime—the justice might have remained at home in Devon or perhaps chosen to entertain officials at his sizable country place, Littlecote, in Wiltshire, nearer to London. Instead he wished to remain an active enforcer of laws, especially treason.

And he would take this time in Exeter to oversee Seymour's work with Skidwarres. Since the natives' arrival, he had insisted all five be treated with respect and kindness. Popham personally apologized for his "rude invitation" to visit England.

Following the prosecution's argument, Popham quietly confers with the other three judges. During this break, Richard softly asks Skidwarres, "Friend, in your land, what is done with those who steal or commit treason?" Richard's eyebrows rise a little. Their friendship often feeds on humor, the humor of young men who have been thrown together, who relish the strangeness but unifying exuberance of the other. Richard asks a genuine question, but one which to Skidwarres has many words and shades of meaning.

"Yes, steal—a concept—is that the word? Steal what? A bow, a meal, a woman? Little to steal," Skidwarres says.

"But, some do steal?"

"Yes. Then the sagamore, the elders, they talk to this person."

"Yes, of course, so rational, your noble people."

It is Skidwarres' turn to raise an eyebrow, a gesture not unknown in his land, but employed more in this strange one. "If poor—as you say we are—is noble."

"And if he steals again?" Richard quips.

"If not liked, he is asked to leave—or killed." Skidwarres shrugs his shoulders as if to say, that is how it is done.

"And treason?

"You explained to me treason. But in my language there is no word for treason. If a person does not like his village, he moves."

Popham slowly rises from his seat and clears his throat. "The court finds the defendants guilty of treason and so will be they punished forthwith. You shall be led hence to the place where you came, there to remain until the day of execution. Then you shall be drawn on a hurdle through the open streets to the place of execution, there to be hanged and cut down alive, after which your body shall be opened, your heart and bowels plucked out, and your privy members cut off and thrown into the fire before your eyes. Then your head will be stricken from your body, pierced by a rod, and boiled, and your body shall be divided into four quarters, to be disposed of at the King's pleasure. And may God have mercy on your soul."

Commotion arises from those awaiting their own trial. A woman moans. A guard casually punches the handle of his spear against the head of the man closest to him. It is enough to regain quiet throughout the hall. The three chained, condemned men begin to mechanically shuffle away, until the youngest collapses without a word. In a soft voice, the guard tells the two others to haul him out. It is awkward because of the wrist and ankle shackles, and they trip over one another three or four times before finally exiting, comically enough for some of the waiting prisoners to cackle. Richard and Skidwarres remain in their seats watching.

"Richard," Skidwarres leans over and whispers, "I do not understand all that Popham said."

Richard's mind has been wondering. He has attended trials and a few hangings. Like Popham, he trained at Middle Temple in London. Hangings were common and often festive, with ale and gin the typical lubricants. He has tried to cloak himself in an educated indifference. The law pronounces guilt. Who is he to second guess? Hasn't the Queen faced assignation plots from poisoning to abduction and murder? Shouldn't the law bend in her direction and now in King James's? And why not intimidate with heads on stakes? Didn't the practice go as far back as Alexander the Great, probably to aboriginal times?

But drawing and quartering? That was cruel. At Middle Temple he'd been introduced to the French essayist, Montaigne. At first his work appeared simply a curiosity, so compelled was the Frenchman to discuss his own foibles and mix his daily musings with the most weighty ideas handed down from the ancients, from Horace, Aristotle, Ovid, and pointedly, the Greek and Roman stoics.

But Montaigne's clear style took hold. Montaigne became Richard's personal, if unacquainted, friend. While in London, and lately in his bedroom at his father's estate, the essays sat on his nightstand, opened to this or that page. He read them daily as others did the Bible. He traveled with the essays in his satchel. Richard knew it was fanciful to think so, but he felt if he kept Montaigne's essays close by long enough, the words might seep into his very skin.

Montaigne had written, "What I fear is fear itself." That sounded lofty and elegant, yet so often true. But what of pain? Wasn't pain real enough? On this subject he wrote, "If you can't bear it, it will bear you off."

Whenever he had a few moments to ruminate, there would be Montaigne and his intellectual mentors, the stoics, beckoning. It was Seneca, Richard thought he remembered, who said, "It's not how long you live but how nobly you live." What possible connection might this have for the three wretches now, thankfully out of sight? Words, frothy things—but there they were, Montaigne's words.

Finally he answers Skidwarres, "They will die, horribly. I will explain later. It is we, the English, my friend, who are the savages."

Skidwarres nods seriously, picking up Richard's mood.

"Friend," continues Richard, "what of heads on stakes, a tradition in the New World—with your noble folk?"

Skidwarres continues to nod. "For some, yes."

CHAPTER 2

April 15, 1607, Afternoon, Exeter, England
Grand Commerce

"I sometimes frequent this part of town," Popham explains to Seymour, Skidwarres, and a business associate, Ferdinando Gorges. They stroll, Popham at the lead talking over his shoulder. "The unscrupulous stories about me—mostly true, my friends. My vagrancies, my wanderings as a youth." Popham points to a narrow street. "Let's go a bit out of our way. I have often chosen pastimes over responsibilities. Though in London, there are so many more pastimes."

As they enter the narrow street, the four men hear shouts, as if from a sporting event, first one group and then another. Where the street opens into a courtyard, they approach a crowd of thirty or so men. Not all the sounds are human. Intermixed with cheering are ferocious grunts and growls.

"Here you see life with all its oddities and basics, life in the flesh." Popham's stern demeanor has vanished. He is now jocular, a man who plays many roles, and like any good actor, is content in all of them. The onlookers encircle two huge, scraggly, brown bears reared up on their back legs. Each is chained to a stake, but with enough length to grapple, swing their sharp-nailed paws, and sink their teeth into one another. One's snout is ripped open and gushes. Dust and shouts fill the air.

The four men watch from a short distance. Popham chides the others. "Richard, haven't you taken in such basic sport in your study or on your horse? There's nothing more absorbing than the fight for life. And Skidwarres, there are many bears in your land, I'm told. These are from Northern France."

"Yes, but black in color, smaller—the word?—shy? Unless they feel threatened."

Richard has, in fact, witnessed bear baiting, as well as dog fights, while at Oxford and London. But he keeps it to himself, not wanting to interrupt Popham's narrative.

"And Gorges, my friend," Popham chuckles, "I wager you haven't been in this section of town. Unless for the women." Popham nods his head to the second story of a building overlooking the small cul-de-sac. Three women stand at an open window watching. When they sense recognition, all three offer exaggerated, pink-cleavage bows. One unlaces her frock, reaches in, and presents to the onlookers her ample left breast. She jiggles it, something between a wave and an offering.

"Welcome, Sir John. Won't you introduce us to your friends?" shouts the one with her breast still in her hands." Popham knows Gorges to be an untiring entrepreneur—and a prude.

"What say, Gorges, do you have time for a frolic?"

"I think not, sir. It is not of my taste." He has quickly turned his gaze away to the battle, which has apparently lost its heat. For the moment the two bears stand like tired boxers, their paws out in front, on the defensive.

"Yes, my dear," calls back Popham, "that would be wonderful, but alas, we are late for an appointment. Some other time."

The woman exaggerates a pout and stuffs her breast out of sight. "That is a shame, a waste, sir. My friends here are so cordial."

"And so lovely, too. Some other day." Sir John waves, as do Richard and Skidwarres in the spirit of good cheer.

"Sir John," Gorges manages a weak retort. "She must have a long memory."

Popham slaps Gorges' back. "Not so, my friend. Some old bad habits happily remain unbroken—though I must admit they begin to fade."

They turn to see the injured bear back up a few short steps, drop to all fours, and bring a bloodied paw up to investigate its snout. "It must be weak from loss of blood," offers Popham. The bear then sinks further into a kneeling position, its head resting prayer-like on the ground. The other bear charges in for the kill. With its mouth wide-open and teeth bared, its head is brought up short by the chain secured to the pole, which bends but holds. The referee points to the snarling winner, again on its hind legs, at least seven feet tall, apparently enjoying the victory. Handlers move in to offer the winner raw meat. The loser is rolled on its back. A man with a long knife investigates the wound, offers an expletive, then slits the furry throat in one quick swipe.

"Shall we proceed?" asks Popham, who has already started back down the alley.

Popham is known as ambitious and crafty—and wise. As with this little foray before lunch, he's comfortable leading others into the unexpected and unknown, be it a business adventure of vast proportion, a political juggernaut, or exploration and conquest. For him, life is most alive and authentic when unpredictable.

The four men wander through the fish market. Here, Popham is also at home. From a few yards away, a fish monger who'd noticed the justice begins to jostle through the shoppers in front of him. Like the water pushed by the prow of a ship, a foul smell precedes the man's bulk. "Your Grace, please come. You are just in time to observe the catch from the New World. Look over there," he says, pointing to cartloads of salted cod, some as large as a man. "Thousands of pounds, sir. They tell me all one has to do is drop a line and haul. No waiting. It is God's smelly gold."

"Yes, my friend, and with it unlimited lumber, furs, and, some say, gold itself. I intend to bring you more. All of it." Popham is expansive and claps the bloody-aproned fellow hard on the shoulder.

Townspeople know of the justice. They congregate closer and lean in to hear him speak. Popham is accustomed to making short, impromptu speeches. "Not as rewarding as pirating—the gold, trading slaves, all that twenty years ago. There is less adventure in fish and beaver—but it is reliable, profitable." The reaction among the claque of men and women is mixed. Some clap obediently. Others laugh, catching the local celebrity's enthusiasm. A few others, perhaps influenced by the justice's reputation as a harsh cruel authority, simply stare.

The justice takes Gorges by the arm and ushers him out of the market, Seymour and Skidwarres following. They pass the grand cathedral, the largest in the West Country and, before Henry VIII less than a hundred years ago, a bulwark of Catholicism—now equally so for the Church of England. Around the corner lies their destination, the Ship Inn, marked by a wooden blue and white sign creaking in the breeze over the entrance. On it is carved a ship, the *Golden Hind*, belonging to one of the inn's recently deceased patrons and England's most revered explorer and privateer, Sir Francis Drake.

Popham arranges everyone around a thick oak table, scarred from the impact of heavy pewter mugs and dishes, and slightly sticky from half-hearted wiping. Popham orders ale, bread, and sausage from the attentive waitress, who has served Popham and Gorges—as well as Richard and Skidwarres—before, though never all together.

As part of Skidwarres' education, the two often traveled the half-day ride from Seymour's estate in Dorset. Skidwarres had come to favor the cathedral. He spent hours wondering about it, simply sitting in silence, or even better, listening to the madrigals spreading out and echoing off the vaulted ceiling.

"Gentlemen, while we are awaiting my cousin, George, please indulge an aging man. I chuckle whenever I frequent this establishment." His companions smile, quite happy to listen.

"Please do," says Gorges. Ferdinando Gorges is a man who has spent many years courting the wealthy and the royally-connected. What brings the two together, Popham and Gorges, is their mutual ambition: the colonization and exploitation of the New World.

"I knew Sir Francis Drake. Not well. But of course, we are a small island and even a smaller segment, we here in the West Country. Extraordinary man. Maybe the most single-minded man I've every met—and for this reason, one of the richest. I'm sure you've all heard the same tale, the one about him standing in a tree somewhere in the New World between the large North and South, where the two meet in an isthmus less than a hundred miles across, they say. And Drake, after climbing high up a tree, was able to see both oceans. One climb, both oceans—how remarkable!"

"Indeed," adds Gorges, "I so wish I might also climb that tree."

"Well, for myself, I am too old and corpulent for tree climbing." Clearly Popham hasn't finished his story. No one interrupts. "My reminiscing is of an older Drake. The incident occurred in 1595, just before he and John Hawkins—the two old scoundrels—sailed in their fatal journey to find gold. And it involves my son-in-law, Richard Champernowne, so I suppose this is a family story."

"Seymour and Gorges, you know well how the extended Champernowne family has been at the hub of exploration and adventuring. Everyone seems to be related to them: the Gilberts—Sir Humphrey, before he was lost at sea exploring the Northern New World—but more important, his son, Raleigh. More important because I have decided that this young man—about your age, Richard—shall be second-in-command. And of course, just to bring matters full circle, Raleigh Gilbert's uncle and half-brother to Raleigh's father, Humphrey, is Sir Walter Raleigh, the owner of the original Virginia Charter. As I said, full circle. I, too, am brought into the Champernowne orbit through my son-in-law—and you, too, Richard, your families are intertwined—therefore you and young Raleigh, our second-in-command-to-be, are, I suppose, cousins."

"Yes, sir, I believe we are second cousins, though I have never met the man."

"Important, important. But the quirky reminiscence: Drake, great as he was, could be petty. Richard Champernowne—that is, my son-in-law—held, for a while, the post of Sheriff of Devon. Drake, who was brought up here, must have had unsatisfactory dealings with him when he returned. Whatever the case, Richard loved music. Many envied him. He owned a band and a consort of singers—quite a fortune he spent— paying for the young boys, the consort singers. You know, of course, how pure the voices are of some young boys—angelic really. Even my dull ear can tell."

The waitress arrives with victuals and drink. They are sampled, and then the three look up for Popham to continue.

"Well, Richard Champernowne received a letter from the great adventurer. In it, Drake accused Richard of gelding some of his boys, one in particular with a stellar voice. Of course, you know this is the practice in Italy, to keep their voices high and pure—to snip off their testicles. It's an honor, some say, but not one an Englishman or boy wishes for—though I suppose one never knows. In any case, Drake should have known better. Maybe he did. The letter and the fact that it was made public, of course, were considered slander by Richard. I agreed. I was in a position to advise, so my son-in-law wrote to Robert Cecil of the Privy Council. But instead of chastising Drake, Cecil wrote that he wished to purchase the boy for his consort singers. My son-in-law, a melancholy sort anyway, fell into quite a black mood. He didn't want to sell the boy, and his honor was still besmirched. Though I have to say, it was hard for me to muster great sympathy; it all seemed more a comic plot for the playwright, Shakespeare. Whatever slight Drake intended, I never knew, but in the end, there were many letters and much public rumor. Folly, really."

The group returns to nibbling and sipping, nodding their approval to this bit of history and entertainment. "Sir John," Gorges asks, indulging the man a bit more, "what of Drake's final voyage? More comedy or tragedy?"

"Ah, fine question. As you know, he and Hawkins were both well into their fifties. Couldn't keep them ashore, they had to sail and plunder. But their day had passed, and I suppose their judgment and luck. First, a failed attack on the Portuguese, and then, instead of death by sword, they lingered off the coast of some puny island in the Caribbean and, within days of each other, died of dysentery. Aging men—great men really— attempting the boldness of youth. You tell me, comedy or tragedy?"

"As you suggest, some of each," Gorges quips, irony really.

"Gentlemen..." Popham changes the topic. "My cousin George's previous engagement should have concluded, and I am eager to proceed with business. Otherwise timidity sets in and plans rot. You, Gorges, have worked hard to raise funds."

"As you say, Sir John." Gorges bows his head to accept the accolade.

"Yes, yes, and as you all know, we have the King's support—last year, the signed charter, our ducks neatly in a row. Cecil stands with us. The Virginia Charter—for our dead stellar Virgin Queen—is a charter for the vast virgin land." The term "Virgin Queen," often accompanied by a whiff of sarcasm, holds no ambiguity for Popham. He looks to the entrance again, then stands. "Ah, George is here."

George Popham, a man in his middle fifties, resembles his elder cousin in breadth and height. Both Pophams are at least five feet ten, and both feature ruddy faces, though George's bears the leathery texture of a man who's spent a good deal more time outside. Both exude confidence. George has a ready open smile, and his eyes, with their crinkles, convey friendliness; whereas, even when jocular, Sir John's never seems to lose their judicial remove. George's eyes are dark brown and a bit rheumy. Regarding the coloring, he tells whoever will listen that during his time in the Caribbean among the Spanish, African, and "Black Irish" sailors, his eyes adjusted their color to the company.

After short introductions, Sir John continues. "All of us here have played a role. You, Richard have miraculously created our ambassador, Skidwarres."

"Sir John, I am a tutor, not an almighty. He is a brilliant student and a forgiving one. A man is abducted and transported to a foreign land... sir, I don't mean to offend."

"No, no. You must speak your mind."

Though the justice may be sincere, Richard isn't sure. "And, sir, our country does appear to him quite fantastic. Though he can speak for himself, England, at least, fits him." Richard refers to Skidwarres' English dress.

"Yes, of course, we English are strange indeed, even to ourselves. And our emissary from Northern Virginia is of fine character and intellect. We chose well. Or should I say, out luck chose well?"

Skidwarres softly interjects, "As you say, England is a strange world. At first, I am angry and want to kill. But they tell me I am to return. They tell me on the ship, soon after capture, and again you, Sir John, and you, Richard. No longer I am so angry.'"

"What you say is excellent," George Popham says into his raised flask.

"Your god or mine, I think, he made this visit so." It is the first time Skidwarres has spoken at any length. Unlike the banter which has filled much of the early afternoon, his message is slightly formal and direct.

Sir John smiles. "Well said, Skidwarres. And this friendship must soon bear fruit."

Skidwarres repeats the phrase and then smiles. "As with your apple trees."

"Exactly," continued Sir John. "George is quite aware how important your participation is, along with Nahanada who, as you know, returned to your land some months ago. George will be my presence there. I am too old. My joints, they all ache. Nothing I'd rather do than sail with you—nothing."

"You sir, cousin," adds George. "You remain essential. My devotion to you I will carry to my grave."

"You have proved yourself: a captain, an explorer, a gentleman—all these essential ingredients. And, dear George, let your grave be in dear old England." The justice pauses to swallow deeply from his mug. "And you, Gorges, my trusted fellow with the purse strings. How go the pledges?"

"Well, sir. We have eighty thousand pounds pledged, half of it already banked. But some request your physical presence before they make good on their pledges."

"Incredible," George Popham continues after refilling his mug. "A land so vast, so many times greater than our England, and we will purchase it. Or be granted it. Inhabit it, in any case. Not the French or Spanish. Not the Catholics. You are acquainted with that remarkable Portuguese, Verrazano? Over fifty years ago, he wrote of such bounty and incredibly, beautiful healthy men and women who go naked except for ornaments of copper and gold, and stag skins across their privates. I, too, have seen these people in my journeys to the Orinoco. Is it true, Skidwarres, that your women are beautiful and go naked?"

"Some women are beautiful, yes, but not foolish. They cover themselves except in hottest summer."

"George, my cousin," Sir John offers with a hearty chuckle, "I am glad to see such prospects still embolden you. Besides, if truth be known, we all lust after the New World. I am envious, and of course, this plan is fraught with danger."

They all drain their mugs and clean their plates in momentary silence, excepting the general clatter and chatter within the small tavern. Gorges hands over the pledges of support to Sir John and begins to discuss further meetings.

Sir John looks at Richard and interrupts. "And you, dear Richard will you return to your studies? Will you be a priest? A professor? A lawyer?

Or do you want to jump into the great unknown and find yourself?"

Richard comes out of a semi-trance. The conversation has transported him to an open ocean. For the past two years, while devoting himself entirely to Skidwarres' English education, it had slowly dawned on him that his future might be tied to this man and not to the practice of law or pursuit of business or diplomacy—both possibilities that had floated through his head at Oxford and at the Middle Temple in London. It was no surprise that Sir John now turned to him.

"Sir, pray, what you are suggesting?"

"I'm suggesting we need a chaplain on this mission, a man of learning, a young man with energy, a lay minister. I'm suggesting an adventure. I'm suggesting you have balls."

"Well, sir, considering an Atlantic crossing and the chancy nature of this new world endeavor, I'm suggesting I want to keep them." Again Richard realizes the ale and self confidence, along with a penchant for wry humor, may have pushed his familiarity out of bounds. His response draws congenial laughter.

"I can have the bishop appoint you. You need not be ordained. These will be rough men, many of them. They need someone with common sense and youth—someone to confide in. We also need a secretary, the council does. You have proven yourself a capable teacher. You and Skidwarres, you two are a natural bridge between our peoples. I assume a yes, but I will give you a brief time to decide. You are not married, correct?"

"I am not."

"I will be visiting your father's estate in two weeks. Please be prepared to give me an answer then."

"No need to wait, sir. I cannot imagine saying no." The answer comes less from a conscious decision than from many months of subtle internal shifting, tremors before a quake. He has watched Skidwarres accept his fate with such grace. Now Richard can not help but imagine the unimaginable venture.

Sir John watches carefully. "Very well, my lad, I am pleased to hear it, very pleased. But you can change your mind. If not you—and I hope you choose so—I know of another who wishes the position."

"As you say, sir." The thought that another might be in competition only sealed the decision for Richard—exactly as Popham had intended.

CHAPTER 3

Fall 1605, Two Years Earlier, Hanford, Dorset,
The Seymours

By 1605, nineteen Richard Seymours (also spelled Seamer, Semer, and eventually the most popular Seymour) inhabited England.

The original English Seymours crossed the channel during the Norman Conquest in 1066. The Norse filled their craft with ponies on the continent side of the channel. After the thirty-mile crossing they disembarked with their riders astride. William the Conqueror, and not Seymer or Seymour, but a descendent of St. Maur, began ransacking and spreading their seed. (During the sixth century a monk named Maur was canonized because of his good works. The Church erected an Abbey of Saint-Maur-sur-Loire in his name. As was the custom, individuals appended the place of birth to their "given" name.)

Waves of Normans followed and invaded the West Country, the arm of England between the Atlantic Ocean and the English Channel. Another Joscelin de St. Maur continued north to Wales.

The determined and battle-hardened Normans seized the land from the Welsh. By the early eleven hundreds, a crude wooden Penhow Castle, surrounded by an earthen moat, dominated the countryside of Gwent. At Penhow, the St. Maurs created a coat of arms, that of wings conjoined that looked much like a hand, thumbs together and fingers spread out as feathers. This symbolized the Phoenix rising. And from this location, the St. Maurs multiplied and spread throughout England. This was the background offered to Richard as a boy. At age fifteen, he received his first ring the night before he left for Oxford—on its small flat surface were two wings, conjoined, embossed in gold—the same insignia adopted by Queen Jane Seymour's family.

In the fall of 1605, Richard resided at his father John's estate, Ram's Head, in Hanford, Dorset. Richard's great-great-grandfather had built the original. Since then, the house had expanded to four times the original size, its thatched roof replaced by stone shingles. His lands, originally a few hundred acres, had grown to over a thousand. As was the case for other families who had gained wealth and prominence, some Seymour women "married up." Women became bargaining chips, often quite willing—even loving—ones.

For Richard's branch, the crowning achievement involved just such a maneuver in 1536. Jane Seymour, daughter of another John Seymour of Wolf Hall, a medieval castle in Wiltshire, stole, some say—those who believe her father and brother encouraged a plot—the heart of Henry VIII. Stories about Queen Jane and her brothers abounded among Richard's family members, spread mostly by Richard's father, Jane's younger first cousin.

Henry VIII considered John Seymour, Jane's father, a supportive member of the gentry, regardless of his reputation as a rake. After John's eldest son, Edward, married, the father began a sexual relationship with his daughter-in-law, and in so doing produced two children. Edward, understandably outraged, denounced his wife and children and had little trouble securing a divorce. She conveniently died soon afterwards. By the time of Queen Anne Boleyn's disgrace, the smudge on John Seymour's character had substantially evaporated.

Jane Seymour befriended Anne Boleyn while they served as ladies-in-waiting for Katherine of Aragon, the first wife of Henry VIII. Jane then became Queen Anne's lady-in-waiting—in both cases a rather ironic title, Richard's father, John Seymour, pointed out. Anne Boleyn maneuvered for seven years before she wore the crown. Jane Seymour waited four days between Anne's decapitation and her own betrothal

When the ax fell, a hundred-gun cannonade reported the event to the populace. Henry went straight away to Jane who, with her family, occupied a house on The Strand. There she prepared for her wedding, apparently little moved by her predecessor's fate.

Soon Jane fulfilled her duty by delivering a son, Edward VI. Henry VIII had what he wanted most, a male heir to the throne.

It was a grueling three-day birth which left the Queen depleted. The doctors had advised the King that they probably could not save both mother and child. Immediately the King ordered, so it was rumored, "Save the child. I can always find another wife." Richard's father would bellow during this part of the story, while his wife, Agnes, rolled her eyes. Fact or fiction, it made little difference. "All history is a mix of overwhelming facts and charming myth," John Seymour would pontificate.

To mark the birth, this time two thousand cannon reports rang out from the Tower of London. A few days later, abiding to the King's demand that she attend the elaborate christening, Jane arrived, carried on a stretcher and exhausted. Within hours, she died of puerperal fever, caused by infection incurred during labor.

With Edward's birth, Henry's ecstatic mood brought fortune to the extended Seymour family. They received gifts of manors, castles, gardens, and forests, some of which had been wrested from the Roman Catholic Church.

Henry quickly remarried—he had been attracted by Anne Cleves' portrait, hastily offered to marry, and then found her unattractive in person. But marry he did, and then months later had the marriage annulled. His sixth and last wife, Katherine Parr, became an attentive mother to Edward VI, as well as to young Mary and Elizabeth, Henry's two daughters. Henry died in 1547, leaving Edward, age ten, the King of England.

Jane's brother, Edward Seymour, became Lord Protector for the child-king, but Seymour preferred the immodest title, Lord Great Master. In this position, Edward Seymour virtually ruled England—and more largesse trickled down to Seymours in Dorset, Somerset, and Devon.

For five years, Edward, who became the Duke of Somerset, hired tutors for the Tudor King and managed his daily routine. However, the Lord Protector lacked diplomacy, an essential ingredient for his position. It did not take long before he provoked the enmity of other powerful men. The construction of the mammoth Somerset House, prominently situated on the Thames between Westminster Hall and Middle Temple, provided one example of Edward's hubris. Many prominent men watched as their expensive homes fell to make room for Seymour's future.

No aspect of the Seymour history interested John Seymour more than the archetypal rivalry between his two elder first cousins, Edward the Lord Protector and his younger brother, Thomas, elevated by Henry VIII to Lord of the Admiralty. For Richard's father, it was a cautionary tale about the evils of ambition and greed.

On a portrait of Thomas Seymour, a poem is inscribed. Thomas is a "rare person with strong limbs and manly shape" who in war displayed "skill great, bold hand—on horse, on foot, in peril, or in play none could excel." To complicate matters, before Henry VIII married Katherine Parr, Thomas Seymour, "in his play" wooed her. Thirty-four days after the King's death—and against his brother, Edward's better judgment—

Thomas married the Dowager Queen. Besides the noble qualities offered in the poem, Thomas was rash.

Rumors perpetually flew from the Royal Court. During Edward Seymour's five years as Lord Protectorate, the Seymour brothers became leading characters in these sometimes comical dramas. One story had Edward's wife, who considered herself higher- bred than Dowager Queen Katherine Parr, purposely sitting in the Queen's seat at Westminster. A verbal harangue ensued between the two ladies, until they had to be separated by their respective Seymour husbands. Other stories involved Thomas waking the young adolescent Elizabeth—who continued to live with Katherine and her husband, Thomas, Elizabeth's step-father—in the morning. Thomas flirted with Elizabeth, kissing her in bed. On one occasion, with the assistance of Elizabeth's step-mother, Katherine, they held the adolescent Elizabeth down while Thomas cut the girl's dress to pieces.

Thomas managed to be accused of trading with pirates on the Scilly Isles, an area he managed in his position as Lord of the Admiralty. Closer to home, and after his wife Katherine's death in childbirth—in the same manner as his sister, Jane, a little over a decade before—Thomas made known his wish for Elizabeth's hand, thereby potentially positioning himself to be prince or even king. The Privy Council and Edward Seymour would not have it. Further rumors had him impregnating Elizabeth, something she adamantly denied. Finally, charges arose that Thomas had attempted to murder the young King Edward in his bedroom. Richard's father thought this business ludicrous, but so entangled were rumors mixed with semi-fact that nobody was sure.

The weight of Thomas's effrontery finally sent him to the Tower. Charges of treason were backed by his brother Edward. In March 1549, Thomas Seymour lost his head on the block, the orders signed by his own brother.

It took only two years for Edward to sink into a political morass of his own, aided to some extent by his brother's behavior. This time, most agreed the charges of treason were trumped up—at least most said so in hindsight. Edward Seymour's beheading in 1552 ended the family's influence at court. In a show of respect, the execution occurred inside the walls of the Tower, rather than on the hill just outside the gates, a place for the more common prisoner.

In his diary, King Edward VI, at this point fifteen years old, showed little remorse. He simply wrote, "The Duke of Somerset had his head cut off between eight and nine this morning." Less than a year later, King Edward himself was dead from illness. After the brief reign of Mary, daughter of Henry VIII's first wife, Katherine of Aragon, Elizabeth, age twenty-five, ascended to the throne. Elizabeth would reign like no other.

Richard heard these stories growing up. They enchanted him. In the listening, he absorbed his father's sardonic perspective. It was the stuff of tragedy, if such stories hinge on fatal flaws—and it did seem so to John Seymour. "Greed and power- mongering—flaws. You see the consequences."

Yet when Richard came into his young manhood, he couldn't help seeing his ancestor's brief glory as part of his legacy. Wasn't his father able to increase his landholding based on the family name and connections? Wasn't his own stature lifted as well as tainted? He supposed his inheritance, like that of most families, came with the good and the bad. At Oxford, at age fifteen, Richard's surname had caught the attention of a few history-keen older boys. They taunted the new fellow from the West Country with, "Off with your head—and no Seymour;" and, evidently in reference to Thomas's rumored shenanigans with the then elderly Virgin Queen, "Seymour under petticoats."

Richard's reaction to this heckling was twofold. Well, he thought, at least he was being noticed, and in an odd way, respected. On the other hand, the tainted family name pushed Richard to make sure his own character could not be labeled arrogant or foolhardy. Richard strove to appear friendly while cultivating a dignified reserve—to the extent such a posture was possible at his age—or so he told himself. But, like his father, Richard's wry sense of humor usually got the best of him. His protection against the older boys' slander came with a piece of advice offered by his father, "Take yourself lightly. That's what angels do so they can fly." So as a defense, Richard used self-mockery, "Seymour, do little."

Richard returned to his father's estate, Ram's Head, at age twenty-two in response to Sir John's request that he tutor Skidwarres. Popham knew John Seymour through the Champernowne family that had become prominent by backing English adventurers like Francis Drake, John Hawkins, and Humphrey Gilbert, as well as Sir Walter Raleigh. While Richard attended Middle Temple, Popham resided periodically in London, nearby at Bishop's Lance. In fact, a gift from Sir John Popham allowed for the construction of Richard's residence, inhabited mostly by other West Country gentlemen.

CHAPTER 4

Fall 1605, Hanford, Dorset
Skidwarres Arrives

In the fall of 1605, Skidwarres joined a lively Seymour household at Ram's Head. Richard had eleven siblings. The eldest brother, Robert, who had also attended Oxford and Middle Temple, would be the inevitable inheritor of the estate, given the laws of primogeniture. At the time, he lived in London and worked as a teller to the Exchequer. Six other siblings lived within a few hours in Dorset and Devon. One younger brother attended Oxford. Two teenage sisters remained with their parents. It was not unusual to find some or all brothers and sisters at home, especially during holidays. The curious presence of a "savage" became an obvious attraction—though what type of savage, their house guest in his English britches and cotton frock, with his friendly dark brown eyes? Jane, age thirteen, and Rosemary, eleven, the two youngest, quickly fell in love with him. Early on, Skidwarres nicknamed them Tidesso (grasshopper) and Kaakw (gull).

How, Richard had wondered, would he begin his teaching? The intriguing prospect and the modest salary offered a break from too many years of books and the drunken gaiety of the student life. Before his teaching began, Richard managed to make an appointment with his favorite don, the prestigious Francis Bacon. Bacon had no specific pedagogical expertise teaching language to a non-native speaker. He was simply the most knowledgeable man Richard and his fellow students knew.

Bacon pondered Seymour's question. Most intellectuals for the past century had contemplated the New World with great curiosity. While Richard sat watching and waiting in Bacon's quarters within Gray's Inn, one of the of the "Inns at Court" along with Middle Temple, the great man—some believed the greatest scientist alive—walked back and forth, hands folded behind his back, his habit when lecturing, something of a caricature of himself. Bacon the parliamentarian, the writer on matters scientific and political, had experienced a good many ups and downs financially, romantically, and in his dealings with the court. However, by the end of Elizabeth's reign, he had attained her good graces. Soon after the Stuart King ascended, Bacon was knighted. Like many of his time, he wore a goatee and dressed in silken, ruffled attire. His face featured a prominent nose in the middle of an often-beleaguered expression. Outdoors and sometimes in, he nearly always wore a high-crowned silk hat. His favorite featured a jeweled band, rather than the feather worn by men in the lower ranks.

His spoken words often came in the form of epigrams, pithy as the ones in his writing, nuggets—but often surrounded by mountains of less precise verbiage. "Begin very simply, as for a child, but make the content for an adult." Bacon also advised a daylong regime, broken up by exercise and excursions. "Throw him into the water of our language and culture, but never drown him." And after a few more turns and pacing, "Join speaking with reading. Write words down. Practice, practice, practice. Then allow rest. The brain craves excitement, but like the muscles, requires rest. Modulate."

"You have become a devotee of Mr. Montaigne? Is that correct?" Bacon inquired while escorting Richard to the door. Due to Bacon's own admiration for the Frenchman's essays, many of his students likewise became eager readers.

"Indeed."

"Then I recommend you comb through his essays. Find short sections. Read them to him. Have him read them. Then talk. Let the ideas bring you together. Again, begin with universal ideas."

"Yes, I understand, and thank you. And I shall do the same with your scintillating essays." Richard realized his words bordered on false flattery. Bacon was a genius, no doubt, but Montaigne the better writer. His words entered the blood stream.

The day Skidwarres arrived from Plymouth with one of Popham's associates—in a stagecoach with a sixteen-foot canoe strapped to the roof—he and Richard began their tutorials.

To Richard's surprise, they were able to communicate a good deal with slightly exaggerated facial expressions, combined with gesticulation and tone of voice. He had never truly considered the repertoire embedded in the facial muscles, shoulders, and hands, or the modulated voice. Richard knew French, Italian, Spanish, even Egyptian and Greek fellow students, but they all spoke English, so their mutual humanity appeared less remarkable. But the representative of the New World, his face reflected curiosity, disapproval, joy—especially on horseback—degrees of disgust, sadness, annoyance, and a broad range of humor from polite to ribald, from out-and-out belly laugh, to subtle appreciation. Only an ignoramus would call this man a savage. Simply, here was a man. The face proved it.

Taking Bacon's advice, Richard began writing down words for common objects: chair, bed, barn, horse, sheep, girl, sister, father, mother. Richard knew natives from the New World had no written language. But the presence of an obviously intelligent man who neither read nor wrote, and most remarkably, lived among people ignorant of the written word—this took some adjusting. And clearly it required even more imagination for Skidwarres. He knew the French and some of the English aboard ship carried "books." At his village, he once met a Frenchman who always dressed in a long black robe and carried a book from which he often read. This was curious, but he had not quite absorbed the enormity of this activity.

"Word," was one of the first words he learned. The scratchings on paper were similar to the symbols some men chiseled on rock or wood, and that men and women painted on their bodies. In one instance, a shaman, a wise man, had cut the bark of a tree in serpentine fashion, some twenty feet high, and then painted it with red ochre. At one time or another, everyone in the village traveled to see this, as well as the sacred etching on rock. What they saw was a woman giving birth to a fish. Next to her, a man held his enormous phallus, the size of his forearm. These symbols sometimes carried meaning, though people argued about exactly what.

But words were different. Ideas could be conveyed in the absence of the writer, precise ideas. Everything, Skidwarres began to realize, had a word. Even feelings and thoughts—not just objects—might land on something called "paper." It took a few days before the power of written words dawned on him. The written word, he fathomed, led to—he did not know what.

Skidwarres adjusted to Richard's single-mindedness. Two hours separated by a half-hour rest, then two more hours of words, walking around the estate, into the countryside, sitting in the library, but always words, and often the scratching, the quill on paper. At first only Richard, but later he, too, held the feather and learned letters. They ate lunch in the library, yet another opportunity to talk; then rest, allowing Skidwarres solitude.

By afternoon during those first weeks, exhaustion hit Skidwarres. It felt as if his skull would crack and then explode with words. During the second month, he began walking during rest periods, sometimes down to the narrow river to canoe alone. Then his loneliness sunk into his bowels with the dipping of the paddle, the silence, only the water. Sometimes the sadness might lift. In its place came a queer, absolute freedom.

The two met again in the late afternoon, and again more words, then sentences and the development of conversation. At dinner the two joined Richard's parents, John and Agnes, plus the two girls. When Skidwarres' comprehension and expressive ability allowed for communication, the two young adolescents peppered him with impudent questions. "What do women wear? (Much like the men, leggings held together at the waist by leather straps, deerskin across the middle and behind, robes during the cold.) How big is your house? (A third the size of the dining room.) "Everyone sleeps in the same, ah, space?" (Yes.) "Where do you, well, go to the toilet? (A hole in the ground, in the woods.) "Oh," the two girls said together. Then the youngest added, "Isn't it very cold?"

It was time again for their mother to step in. "That is quite enough, girls. You can continue this conversation some other time."

Into their sixth month together, Richard greets Skidwarres at eight o'clock in the library, where breakfast is habitually served. He holds two books, one in each hand. "The essays of Montaigne," Richard explains, placing the fat book in his friend's hand, "and the essays of Francis Bacon." He hands this one over. "I wish to talk about some of the ideas in these books. These are wise men." Here Richard again finds himself trying to communicate a complicated word, "wise." He has used the word early on, but isn't sure how to communicate the meaning. Now he'll try.

Richard points to his head. "Very intelligent. These men know a great deal." Richard stretches his arms out. "They know many, many things, ideas." Then he raises one hand high in the air, the other low in an exaggerated fashion. "Their ideas are very deep. Not like the river. Deep like the ocean." This time, Skidwarres displays no confusion. These physical efforts, so necessary at the beginning of their work, were becoming superfluous. He speaks with confidence. "Wise. Wise is to know many things. Wise is deep. Important ideas."

"Excellent, my man." They had begun sharing progress with deep laughs of satisfaction.

"All right then, my savage." Richard occasionally addressed Skidwarres so, with the ironic twist intended: here is the opposite of a savage. "Let us examine a Montaigne sentence."

Seymour opens to a leather marker. "What of a truth that is bounded by mountains and is falsehood to the world that lives beyond?" Richard reads it twice. "What do you make of it?"

"Bounded by mountains? Mountains, you have taught me that word. But bounded?"

"Yes, difficult. Let me try to explain." Seymour takes his quill and makes an X. "This is a person. Around him are mountains." He scratches these in. "You see the man is bounded by mountains. He is enclosed. He has these limits. He cannot go over the mountain, so he is bounded by them."

Skidwarres nods his head, though Richard isn't sure he understands yet.

"Before the English came, you, Skidwarres, were bounded by the sea."

Skidwarres looks up and stares at Richard without expression, not sure where his tutor is heading. "Montaigne tells us what might be a 'true' idea—say about religion—is not true or may not be, on the other side of the mountain. We are bounded by geographic limits. The limits might be mountains or seas—and not just geographic boundaries. Some, many, are bounded by stupidity."

"But, Richard, my friend, I am not bounded by sea. It is you who have not crossed the sea."

"Yes, you have bounded over the sea." Skidwarres looks at Richard a bit askance.

"Yes, I'm sorry. Again, the English language plays tricks. Bound can also mean to jump over—or another word, leap. The devilish word appears to have opposite meanings, to set limits and to jump over them. Best to write it down." Skidwarres does so in his improved penmanship. "And you are correct, it is you who have made leaps and bounds." Skidwarres nods while he writes, "You were bound, but then bounded." Skidwarres looks up and smiles in appreciation.

"Let me show you another Montaigne sentence. It is one of my favorite. And the idea is similar." Richard opens to another marked section. "'Nothing is so firmly believed as what is least known.' You see, the Frenchman believes we all fool ourselves. We, we humans, are more likely to believe something if we know very little about it."

This time Skidwarres nods and smiles. "This I understand. Both sentences are true."

"Excellent—and so Bacon has a similar thought. He writes..." and Richard takes Bacon's essays from the table next to Skidwarres' notes.

"Here, I want the exact words. "Yes," he points. 'They are ill discoverers that think there is no land, when they can see nothing but sea.' Let me try to make it more clear if less literary. At sea, just because you can't see land, doesn't mean is doesn't exist.'"

"Ah, that thought I have had, and not long ago. Standing on deck of your English ship. Nothing but sea. Difficult to imagine land."

"And the more general meaning? What is it Bacon wants us to know?"

"I think, Richard," Skidwarres says, "it is not just land we don't see, even though it is there—beyond what can be seen. Because we don't see— or does he mean understand—something, doesn't mean it is not true."

"Brilliant! Excellent! And finally, another from Montaigne. This one I know by heart: 'A man must be a little mad, if he does not want to be a little stupid.'"

"So," points out Skidwarres, "you try to fool me again with the word mad. It has two meaning. This I have written."

"True."

"Here it means to be..." Skidwarres scratches his head, then pantomimes by widening his eyes and shaking his head, as if deranged.

"Excellent again—crazy, a man who has lost his mind." Richard points to his temple. "So the meaning: one has to be a little mad in life. Life requires it. If you don't understand this, one is stupid."

Skidwarres nods his head with a sober look. "This, Richard, I believe to be true."

Though Richard and Skidwarres' rigorous daily schedule included at least six hours of reading, talking, and writing, they held to Bacon's advice: each day must allow for exercise and rest. Travel was essential as well. By the spring of 1607, Skidwarres had walked the gardens of Middle Temple in London; he had sat silently for three hours at Saint Paul's Cathedral and stood at the hill at the Tower of London, the site of most executions. They had met Bacon and members of the Privy Council; they frequented taverns, plays, concerts and dinner parties. On numerous occasions, they visited Exeter, only four hours away. Each time, Skidwarres insisted he visit the cathedral whose Mass he found intriguing. Even more, he relished sitting in the immense, stone enclosure—the dank, musty smell of the past, the sounds of soft footsteps, of hushed voices. These had no equivalent in his previous world. Mostly, he delighted in the amplified silence of the empty cathedral. This he could compare to the sounds of the forest, to the wind rustling the upper branches. It was not the same, but he could make these comparisons.

At Ram's Head, the two men took daily walks. In the spring and summer they swam in the small river that ran through the estate. When Skidwarres first arrived, he often wandered on his own down to the barn. It was to him the same as for Richard when he visited the zoo in London and stared at the exotic animals. The natives of the Northern New World had no domesticated animals excepting dogs. No chickens, no goats or cows. No pigs or sheep. And most astonishing among these animals at Ram's Head—a horse. Within the first month after his arrival, Richard taught Skidwarres to ride. This, above all, became the native's passion. It was—Skidwarres told Richard some months after learning the pleasures of galloping at full tilt and learning the words to express himself—like changing oneself into another species. "With your teaching I am becoming an Englishman, but riding, I become a god."

"Exactly," replied his tutor. The two and their panting mounts were resting at a stream after galloping full-out for five minutes. The men knelt at the water's edge sucking water from their cupped hands, while their mounts sucked even louder.

CHAPTER 5

May 3, 1607, Ram's Head, Hanford, Dorset
A Canoe Ride

On a warm spring morning three weeks after meeting with Popham in Exeter and dining at the Ship Inn with Gorges and George Popham, the two young men are sipping tea in the library following lunch. After nearly two years together, they now fall into easy conversation with only brief interruptions for clarification.

"I have thought of this often, friend, but said little," Seymour offers, "that before, you did not read. No written language."

"This is true. Only a few symbols. Yes, and I, too, think of this. This written language is strange. Our stories come from…how do you say… time to time?"

Richard completes the sentence, "From generation to generation?"

"Yes, generation to generation, and I've told you these stories change, as you say from generation to generation. But the written word is so…I don't know how to say this."

"Change, do you mean the word doesn't change, it's somehow more substantial, or I don't know, immortal? Because if written it is—well, almost as if you can touch it. It makes it more real? And whatever is said doesn't die?"

"Yes, I think something like that, but something more, more like the opposite. By writing it, that is whatever is written, it makes it dead. It is like those paintings you showed me of your grandfather. It is like that deer head on the wall, over the fireplace. I can touch and see that deer. Dead. When alive, it was a real deer. My people don't have books. That is true. I begin to understand this and I don't mean disrespect. But there are so many dead words." Skidwarres holds up his own copy of Montaigne that Richard has given him. "I have been thinking how my people live more in the moment they are living. I don't know if that makes sense—or if it is true."

"Skidwarres, you should be lecturing at Oxford. But, and again, no disrespect meant, do not your people also have no science, no philosophy, such as you hold in your hand, no written music? To me these words, especially Montaigne's, are alive. He though is dead--but not his words.. Children live for the moment, and they are ignorant. Is that the exchange for living, as you say, to be childlike?"

Richard laughs and picks up his copy of the Bible. He stands, holds it out at near arm's length, and begins reading Genesis with the deep, pompous authority of an Anglican Priest. "'But of the fruit of the tree which is in the midst of the garden, God hath said, ye shall not eat of it, neither shall ye touch it, lest ye die. And the serpent said unto the woman, ye shall not surely die: for God doth know that in the day you eat thereof, then your eyes shall be opened, and yet you shall be as gods, knowing good and evil.'"

Skidwarres remains seated and watches Richard's eyebrows raise, a slight grin on his face.

"You see, my savage friend, you are Adam and have eaten the apple of knowledge, the written word—and we, the beguiling English, we are Eve."

Skidwarres knows this section of the Bible. It, too, has become their text. He offers a broad smile. "Ah, then it is Eve who is my teacher, not Richard. You have tricked me. You are a shaman who changes form."

Richard slaps Skidwarres on the shoulder. "And so then let this shaman and his Adam take to the outside. It is a warm spring day in England. We have been too long marooned in this dank library, surrounded by useless knowledge. We will leave our dead deer and words and commune with nature. We will live." His tone is self-mocking.

Before Skidwarres gets up, he looks at Richard, demanding eye contact, and in a more serious mood, slowly states, "Richard, you are playing and that is good, but you must know, my people are not ignorant. Not children. I don't know how long my people, the Mawooshen have existed, but I am told for many, many generations. Our stories are not so different from your Bible, but yes, different. We don't have this thing you call sin. And your god, he seems very angry. Very, how would you say it?"

"I think I would use the word vicious."

"Vicious," repeats Skidwarres, "Yes."

"Vengeful, brutal...maybe sadistic."

"So many words you English have. Are you sure you need them all?"

"Every one, my friend." This time he places his hand on his friend's shoulder and lets it rest momentarily. "I'm sorry. I have offended. Please excuse me. This spring puts me in ludicrous cheer. We must leave this grimness." Richard guides Skidwarres out of the study, through the entrance hall, and out the large wooden main door.

Skidwarres shifts his mood to join Richard's. "Is it the spring, Richard—or is it your friend Margaret that makes you like the colts in the field?"

"Yes, yes, I think of her and my spirit rises. It is you who will be the shaman when you return."

The two men port Skidwarres' canoe from the barn to the river. Today Richard stands near the stern and poles, English style, pushing them forward along with the easy current. The countryside is abloom, the smell so profuse and mixed one cannot discern lavender from lilac from lily from apple blossom from the damp earth. For long stretches, they don't speak. Richard's attention drifts. Like feelings, like emotions these smells are, one mixed or overlaid with the other, and then they fade, only to be replaced by others and to fade again. Richard wishes he could travel to France and sit with Montaigne, share wine and thoughts. Dead though, fifteen years ago. Only those words, his fleshless thoughts, remain. Yes, he is immortal.

Skidwarres rests on the bottom, his back against a seat, his legs stretched, his feet on the gunwales. They both smoke long-stemmed pipes, an indulgence encouraged by Sir Walter Raleigh after his failed Roanoke colony. Richard breaks the silence.

"Tell me my friend, do you often pine for your wife and daughter? You say little of them. If I were taken from Margaret, I would be heartbroken. And we are not yet even engaged."

"Yes, I think of them. And pine? You do not speak of the tree?"

"No, the other meaning, to yearn for someone." Richard holds his pole and pipe with one hand, the other he places across his heart. "To pine, that is to wish for something or somebody that is loved."

"Love. You speak often of this word. It, too, has many meanings. But I'm not sure. Our women, a few of them who have lain with white men, the women say they—those Frenchmen—mean fornicate. No, that might not be the best word—you have so many words for it."

"Fornicate, yes, is perhaps the correct word. Fornication and love, for these things the English—and the French and Spanish—have many words."

"The 'pining' that does not mean to fornicate?"

"No. Let me see. So, you can pine for one you've fornicated with, or loved. But you can also pine for your people, your land—your land of pine trees."

"You play again. Richard, I do pine for my wife and child. And I do pine to fornicate with my wife. And I think this is something like your English love, no?"

"And now you are confusing me. But yes."

"It is not for me to ask, I think. But do you fornicate with your Margaret?"

"Skidwarres, we are, I may say, sweethearts. But fornicate, not yet. Margaret and I, we are waiting. That is our custom. I met her only months ago. You were there at the concert. You attended when she and I played music. She is forever chaperoned and I busy. We have found moments to kiss and fondle. But fornicate, not quite yet. If we become engaged, probably. You wonder about our English love and fornication. So do the English, nearly all the time. And just recently I read of a French explorer who visited Acadia, near your Sagadahoc. This fellow reports the natives are—and these are his exact words—are "strangers to the blind fury" which we call love. Blind fury? Was he correct or was he just one of those puffed-up frogs who think they know so much and are themselves so easily stricken by love?"

"I'm not sure I can answer. This 'blind fury,' I have felt something of that. He pats his heart, his stomach and groin, with the hand not holding the pipe. "It is not a bad storm to be in, do you agree? It is short but strong. But I think the Frenchman speaks of something more, something in the head. No?"

"Yes, I think so. We English—and French and Spanish—we are stricken with chivalry. We have myths too. We make our women mythical. Maybe Margaret is my mythical woman. We worship them." Richard's tone is again becoming ironic. "Is it not strange that Margaret and I do not fornicate? What a stupid thing—the sin of sex, unless you are married. It's a myth I can do without. Skidwarres, do your people not live by such myths?"

The countryside moves by. They are now drifting. Richard uses the pole more for balance than locomotion. The pipe hangs from the corner of his mouth, no longer trailing smoke.

"I believe I know what you mean. And yes, we follow the stories of our ancestors and, as you say, myths"

Richard continues, his mind still on Margaret, "Of course, this urge young men have, is strong, no? And in our youth, we are inventive and naturally disrespectful. At fourteen, I was seduced by a very pretty maid whose mother and grandmother worked for our family. She was eighteen and is now married and living nearby. We met as often as we could. We smile at one another now, remembering that secret. Ah, the blind fury of fornication, but I only briefly pined for her. And I felt no sin. No romantic blind fury and no solemnity of marriage."

"But you soon will be married?"

"Margaret, she still does not know I will become a chaplain. I don't know how she will take my decision. She might have known my intention before I did." A long moment of silence settles before Richard again picks up the conversation. "This Frenchman also says your young men and women are quite free with sex. Is that true?"

"Free? Yes we are free. If you mean we practice before we marry. Is that what you mean? After marriage, not so free."

"Interesting."

"I will tell you a story," Skidwarres says. His tone is an attempt at Richard's teaching voice. "It is a bit unusual, but it will help you know our people. From what I know of the English, I don't think you would use this kind of cure."

"Cure?"

"Yes. Once, a grown woman turned quite ill. She lay on her mat for days and wanted nothing but to die. Her husband had drowned fishing. She had no physical problem. It was her spirit that didn't want to live. A woman of the village, known for her healing talents, came to her. They spoke, and then all the young women were invited to join them. When—I think you would call them girls—arrived, the woman healer asked each which young man of the village she would like to be with. They laughed together as young women do. They 'negotiated'—that is the word Sir John uses. That is what the unmarried young women did. And when they came to some agreement—some got their first choice, others not—they were told to meet at the main lodge the next night. While this talking occurred, the sick woman sat up on her mat and listened. She became interested. She made suggestions and helped with the negotiations. The next day the healing woman visited the chosen boys and told them to visit the lodge that night."

While Skidwarres spoke, Richard remained standing, listening, pole across his chest. Skidwarres grinned. He had heard many stories. He knew when to stop and wait while the listener absorbed the narrative. After this brief silence Richard asked, "Yes?"

"The next evening the young people arrived. The sick woman greeted them. It was the first time she left her hut. The healer told the girls to sit with the one they had chosen. Then we were told—to enjoy each other."

Richard interjects, "We?"

Skidwarres smiles. "We did enjoy one another. Much laughing from us, and from the sick woman. She also encouraged and instructed some of us. We drove the sick spirits out of her with our good spirits."

Skidwarres looks at Richard with a constricted, feigned seriousness around his mouth that then flitters into a smile—and then the two of them begin laughing from the stomach up. Richard loosens his grip on the pole long enough for it to slip a few inches. His readjustments tip the round-bottomed canoe. Noticing his opportunity, Skidwarres shifts his weight just enough to topple Richard overboard. He splashes with a sputtering curse and stands in the cold, shoulder-deep stream.

"Treachery!" Richard mutters while guiding the canoe to the bank with one hand.

"But Richard, you say we are diplomats. You must not always be the teacher. So I teach you to balance."

"Ha! A diplomat who takes advantage of a weakness." Richard pulls the canoe up on the bank. He strips off his soggy clothes and places them over a bush to dry. "And I say we equalize the power by becoming naked children of God." Richard dives back in while Skidwarres peels off his English clothes and follows.

Richard and Skidwarres lie naked, half-asleep on the grassy banks of the stream. Heads on the soft ground, they momentarily open their eyes to the high cirrus clouds. The bright sun bakes them.

"Skidwarres, you were not telling me a myth or joking?"

"No, my friend." His voice is soft, his thoughts distant.

"And what of the woman? You said, 'cure?'"

"That evening she walked about the village for the first time. She ate. The next morning she greeted others outside her hut and later that week—cured."

"Hmmm," Richard offers. "You and your friends, you reminded her of joy?"

Skidwarres answers, slowly and circumspectly in his native tongue, "Life wishes to be lived." Then in English, "Something like that."

Richard sits up. "My clothes should be dry enough. The stable boy will be waiting for us not far from here with the horses. We still have some hours before evening, before the dinner party."

Skidwarres doesn't open his eyes, "I am at your command, Sir Richard." His voice, still distant, sounds tired.

CHAPTER 6

May 3, 1607, Early Afternoon
Highwaymen

Skidwarres relishes putting his five-year-old mare, Silk, into a sustained gallop. When the stable boy offers him the reigns, he quickly swings onto the saddle, and with a warrior's scream, kicks Silk's withers. Horse and rider take off down the dirt road that crosses acres of open countryside. Richard grabs the challenge. He leaps onto his mount, a six-year-old stallion named Dancer.

"I will catch you—unless you break your neck first," he yells, but is only faintly heard by Skidwarres a good thirty yards ahead.

For more than three minutes, the two push their horses. Richard gains slightly, but does not catch up before Skidwarres enters a wooded section and slows to a lope. Richard reins in when he comes abreast. Both slow to a walk. Skidwarres turns and smiles boyishly.

"All right, well done—though soon I would have caught you."

"If you say so, instructor. But I think it not safe in this part of the road. There are holes. So I slowed."

"That was wise—and a good excuse."

The two continue in the shade of the oaks and elm, letting their sweaty horses catch their breaths. "We'll cut off this road up ahead a mile or so and return, give our mounts a drink, and be back in time to greet Sir John and Margaret—and her friend, Emily. You remember beautiful, spirited Emily?"

"Yes. And those are the words you used to describe my horse, when you introduced us."

"Indeed, and for good reason. I will need some time to explain my plans to Margaret. Perhaps you can entertain her."

As the two converse, they are unaware of the five men who have emerged from the woods, until one steps into the road with a musket pointed at them. "Halt."

The other four brandish long knives. All are ragged and thin. Three are English with long scraggly brown hair. Two appear to be Gypsies: olive skin, skinnier, with matted, curly black hair. For years highwaymen have menaced the countryside. Unlike John Popham, when he practiced being a highwayman nearly half a century before, most are poor, out-of-work men, many with military experience. For them it was not a caper. This is not the first time Richard has been waylaid. Before, he had been relieved of his saddle bag and small amounts of cash. Though the victims were sometimes tied up and left horseless and naked, these misadventures typically didn't end in violence.

Richard decides to act bemused. "Good afternoon, gentlemen. A fine day for banditry."

Two of the Englishmen come closer. Richard's horse snorts and shakes his head.

"Easy, Dancer."

"Your money or your throats," says the one with the firearm.

"In this regard, you have barked up the wrong tree. We are without valuables. I suggest you go back into the woods and wait for a carriage."

"Empty your pockets," the one with the musket demands."

Richard stands in his saddle and turns his pockets inside out. Skidwarres takes his cue. "As you can see—penniless," adds Richard, "and without saddle bags. We are simply out amusing ourselves."

"We are not amused," answers one of the knife holders. "Dismount. Your horses are worth much, and your clothes will be useful," says the one with the rifle. His voice has lost some of its resolution.

Richard looks over at Skidwarres. "Before I do as you say, I must tell you about my friend." Richard had noticed all of the men glancing suspiciously at Skidwarres. "Skidwarres, open your shirt and let them see. I must inform you, he has powers that might affect your long-term health."

Skidwarres slowly unbuttons his shirt. The three English take a few steps closer to inspect the black triangular design across his chest.

"My compatriots, you are gazing at a savage from the New World. My friend, he is called a shaman. In this country we have our witches, our wise men, our soothsayers. This shaman has powers we do not have. My friend is able to lay a curse on you. He, for instance, can make your privates shrink into your groins. Is this not true, Skidwarres?"

Skidwarres, steely-eyed, shifts his gaze from one man to the next, uttering threatening sounds in his native tongue, and then in English adds, "True." The two Gypsies back off a few feet and mumble to one another.

"This horse has been my companion for his entire life. I do not intend to give him up."

Richard knows that Gypsies tended to be superstitious. It was also likely that the remaining three were illiterate, with a susceptibility for black magic. "You will notice the red hue of my friend's skin. If this is not proof of his people's devilish ways, then I must condemn you for lack of imagination."

The smallest man with the knife blurts out, "Fuck!"

Richard continues, "Shaman Skidwarres, perhaps you would get off your horse and address these men at closer range. Let them see your eyes, where your power is obvious."

As Skidwarres drops to the ground, the two Gypsies walk backward and then turn and run into the woods. The other two with knives back up, their weapons pointed straight-armed in front of them. The one with the gun shouts, "Fie on you, stay there!"

"Sir," Richard softly commands, "pray, put down your musket before you do us all ill."

The gunman obeys, incredulous now that two of his companions have disappeared and the others continue to edge backward as Skidwarres advances toward them, one hand on his horse's reigns, muttering a menacing, "*Moz wiagzi, moz wiagzi*" (you are moose entrails) over and over. Richard softly urges Dancer forward. The man, his musket now pointing at the ground, looks up at Richard, at his commanding height.

"Thank you," Richard says with a small bow of his head. "You are a gentleman."

The gunman stammers, "Tell your crazy friend to back off."

Richard bends over slowly and lays a hand on the weapon's barrel near the stock. He receives no resistance, so lifts it and takes possession. From atop Dancer, Richard aims at a tree and squeezes the trigger. The mechanism clicks.

"Beg your pardon, sir, but we could not afford the powder." The embarrassed highwayman smiles sheepishly, displaying a missing tooth and bloody gums, suggesting malnutrition.

"An unloaded weapon can be just as effective. It is not every day you come upon a shaman from the New World."

"Yes, my lord."

Richard does not feel superior. Friends of his brag about charging their horses into the sorry highwaymen or even using their swords, severing a hand, jabbing into a stomach, and charging off, later showing off whatever blood remained on their weapons or splattered on their pants. Sport of a kind, though one had to exercise good judgment. Highwaymen could be deadly. Rather, Seymour remembers his recent visit to the court where Sir Popham presided. These men on the road, like those hanged, are more often than not hapless, ludicrous men, mostly just desperate.

Richard looks over his shoulder. Skidwarres has remounted. The two other men, now yards away, daggers at their sides, watch slack-mouthed. Richard stands up in his saddle, jams a hand into his back pocket, and gropes for a moment before retrieving six coins. "In these highway matters, lying is part of the game." He leans from the saddle and with his right hand drops six pennies into the hand the highwayman automatically reaches out. "This is not much, but I see you need sustenance. May you purchase some—and share with your...friends. England is great, but it is flawed. Richard returns the firearm. The dumbfounded man reaches again. "Good day."

"Thank you, sir." The two Englishmen have cautiously approached their leader. The two Gypsies stand at the edge of the forest.

Dancer and Silk break into an easy lope. Their riders settle and don't speak for ten minutes, not until they water the horses in the stream.

"And what are you thinking?" Richard asks. His own mind has wandered from Popham's offer, to Margaret's soft skin above the scoop of her dress, to the vagaries of fate.

"I think the word is sadness. Is that correct? They are thin. They need food. So they must...steal. In our villages, if one is hungry, then we are all hungry."

Richard looks at Skidwarres, nods his agreement, and then commands, "Homeward to roast beef and duck, to the guile of our elders and the calculated charm of women." They pull gently on Dancer and Silk's heads, interrupting their slurping. Aware of their proximity to the stable, both snort, quiver, and glimmer with sweat in the late afternoon light. Without urging, they move into a gallop.

CHAPTER 7

May 3, 1607, Evening, Ram's Head
Hosting Popham

Richard's father, John Seymour, presides at the head of his oak dining table, Sir John Popham at the foot, some twenty feet away. Dinner party neighbors chat amiably, except when either Sir John Popham or John Seymour addresses the other loudly in order to be audible. In turn, the others hush and let the senior men speak without competition. John Seymour holds a solid reputation as a steward of Ram's Head, which has expanded during his and his father's lifetimes due to shrewd investments and Seymour family connections. In his later years, he spends hours in his well-stocked library reading philosophy and astronomy and writing the history of the Seymour family, though he has graciously given over this sanctuary to Richard and Skidwarres and settled into the sunny anteroom off his bed chamber.

Amy Popham, Sir John's sixty-year-old wife—round, pink, and powdered—sits to her husband's right. As with many of her age and station, she remains steadfast and loyal to her ambitious husband with his business and legal responsibilities. She has weathered his frequent absences while raising seven children. Behind her pleasant smile and apparently rapt attention with those she converses, a keen observer might look carefully and still not discern her true nature beyond her dedication to others.

Margaret commented later how the prodigious energies of men like Sir John Popham can take the air out of a room, and perhaps out of their wives, as well. "Don't most gentlemen of his age—and your age too—take mistresses as a born right, leaving their wives holding begrudged love?"

"Never," Richard responded.

Next to Mrs. John Popham sits Robert, John's eldest male child, and therefore the rightful heir to Ram's Head. Robert precedes Richard by seven years and predated him at both Oxford and Middle Temple. Lean and tall since childhood, by adolescence he began wearing a serious look, so much so that his siblings and friends began calling him "Sir Robert." He didn't seem to mind, as his demeanor apparently derived from his image of himself as a future large landowner and a man who would manage prodigious responsibility. Unlike his younger brother, Richard, who loves music, horsemanship, dancing, literature and philosophy, Robert gravitated to economics and the law—and little else. At the time of the dinner party, he is working in London for the Exchequer. In the not too distant future, he would live up to his nickname and be knighted for his work in that realm.

George Popham's third wife, Penelope, is to Robert Seymour's right. George's first died wife in childbirth, the second from tuberculosis. Penelope, a commoner, responded to George's reputation as a bold explorer and raconteur. He—or at least his reputation—enlivened her heretofore spinster existence for a while. They met at a similar dinner party, she brought by a sister who had herself "married up." He succumbed to her abundant bosom and sweet modesty. These qualities allowed him to overlook her dullness that he at first misread as shyness. On the bridal bed, a twenty-eight-year-old virgin, she lay with her then forty-year-old husband. He had his way, as they were now of one flesh. Neither that night nor during their entire marriage did she ever experience desire. George remained oblivious to this fact. After all, her body reacted with dampness to his touch. Her taut nipples provided evidence that she wanted him. Yet the connections between bodily reaction and desire did not exist for Penelope. Her lack of enthusiasm, he took as a sign of her parental training, derived from biblical teaching, and her God-given modesty. A few years into the marriage, she learned from one of their servants the simple unadorned truth the Puritans offered. To George's consternation, she became a follower. Her taciturn nature now earned the Lord's blessings, as she saw it. At first, George tried to browbeat her. He was a reformist, but adherence to the Church of England was synonymous with allegiance to the English monarchy. She remained adamant. Years into the marriage, his disappointment occasionally dissolved in the face of her apparently responsive, abundant, and well-placed flesh. George remained, at least periodically, attentive.

Richard is between Penelope and his mother, Alma Rosque Seymour, she next to Sir John at the other end of the table. In her mid-fifties, the mother of fourteen children— three stillborn, two dead after six months, but nine raised to adulthood, all but two teenage girls—Alma carries with her a rather tired cheerfulness. "With all her heartaches," Richard once commented to Margaret, "you talk to her or she pats your cheek, and she's able to let you believe you are the most important thing in the world."

Margaret had smiled. They were lying in the grass on a blanket, miles from her estate, their horses grazing nearby, his hand lazily cupping her left breast under her chemise. "Richard, you are the only person in the world." She looked quite serious before giggling. For that she received a little pinch on her nipple followed by a serious bout of tickling.

Margaret, age twenty, is to John Seymour's right, her long, curly, strawberry-blond hair reaching her midriff. She tends toward shyness in a formal setting, though a little wry smile often appears on her face while she listens. Her eyes dart about and sparkle. Richard learned early that her sweetness was intertwined with a barbed sense of humor and a tendency to be headstrong. Some months before, a year after Skidwarres' arrival at Ram's Head, Richard took his pupil to a concert. There Richard and Margaret had met. Periodically, they began meeting at Margaret's estate to practice music: Richard on the harpsichord, Margaret, the cello. Emily had been Margaret's guest twice. She was an accomplished violinist. Skidwarres had fashioned a drum from a kitchen pot and leather and quietly provided a steady beat. Richard and Margaret's ardor deepened and warmed. They found time alone to kiss and fondle within the occasionally relaxed Elizabethan constraints of a young gentlewoman wishing to maintain her virginity for the wedding night—or at least until her betrothal.

Having been reared in the Elizabethan era, educated women like her were willing to listen to their parents' suggestions for marriage, but not necessarily to follow any orders, though arranged marriages remained commonplace among the nobility and gentry. In their case, both sets of parents smiled upon the potential union between landed families within a two-hour ride of one another, even though Richard's inheritance did not promise to be substantial. At least his education ensured him an entry-level placement with some branch of government, some aspect of commerce, or the law.

George Popham beams with delight at his two dazzling neighbors, Margaret and Emily. He turns to his left and right, back and forth, trying his best to keep the two entertained and focused on himself. Eventually his right hand finds its way under the table onto Emily knee. She doesn't appear to mind.

Emily's height—five feet five inches, tall for her time—and her upright posture gave her a regal bearing. Of all Margaret's friends, Emily appeared the most proper and well-reared. She played the violin and recited poetry. She danced the most recent French dances. She spoke French, Spanish, and Latin. Emily read prodigiously, could converse about history, philosophy, and economics, and did so with knowledgeable men—as she in fact did with George. As was the case for some aristocratic young women, she had spent two years in Paris augmenting her education. Margaret also knew something few others did, and the reason she found Emily intriguing—if not necessarily one in whom she might confide—was her wildness, the exact opposite of her public persona. Under the guise of music lessons, Emily traveled regularly to London to stay with an eccentric aunt. There she was free to be with male friends. It was in London that one such friend escorted her to a parlor off a side street frequented by sailors. Emily left some hours later with a small, delicate mistletoe tattoo artfully placed four inches below her navel. Richard heard of this from a male friend who came across the artwork during an amorous encounter.

While Emily converses with George about her favorite cafe in London, his right hand wanders to a thigh insulated by a silky dress and chemise. Her animation and composure don't flicker.

Skidwarres sits to Emily's right, Robert's wife, Ann, between him and Sir John.

After Richard and Skidwarres arrived back from their encounter with the highway men, they washed and with aplomb presented themselves to the guests when their carriage arrived at the large stone front entrance. Skidwarres agreed to walk Emily around the estate, while Richard gathered his wits to tell Margaret of his dilemma. He has taken Popham's advice and given himself the opportunity to back out, even though he had no such intention. But he hasn't yet told his parents. His angst grew as he contemplated leaving Margaret just as their love was flowering. It seems a repudiation of her, or so he thought, putting himself in her position.

As they enter the formal gardens to the side of the house, they clasp hands.

"Oh, Richard, I am so glad to see you again. It so difficult to leave you, and then there you are on my mind. You are a pest—sometimes. I can't rid myself of you." She stops, pulls his head down to kiss each cheek. It is enough to spill warmth through his stomach, up to his chest, and down to his groin. Their hands join again and they continue the walk.

"Do you wish me gone, to pester you no more?"

"No, you silly fool. It is I who have placed you there next to my heart. I have a wonderful imagination." The path has taken them behind shrubbery and out of sight of the older guests who are now enjoying the late afternoon light in the confines of the sunroom. Again Margaret stops, this time to push her index finger into Richard's belly. "You are real, are you not? I am not conjuring you?"

"I am real—though I admit I wonder sometimes myself." He wraps his arms around her. She is small, five-two, delicately-boned but muscular from dance. He loves her light walk, the way her thighs grip the cello, the strength in her right bowing arm, her fingers moving up and down the stem, and at this moment the whiff of lavender in her hair. "Your smell—that is what is real." While holding her he begins, "Margaret, I have something to discuss." He has tried to prepare for this moment, but having gone so far, he isn't sure which alternative to use.

Margaret straightens. "Your tone sounds ominous. Not like you."

"Yes, well I have not been this way before. I have made a decision. At least some part of me has made a decision. Perhaps I am coming to you for reassurance? Or you may find me a fool."

"Shall we sit? Over there." She points to a curved stone bench. "Let me guess? Or would you simply prefer to tell me?"

"Guess? You think you know the burr under my saddle?

"Remember, you inhabit my thoughts."

Richard wonders if she worries about another woman. "Margaret, there is no one but you." He is as much reassuring himself. On his last trip to Exeter with Skidwarres, he had struck up on a long conversation with an intriguing woman, quite different from Margaret. Dark haired, solemn, he perceived an invitation in her challenging stare. For that moment, Margaret had disappeared. He had undressed this stranger many times since in his mind. Only, with the corset unhooked and the chemise lifted, it was Margaret's body—pink and white with occasional freckles—that appeared instead.

"Perhaps, my unsettled love, but I do believe I have one competitor for your affection—for your love."

"No," insists Richard, "There is no one. Whom do you speak of?"

"Why, it is obvious. Skidwarres."

"Skidwarres? For my love?"

"Yes—even love. No, not the same love we have. No." To seal this thought, she takes his hand, kisses it, then places it over her small, firm left breast, leaves it there a moment, and again with her other hand pulls his head toward her and kisses his lips. Then she draws back a few inches. "Not this flavor of love. But love, I do think."

Richard removes his hand from her and kisses the exposed skin just above the scoop of her dress. They stare at one another, their eyes crinkled with amusement.

Richard finds some of his prepared words. "Sir John has asked me to join the expedition to the New World. He thinks Skidwarres and I would be of service. He thinks I could serve as chaplain."

"Richard, then my guess, my intuition, it is not wrong?"

"That was your guess?"

"An intuition. And now that you tell me, it appears obvious."

"Then I must be finding my way to your bedroom without my knowing it. Margaret, what should I do? I have not made a final decision."

"What do you want, my love?"

"I want you. But what do I have to offer? Robert will someday—perhaps soon, who knows?—be the master of the house. I, if I'm lucky, if he is generous—and I know he is just—I will own a patch of land, one of the houses nearby, and like a wayward planet, I'll orbit around this manor where I now still live like a child with my parents. I am undecided what to do. The life of the law and commerce, it bores me. Should I teach? I am not ready for that, if ever. How could I give you what your father provides you? My prospects are vague to me. These two years with Skidwarres, they have given me more purpose than I've ever known. But then you—you, too, are my purpose. I cannot lose you." His gushing forth brings together a jumble of considerations he's mulled over during the past three weeks, though to himself he sounds desperate—an accurate display, but one he wishes to control better.

Margaret waits expectantly. For a moment Richard looks to her, unsure what to say next.

"How long? When would you return?"

"A year, maybe two."

"And you would be in danger?"

"I suppose. There are unknowns."

"Richard." Margaret, too, has thought about what she might say if her own hunch proved to be true. "Richard, I will wait. Popham chose well. He probably had you cast in this role from the beginning. Richard, do you know how you've told me about your traveling on Dancer, exploring the countryside for days at a time? How much you welcome your own wanderlust? How would you feel if you decided to remain?"

"I'd feel warm and dry in your arms, in a large bed."

"You'd end up resenting me—I do think."

"Never! But your point, Margaret, I understand."

"Then you must go. And I must wait for my love to return. I can do that, you my Odysseus, I your Penelope."

"In the meantime, others will pursue you."

At this Margaret shifts her body so to face him. She bores her large green eyes into his brown ones.

"Yes?" Richard responds, not sure of what he sees.

"But not if I'm betrothed."

"Betrothed. Well, then." The simplicity of it all. Of course, he had considered it. Only he wasn't sure she'd accept. "Well, yes." Richard stands and offers a broad smile, then drops to one knee in front of Margaret. The gesture hints of broad humor, but not his voice. "Then, dearest Margaret, I beg you to be my wife. I beseech you."

Margaret holds her immediate response on her lips, just so, just enough to match the small drama of Richard kneeling. Then she says, "Yes, Richard. I'll be your wife."

He lowers his other knee to the ground and buries his forehead in her silken lap, a thankful supplicant. "Thank God," he utters, his voice muffled in her clothing, then rises.

Margaret rises too, and they embrace tenderly, cautiously, as if their newly-born mutual decisions might bruise with anything more robust.

"Best we get back to the others, before Emily eats Skidwarres alive."

"Now Richard, I'm sure she's behaved herself marvelously with him."

"Margaret, your parents?"

"They will accept our decision. Father is not well. He wishes me married and pregnant. We've discussed it—that is, you."

They reluctantly release one another. Hand in hand, they head back on the path. "Margaret," he says with a wry smile and a raised eyebrow, "Perhaps Popham isn't the only one plotting my life."

Richard's father had described Sir John succinctly to his family the night before. "If he told me to walk into battle, and I knew my chances for survival were nil to none, I'd march. If he told me to jump out a window, I'd jump. He's a leader, pure and simple." While the two young couples tarried outside, John Seymour agreed to commit another sum to the Virginia Company's northern settlement. He had invited Sir John because of his effusive manner. He had visited twice since Skidwarres' arrival. At his Littlecote estate in Wilshire, Popham had hosted the Queen more than once during her forty-year rule and, since 1603, had continued the tradition under King James. Likewise, Popham's attendance was an honor.

A council of merchants, a few influentials at court, and other landed men located in London would be responsible for the planning and financing of the southern colony. Popham's energies focused on the second similar group of men from Dorset, Somerset, Devon, and Cornwall. This group oversaw the proposed northern operation.

When the party is assembled around the table, John Seymour rises to sharpen the long blade of his serving knife, just as a gigantic rib roast is delivered by a male server. All offer polite applause. He brings the chatter on both sides of the table to a halt by directing a question to Sir John.

"We are, of course, eager to hear when you will set sail. I failed to ask."

"Thank you, sir, for your interest, and of course, for your additional contribution and this gracious dinner." He raises his glass as the others follow suit.

"If only others might have your foresight. There is no more important activity for England. Our Queen knew this, even if His Highness King James is less bold. We are a small island in a sea of predators. We all know the French have sent their infernal Jesuits to infiltrate the New World. They befriend and ally themselves with the natives—just as they attempted to undermine the Church of England only a few years ago—and I can say with some satisfaction, I was able to condemn more than a few to death. We know their explorer Champlain sailed up the rivers in the lands occupied by Skidwarres' people. If we do not act, the French, the Catholics, the Spanish—and again the pope, the same sly dog whose murderous plans nearly ended the Queen's life—they or the Dutch will occupy this gargantuan land."

As Popham holds forth, three serving maids and a butler fill glasses, deliver slivers of beef, and busy about with steaming serving dishes of fish, breads, white sauces, peas, and squash. Popham occasionally interrupts himself to sample his food, while the others wait for him to continue.

"This emptiness is starring us in the face, this opportunity for riches. But so much more. If England does not act, we will shrivel. And what of our vagrants, the unemployed, the riffraff that scourge our countryside? I have been quoted as saying I would take them out to sea and throw them overboard. Nonsense! I said that to the ambassador to Spain. Am I to tell him the truth, that we will send rabble to inhabit the New World? And maybe a few Puritans? Of course not. Anyway, our activities will be circumspect as much as possible." Aided by Seymour's good wine, Sir John has warmed by his favorite subject but is now aware he's insulted his cousin's wife's religion. "I beg your pardon, dear Penelope, I get carried away. My sentiments don't apply to all Puritans. You, of course not. Indeed, my own religious views have been influenced by the works of Luther, Erasmus. In any case..."

Penelope offers up a quizzical smile. Her thoughts had been elsewhere, as they often are, and she had only a vague appreciation she'd been slighted. Soon her often- odorous bulk of a husband would sail away. She cared little what her famous brother-in-law thought.

"If England is to grow, we must conquer. We must inhabit this vastness," Popham continues.

Richard listens intently. He wonders if—or rather, when—Popham will ask for his decision. Will it become part of the dinner agenda? The wine and John's mood embolden him as they had in Exeter three weeks before. "Sir John, you use the word conquer. Is this a term reserved for the land or do you include its people?"

"Ah, an excellent question. I am referring to the land. The people, Skidwarres' people and other groups, they must be handled with diplomacy. I think there is enough space for the English and the savage alike. Indeed, I must admit we know little of them. If our friend here is any example, though, then reason should prevail. In fact, we have no idea how large a population inhabits the land. Is that not correct?" John does not wait for an answer. "Nobody knows, is my wager. And what expanses of land have we? Some say a short route to China is not far from the Sagadahoc River. Is that not true, Skidwarres?"

"I do not know of such a route. Some say within a six-day journey from my village, a large body of water exists. Some say it is a sea."

"Yes, I've heard. Fascinating. And to return to your father's question, Richard, we plan to set sail by late May, though I swear it should have been six weeks ago. As it is, we will land with only a few months before the snows arrive. I am told the weather is rigorous. We have commandeered two ships—a third we sent some months ago, but they did not following my orders. They sailed too far south and, damn it all, were captured by the Spanish, the crew, including two of Skidwarres' fellow natives, jailed. In any case, we've recruited men with essential skills: carpentry, soldiering, masons, shipwrights, cooks, and hunters. Others will provide the muscle we need for felling trees, for building a fort, for mounting cannon. Those we will find on the streets and taverns, jails—dragooning, a fine old tradition wouldn't you say, George? An adventurous future will look better to them than their desperate present. Which, Richard, brings me to you."

"Sir, I am to be dragooned?"

Popham replies without recognizing Seymour's lightness. "A year ago when I engaged you as Skidwarres' instructor, I knew I had chosen well, but I did not anticipate the level of knowledge you've both accrued, or the camaraderie."

Richard bows his head slightly in recognition and follows up, "Sir, as you know, it is the pupil who is to be congratulated. Besides, in this case, the teacher and student constantly reverse roles."

"Said well, and it is this knowledge—from both of you—that is so essential. Projects like ours succeed or fail because of the leadership. That is why I have chosen George. However, he needs help. We expect one hundred and thirty men, thereabouts. No women. They will come later. At this first stage we need brawn—and we need brains. Stupidity is to be expected from the average man. No doubt among our men lies the potential for disharmony, ignorance, fear, greed. Good discipline will require good leadership. That is why I am entreating you, Richard. You will, I deem, accept?"

"Sir John, I do."

"Excellent, excellent. And in anticipation of such a decision, I have received the Bishop of Exeter's approval for you to represent the Church of England. In this role, you will counsel the men, ward off trouble, be an ear for George. After a year or so, you will be able to sail back to this lovely woman."

Given his position of host and patriarch, John Seymour feels he must speak. "My son, I have to add that I concur with Sir John." Weeks ago Popham had informed John Seymour of his intent to enlist Richard, a matter father and son had kept from one another. "A wonderful opportunity. I'm sure you'll represent the family with great honor. A toast to my son."

"Here, here!" all add in unison.

Richard rises. "And let me add another toast—to my just-betrothed Margaret, the future Mrs. Seymour."

Richard's mother, somewhat wide-eyed entreats, "My dear Richard, why didn't you let us know?"

"Mother, I didn't know myself until only minutes ago—about

Margaret, that is."

"Well then, indeed, you will make a fine chaplain and diplomat, as Sir John suggests, for you have held not one but two secrets from those most dear." Her comment is double-edged.

"I'm sorry, Mother, I should have spoken."

"Nonsense. On these matters, you must keep your own council," John Seymour intercedes. "Here's to the launching of your adventurous career and— let us hope—your less adventurous future domesticity."

CHAPTER 8

May 3, 1607, After Dinner
A Walk

Except for sipping during the toasts, Richard, Margaret, and Emily refrained from wine an hour before they excused themselves from the table to set up and practice two pieces they would perform in the large main reception room. Richard had begun playing the harpsichord when he was eight. Since his return to his father's estate, he had made it a habit of practicing an hour in the morning, beginning at sunrise. Both Margaret and Emily were proficient at their instruments, the cello and violin respectively. It was music that had brought Richard and Margaret together. Music provided an excuse in the beginning for Richard's two-hour ride to practice duets. Music became their primary language during those first few months. These musical conversations, their bodies as extensions of their instruments, allowed them to forego the artless conjuring of words— words that never approached the pure joining together along a multi-dimensional chord. How lovely, the harpsichord having its say, followed by that first cello note, andante con moto, that sucks at the heart. Their flow, fingers, hands, arms, upper body—when practiced, when in tempo—went way beyond words to a nearly embarrassing intimacy in those early days, weeks before their tentative first groping. At one point at the end, while Margaret was loosening her strings and readying her cello for the case, Richard had commented, "The entrance of the cello in the last movement—that note felt like a kiss." She had wiped the moisture off her instrument and laid it in its place. "Why, it was—a kiss."

After dinner and before the recital, the older men, John Seymour and George Popham, adjourn, so John can demonstrate a radical addition he'd made to his estate. He plays with his guests. "It's not new. The Romans right here in England had something like it. The Queen had one at Richmond Castle—but she decided against, well, against putting her royal self on it. Made too much noise, so I've heard from Mr. Green, who installed it for her. Unseemly for a queen." He walks them up a long stairwell to the living quarters. "You know, gentlemen, I love inventions. I predict it will be with the making of inventions, not the conquering of land, that England will dominate the world." He opens the door to a once-small bedroom. "There," he says, pointing to a toilet at the far end of the room. "You see the chain? It releases water from that bowl up there, filled by the servants, of course. It flushes everything away. Hence 'flush toilet.' But we have not yet solved a problem. All that water and its contents create quite a mess."

"Very fine," adds George, "but a ways to travel on a cold night from your bedroom. Like the Queen, perhaps, I would better prefer a groom of the stool."

"Nothing, I think, compares to a balmy night in late May," Margaret tells Richard, giving his hand an extra squeeze while they walk in the full moonlight. His other hand holds the neck of an open bottle of wine he decided they'd earned from their performance. The path meanders through the garden and over a grassy hill to the stream. It is near midnight. Skidwarres and Emily accompany them, four abreast, another bottle of wine in Skidwarres' hand, courtesy of Richard. The two couples separate a short distance from the house where the path forks.

Skidwarres and Emily had chatted during the period before dinner, she asking many questions about his life before capture. Finally she wanted to know if he had been with any women, English women. The question overstepped boundary lines, she knew, but with such directness and courtesy, and only after continuing the conversation for nearly an hour, Skidwarres felt obliged to answer. Besides, his people often preferred directness. He told her of the shabby little room over the tavern with the foul air of smoke and stale ale. Skidwarres had let himself be undressed and washed. He'd been put up to it by the sailors. During the voyage, they'd learned to like him and began teaching him English. The suspicious and sodden teenage girl with long dirty blond hair, who'd been told he was a savage from across the seas, looked at her unlikely customer and exclaimed, "It's just like all the rest of 'em, except not much hair." He didn't understand much of her content, only her surprise and acceptance.

At dinner he and Emily continued to chat when the conversation wasn't directed by Sir John, or when George wasn't trying to get her ear. At one point, she let her right hand slide under the tablecloth to rest on Skidwarres' thigh. While her hand remained there as Sir John spoke of plans, George's fingers crawled from her knee to her thigh like a large spider. Finally, she gingerly plucked it off.

After the couples part ways, Emily asks her companion for the bottle and takes a long swig from it. "Shall we continue to the river, where you took me earlier? It's a lovely spot."

Margaret and Richard settle on a blanket over recently-cut grass alongside the riverbank. They remain quiet until he asks about her mood.

"I am thinking how it will be with you sailing away. Oh, I don't know what, this Popham's folly—that is what I think sometimes. He is so headstrong. He's old and full of himself. About all this importance of England, as if he were England."

They sit facing one another, knees drawn up, hugging each other for support. The moonlight allows each to discern the other's expression. Margaret is uncharacteristically pensive, slightly sad around the mouth. In response, the skin around Richard's eyes crinkles in worry.

Margaret sniffles. "I'm sorry. I don't want to be in your way. Really, I'm so happy. I know this is a…well, I don't know what, but I can understand how you are excited, especially to travel with Skidwarres and everything."

Richard pulls himself even closer, spreads his legs apart, and brings her in tight. His hands reach up to her cheeks and he wipes the tears away with his thumbs. "Margaret, I am not without trepidation or regret."

"Thank you." She adjusts her legs, straightens them out, and places them over his calves.

"More wine?" He offers her the bottle. She accepts and takes two long slugs. He does the same, and then they remain quiet, his arms resting lightly on her shoulders, caressing her hair, ears, cheek, the back of her neck. Her hands rest on his thighs. She kneads them gently.

"We played well tonight," Richard says after a long interlude. "I really practiced this time, and not just my mistakes. Emily's instruction helped."

"And Skidwarres and she, what do you suppose?"

"I suppose nothing." He bends over and kisses her nose and then her mouth. She giggles and adds, "I'm thinking maybe she takes it as her duty to flummox men.

"And you, dear Margaret?"

"Tonight I think not, but are not women—as with Eve—put on earth to set it topsy-turvy?"

"Indeed, dear Margaret."

For a long moment they sit quietly, their foreheads resting against one another. Crickets' song fills the night. Then they let go and stare upwards. Hundreds more stars emerge as the couple's night vision improves. Margaret speaks first. "I have something to give you before your journey, and I don't know after tonight when we will see one another again, if we'll be alone." She moves to perch upright on her knees, still between his outstretched legs.

"You have something to give me? What…where?"

"Here, Richard dear, right in front of you. I want to give you myself." As she stands he remains seated, arms behind him, looking up at her, not comprehending.

"I want to give you all of me."

"Oh?" He thinks he understands and rises. They face one another, four feet or so separating them.

"Richard, I've thought about this for days, and here we are." She drops her shawl, unbuttons her frock, and turns her back to him. "Please unlace my bodice." She wriggles out of it, bends, and removes her stockings. Finally she wears only her linen chemise.

They stand under the light as the sky darkens and brightens from the few gossamer passing clouds. After watching her in happy amazement, he, too, begins slowly undressing, beginning with his boots. They gaze at one another, savoring the moment. They have caught one another's tranquil, seductive mood. Little by little, exposed patches of skin feel the warm night air. They stare at one another. Richard removes his last article of clothing, his underpants. Margaret brings the chemise over her head. They stand naked. Margaret then turns in a full circle and ends with a little curtsey, as if she were showing off her new dress.

Picking up on her playfulness, Richard smiles. "It fits well."

"Your breasts," Richard had commented a few months before, "they might each fit perfectly in a tea cup. This is not a complaint," he quickly added. "The association is meant to conjure up their delicate, exquisite nature." Now he refers to that night, "Still exquisite."

"And you do not wish for soup bowl breasts?"

"No, thank you, madam, I prefer petit to ponderous."

Richard admires her from head to foot. Because of this brief distance, her beauty feels more objective, as opposed to the sometimes wanton focus that comes through hands and lips. Not that she isn't enticing— rather that her aesthetics absorb him for the moment. In contrast, her eyes are half-closed, the objects of adoration. For the moment, for both, wonder overrides desire. His phallus is engorged, she notices, but not erect. He feels this and is glad. A full erection, under the immediate conditions, would be impertinence—or so he feels she might think.

A cloud crosses the moon, shading them both. Margaret steps forward, only inches away. A slight lilac scent comes off her body. At five foot eight, his nose brushes the top of her head and fills with hair lotion and musky sweat from the hot day and hard work bowing. Immediately he feels himself rising and touching her belly.

"Hello," Margaret says in response and reaches down to touch him, but stops. "May I touch you? I want to. I'll be gentle, as you must be with me. You know I am your virgin."

"Yes, touch me. We will take the next step carefully."

Margaret caresses him softly, as she might the ear of a puppy. She lifts her head. They kiss. His hand drops to cup her bottom. Interrupting the kiss, she whispers, "Amazing."

"Mmmmm," they say in unison, and then Richard adds, "It won't be amazing if you keep touching me like that. It will be over."

As from the start, Margaret takes the lead. She steps back, kneels on the blanket, looks up, reaches for his penis and kisses it briefly, then lies down on her back. "All right, my lionhearted, it is time for you to take command. I am the land you must conquer." Margaret allows humor to lubricate her moment without dissolving its small momentousness, tiny against the immense night sky.

He has not lain with a virgin. Without sexual experience, he might have felt some trepidation, but not tonight. His heart and his groin feel allied. "I will go slowly. Open your legs, just so. I will bring myself up to you and you can raise yourself." She does so, and he pushes some of the blanket under her. "Do you feel me now?"

"Yes, yes, of course. What do you want me to do?" asks Margaret.

"I will press just a bit and you can tell me to stop or continue."

She obliges. "More."

"That is all right?"

"Yes, a little more."

"Yes." Richard is now aware of his gathering sweetness. He continues.

Margaret utters an "Oh!" and Richard hears pain. She withdraws just an inch or so.

"No, continue. Push." He does, much harder, as if diving off a steep bank into deep, warm water. Her blockage breaks and he sinks into her. Her arms cling to his neck, her legs wrap around his thighs. He cries out,

"Margaret!" as if wounded.

As their breathing returns to normal, he settles some of his weight on her. He also braces himself on his elbows and places his mouth next to her right ear. They lie motionless.

"Does it hurt now?"

"No, just a little ache. I feel wonderful. Thank you. I hope I wasn't too bold and too inexperienced at the same time."

"You were marvelous." He presses into her a bit more and then withdraws and shifts his body off hers, so she is lying on her back, he on his side. He strokes her breasts.

"Richard?"

"Yes?"

"Do you believe in God?"

"Do I believe in God? Well, I should say yes, after tonight."

"No, I'm serious. You are to be a chaplain. Don't you have to be rather like a man of God?"

"We've talked of this before, no? Haven't I said something about not being very sure about God the Father or God the Son, but very sure about the Holy Ghost? I'm serious, that's what I think. And seriously, I think the Holy Ghost is with us tonight. I guess one part of the Trinity will have to do."

"But you believe in the Church of England? I mean, you are comfortable representing it?"

"I am. But what it represents differs from man to man. Richard's hand moves across her belly and over her soft patch of strawberry pubic hair. He had wondered about her coloring there, his theory being a woman's eyebrows were the giveaway. And so it was. "Margaret, to change the subject to something more...well, at hand. What color are you down there? The light is not quite strong enough."

"I guess I'm like the hair on my head. Does it matter?"

"You could be dark green and I would love it." His hands twirl a bit in her hair.

"The Holy Ghost," Margaret repeats. "I suppose that means mostly that God is mysterious and maybe around when we don't know it. And says 'boo!' Maybe you're right, he's here tonight, right next to us on the blanket."

"Welcome," Richard adds, looking over his shoulder to the invisible guest. "Yes, and I suppose I will have to offer up sermons as part of my responsibilities. So I will let the men know of our encounter here tonight, proof of God the Holy Ghost. I will speak in great detail about it—a miracle."

Margaret cuddles in closer. The air around them has cooled. Her hand finds its way. His tumescence had receded, but returns with her touch. He groans softly. "Would you like to return to me?" she asks.

"You are not too sore?"

"A little, but I want you."

Richard rises to his knees and slowly reenters. "Should I continue?"

"Please."

He slowly moves back and forth, slowly sinking." He stops for a moment and Margaret opens her eyes to his face and the stars beyond. "Excuse us, Holy Ghost," she offers to the heavens.

Richard slowly glides, gathers momentum, and falls. For a moment, the image of a hawk—descending, circling in the thermals—comes to him. He hears himself whispering, "Thank you, Margaret. Thank you." His words have quickened with the tempo of his passion and then trailed off. "Thank you, thank you, thank you, thank you."

Then he is quiet. The cicadas, too, have ended their song. It is late. "Please, Richard, return to me." Off in the trees, an owl hoots softly. After the two have returned to their respective rooms only hours before light, he remembers the Roman myth—an owl's hoot the harbinger of death. Or was it, as Skidwarres has told him, a sign of a fortuitous event?

CHAPTER 9

May 3, 1607, After Dinner
Cultural Exchange

Emily's presence reminds Skidwarres of his capture: the initial moment, having his hair grabbed, his body slammed to the boat deck, his realization that he was a rabbit in a trap, that it was pointless to struggle. The large floating object that had caught the wind, the men from another world and their shining objects—iron pots, beads, gunpowder, and powerful drink—this mesmerized many of his people. He was now among them, these others. But why does Emily make him think of this? He also feels desire.

Soon after Skidwarres had been carried under the deck into a small room and lashed into a hammock, the captain entered. He said two things: "You will not be hurt. You will be returned to your people as will your friends." At first Skidwarres didn't understand, but the tone offered comfort, so he nodded.

When he was released, he stood in front of the captain. His now-free arms wanted to attack. He felt his chest heaving and his heart racing. But Skidwarres knew a warrior must learn to calm himself. The captain smiled. "I'm sorry. I know this is cruel. I have my orders. I can see you are a reasonable man." And he took Skidwarres' hand and shook it. Another man handed him English clothes.

On deck, Skidwarres looked at the horizon and saw only water. The English showed to be in good spirits, heading home, drinking rum. In the fresh air, Skidwarres rejoined Nahanada, a man in his late thirties. Nahanada, the sagamore, the village leader, had encouraged the others to meet with the English.

As time passed, his friend's company and good cheer offered

Skidwarres some optimism. They reminded each other that they were not the first to be taken away. From village to village, fantastic stories were told of strange food, tall stone buildings, animals doing human work, huge guns, unbelievable wealth and poverty. These stories were as unlikely as the native legends of Glooscap changing himself into a gigantic bear or the wind.

Later Skidwarres accepted Richard's kindness and generosity. His captor, as Skidwarres sometimes thought of him, became the closest friend he'd ever had. His grandfather's words might have applied: "Even your enemy is a human."

At dinner, with Emily next to him, he thinks yet again of his wife, Sokw. Did she think him dead? During his two-year absence, had she remarried? Did she want him back? Did she remember their long afternoon in the canoe after they paddled up the gentle river, way up and then turned, settled together on the canoe bottom, floating back with the current, bumping into the bank turning and flowing free. When he returned—not if, he knows this now—would Nahnibssat, his two-year-old daughter, now four English years old, remember him?

Skidwarres considered himself disciplined. Never had he been more so than these past twenty months. His work with Richard required much more rigor than his training to be a warrior. Reading, hours of conversation, writing, time alone with books—how different, how much more demanding than practice with the bow and spear, or even surviving alone in the snow. Recently he realized he'd spent the last two days without thinking of his previous life. It felt as if he were growing into something other than himself. He would look in a mirror and see a dark Englishman and hear the words coming out of his mouth or feel the camaraderie with Richard. At times he felt himself hovering over himself, watching himself as someone else, at the same time knowing the reality—he was this person—but who? At other times he felt split down the middle, his past and his present with an ocean between. Sometimes he wasn't sure if he had a self anymore, or rather, he now felt apart from his land, his ancestors, his people, apart from whomever he was. The other Skidwarres was an extension of his people. Individuals are not separate from their people and their land, rivers, and sea. Of course, in his hut lying next to his wife and child, waking in the morning, hunting, paddling his canoe, he knew he was a separate being. His mother had borne him, a separate individual, and he would die so. But in his mind and in the minds of all his people, they were not separate. Everything held together and was whole. No mind was separate. In fact, he wasn't sure he had ever considered his "mind" as the English called it, before— at least not separate from the mind that was everything.

Yet another sensation occurred to Skidwarres. Instead of feeling part of a whole, or that sense of looking at himself from afar, or being two people disconnected, sometimes he felt a great emptiness—that he was hollow and at other times invisible. He wasn't sure, maybe these sensations were all one. It began to dawn on him that the English language, with its thousands of words, identified thoughts and feelings his own language didn't touch.

His sense of being invisible usually arose in Richard's company. He was always kind or funny, and unflinchingly supportive and respectful. So what was it that led to this sense that Richard was blind to him? Or that he, the native, was invisible? Never before had Skidwarres been forced to look inward and to sort out thoughts and feelings, and this last one was most confounding. He was coming to believe that the English considered their world, the English world, to be the only real one. Even the French and the Spanish did not occupy English reality and were therefore suspect. Richard simply saw him, Skidwarres, through his English eyes, and they apparently could not see him, at least some essential part of him. And most confusing, he accepted at times Richard's perspective of himself—invisibility, nonexistence. These thoughts, with their moods of near dizziness and occasional small bursts of anger, faded fast with life's daily demands.

Fleeting thoughts of his own insubstantiality caught him during the dinner when Emily eagerly and politely queried him about his life, as if he were a specimen. Now she carries the wine bottle Richard gave him. She sips as they walk. When they leave Richard and Margaret and head on the downstream path, she locks her arm around his, sips again, and asks, "What have they told you about me?"

"Very little, Emily." His voice, as with everyone except Richard, contains a respectful remove.

During the evening, her voice had carried a lightness and a rather singsong ease. During dinner, in response to Emily's questions about native religion, he told her about how some believed ghosts lived deep in the forest, ghosts of men who had died of starvation. They attacked hunters and sucked their blood; or they'd run a cold bony finger into the hunter's entrails or snatch out their steaming livers as they slept. Skidwarres found he enjoyed recounting this in English. As he did, conversation quieted around him, so by the end he was the only speaker. When he had finished, he received applause.

"And do your people have a god?" Sir John Popham wanted to know.

"Not quite like your god. Though I'm not sure I understand your god. We have a giant who lives on the highest mountain, so far from my village that I've never been. It has snow even in the springtime. His name is Glooscap. That means in my language 'liar.'"

John Seymour added to the conversation. "Liar, that is noteworthy. A god who is a liar. Would our archbishop admit to such a thing of our god? Some of our poor might think so."

Skidwarres knew something now of English humor, and indeed appreciated its twists, often cruel or biting. He smiled, something he did not do often outside of Richard's company.

After the conversation had moved on, Emily's hand had found its way back under the tablecloth and onto Skidwarres' thigh, this time higher up. It offered a small caress and retreated back onto the table like a small animal testing.

Now that they are on the path, her tone shifts. Her voice becomes firmer and lower in register, conspiratorial but without losing its playfulness.

"Well, that was an interesting encounter—you, Richard, and the highwaymen, and you posing as the devil!" Richard had regaled the group about their afternoon holdup, and Sir John had followed up with his escapades while at Oxford.

"Yes, I think they were convinced."

"You have powers you may not know about. I believe in power. I was born during Queen Elizabeth's reign, a woman all men near-worshipped. Even her most feared enemy was a woman, a cousin who plotted to overthrow her—and who lost her head in the process. We women, born of this generation—many of us anyway—feel this power. And we don't all lose our heads, though many men think us brainless. Do you have women who rule in your land?"

"We have strong women. But to rule, I think not."

They come to the end of the path at the shore of the stream and stop. Emily hands the half-full bottle to Skidwarres. He drinks from it. Emily holds out her hand. He gives it back. She consumes the remainder and tosses it into a bush.

"Skidwarres, I don't think you have been with a woman for a long time."

They are standing in the cloudy moonlight. He nods once in agreement. He understands her comment.

"And you will sail soon, back to your land. So do you not believe it is important to expand your experience of women? Will you not wish to remember an English woman, not a bar whore, a lady? An English lady?" Emily draws the "isshhh" from "English" as if she were calming a horse while saddling it.

This time Skidwarres simply stares expressionless. The young village girls knew how to play with their sex. They could show themselves off. His first girl, the same one he told Richard about in the curing story, could be coy and playful. Emily played by different rules.

"Would you not consider it rude not to offer a willing woman the chance to lie with a savage?" It was not a question.

Again, Skidwarres offers a nod.

"So then, I would like to see your tattoo. And I, too, will show you mine." Emily unbuttons Skidwarres' shirt and slips it down his arms. "Ah," she says, "a fine piece of work." Her hand follows the outline of the design, two triangles interlocked. Then she raises her petticoats and dress to expose her nakedness.

"There, below my navel. That, my alien friend, is mistletoe."

He steps back. His eyes lower and focus. They wait for a cloud to pass by. More light shines.

"Do you know of our English tradition, a Christmas tradition?"

Skidwarres does know. He remembered the mistletoe in the entrance way to the Seymour dining hall, how Margaret had kissed first Richard under it and then Skidwarres. He nods again.

"Then would it not be rude for you not to practice this tradition—to obey?"

Emily drops her gown, then begins unfastening her hooked bodice. She stands in her chemise, her last undergarment. Then that, too, is slipped from her shoulders. He smells her perfume. In the summer, native women might uncover their breasts. Men took an interest, but it was accepted, and by mid-summer they might pay only scant notice. Because the English always cover themselves or push the flesh up from their dresses, Emily's exposed breasts stir him.

Her hand moves to his pants with the same adroit quickness. She frees six buttons. Skidwarres helps by stepping out of his boots, pants, and underwear. She watches and touches his hair and shoulder as he bends.

"Thank you," Emily says. She returns her hands to his shoulder and pushes down. "To one knee, sir," Skidwarres, accustomed to obeying the English, feeling the effects of the wine, and also now aroused, follows her command. One hand rests on his shoulder, as if it were a sword. "Sir, I Queen Mistletoe hereby knight you. Henceforth you will be known as Sir Skidwarres, Earl of the Mistletoe. You may now kiss me. Kiss the mistletoe." Skidwarres lowers his other knee and braces himself. He brings his own hands up to the back of her smooth thighs. These oral attentions are not new to him. He and Sokw had played freely with one another.

Standing still, Emily spreads her legs, thrusts herself forward, stretches her arms out, and gazes into the sky. She hisses her esses... "Queen of the Missstletoe." The wine and her design on Skidwarres are more successful than she had anticipated. She begins laughing. Unlike the native girls' giggles, Emily's laugh is deeper and self-satisfied. Her scent is not repellant, but it is foreign. For a few seconds he finds himself watching himself again, the man licking this English woman, this man—him and not him. Then lust, unlike anything felt before, surges, charged with pent-up anger. She is taking him prisoner, making light of him, making demands. He quickly stands, grabs her waist and raises her off her feet, places one hand under her buttocks, and not so gently brings her to the ground on her back. The restrained aggression excites her more. She grabs fists full of his hair and directs him back between her legs.

After a few moments of following her lead, of mutual grunting, Skidwarres abruptly pulls away and speaks as if a curse, "*Wabi behanem*" (white woman). He catches Emily by surprise. "Ah, my savage, I have awakened you." She sounds in control, but in fact is surprised, on the edge of being frightened. He repeats, "*Wabi behanem*." On his knees again, he leans over and bites the mistletoe, not viciously, but enough to hurt.

Emily startles and cries out, "That hurt!" Skidwarres places his hands on her waist and roughly swings her onto her stomach. His aggression heightens her fear, but passion overrides, or rather fear becomes an essential ingredient. She thrusts her bottom up toward him. "Yes!"

But Skidwarres is following his own course. As she spreads her legs he plunges into her, aiming for and penetrating her upper and smaller orifice. Again she is unsuspecting and cries out without words. Skidwarres enjoys her pain nearly as much as his own pleasure, and slowly rams into her three, four, seven, eight times—and then, just as suddenly as his entry, pulls out and slips below and into her more accepting place. He is consumed by lust and anger. He doesn't even hear or care that Emily herself has moved from pain to a shuddering orgasm.

Finally exhausted, he drops, pressing her onto her clothes, against the ground, his chin resting on her upper spine. Their panting slows. All is quiet.

When their breathing returns to normal, as unpredictably as before, Skidwarres pulls out of her and stands without comment. He looks down. Spent, she doesn't even roll over. He grunts, turns, and walks the short distance to the stream. He wades in up to his groin. The cool water, the sand underfoot—these sensations now fill him. He dives, swims underwater in a black, liquid world that feels, finally, like home.

CHAPTER 10

May 23, 1607

A Journey Begins

The four-horse carriage carrying Richard and Skidwarres rumbles over the main road from Exeter, where they spent the previous night, to Plymouth some ninety miles southeast. In silence each looks out an open window, reminiscing, consolidating, and anticipating.

A week before, Richard and Margaret had celebrated their betrothal, hosted by her parents. Margaret's household—especially her sisters—was atwitter with questions for Richard. For most young people, the New World conjured up primitive naked people, gold, silver, monster-sized animals, seas where leviathans roamed and even attacked ships. It defied the imagination, and it was dangerous. Many adults thought the same.

With so much commotion during the weekend affair, Richard and Margaret found little time alone. Their only escape involved an early morning horseback ride, where, far from all, they could dismount, disrobe, and renew themselves with one another under an open sky and a soggy riverbank. Richard would part in three days, so to allow a few days' stay in Plymouth. Popham insisted he must stop there to acquaint himself with various principals and assist with preparations.

Emily had written Margaret's parents explaining with heavy regrets that she would not be able to attend, as her elderly aunt in London had fallen ill and required assistance. Skidwarres had not been forthcoming when Richard asked about his evening with her. "Interesting woman, Richard," had been his reply. Both had left it there.

In the coach, Richard rereads the letter Margaret gave him while he stood holding Dancer's reigns, ready but reluctant to leave, as it would mark a departure of unknown length.

"Richard, my dearest, there is so much to write. I have already torn up two attempts; they both seemed so superfluous. So I conclude I must be brief and direct. Sir John suggests you will return within a year. Please not two. As I have promised, I will wait for our love to flourish. In the meantime, I will tuck it away tenderly and care for it daily with my thoughts and prayers. To fill the lonely time, I have decided to take Emily's advice and become a more serious student of the cello. I will even travel with her to London for lessons—ah, I know what you are thinking—that you will return to find a hidden tattoo. Do not fear, my boldness has its limits, unless you'd wish your initials somewhere?

"But I do enclose a not very modest offering for your departure. Richard, does not intimacy destroy false modesty? We have been of one flesh. This is to help remind you. My handkerchief in the other envelope carries my scent. I hope you don't think me outrageous. The other night I thought of you. My scent is the result. Please take me in, and when it fades—and I hope it never disappears—remember that my ardency for you will never end. Your beloved, Margaret."

In the coach Richard again reaches into his satchel, removes the silk cloth, and brings it to his face. Skidwarres looks at him dubiously, grins, and shakes his head. Yes, Richard thinks—her personal elixir and my touchstone.

During Richard's recent visit, he offered Margaret his grandmother's gold bracelet. He felt a fool after riding off. He hadn't written anything. So in the early morning before leaving for Plymouth, he penned a note:

"When I left on Dancer, it took me only moments to feel unworthy, as I had left you only a metal heirloom, while your imagination and generosity gave me yourself, your words and your glorious sweet scent. I will honor it and you.

"I can offer you one curious aspect of myself. I awoke early this morning, before sunlight. A dream haunted me while I lay in bed. All was quiet outside, before the sun and the complaining crows. In the dream, I stood at the top of a stairwell, a bit like the one at my father's estate. Next to me I felt warmth and light. It was you, I believe, but without embodiment. I descended into the dark, leaving your presence. One does not have to be a soothsayer or one of Skidwarres' shamans to decipher meaning. Am I correct? It was you, our love I left at the top of the stairs?

"Upon waking I felt a strange fear. I don't know exactly how to describe it, except as a sense of groundlessness. Do you know that feeling one can get in the early morning, when it's no longer night and not yet day? I felt an eerie nonexistence. Do you not think the dream says I'm going into the unknown, and that unknown is me as well as the New World? That is what I make of it. I remained awake. Soon, the sky lightened and the crows did squawk and the strangeness disappeared. I felt more rational. and I remembered one of Montaigne's quotes: 'Those who have compared our life to a dream were right...we sleeping wake, and waking sleep.' The dream is less rational, but perhaps more real, more real to my sensibilities.

"In any case, dear Margaret, I shall write from Plymouth, from aboard ship, and from the Sagadahoc River. One of the ships will return before winter. Until you receive more news and forever, I remain your devoted love, Richard."

Skidwarres' thoughts are of the future. Soon he would be back in the land where fields were so much smaller than the ones passing by the carriage window. Only with his father's generations did his people begin burning and planting, as was the custom for other tribes to the west and south. Now maize and squash joined the wild plants as part of the diet. The land of the Mawooshen opened itself in other ways, especially the broad expanses of sea grass and marsh with their meandering tidal streams. There fish spawned and life oozed. Nowhere in England had he seen such a great vista as the Sagadahoc, the tunnel of green forest and rocky shores or the ocean beyond with sparkling offshore islands. The light here in the English countryside appeared dull in comparison. That was one of his first impressions. At the meeting of ocean and river and rock between the Sagadahoc and the Penobscot, everything shone sharper, brighter, clearer. Everything appeared more defined.

Skidwarres remembers aspects of Richard's instruction as they bounce along the pocked road. Some four hundred years before, Richard's people had traveled across the waters from Europe. They also came upon vast forested lands, the native peoples living in small villages. Cities such as Exeter and Bath were much smaller then. The Normans cut the forests, populated the countryside, built up the towns, and finally grew into a society where land no longer belonged to everyone, no longer "common property" that anyone could use for grazing and planting. Wealth accumulated in the hands of royalty and other "noble" families. Skidwarres, then and now, wondered if it would be the same for his land, once the English landed. He had raised this question with Richard. "Will you English make an England of the land of the Mawooshen?" It sounded preposterous, but it came out of his mouth anyway.

Questions such as these amused Richard. They were said with such straightforwardness. "The channel from Brittany to England is narrow enough to piss over. Easy for those Normans. And your land, as far as I've been told, is much vaster than tiny England. Besides, we are only a hundred-plus men, no women, therefore no babies, no overrunning your land by fucking."

Skidwarres had nodded his head and simply added, "But you English are a determined people."

It was Richard's chance to nod his head. "Yes, Skid, you have noticed."

Skidwarres struggles to recall the face of his wife, Sokw. The growing vagueness of her image frustrated him. Yes, her dark brown eyes, darker than most English, those he held in his mind's eye. He could also remember the fresh scent of his hut—not in winter, when it was smoky, but in summer, the deep scent of cedar—and he could remember the smell of her hair, freshly cleaned in pond water, and the warmth of her body when she lay next to him, pulled up against his back, her belly and groin snug against his bottom. This he could remember, but should he expect it upon his return? And what of her smile or the exact color of her skin? Of these he was less sure. He had been told that Nahanada sailed home last October in a ship captained by Sir John's grandson, a Thomas Hanham. By now she'd know he was alive and would also return. Would his daughter, Nahnibssat, remember him?

CHAPTER 11

May 28, 1607, Plymouth
The Virginia Company

Eleven gentlemen occupy a large table. They face a group of nearly one hundred men. Sir John Popham sits in the middle, head of the Council of Twelve which governs the Virginia Company's northern expedition. To his right are George Popham, president in charge of the colony in the New World; Sir Ferdinando Gorges, the other initiator and fund raiser of the expedition; Captain Raleigh Gilbert, second-in-command to George Popham; and John Evans, fur trader and major contributor. To Sir John's left sit Richard Seymour, chaplain; Skidwarres, representative of the Mawooshen; Gome Carew, chief searcher for mines; James Davis, captain of the fort; and finally Robert Davies, captain of the Mary and John and adjutant for Gilbert.

Sir John Popham stands and clears his throat, "Gentlemen, soon we—that is some of you—the essential men and others who will join us in the next few days, some honorable and skilled, some no doubt who tire of prison and now choose adventure—soon you all will set sail. Welcome, all of you." Sir John sweeps his arms in a large arch that includes all in the room. He is expansive.

"Those of us at the table have for some years labored to make today a reality. And many of you not at the table have played a role, a crucial role, as you will continue to do. Welcome, all of you. Now let me begin with some introductions, though many of you know one another by now. Then I will speak more to the particulars of this small but important expedition, this gallant endeavor for His Highness King James—and for God. And yes, for ourselves."

Some around the table and many watching utter in unison a grunt of approval, as if a large dog has been awakened, takes note, and then falls silent again.

"I will begin with my nephew George, president, your commander. George comes extremely well qualified. He combines courage and practicality. I so wish I could be in his place, but my age..."

Still seated, George Popham interjects, "Dear cousin, so I wish you to be with us, to share the soggy journey, the maggots in the bread, the cold and the hard beds with no female warmth." As intended, George's comments are followed by throaty chuckles.

"My younger relative knows whereof he speaks. He, as you no doubt know, has had a brilliant career as an explorer, and for the past decade and more has been a customs officer at Bridgeport. So he knows our business well. Most important, he is a fair man, a man of honor to whom I entrust the day-to-day affairs."

George stands, gracefully bows to Sir John, and simply adds, "I intend to honor that trust, dear cousin and Chief Justice." His tone has changed from light to solemn. George sits and nearly everyone approves with a "Here, here!"

Sir John remains standing. He looks next at Sir Ferdinando Gorges. "This expedition is the creation of Sir Ferdinando and myself. He is, of course, also a Devon man, and has for the past ten years been involved with many who have plied the seas in search of riches. He is a man of great insight and foresight. He will work in your support as a member of the Virginia Council here in Plymouth. He will steadfastly assist my son, Edward." Sir John points out Edward in the front row of the audience. "He is treasurer and so responsible for supplying the project. Gorges will reap the funds so Edward can manage them." Gorges and Edward stand, bow, and receive everyone's approval.

Sir John continues, "Next I wish to introduce Raleigh Gilbert." Gilbert has a striking bearing. He wears a military uniform, topped with an admiral's cap, navy blue against his curly reddish-brown hair and dark brown eyes. His pointed goatee and mustache mimic those of his uncle, Sir Walter Raleigh. He sits staring out at the observers, his intention, Richard assumes, one of commanding respect. Popham continues, "Though a young man, Admiral Gilbert represents a courageous and heroic family. His father, Humphrey, as you all know, was lost at sea in a small ship near the Azores during a gale some fifteen years ago. And he had the temerity, the cheek, to yell out to another ship that came near wanting to know if Gilbert needed assistance, 'We are as near to heaven by sea as by land.'" Again the listeners mumbled their acknowledgment.

"Exploration is deep in Admiral Gilbert's bones. He is an experienced soldier and sailor, eminently qualified to be the president's second-in-command."

It is Gilbert's turn to stand. "You are very gracious, my lord." His tone is formal and slow. He nods his head, a gesture more constrained and theatrical than those offered by George and Ferdinando. Gilbert then slides his gaze from the Chief Justice to the men in the audience. He nods slightly four times as he surveys the silent room. "Sir John, I relish my command and to all in this room, I pledge we will succeed." His tone is as much an order as a prediction. Some in the room think that the title of admiral, earned more by birth than by deeds, is intended to compensate for his youth and inexperience.

Richard listens. This man, Gilbert, blends audacity and credibility. Without hesitation he has grabbed center stage. Richard's knowledge of the man began the night before over dinner with Sir John and Skidwarres. Popham's mind seemed always restless with plans and calculations. The older man at first asked light questions about Richard and Skidwarres' activities of the past two years. He bantered about the difficulties getting merchants and the landed gentry to part with their money over what most considered to be a risky venture. Over the third glass of port, Sir John leaned toward Richard and lowered his voice. "Seymour, we are here to speak privately—and with our ambassador, Skidwarres. As in our previous conversations, I have told you how I wish you to be the eyes and ears for my cousin. True, he is advanced in years and not the healthiest. However, I simply do not know anybody of his caliber whom I trust more. But he will need your advice. Your knowledge, your power, will come from listening. Get to know the men. You will become the confessor. Offer comfort and provide moral leadership, but above all, listen.

"Yes, I admonish as well. I have agreed to make Raleigh Gilbert second-in-command. Gorges insisted, as their two families intertwine. But I have done so with some trepidation. It is true he is brave. It is also true he carries resentments, and I am not convinced his judgment is sound. He is, of course, young. His father, Humphrey, and Raleigh controlled a major share in the first Virginia Company, granted by our late Queen. With Humphrey dead—Sir Walter Raleigh, you are probably aware, is Humphrey's half-brother and therefore Raleigh Gilbert's uncle—the Queen revoked the grant. The resentment—so I hear from my informants—is directed at me, first for my role in Raleigh's imprisonment, and second as a principal in gaining the renewed

Virginia Company grant from King James. I do not know if Humphrey's son, Raleigh, has any mischief in mind. I do consider him a potentially strong leader and—I'm not quite sure what word to use here—so be alert. I suggest gaining the man's confidence."

"As a matter of fact, sir, as I have mentioned, according to my father his family and mine are distantly related, second cousins. But we have yet to meet."

"Yes, yes I am aware. You will have many topics about which to converse, as you are also both members of the council, both educated gentlemen. My request again: be sagacious. Listen and learn. And when appropriate, advise George."

"And let me add an amusing piece of information about Sir Walter Raleigh and myself. As you know, he has been in prison for the past four years. There he requested my help in legal matters regarding his estate—I, the judge who condemned him. You may know he is quite well regarded for his medical potions. He talked a good deal about these and gave me a tincture he said would cure the aches in my joints. I began taking it recently, and indeed, there was less pain, though instead I complained to my wife of stomach cramps and fatigue. Raleigh had predicted these side effects and told me they'd be short-lived. But I discontinued the treatment. I will try again when I return home and have more time to rest. Fascinating man. So I condemn a man, and he becomes my doctor!"

Richard recalls these comments made by Popham, while Raleigh Gilbert completes his brief address. The man, Admiral Gilbert, is certainly self-possessed, especially for someone in his early twenties.

The next to be introduced by Popham is John Evans, the furrier. "If you don't know it now, let it be known that the Virginia Company's fortune, especially that of the Plymouth Company, will in good measure depend on this gentleman. Mr. Evans, might you offer us a few words?"

Evans is a large, prosperous merchant in his late forties. The fashion during the later part of Queen Elizabeth's reign had turned decidedly colorful, ornamental, and feminine. Mr. Evans has not changed to suit the plainer dress worn by the younger men of the new millennium. He represents an older generation with his bright red doublet, its sleeves tied to the shoulder, covered in part by a green jerkin with a high ruffled white lace collar. His puffed-out breeches come to his knees; below them he wears silk hosiery and leather boots with inch-high heels. His long hair is artificially curled. Through his pieced ear, instead of jewelry, Evans has threaded a piece of thin black silk long enough to drape across his shoulders. He rises and simultaneously places on his head a beaver skin hat with a broad rim. He offers an infectious grin, and a number of men chuckle. It is a relief from the ponderous mood imposed by Raleigh Gilbert.

"Yes, well, some of you may prefer the beaver of a different species, but this pelt comes with a high price tag. Across the channel from France to Italy, the price of beaver hats has risen as the little creatures become scarce, nearly gone here in England. Where to find a plentiful supply? That is why I am here and why I will be aboard the good galleon, the *Mary and John*. That is why I have invested. The world turns in strange ways, my friends. We follow profits like bird dogs, and who knows what we will scare up. The fort and afterwards the community we will build must have an economic base. The fort, Fort St. George, England's foothold on the New World—indeed the future of England—depends, my friends, it depends upon what sits atop my head." The gathering, catching Evans's good cheer, responds in kind with clapping and laughter. He lifts his hat in salute and sits down.

"Thank you, Mr. Evans." Sir John is obviously pleased by the change in mood as well. He smiles broadly for the first time. "Now I introduce Richard Seymour. Mr. Seymour derives from royalty—his great aunt, Queen Jane—and more to the point, he has been granted by the Bishop of Exeter the status of chaplain. His studies and his fine character will enable him to represent the Church of England. He has my utmost confidence, especially since he has for the past two years so adeptly tutored the man to his left. I ask you to turn to Chaplain Seymour for whatever support you may need, be that personal or spiritual."

Richard stands, bows slightly to Sir John, and addresses him. "Sir, I say simply that I will attempt to uphold your trust." Then, turning to the men at the table and finally to the audience facing the principals, Richard continues, "I look forward to meeting all of you. Those of you assigned to the galleon *Gift of God* I will, of course, have some weeks on board to get acquainted. Those of you on the *Mary and John* I will endeavor to get to know as soon as we rendezvous in the New World. May our journey be safe and may our work there be considered righteous in the eyes of God. Amen." Richard had not planned his words. As he heard them tumble out of his mouth, he was simultaneously amused and disconcerted. Whose voice was this, himself or the chaplain? Had he become the voice of the Church of England? For the moment it felt absurd. But as far as he could tell after sitting down and hearing the group's mutual "Amen," he had carried off his first official act successfully.

Sir John continues his introductions: "Next to Richard—indeed for the past two years Skidwarres has found himself next to Richard—is a man of uncommon nature. When abducted by Captain Weymouth he wore but a loincloth—and he fought. And now, as you see, this well-appointed representative from the New World, this good man who will be our ambassador to his people, speaks and reads English with great aplomb. It is fighting we wish to avoid. It is imperative we not repeat the mistakes made by those at Roanoke, as their relations with the natives turned sour quickly. That must not happen, and I am confident with Skidwarres' assistance it will not happen." Sir John gestures for Skidwarres to speak.

The native stands but does not nod or bow. Nor does he smile, though he knows a smile might be what the English expect. He fully understands Popham's words but is less sure what his elders, especially Nahanada, the sagamore of his village, might expect. During the year of Nahanada's captivity, the two natives met only once. Nahanada and his tutor did not become friends. His studies were less rigorous, and as a result, after one year Nahanada knew far less English than Skidwarres. Instead of embracing his time in England, Nahanada nursed his anger, though it remained mostly undetected. His unbending resentment, with its veneer of pleasantness, allowed the sagamore to maintain his dignity while not offending his captors. Skidwarres had detected some of this during their brief reunion. He didn't know if his people would welcome or wish to destroy the English, given Nahanada's inclinations.

Skidwarres decided to say but a phrase, first in his native tongue and then a translation: "*Kway ki*. Welcome to my land." The impression given is similar to that of Raleigh Gilbert's: cool, determined, reserved; though just before he sits, Skidwarres offers a small nod to Sir John and a blank stare at Richard. It is the first apparently unfriendly sign Richard has ever detected, and it confuses him. The room is silent, then some murmur, and finally there is a scattering of applause. Politeness rules. No one quite grasps Skidwarres' mood. Skidwarres himself realizes his words were less gracious than intended, especially given Popham's laudatory introduction. Without fully intending it, he spoke out of respect for Nahanada. With this surprise shift in Skidwarres' mood, the two unlikely friends, the Englishman and the Native American, not yet on board the *Gift of God*, find themselves momentarily adrift.

Sir John maintains his commanding equanimity. He introduces other members of the expedition who sit at the table and in the audience, as well as the craftsmen so necessary for success: crews of both ships, carpenters, smiths, smelters, shipwrights, farmers, fishermen, woodsmen, and cooks. "Other will join us," Popham quips. "They have yet to be pressed into service."

With the introductions concluded, Sir John stands and arranges himself, hands on the lapels of his crimson judicial cloak. He turns and, for the first time, acknowledges a large map of the outline of the East Coast of the New World that has been erected behind them. "Gentlemen, this might as well be a star or a planet, so little is known of the terrain, yet, we do possess a map. Notice, behind this rim of a coastline, we know not what exists. Here we can see a great expanse of land. Thousands...no, what must be millions of square miles. Below this point," he continues, picking up a wooden pointer, "the Spanish rule and have since before I was born. Above..." The pointer hits the mouth of the St. Lawrence River. "Here the French hunt and fish. They bring with them their Jesuits who spread papal influence. And don't forget the Portuguese; along with the Spanish, they thirst for more, for riches, and for the pope. So what is England to do? Here..." Popham's pointer hits the middle of the map. "Here Roanoke and soon Jamestown."

The soft conversational commotion rises softly and falls. "A bit over a month ago, two ships departed to reestablish a settlement. They, too, are part of the Virginia Charter and backed by London gentry and merchants. They took with them women and some children. I think this was a mistake." The pointer slides north. "When we soon set sail, men and only men will be aboard. Too much is at stake. This is a beachhead. In a year or so, women and children will arrive. Then we will have a settlement. You, you men must be of strong minds and sprits. You will build a fort." Popham taps the pointers at the mouth of the Sagadahoc. "You'll establish good relations with the natives, develop commercial alliances, establish profitable mines of silver, perhaps even gold, harvest great trees, fish the bountiful waters. Others of you will explore. A route to the Orient—be there one—will be found by the English." Again the group responds to Popham's growing enthusiasm.

"This is not just about beaver hats—though God praise the beaver." Popham smiles at Evans. "It is not only about fish and lumber and mines. This is about England, about King James and the Church of England. We must prevail. No?"

Popham hears what he expects: "Here, here!"

"Exactly! This charter, the Virginia Charter granted by His Majesty King James, bestows upon us the right to all these lands." Popham grabs the written charter from the table and reads a portion of it. "'We are to propagate the Christian religion to those who now live in darkness and miserable ignorance of the true knowledge of God. And may we in time bring the infidels and savages living in these parts to civility and to our quiet government." He puts the document down, realizing how the words written by the court might offend Skidwarres. "Of course," Sir John offers, "not all our natives are savages. This is simply a term, a poor one. The document is a general statement, written by His Majesty's advisors."

Popham trails off. His inclination is to offend the King's underlings, but he doesn't. "In any case, the Council of Twelve in the New World will govern. The Council will have the authority to coin its own money and to establish and uphold its own laws, some of which are set forth in this document: thievery, sodomy, murder, of course, punishable by death. Gentleman, under such harsh conditions, we must be as determined and organized as an army. Indeed, we will be an army. The fort will erect nine cannon. Among you are experienced soldiers and sailors." Popham hesitates. He puts out a hand in recognition of the soldiers present. The group responds, "Aye, sir."

"The Plymouth Company, an entity, a legal reality, an extraordinary invention. Like a person, a company thinks and acts and governs. Finally, it is here you will build." Sir John stabs his pointer. "Here at the mouth of the Sagadahoc River is the location of your Fort St. George. Here my grandson and the well-known explorer, Martin Pring, recently visited. Here on the shores of the mightiest of rivers, you will gain access to the interior of the country as well as the fishing grounds. Captain Pring and others such as Weymouth have searched for the optimal location. It is here, gentlemen. You will sail in three days, May 31. Godspeed—God save the King!" Again the men respond, "God save the King."

Popham's enthusiasm and purpose is contagious. While the group leaves the building, the conversations are loud and positive. Members of the council shake hands. Sir John puts a hand on Richard's shoulder. "Chaplain, tomorrow morning meet me at the dock so that I may introduce you to your ship and some of its mates. At ten o'clock."

"Yes, Sir John. I will be there, if it pleases you."

"And you, Skidwarres. You join us."

"Yes."

Popham heads for the door in a flourish, followed by his son, Edward, nephew George, and Gorges. Before exiting he turns and shouts, "Richard, that map is now yours. Make good use of it." Before Richard can respond, Popham's magisterially-robed bulk flows through the open door.

As the remainder of the group departs, Skidwarres signals Richard to remain. "Richard, you have shown me maps like this. I like this one." Skidwarres appears to have lost his earlier cloudy mood. "I have not traveled much beyond here." He points west of the Sagadahoc, "or here," now pointing east of the Penobscot. "Nor have I journeyed up the Sagadahoc more than a day or so. I do know of the location Sir John pointed to. It is well protected, and as he states, a good place for trade."

Skidwarres' tone suggests more to come. "Yes?" asks Richard.

"But I am also troubled. My people live between these two rivers." He points to the land between the Sagadahoc and Penobscot: "The Mawooshen. To the east of the Penobscot live the Micmacs. For many years we have engaged in warfare. I have told you this. They encroach, they fish and hunt on this side and we sometimes on theirs. There are skirmishes. They have kidnapped our women and children. We do the same to them. We have made peace. But peace usually does not last. This may be of little concern to you. They are far from the Sagadahoc. But here," Skidwarres points again to the intended site of the fort, "this is on what you call the west side of the Sagadahoc. The tribes that occupy that land are ruled by Sabenoa. He, like his grandfather and father, names himself Lord of the Sagadahoc. He is ill-tempered. No war with the Mawooshen, just disagreements—hostility sometimes, killing sometimes. He is difficult."

"As I understand, this location is the choice of Sir John because of advice from many. But you suggest this location may bring trouble with tribes on the west side? Would Nahanada—that is his name?—not have made this case to Popham?"

"I do think so. And Nahanada is a wise man. But I am surprised."

"If you are to be a diplomat, and I, too, then we should begin now. Tomorrow we bring this matter up with Sir John—though I have to say, Skidwarres, he appears to be a man with an unbending will—once a decision has been made."

Skidwarres utters a phrase in his native tongue and then offers a rough translation, "It is beguiling to believe what you know."

My savage friend, you begin to sound like Montaigne."

CHAPTER 12

May 30, 1607, Plymouth
Ships, Goods, Purpose

At the Port of Plymouth, more than a hundred ships lie at anchor: galleons big and small, barks, pinnaces, shallops, warships—some part of the Royal Navy, others privately owned. Scores of rowboats are shuttling goods and people between ships and wharf. Some ships lie at anchor with their sails furled; others ready to sail. Richard and Skidwarres watch men scurry over their decks or balance with their feet on ropes, their hands loosening sail. Some are ready to land and unload, others to take on provisions and cargo. The late May morning breezes are offshore, bringing a potpourri aroma of vegetation, smoke, manure, fish, garbage, and sewage mixing with the sweet scents of spring. The temperature is already in the muggy seventies. A few drunkards from the night before lie in fetal positions against warehouses. A cadaver is casually thrown onto a cart, the same type used in the most recent outbreak of the plague. The docks buzz with activity.

Twenty or so ships of varying sizes are loading or unloading. A massive draft horse pulling a cart stacked with bags of gunpowder parts the street crowd. Richard and Skidwarres quickly move aside. The driver's eyes are fixed ahead. He has little regard for anything but his destination. "Sir," Richard shouts as horse and cart pass by within inches, "where to the *Gift of God*?"

"Follow me," grumbles the driver without turning his head.

The two men follow quickly in the cart's wake over cobblestone and grime. In less than a minute they stand before an English flyboat.

Men in twos and threes unload barrels of water, molasses, rum, flour, and port wine. The coming and going of thirty or so men, their weaving in and out, the turning and maneuvering to get out of one another's way, appears as orchestrated as a country dance, all directed by Captain John Elliott who stands high on the quarterdeck overlooking the dock and the hold. George Popham stands next to him. "Good morning, gentlemen," he shouts. "Come aboard."

Richard and Skidwarres approach a gangplank and wait for it to clear. A tall, thin man scurries across, readying himself to haul yet another barrel. As he steps onto the wharf, his eyes meet Richard's. The man then looks over at Skidwarres. All three come to the same recognition together.

Richard is the first to speak. "We meet again, sir—under more propitious circumstances."

"Aye, my lord. I dare say." The three men move aside, out of the way. "As a highwayman I was a miserable failure. The day after you embarrassed me, the sheriff's men apprehended me."

"And now the docks of Plymouth," Richard interjects.

"Since then, prison—until this morning. When they heard I was a cannoneer, Sir George offered me passage in trade for a long sentence."

"Some might choose the safety of a cell."

"Sir, I know the hazards of the sea and the cannonball. Five years in the navy. And while I was there, my family—obliterated. Parents burned to death for being Protestants. Wife died in childbirth—to a stillborn. No work after the Spanish wars." This information gushes out of him, a confession from a man starved for receptive ears.

"Yes," says Richard, "Nothing like peace to put the economy in the doldrums."

"Said well, sire. And are you here to say your farewells?"

"No indeed. Here to be your chaplain." Richard smiles. Even when this thin, sad-faced man was brandishing the empty gun some weeks ago, Richard found—and finds—him likable. His belligerence on the highway, even for a seasoned fighting sailor, wasn't authentic. His good nature leaked out. "Your name, sir?"

"Fletcher, John Fletcher." He bows. "Chaplain?"

"Yes, Mr. Fletcher, and—as much to my surprise as yours—here to save your soul when it finds itself surrounded by heathens on ship, and then in the land of non-Christian savages." Richard puts a hand on Skidwarres' shoulder. The purposeful work on the docks, the presence of the ship have excited Richard like drink and loosened his tongue.

Skidwarres' shoulder tightens. He knows Richard doesn't mean to insult, yet "savage" roils him today, a stale joke. The previous day's meeting had left Skidwarres irritated. For months the word occasionally tripped out of Seymour's mouth good-naturedly. And if he, Skidwarres, is hearing his friend's tone correctly—his authority, the educated accent, the assurance—Fletcher, too, is being subtly demeaned. Richard, his kind friend, is at times numbed by privilege.

"My lord," Fletcher interjects, "I am so pleased. All I know is that we sail soon and that I will not rot in Plymouth. Beyond that I know little of Popham's purpose. He, Popham—the president I think he is—asked me if I wanted to conquer the New World."

"And so do you?" Richard inquires.

"Sir, I only wish to save my sorry ass." Fletcher, realizing he might be reprimanded for interrupting his labor, or even sent back to prison, bows, turns, and grabs hold of a barrel of rum with a waiting fellow seaman. They lift it with grunts and haul it up the gangplank.

"We'll continue this conversation soon, Mr. Fletcher."

"Aye, sir." Fletcher's voice strains with the weight.

Standing with the captain and George Popham, Richard and Skidwarres watch the parade of men carry an astonishing array of provisions: salted dried fish, boxes of muskets, cannonballs, carpenter's tools, lumber, a crate holding two roosters and eight hens. Joining the procession, a reluctant billy goat is hauled up the gangplank along with six cooperative nannies. Following right behind and indifferent to the goat droppings, an incongruous Sir John does his best to stride onto the ship and slowly up the ladder to the quarterdeck. He stands and smiles.

When he's caught his breath, Sir John slaps his cousin, George, on the back and nearly shouts, "This is my favorite spectacle, the materialization of plans. Desire and energy give birth to the tangible. Men, ships, goods—purpose. By god, it is about time!"

For a while the five men share Sir John's expansive mood in silence. Richard is the first to speak. "Sir John, I don't want to spoil this moment, but I have one concern—a point made by Skidwarres to me yesterday—and since we sail tomorrow, this will be the last I see of you."

"Yes, yes." Sir John doesn't take his eyes off the activity below.

"As you have said, Skidwarres is an ambassador, and in that capacity he has raised a concern about the location of the fort. It is to be on the west side of the Sagadahoc in territory not—'controlled' I suppose is the correct term—by his tribe, but rather a potentially less friendly group."

At this Popham looks at Richard. "Yes, sir, I do respect your concern. I am aware of this. It was given some attention. Nahanada raised this before he returned, then dropped it. Besides, as I made clear yesterday, other factors predominate: the safe harbor so near to open sea, the presence of drinking water, and most of all, access to the interior by river. It has been decided."

"Yes, Sir John," Richard responds with a nod, "and I'm sure you have chosen well."

"George!" Sir John barks. "Why don't you show these gentlemen to their quarters below deck. Show them around."

"Excellent idea, come with me. Everything is modest and cramped below, but you will find it sufficient, I trust. But before we go below deck, let me point out a few things to you gentlemen of the land."

"Very well, I'd be pleased to be informed." Richard, in fact, knows little of ships, though he's tried to educate himself recently.

"The *Gift of God*'s a fine ship, a flyboat, a hundred and twenty feet in length. Smaller, you see, than the *Mary and John* just over there. She's closer to one hundred and eighty." George points to what Richard understands to be a galleon nearby, also being provisioned. "Very much the same design, you can see, each with a main, fore, and aft mast, the mizzen. Only she's about two hundred ton and we only a bit over a hundred.

"And tonnage I believe refers to the weight the ship can carry? And there is a formula by which one calculates tonnage?"

"Indeed. Very simple. You take her length at the keel and multiply it by the beam, the width at its widest, and then divide by the depth. And you don't get more versatile than these working ladies. They can be armed. Ships just like these—for that matter maybe the *Mary and John*—outsailed the fat Spanish Armada galleons. The *Gift of God* is recently built. She'll be used to sail river waters. Less draft."

The three men duck through a door off the quarterdeck. "This is the chartroom. We'll begin at the top. I spend most of my time here, if not just below in my cabin. Below here she's got three more levels, five levels in all if you include the poop deck above us. Rather a tall building afloat, no?" Richard and Skidwarres look at the large table, the lanterns, the upholstered chairs, the rack of muskets, and the light streaming through the windows that line the rear of the ship, the transom. It is a well-appointed parlor.

Popham enthusiastically guides them down a few steps. "Watch your heads. You can always tell a sailor, he's the one walking with a stoop, so used to ducking in these close quarters. And feet apart to keep his balance." He carries a lantern fueled with whale oil.

Popham opens another door. Their eyes begin to adjust to the dark. "In this section, are your quarters along with the other gentlemen's. We've partitioned it off into small cabins. The two of you are here." Popham opens a crude door and points to a cubicle about seven feet by four with two wooden bunks. "Sides here, you see, make it look like a child's crib, but rolling out is a mean way to wake up." The air is close and damp. Though the ship has recently been scrubbed clean, the small space smells slightly of rotten vegetables and brine. Clean wool blankets are folded at the head of each bunk.

Again they descend, moving through the galley and into a large section filled with hammocks hanging as close as coats in a closet. "This is for most of the men. Close quarters. Fifteen or so always on deck, so we can reduce the number of hammocks by having men share them." Popham continues briskly, "Might as well show you the hold." They climb down a ladder and join men stacking casks of fresh water, barrels of salted meats, crates of vegetables and fruit, and bags of flour, dried beans, butter, oil, and salt. The goats bleat in a fenced-in corner.

Popham points to and opens a trap door. "That leads to the lowest level and the ballast, stones. If you include that section, we have six levels," Popham adds with some pride. Richard and Skidwarres lean over and stare into the dark. A sour, cold dankness arises. Richard steps back, propelled by tiny ripple of fear. It smells like an underwater crypt. The notion of living on this ship for up to two months seems preposterous.

Finally, Popham escorts the two up to the forecastle, a room on the same level as the main deck. Beyond is the beakhead. "Just as it sounds, like the beak of a huge bird, isn't it, sticking out over the bow." From its middle arises a long pole at about a thirty-degree angle shooting out another twenty feet past the bow. It's a long finger pointing straight ahead. Again he points, "That's the bowsprit—sometimes tied to it a spritsail. It's old John Hawkins who designed galleons and flyboats to be longer, with additional sail, and more maneuverable as a result."

"I'll spend some more time with you two gentlemen later. Now best I get back to the quarterdeck. Busy, as you see.."

"Thank you, sir, for your time. Much obliged," Richard answers. "We'll find our way around."

"Very good." And for a portly man, George Popham rather nimbly weaves his way along the main deck avoiding seamen polishing brass, scrubbing the deck, and attending to four cannon.

The two men take in the fresh air and look out over the active harbor. "What are you thinking?" Richard asks finally, still staring into the distance.

"The other ship was bigger, the one I arrived on. I slept on a hammock—that is the correct name?"

"Correct," Richard turns and faces Skidwarres.

"I haven't heard the word in two years. I told you for a long time I was sick. This time I am a gentleman. This gentleman will not get sick. Better to die." Richard, hearing some lightness in Skidwarres' voice, reaches over and shakes his shoulder. It is a welcome opportunity to adjust their friendship to more familiar terms.

"Do you have any thoughts, Skidwarres, about Sir John's comments? About the location of the fort?"

"Yes. Two possibilities, I think. I have been in England for all this time. Things change. Nahanada too, was away for so long. My concern may be—how would I say in English?"

"Without grounds?"

"Yes, I like those words: without grounds. But I have another thought. Not all elders think the same. Some enjoy the trade during the summer months. But they will be less happy, I think, if the English remain and build forts. Some think it better the English not settle between the Sagadahoc and Penobscot. Some wish the English harm. Nahanada would consider this, I believe."

"An interesting prospect. Is this not the life of a diplomat: to have knowledge and little power?" Richard laughs and this time slaps Skidwarres on the shoulder. "Let us find a tavern, some grog, and a solid meal. Our immediate future presents itself with a good deal of dried cod, probably poor wine and ale, and cheap rum."

CHAPTER 13

May 31, 1607, At Sea
Wind Fills the Topsail

T he next morning's high tide coincides with a gentle breeze. The *Gift of God* and the *Mary and John*, now untethered from the dock, are each pulled by two longboats, manned by six rowers, all straining with legs and arms, hands on twenty-four oars. At first the two massive hulks inch along, not yet in their element. It would only be a few hundred yards before the tide drew them out the harbor's entrance with the breeze, first luffing the topsails. The rowers ship their oars and scurry up the rope ladder, followed by the winching of the longboats up on deck where they are lashed down.

Richard and Skidwarres again join the officers on the quarterdeck. President Popham continues his lecture. "Galleons and their smaller version, the flyboats, were built as merchant ships or to hold many cannon and fight. Galleons were normally two- or three-masted and carrying three to five square-rigged sails per mast. They were the most ubiquitous ships sailing the Atlantic, be it under a Spanish, French, Portuguese, or Dutch flag." The information flowed. The larger ships required more than two hundred crew members when prepared to do battle, less when simply carrying cargo. The *Mary and John*, a mid-sized galleon, required fewer sailors, the *Gift of God* fewer yet. Because the new settlement needed men of varying skills, it was necessary that non-sailors aboard both ships be trained for various sailing duties. The same would be true once they reached their destination and building began. Richard and Skidwarres, for instance, would help haul lines. The shipwright would work the winches. At the fort, sailors would dig ditches, fell trees, fish, hunt, and learn marksmanship—those, that is, who didn't return in the

Mary and John before winter.

As both ships slip into open water, no longer in the lea of the land, breezes fill the lower sails. Experienced sailors bustled about deck, yelling orders at the neophytes.

These square riggers, as George Popham has explained, do not have much range of motion. "Mostly or optimally they 'run with the wind'—that is, when the wind is at our backs. Or we will sail a 'beam reach,' with the wind behind us, but at an angle. This tack also allows speed. If we want to head slightly into the wind, at a narrow angle, this is called 'a full and bye.' The galleons are poor at this maneuver, the flyboats a bit better. Much speed is lost. The galleon is a cow, not a fine horse—but a good beneficent cow."

The route to the New World from England or Europe and back again is circular, at least that was the route taken by most ships. First they sail south to the Azores, a group of volcanic islands nine hundred miles west and south of Portugal. Then, with the current under them and the wind often behind, they run southwest with the northeast trade winds, eventually to the Caribbean, where currents and wind allow ships to turn north along the coast, eventually reaching Northern Virginia, or Norumbega, as it was called before. Traveling back home, the prevailing westerlies and the Gulf Stream complete the circle. The temperate sailing season runs from early spring to early fall.

A quicker, but more dangerous and colder route begins north of England and continues south of Greenland. There, mountainous, shiny, bluish icebergs float about. Here too, currents and winds oblige. If all goes well, a ship might complete its journey in only three weeks rather than the five to eight or more on the southern route. On the other side of the ledger, the northern route promises stronger squalls that might interrupt the journey or obliterate ship and crew. It is best to sail this route only in summer.

Richard finishes helping to haul up the sails. He stands at the port rail watching the *Mary and John* only forty or fifty yards away. A few days before, he lay in bed the first night at the Plymouth Inn—listening to the cacophony of iron wheels on cobblestone, the loud bravado of drunks, the high-pitched screeching of women in the tavern; and inhaling smells of cooling manure, tar, grease, ale, and the stale perfumed pillow his head rested on. All this reminded him of his removal from his father's estate, especially its immense quiet at night and the various seasonal smells, recently that of the garden wafting up its sweet fresh scent of rose, lilac, honeysuckle, and wet grass along with the cooling breeze, sharper, cleaner. In Plymouth, Richard had groped under his pillow and found his treasure, Margaret's handkerchief. He smelled its musky, slightly rosy sweetness, her female garden. Had it faded? He thought not. He saw Margaret's naked body, silky, curvaceous, always intriguing to the touch. "I will not forget," he told himself and vowed to practice remembering every night. And how strange this cramped life here in Plymouth, he had thought. It would take a long time for him to accustom himself, yet the third and last night, tired and full of expectation, he lay his head on the pillow and heard or smelled little of his environs.

Now he marvels at the two ships under sail, straining with a stiffer wind like two horses eager to stretch their legs on an open field. He will miss Dancer, but there was little use for horses in a world with no roads. What a wondrous sight, what ingenuity is a ship under sail! Thousands of working parts, over a year of construction, requiring handfuls of money, centuries of accumulated knowledge, the harnessing of something so magical and everyday as the wind. And the sea, so…and here he was not quite sure what to think. He'd traveled across the Channel twice, been to Amsterdam and Paris, but this was different. The sea was a welcoming temptress, he decided. Anyone but a fool knew how duplicitous a gorgeous sea can be. Like love, the ocean can destroy. Admit fear. Would he, he wonders, accustom himself to nothing but water under him for five, six, eight weeks? He thinks not.

On the *Mary and John*, standing next to the helmsman with his hands on the four- foot diameter wheel, is Raleigh Gilbert, behind him his two Mastiffs the size of ponies. His father, Humphrey, became known for these ferocious dogs. Raleigh, in turn, looks over at the *Gift of God* to see Richard gazing at the ocean. Their courses slowly separate them, but the two ships remain within shouting distance. "Cousin Seymour, how fare you? Not seasick yet, I trust?"

Richard lifts his head, smiles and waves. This is the first time Admiral Gilbert has addressed him. He didn't know Raleigh had made this connection. That places them in a more intimate relationship than he expected. On the other hand, he flinches at the mild rebuke that he might be seasick.

"Ahoy, Admiral. No indeed, so far I feel only exhilaration."

"Very fine. Sorry not to have made acquaintance on land. So it will be at Northern Virginia or the Azores."

"So it will be!" yells Richard at the top of his lungs, over the clanging of the rigging as the wind shifts, and the widening space between ships which brings the conversation to an end.

While Richard is watching the *Mary and John* grow smaller, he hears a commotion behind him, something other than the crew shouting to one another as they hitch and coil lines and swab the deck. Instead a burly man, a soldier by his dress, wearing a frayed and faded tunic with puffy sleeves over the upper arm with the red cross of St. George on the front and back, is grappling with a boy. The soldier's huge hand nearly encircles his neck. The boy cradles a small black and white object in his arms. "Damn you, son of a whore, that little bastard will be eating our share and shitting under our feet." With his free hand the sailor tries to grab the object, but the boy bends over, knees on the deck, protecting his possession. He screams, "Get away!"

"Get away, hell, that little shit is going overboard!"

Richard hadn't noticed the boy before, although he'd greeted a few others. He couldn't be more than fourteen or so. The soldier, angrier yet, kicks the boy in the back. A chaplain shouldn't just watch, Richard quickly decides. "My good man," Richard says as he strides up to the two, "this is not a good way to begin our journey. I'm Chaplain Seymour. What is the problem?"

The soldier steps back, recognizing that a gentleman is addressing him. "Sir, this little bastard's got a dog. Had him in a sack. Snuck him on board. Against the rules. Dogs eat meat. In a month we'll have precious little of it."

The boy remains doubled over, protecting his small charge. "What's your name?" Richard addresses the sailor.

"Hawkes, sir."

"Well, Hawkes, I appreciate the dilemma, but why not let me handle it. I'll speak to the boy and to the captain. Will that suffice?"

"If you say so, sir."

"Thank you, Hawkes. I'll personally let you know the outcome. But I have to say," Richard then points to *Mary and John* and to Gilbert, still in sight beside his Mastiffs, "those animals will eat four times the food as this little fellow."

"Thank you, sir." He backs off a few steps. His commanding officer shouts, "Hawkes, over here, we need you with this winch."

Richard gets down on one knee and puts a hand on the boy's back. "What's your name, lad?"

The boy looks up. His face is small-boned. Matted, curly black hair covers his forehead, and his cheeks are flushed pink. "Lance Ludlow, sir. I'm the drummer and bugler."

"So what do you have here?"

The boy sits and cradles the black and white fluff of a border collie puppy. "I'll give him my food. He won't be a problem. Anyway, one seaman has a parrot. Some ships carry monkeys and cats. Thank you, sir, for mentioning the admiral's dogs."

"May I hold him for just a minute?"

"You'll toss him overboard?" It was part accusation, part question.

"No, no, I wouldn't do that. Looks like a fine pup," Richard says with a smile. The boy's expression is wary, but when Richard puts out his hands, Lance passes over the warm soft object. Richard brings it to his face, nuzzles the button black nose, and receives quick little licks in return. "Does he have a name yet?"

"No, I just got him yesterday. He belonged to a farmer who said he'd got plenty more and would be drowning this one. It's a male."

"I can see that. A little male stowaway."

"I guess he is. Will you help me keep him?"

"I'll speak to President Popham. Tell you what, I'll donate a small portion of my food, and I'll try to get a few others to do the same. Maybe then we'll get permission, though I think we'll get it anyway."

"Would you do that, sir? I'd be grateful, sir."

"I can do that. So what about Stowaway or Stow for short? Seems like a good name for a male."

"Yes, good, I like that, Stow."

Richard hands him back. The puppy is all wiggle and tongue. "Tell you what, Lance, I'll introduce you to a cannoneer named Fletcher. He can keep an eye out for you. Like anywhere, on board you're going to find good men and mean. How old are you?

"Fifteen, sir."

"Family?"

"Got none, sir. Mother died of the pox. Don't know my father. Lived with an uncle. I hated him and ran away."

"Yes, you and Fletcher might get along. I'll have a talk with the president."

"In the meantime, make sure to clean up after him. That seaman has a point."

"Aye, sir. Are you a priest? You're not all in black."

"No, just a chaplain, not ordained. But I do represent the Church of England."

"Then what do I call you?"

"You can call me your friend. Call me Richard. We are all employees of the Plymouth Company."

"Thank you, sir...Richard."

"Take good care of Stow."

"Yes, my-, my lord...Richard."

CHAPTER 14

June 2, 1607, At Sea
Old Sea Dog

In George Popham's cabin, around his table, sit Richard, Skidwarres, Captain Elliott, skipper of the *Gift of God*, and James Davis, who will be captain of the fort. They drink good ale over a meal of roast chicken. George, jovial, loquacious, and confident, holds sway. His beefiness, like that of his elder cousin, Sir John, offers up a yellow pallor with pink that, to Richard, resembles a sunset of the skin. The president's eyelids fold like heavy drapes. His guests have become a rather abstract audience, he is so full of reminiscence, gazing often toward the overhead or with his eyes closed.

George is said to be in his late fifties or early sixties. The gossip heard in the taverns and on deck went, "The man is trying to relive his past. He ought to be drinking tea in Bridgewater, not looking for gold and bare-assed natives and doing his cousin's bidding." But all agreed George had earned his aging swagger. He'd sailed with the best of the legendary sea dogs, Sir Francis Drake, John Hawkins, and Sir Walter Raleigh included. Beyond that he is courteous and optimistic. His company is infectious.

"Lads, how is it, having this ship under your feet—her sway, her groans and promise? You know ships, like women, offer promise. Have you ever walked under a galleon or bark, like the *Gift of God*, while in dry dock, sitting there naked, her bottom scraped clean of barnacles, ready for a fresh coat of paint or copper. I tell you, underneath her nether immensity lies a fullness, nay, a pregnancy of promise. And here we are swaying in her and moving ahead to—let us be honest gentlemen—to what and where? No different from crawling into bed with a woman for the first time."

George's company smile and lift their drinks. Richard wonders if George is soft in the head—that is the phrase that comes to mind. Probably not, at least he hopes not. English "sea dogs" are famous for their plunder and sailing expertise, but many also for their wit. How does one parcel out a fool from a sly dog? Sir John Popham is too cunning to offer up a fool for his president. Or did greed and nepotism come into play? Indeed, many of the leadership, including himself, had family ties.

"My friends," George continues, "you all have heard of El Dorado, no doubt, but what better time, with all of us heading for a wilderness of riches and savages, what better time to tell you about my voyage with Sir Walter Raleigh to Guiana. Not so long ago—a bit over twelve years, 1595—and now Sir Walter is in the Tower. But that is his problem—first in the Tower for diddling with the Queen's lady-in-waiting; and now, under James, for diddling with royal intrigue. With Raleigh, his pen, his prick, and his starry-eyed ambition get him in trouble.

"But gentlemen, let me take this opportunity to regale you with a few facts of Sir Walter's and my excursion to Guiana. True, many thought him a wild promoter of himself. You may have read his *Discovery of Guiana*, the account of this adventure written soon after our return, and true enough, half-propaganda for the Queen. But is it all bluster? I am here to tell you otherwise." His tone suggests his guests prepare themselves for a long tale.

"El Dorado. True, we never did enter its gates and witness the king bathe in turpentine and then dust himself with gold. We never ate off their golden plates or drank from their golden chalice. But keep in mind, sirs, we know of the Incas and their gold, as well as the Aztec civilization and the tons of gold carried in galleons to Spain to this day. Should there not be another great city miles up a river, through the jungle high on a mountain plain? Raleigh believed so. The Spanish Captain Barrero thought so. These two gentlemen became possessed by El Dorado, or what we came to know as the city Manoa—and Barrero became Raleigh's prisoner. But I rush myself.

"The island of Trinidad lies just to the north of the great river, the Orinoco, in Guiana. Here the Spanish, under Barrero's command, sat with a small garrison guarding the mouth of the Orinoco like a cat sitting at a mouse hole. By this time Sir Walter was over forty years old, some years past his privateering days, a long time since he'd seen battle. After the first time in the Tower, followed by years on his estate writing poetry, Raleigh was primed for action. We attacked the poor Spanish in their puny garrison, ran many through with our swords, and burned the town and garrison both. Raleigh was back in his element. Captain Barrero was captured. A year before, Barrero had tricked an English scouting party, one charged by Raleigh to explore the Orinoco. He captured and killed eight Englishmen. Now we wanted revenge.

"But Raleigh insisted Barrero be treated as the gentleman he was. He said of him..." At this, George moves his seat back from the table and pulls out a drawer. From it he retrieves a copy of *Discovery of Guiana.* "Why not read from Raleigh's own words in regards to Barrero, 'very valiant, of great assurance and heart, long serving the King of Spain.' So Raleigh treated him, Barrero, gracefully, even lavishly, to the extent our supplies allowed. And in return we learned how better to find El Dorado. He spoke of silver mines and confirmed the existence of Manoa—El Dorado—though he himself had never seen it with his own eyes. He warned us of the Orinoco River, of its dangerous swiftness. An expedition would founder without ample supplies and a native guide.

"The Spanish are bullheaded fools. Wherever they plundered, they killed and tortured. So, of course, the savages didn't trust them. On Trinidad, just before we vanquished the Spanish, Barrero captured five Trinidadian chiefs and enslaved them. When we arrived, all were chained together and staked out to starve to death as their Spanish guards dripped burning bacon fat over their naked bodies. But Raleigh freed them. He showed them pictures of Queen Elizabeth. Our interpreter called her Ezrabeta Cassipuna Acrewana, the great princess Elizabeth, the virgin, and said she would protect them from the Spanish. It was a great success. In return we received provisions and a navigator from the native population.

"The mouth of the Orinoco is a vast delta. There were a hundred of us, more or less, in that oppressive hot air, wearing heavy, sticky, scratchy English clothes, some of us with helmets and breastplates on ships that could not navigate the shallow river. About eighty of us transferred to five rowing vessels, all loaded with victuals and arms but open to the elements— heat, rain, insects, some as large as bats. And what a confluence of streams, branches, and islands—a maze, this Orinoco.

"Our guide eventually did not know the waters. We wandered and circled until we spotted a canoe. Its occupant became our new guide after we offered him food, drink, and assurances we were not Spanish. Days later, we were hungry and dispirited—our new guide telling us upon the fall of each day how we had only a small way to travel until we would be able to re-provision ourselves—and then the next day the same promise.

"Not without reason did Raleigh have a reputation as a braggart, always claiming more than he could ever perform and taking credit for more than he deserved. But here he was, in the middle of a sweltering jungle, in charge of eighty disoriented men whose rations were low and tasteless, facing possible hostilities from the natives or the Spanish, heading into a nightmarish place, trusting in those who might well have been laying a trap. And did the men grumble? Of course, soldiers everywhere live on complaints. But were their spirits low or was there talk of mutiny? No. They believed in Raleigh. His optimism became theirs. He was a true adventurer, a true leader—and yet a man in his forties gone a bit soft from his life in the Tower and at his estate.

"We grew hungry on small rations of beer, hard biscuits, butter, cheese, pickles, smoked herring, dry sprats, oil, vinegar, mustard, and onions: an English diet in the middle of hell, supplemented with the strange eels we caught from the river. The provisions grew smaller and smaller, and yet the men remained healthy and alert. Yes, many hours were filled by rowing against a strong current which only grew stronger; and each day's journey extended into the night. Raleigh himself commented to me how he'd rather be in the Tower than here in this hell. And that he'd considered murdering the native, our guide, whom we had more or less shanghaied. Would we ourselves be murdered by his tribe? Would the Spanish be waiting for us, kill us and leave our bodies to rot in this sponge of a jungle? But he and they—and I—we were driven by silver and the Madre de Oro, gold.

"After days—I had lost track—the guide pointed to a branch of the main river. We should travel up it. One of the smaller boats was the only one with a shallow enough draft to navigate this stream. We kept rowing late into the night. The old guide kept promising. Then, just as his credibility was finally running out, yes, we finally saw light, a village, and safety. The natives were hospitable, just as our pilot had promised. They gave us some kind of cornbread, fish, chicken, and drink, a local wine. We slept with our bellies full and the next day awoke to a beautiful countryside, rolling and soft, a veritable parkland. Deer, almost tame, came down to river. And then the mood changed immediately. A young native in our employ as a bearer, he jumped exuberantly into the river for a swim and was promptly devoured by a crocodile. But we soon forgot, since he was but a native and because the next day, our fifteenth, we sighted the mountains of Guiana far off, the highlands, the site of El Dorado."

"Then another two-day journey up the main river. At this point we met another chief who supplied us with fish and turtle eggs. We in turn offered him two bottles of Spanish wine. With this, we were invited to his village. There we encountered other chiefs lying in hammocks. They sipped wine ladled by their womenfolk. Topiawari, our ancient guide at this point, offered Raleigh presents of miniature parakeets and an armadillo that looked like a small rhinoceros.

"One of these chiefs had a wife who greatly took Sir Walter's fancy. He wrote in his report to the Queen—again, I will read from *Discovery:* 'She was of good stature, with black eyes, fat of body, of an excellent countenance, her hair almost as long as herself, tied up again in pretty knots.' She was entirely naked, as were all the women, old and young— that he didn't write that to the Queen. Another native girl, quite like the one Sir Walter wrote about, took a fancy to me, I do believe. She was indeed friendly and hospitable, that I can attest to."

George sips again from his glass to emphasize his point. "She was quite small, no more than four and a half feet, and I suppose not yet fourteen. She smelled strange, but not unpleasant, something nutty. They, even the men, were nearly hairless. Indeed, these women were quite liberal and generous with their affections.

"We were by then on a branch of the Orinoco named the Caroni River. Up this river we were told by Topiawari—he didn't know how many miles, he had never ventured there—lay the golden city of Manoa, El Dorado.

"The strangeness of this land, the geography, the weather, the insects and animals, and the native customs made the legends Topiawari and others told us all the more believable. Along the banks of the Caroni lived—and here I will again resort to Raleigh's own words—'a nation of people whose heads appear not above their shoulders; which, though it may be thought a mere fable, yet for mine own part, I am resolved it is true…They are called the Ewaipanoma; they are reported to have their eyes in their shoulders, and their mouths in the middle of their breasts, and…a long train of hair growth backward between their shoulders.' And I have to add myself that this all seemed at the time quite plausible.

"Another fable is even more likely: the Amazons are a tribe of female warriors who live to the south of the Orinoco, on what is called the Amazon River, even more immense than the Orinoco and over thirty miles wide in places. We were told that once a year the local chieftains assembled with this tribe of women only. The brave ladies would, as we were told, again from Raleigh, 'cast lots for their valentines' and then for a month all would feast, drink, dance, and make love nonstop. If these women conceived—which was their purpose—a son would be given to the presumed father, but all daughters kept and raised in the 'cruel and bloodthirsty ways of the female warriors.' The next year the chieftains were invited back to repeat this ritual. To prove their point, Topiawari and others showed us beautiful green, jade-like stones, given by these women to the men in exchange for gold.

"It was up the Caroni River we continued in our search for El Dorado—our quest. More mountains rose in the distance. Raleigh asked who lived there. Topiawari answered—again from Sir Walter's *Discovery*: 'He answered with a great sigh...that he remembered in his father's lifetime....that there came down into the valley of Guiana a nation from so far off as the sun slept...and they had slain and rooted out so many of the ancient people as there were leaves in the wood upon all the trees, and had now made themselves lords of all. They built a great town at the foot of their mountain and with great houses containing many rooms, and that they all abounded in gold and consequently guarded constantly with three thousand soldiers.'

"Another tribe appeared on the river and confirmed Topiawari's story. It was also along this river thereabouts that Captain Barrero, the captured Spaniard, reported the existence of a large silver mine.

"At this point, the English grouped themselves into three parties to explore on either side of the river. I joined Raleigh and was glad I did. We witnessed great waterfalls, one after the other, all larger than I had ever seen, creating above them a mist miles long and giving us initially the impression of smoke—and therefore the existence of a large city. And then, when many of us, especially Raleigh, became profoundly tired, as we had traveled many miles Raleigh himself complained he was not strong afoot—it was then we came upon an enchanting spectacle. And here I will read for the last time from *Discovery*: 'I never saw a more beautiful country, nor more lively prospects, hills so raised here and there over the valleys, the river winding into divers branches, the plains adjoining all fair green grass without brush or stubble, the ground of hard sand easy to march on either for horse or foot, the deer crossing on every path, the birds toward the evening singing on every tree with a thousand several tunes, cranes and herons of white and crimson, and carnation perching on the rivers side, the air fresh and gentle, and every stone that we stopped to take up promising either gold or silver by its complexion.' It was indeed a Garden of Eden.

"The men fell to their knees and dug as many of these rocks as they could carry. We had now proof of the country's wealth. When we regrouped the next day, we found the others burdened with sapphire-like stones and golden rocks as well. The natives told us they could show us much more, and they urged us to join them and other native tribes to invade and conquer the mighty rulers of El Dorado. We, the English, would take the gold; they, the natives, would take their women.

"However, it was time to go home. After a month we were exhausted, weary of living in one shirt and pair of pants, and nearly out of our own provisions. The men had little left in them. And Raleigh felt vindicated. We had found the land of his dreams. The evidence was in our hands—not enough for sure, to pay off even a fraction to the financial backers, but enough to prove to even the most skeptical that another voyage would be profitable—so Sir Walter argued—that all was not in vain. Far from it.

"Another pressing matter: the river was rising and becoming even more treacherous. We would either lose our way or be swept into the trees. A few days after reaching our mother ship at the mouth, we joined with two other English galleons and searched for gold-laden Spanish vessels as they departed from Havana Harbor. We were prepared to plunder. The men were eager. But none did emerge, and we so turned and headed east, back to Plymouth."

George places *Discovery* back in the drawer and closes it with a bang, punctuating the end of his story. He then takes a long swallow of his wine and smiles at his audience. "So, there you are."

"Sir," Captain Elliott offers after a brief silence, as all the others take up their glasses. "That is a wonderful tale indeed, but the rumor I heard was that this was but a lie, a means for Raleigh to worm his way back into Elizabeth's court. I heard he went nowhere except an obscure cove in Cornwall. There, they say, he anchored and lay low."

"Yes, I have heard that. But now you know otherwise—for I was there, in truth."

"Is it not true," Elliott continues, "that the gold rocks returned were assayed and found to be merely pyrite, fool's gold?"

"Ah, you are well-informed. Indeed, though we had some evidence of gold given to us by the savages, the rocks were a great disappointment. But gentlemen, I believe you miss my point. Raleigh's *Discovery*_is the documentation of a great man undertaking great deeds. That is my message. And do not be fooled by the small minds of court officials who are afraid to dirty their feet in exploring anything beyond their silken bed sheets. I contend, Raleigh will return. Gold will be found."

"And, President, what, if anything, does this story portend for our quest?" asks James Davis, appointed captain of the fort"

"Of course, we seek gold—though there is no evidence of its existence in the north. Some say yellow gold can be found only where the sun is hot year-round. But other riches—fish, lumber and, above all, beaver— are their own kind of gold. And are we not Englishmen? Did we not spoil the Spanish domination of the seas? If we rule the sea now, should we not rule the New World? Is this not treasure enough—a New World yet closer? Though I dare say, we will not encounter native women naked for all to see. No tropical Eden. A different terrain and different customs, no, Skidwarres?"

Skidwarres has been deep in thought, more removed than usual, and groggy with wine. As Popham rambled, Skidwarres' mind strayed and bent. He thought of his people, how they might greet him. Would they treat him as a mother bear might her cub who, fed by humans for a week, is returned only to be killed? He thought not.

"No, sir, you are correct. The air is cool much of the year. From our feet to our heads we are clothed much of the time—like the English." His voice is tired.

"And what of strange peoples or beasts living in your lands, your forests?" Elliott wants to know.

Skidwarres' mind shakes off its fog as he returns to his role as respectful and patient chronicler.

George ends their evening by addressing Skidwarres. "There are some parallels, Skidwarres, between Raleigh's adventure and ours. We would not have survived on the Orinoco without our native guides. Naked—primitive—as they were, they knew the land and water. They fed us and we became merry together. Those at Trinidad even adopted the Queen as their protector. May we grant respect to the natives of Northern Virginia, the Mawooshen. I lift my last glass to you, Skidwarres, and to your people. May we live in peace and prosperity."

All lift their glasses and consume the remains. "Here, here!" Still feeling his isolation, Skidwarres is last to accommodate. He lifts the goblet and looks into it, tips his head back, and swallows a mouthful. All watch. He remains an enigma. He is not sure how to respond and so resorts to his new diplomatic role. He raises his empty glass, "To prosperity for all of us."

CHAPTER 15

June 25, 1607, Off the Azores
Interception

In the Atlantic, south of England and west of France and Spain, the tips of volcanic mountains emerge from the sea, appearing as a collection of floating islands hundreds of miles from the continent of Europe. Here a confluence of water and winds creates a veritable funnel for ships heading toward the Caribbean and the Orient. Long before Columbus landed on Hispaniola, the educated knew the world was not flat. One only had to live by the sea and notice a topsail appear over the horizon, then the mid-sail, then the lower mizzen, and finally the hull, to imagine a roundness of ocean and therefore earth.

1492 was a century ago. For decades the Spanish, French, Portuguese, the Iberian Basques, the Flemish, and finally the English visited the New World. In one sense, it was a great inconvenience. All competing interests wanted a route to the Orient, to civilizations older and richer than anything imagined. But there it was, huge and tantalizing. The winds and currents offered up this New World with its gold and fish, beckoned ambitious explorers, backed sometimes by their governments but mostly, at least in the case of England, by wealthy aristocrats and merchants.

On the deck of the *Gift of God*, at the break of morning, the fog hovered over the chop, the wind slight, the sun pushing over the horizon through the mist and brightening this June morning, the watery earth so expectant. Hot tea fills Richard's mug. He stands half-awake and conjures the sun, he the supplicant. The *Mary and John* is no more than a mile off the starboard bow, churning in rhythm with the vessel under his feet, this creaking glorious invention which on occasion, he thinks, might open up its heavy belly, disgorge its ballast, and empty him into the interminable dark abyss.

Breaking the quiet, except for the soft slosh below and the knocking about of lines above with the occasional snapping of sail as the morning breezes slowly build, Jimmy, a fourteen-year-old, thirty feet above in the nest—a round observing platform between the foresail and to top-foresail—yells, "Ship, ship away! No, two ships!"

President Popham and Captain Elliott appear on the quarterdeck from the chart house. The ships for those on deck remain over the rim of the earth. "What is she flying?" shouts the captain to the boy.

Jimmy reports in his high voice, "Flemish, Flemish flags," horizontal red, white and blue. Within moments the two larger ships come into view six or seven miles off the starboard bow.

Neither the *Gift of God* nor the *Mary and John* was well-armed. In their holds they carried nine cannon. On deck, the *Gift of God* carried four small brass cannon, the *Mary and John* six. The Flemish and English were not at war. Indeed they were trading partners. Nonetheless, historically the English had plundered the oceans with their smaller and faster privateers, giving little heed to the nationality of their prey. Goodwill between ship's captains remained tenuous and the action of one ship toward another in the expanse of ocean unpredictable. The two ships are clear now, well-armed men-of-war, all sails flying, advancing. It is unclear if the *Mary and John*, which lay between the *Gift of God* and the Flemish, is aware of the situation. At the moment, apparently, they have posted no watch aloft.

Lance, the drummer boy and musician, is assigned to signal the other ships. President Popham orders a succession of three staccato blasts on the bugle. Within the moment, the *Mary and John* is awakened to possible trouble.

The smaller *Gift of God*, with its relatively larger spritsail, could outmaneuver the *Mary and John* and certainly the much heavier and cumbersome Flemish ships, with their two tiers of twenty-four cannon each, built essentially to deliver broadsides to rivals. Popham does not want to chance interception. After briefly consulting with Captain Elliott, Popham orders they head a bit more into the light morning breeze. This tack none of the other three could manage. Nonetheless, he expects the *Mary and John* to follow, if only a bit downwind.

Captain Elliott barks out orders and takes the helm. The *Gift of God* edges into the wind a few degrees. They lose some speed but create an angle that will put them out of range of cannon and eventually out of sight, however hard the wind might blow. Following orders, Lance blows another signal to the *Mary and John*. A few minutes later Elliott says to Popham, "Sir, I do not think she is capable of this tack. Do you wish to leave her behind?"

"I think you are correct. But how are we to help? If their intent is hostile, our presence will not change matters. They will need to fend for themselves. I presume no hostilities, but we must take precautions."

"Aye, sir."

On the *Mary and John*, Admiral Gilbert watches and listens in astonishment. "By God, they are running, leaving. Cowards! This is our president with seadog balls? A plague on him," Gilbert snorts to Captain Davies.

"Apparently so, sir. Perhaps he thinks we can follow their course. We can try, but I'm afraid we'll fail. We are at the mercy of the Flemish."

"Captain Davies, Popham is our president. He possesses experience, no? The calm negotiator? Are these not attributes his pompous cousin attributed to him? If I were he, I would not abandon more than half my troops. That is not what I learned as a military officer."

The *Mary and John* does not change course. Instead it raises the white flag of truce. Davies heads her into the wind and waits for the two men-of-war, now only a couple of miles off.

Soon the Flemish ships align themselves broadside to the *Mary and John*. Gilbert can see the cannon rolled into place with their gunners at the ready, torches in hand. It will be a slaughter—if they so choose. The scent of bacon from their galleys drifts by.

Instead of cannon fire, a longboat lowers. Six Flemish crew members row a well- appointed military officer through the mid-ocean chop and alongside the *Mary and John*. Crew members throw down a ladder so the young officer can scramble up on deck. He salutes and in perfect English asks, "Aye, Captain, whom do I address?"

"I am Admiral Raleigh Gilbert; and you, sir?"

"Captain William Van Delft. An admiral so young and with two auspicious names from British history? My congratulations." Raleigh's two Mastiffs, Dumb and Dumber, greet the dubious guest with low growls. "Charming." Van Delft's tone is just a touch mocking.

"Quiet, boys. Your English, sir, did you study in my country?"

"Indeed, Oxford. And not to be impolite, but to change the subject, what might your mission be, and your cargo?"

"We are bound for the New World. To fish and hunt." Rather than be caught lying he added, "We will establish a trading post in Norumbega," The word "fort" seemed ill advised.

"Ah yes. You English claim the entire coast."

"No, sir, only that not inhabited by Christians."

"Well, that leaves quite a piece for yourselves. As I understand it, no settlement has taken hold, not by us, not yet, nor the French—though I hear they tried—nor the Spanish, not in the north."

"This is my understanding as well. May I offer you some French wine?"

"Yes, fine idea, but after you introduce me to your cargo."

After a half-hour inspection, the two gentlemen retire to the captain's cabin. There the Flemish officer and the admiral remain for over an hour. In that length of time, two empty bottles of the admiral's favorite Bordeaux sit on the table. Another empty rolls lazily back and forth on the floor with the boat's sway.

At first the conversation centers on London, especially the alehouses, the Globe theater across the Thames from the Tower, and the frolicking life abounding in that district. When Captain Van Delft begins asking about the contents of the *Mary and John*'s hold, the mood stiffens. Finally Van Delft comes to the point.

"You see, dear Admiral, given the curious nature of your cargo, your cannon and powder, and given those chaps on board—not sailors, I'd wager, more like soldiers. But let me not dwell on that, rather let me repay your kindness. Come visit my *Maria*, she's a fine vessel. Let me introduce you to Flemish craft, and let me offer you some fresh pork and eggs."

Raleigh stands, keeping one hand on the table as if to steady himself. He isn't entirely sure if it is the boat's rocking or the unsteadiness of drink that makes him take this precaution.

Admiral Gilbert and First Lieutenant Adams are greeted aboard the Flemish warship *Maria* with the roll of drums and the high-pitched salute of a fife. While Captain Van Delft escorts the two on the top deck past cannoneers standing at attention, their torches still lit and held upright beside them, one seaman after another is heard to offer up greetings—in English: "Hello, sir," "Right fine day, Admiral," "Greetings, sir. Are you From Plymouth, sir? How are the lovelies at the Tarnished Wife?"

Raleigh is left rather incredulous and still shaking off the Bordeaux. He looks to Van Delft. "Your crew appears half-English? Could that be?"

"Not exactly, not half; perhaps forty in all. We sank a privateer a few months ago. Full of himself with his cleverness, the captain. Thought he could come in close, do damage, and then run. He should have known better. The wind was already dying. We caught him, put him under in half an hour. These boys who greeted you, they were glad to come out alive, and gladder still after they'd had a few nights with some spending money to drink and whore in Amsterdam. Most returned, depleted and happy for a dry hammock."

The admiral and his Flemish host sit alone in the spacious captain's cabin, finishing a second plate of omelets and large slabs of pork. Van Delft pushes back his chair. He has, during the second helping, returned to the matter of the *Mary and John*'s mission. In response Gilbert becomes increasingly vague.

Finally, Van Delft says, "Admiral, if that is how I am to address you—though I question your credentials—I regret to inform you that I must escort you back to port. There you will be questioned. You are being less than truthful. It is evident your intentions are as much military as they are commercial."

Raleigh rises before pushing back his chair. His thighs tilt the table. Two goblets of wine overturn and spill. "You threaten a vessel under the auspices of the King of England, or under..."

Captain Van Delft remains seated while Raleigh looks down, unable to find the next words. "Enter," he commands in Flemish, in a tone that washes away all geniality.

Three soldiers barge in. Two carry large buckets of water, the third a funnel and cloth straps. Their captain addresses them. Although Gilbert knows only the rudiments of Flemish, it is clear what they intend. He will be tied to his chair. The funnel will be shoved into his mouth, and he will be force-fed water. The effect will be that of downing. Gilbert knows well the effectiveness of this technique; he's administered it himself. Within moments, the victim is usually ready to confess to anything. It is that simple.

Raleigh sits down hard, briefly defeated and confused. What would his father do in such circumstances? Though his father had died when Raleigh was only two years old, stories from his brothers gave the man mythic proportions. If one is overwhelmed, bribery becomes one's best weapon. Wasn't that the moral of one such story? He wasn't too drunk to forget this, or did the Bordeaux allow for cool reflections?

"Captain Van Delft. Do I pronounce that correctly?"

"Yes, well done."

"As I say, our mission is on behalf of King James, and I'm sure your superiors do not wish him ill. Might I offer you personally some token of my appreciation, and in return might you allow me to continue my course—so that someday we might reacquaint ourselves and that encounter be a merry one?"

"And your suggestion?"

"Captain, you did appear to appreciate my Bordeaux."

"Yes, indeed." The Flemish captain found himself in a quandary. The events began to upend much as the wine glasses, now that he began taking stock. The three men with water and funnel were probably premature. A military presence in the New World by the English would be prime information for his superiors. His stock would rise. But would abduction be necessary? The other ship had escaped. His capture of the lightweight admiral would probably only delay, not destroy, their plans. And it was fine Bordeaux.

While the two men ponder for a few moments of silence, someone raps hard on the cabin door. "Come in," Van Delft grumbles.

"Sir," the Flemish first mate offers rather sheepishly. He stands in the doorway, reluctant to enter. "We have a small problem. The English, the seamen, they've gotten word that the admiral here might be in some harm. All of them are making a good bit of noise. They refuse to follow orders. They've been told to go below, but they are standing their ground—with knives and firearms. They want to see the admiral—that is, unharmed."

Raleigh grabs the moment, though it grieves him. "The wine, yes? The Bordeaux will provide elegant libation. Four cases seem appropriate for the moment." Already he feels vindicated.

Within two hours, both ships are under sail in different directions. The Flemish, besides establishing dominance and taking on good wine— six cases not four—have gained strategic information about the English. Gilbert admits to the English intention to establish a colony but lies about its location.

Admiral Gilbert feels his father's presence. For a brief moment, while being rowed between the two ships, he's sure his father has inhabited him. On board he shouts to the young man in the crow's nest. Could he see the *Gift of God*?

After searching the clear horizon for a few minutes, the lad yells down. "Sorry, sir, she is nowhere to be seen." This will be the case for the next six weeks.

CHAPTER 16

June 30, 1607, Mid-Atlantic
Montaigne on the High Seas

Richard insisted that the five boys—Lance and four others, all under age fifteen—attend instruction. Lance and a Jimmy Smith could read and write. Two knew their letters and a few words. The fifth, Paul Meeks, has never attended school. "Dumber than a flounder," the boys insist. To make it more difficult for Richard to decide upon a curriculum and meeting time, Fletcher and two other men, the goatherd and a shipwright, asked to be included, but not because they were illiterate. They simply craved company beyond the daily doltish chatter. Skidwarres, too, would participate.

Popham agreed. They'd carve out chunks of time on an ad hoc basis, in good weather up in the bow, outside in the forecastle, or high on the poop deck in the stern. In bad, they'd squeeze into the gentlemen's quarters below deck or even the chartroom.

Richard first discusses his pedagogical dilemma with Fletcher. He'd attended grammar school and taken to reading Chaucer, history, and even Plato. The goatherd, Erasmus Bean, a man probably in his early thirties, looked less than five feet tall, not a dwarf but nearing that stature. His large head with protruding eyes sat on miniature shoulders, absent a neck. As a result Erasmus had endured much verbal and physical abuse from his peers over his lifetime. He'd learned to be taciturn and stay out of the way and, even more than Fletcher, had turned to reading as a salve for his woes.

"So, Fletcher, what do I do," asks Richard when they were alone. We study at a level somewhere between illiteracy and the classics?"

"Well then, sir, I have a question."

"Yes, good."

"How do you best learn?"

"Ah, you, Fletcher, should be the instructor. It is the best of questions."

"And the answer?"

"For me, I learn the most through dialogue. No different from Socrates with Aristotle. At Oxford and Middle Temple—dialogue, that is how I learned, and by writing."

"Then why not talk? I mean, find something interesting to talk about. And then, well, just proceed from there. Ask questions. You have books. You could read to us. The boys could copy the words."

Fletcher confirms Richard's hunch—a man worth his salt. "John, that makes perfect sense. In fact, I'm not sure what else makes sense."

They hold their first session on a mild evening after dinner in the bow section. The boys sprawl on deck or sit backs against the railing. The four men find crates or sit on the railing, holding onto a stay.

"Boys," begins Richard. At first he stands as if to lecture. But that feels too formal, so he sits cross-legged. "Fletcher has suggested we begin by finding a topic of mutual interest. So that some of you might begin learning to read and others of you might delve more deeply, I have brought with me three sources: the essays of Montaigne, those of Francis Bacon, and the Bible, the Geneva Bible translated into English. It would be difficult to find a subject not included in these books. Those of you who can read may borrow them. The others can help those who can't by copying words and sentences and teaching. And we will talk. When we find a topic, I will try to ask questions, in the manner of Socrates— though I'm a poor stand-in."

All nod their heads, not sure how else to react.

"But, Chaplain. What? What do you want us to talk about," asks Lance.

"Mr. Fletcher suggests we decide together."

"How about the piss-poor food," offers James Smith with a snicker.

"That's one suggestion," comments the shipwright. "Or we could examine your empty head."

"Can Mr...you," Paul Meeks points to Skidwarres. "Can he tell us about monsters where we're going?"

"Call me Skid. I will tell you about *moz* (moose), larger than a horse with antlers wider than this." He stretches his arms wide. "And a little black and white creature, a *segogy*, that sprays stink on you from its anus."

"Stink from its butt-hole?" all five boys ask, more or less together.

"Yes, that kind of monster," Skidwarres replies with a smile. Were there monsters living in the deep forests? Even Skidwarres couldn't banish all possibility. In the dark, immensity of night, he wasn't sure himself. As a boy he had sat around fires and listened to stories of battles and the mysteries of those living at the great mountain, Katahdin. He, like Popham, thought possible the story of the tribe without heads, with eyes on their shoulders and a mouth at their chest. One should not dismiss strangeness.

"All right, two suggestions," comments Richard. "We can talk about anything. But you boys, three of you, are going to learn to read. You other two will get practice."

"Chaplain," Erasmus speaks in a low, measured voice, "for myself, I wish to read Montaigne and Bacon. What subject might touch these lads, besides monsters and food?"

"Well then, thank you." Richard opens Montaigne's essays, happy to oblige. "Here are some subjects." He reads from the table of contents: "'fear, learning how to die, on cannibals, on solitude, on drunkenness, on lies, on cruelty.' Many others."

"Tell us more about monsters, Mr. Skid," Paul Meeks insists.

"Meeks, shut your yap. Monsters don't exist, just animals."

"Hold on, Smith," Richard intervenes. Monsters or not, let me read you from Montaigne." Richard thumbs through his well-worn copy. Here we are. I'll read. This is from an essay called 'That it is madness to judge the true and the false from our own capacities.' It starts like this: 'It is not perhaps without good reason that we attribute to simple-mindedness a readiness to believe anything, and to ignorance the readiness to be convinced, for I think I was once taught that a belief is like an impression stamped on our soul: the softer and less resisting the soul, the easier it is to print anything on it.' He goes on to say, 'That is why children, the common people, women, and the sick are more readily led by the nose.'

"Who'd like to put this in his own words?" Richard asks.

James Smith blurts out, "It says Meeks is like a woman or sick in the head."

"Ah, but wait before you throw any more insults—which, by the way, Smith, insults are not allowed. Listen. Montaigne goes on: 'I used to feel sorry for the wretched folk who were taken in by such madness. Reason has taught me that, if you condemn in this way anything whatever, as definitely false and quite impossible, you are claiming to know the frontiers and bounds of the will of God and the power of Nature our Mother...that there is nothing in the world madder than bringing matters down to the measure of our own capacities and potentialities.'

"Which means?" Richard again looks for a translation.

"It means," Erasmus offers, "don't discount things based on your own experience. It says don't believe—absolutely—what you know."

"Excellent. And nearly everything you read from Montaigne says keep an open mind."

"Can we talk and read about cannibals?" Lance asks.

"I know something about cannibals," pipes up Smith again. "Be careful when they ask you over for dinner."

"Smith, you're improving." Richard thumbs through the essays. "All right Lance, let me find the place. Here. To begin, Montaigne knew a man who lived for over ten years in a part of the world called Antarctic France (Brazil), south in the New World, near where George Popham and Sir Walter Raleigh traveled up the Orinoco. So Montaigne writes from what this man reports: 'I think there is nothing barbarous and savage in that nation except that each man calls barbarism whatever is not his own practice...those people are wild, just as we call wild the fruits that nature has produced by herself and in her normal course; whereas really it is those that we have changed artificially and led astray from common order, that we should rather call wild. The former retain, alive and vigorous, their genuine, their most useful and natural virtues and properties, where we have debased in the latter in adapting them to gratify our corrupted taste. It is not reasonable that art should win the place of honor over our great and powerful mother, Nature. We have so overloaded the beauty and richness of her works by our inventions, that we have quite smothered her.'

Well then, can anyone explain? Fletcher?"

"Not sure I've got it all, sir. Maybe something like Mother Nature, which is not artificial, is more beautiful than what humans make—painting, pictures for instance."

"Excellent. Does that not make sense?"

"As the beauty of a butterfly wing or the sunset," Lance adds.

"But what does that have to do with cannibals?" Smith asks impatiently.

"Because what they do is natural, not artificial," interjects Erasmus, "unlike the debased English."

Fletcher decides to respond. "Coming from the Irish, who I guess Erasmus here might consider untouched by Mother Nature."

"Yes, yes, well let's go on," Richard interjects. "Montaigne goes on to describe these peoples: 'They'—here Montaigne refers to Plato and other ancients who wrote about such peoples untouched by science or letters—'they could not imagine a naturalness so pure and simple as we see by experience; nor could they believe that our society could be maintained with so little artifice and human solder. This is a nation, I should say to Plato, in which there is no sort of traffic, no knowledge of letter, no science of number, no name for a magistrate or for political superiority, no custom of servitude, no riches or poverty, no contracts, no successions, no partitions, no occupations but leisurely ones; no cares for any but common kinship, no clothes, no agriculture, no metal, no use of wine or wheat. The very words that signify lying, treachery, dissimulation, avarice, envy, belittling, pardon—unheard of.'"

Richard looks up. "Skidwarres, do you wish to add anything?"

All turned to where Skidwarres sits cross-legged, back against the railing. For the first time, all but Erasmus and Richard realize the connection between the essay's content and the native. "These people are a long distance from the Mawooshen. I listen carefully. Many similarities."

"All right then, some more about the people themselves. 'They live in a country with a very pleasant and temperate climate...rare to see sickness. They settled near the sea with mountains behind them...fish and fowl of great abundance and little resemblance to our own. Their buildings are made from hardwood and covered with long strips of bark... a few buildings, long and capable of holding three hundred souls. They have one meal in the morning but drink throughout the day a bitter beverage made from boiled roots. In the morning, in one of the large buildings, all sit to eat, while an old man, a preacher of sorts, walks from one end to the other repeating two things: Valor against the enemy and love for their wives...They are close-shaven all over and shave themselves much more cleanly than we, with nothing but a wooden or stone razor. They believe that souls are immortal, and that those who have deserved well of the gods are lodged in that part of heaven where the sun rises, and the damned to the west.'"

"Skidwarres," Fletcher interrupts, "You are very clean-shaven. Is that true of your...friends?"

"It is true. But we do not use stones. Most pull the hairs out, but we have many fewer hairs than you English."

"And valor and love for your wives?" asks Fletcher.

"I think the Mawooshen are similar."

Richard continues his reading. "'The men there have several wives, and the higher the reputation for valor, the more wives they have...and apparently very little jealousy, as the wives are more concerned for their husband's honor than anything else.'"

"And it is the same in your land, Skidwarres?" asks Fletcher again."

"Yes, some have more than one wife. But no jealousy? These indeed must be noble savages." The men catch his sarcasm with grunts of approval.

"But they're cannibals? Isn't that the name of the story?" Smith asks.

"Yes," says Richard, "I'm about there."

"Are you a cannibal?" Meeks blurts out.

The boys turn to look at Meeks as if he'd just passed gas.

"No, Meeks, I prefer venison and sturgeon to boys. But it's a reasonable question."

"I'll continue reading," says Richard. "'They have their wars with the nations beyond the mountains, to which they go quite naked, with no arms other than bows or wooden swords. Each man brings back as his trophy the head of the enemy he has killed, and sets it up at the entrance to his dwelling. After they have treated their prisoners well for a long time with all the hospitality they can think of, each man who has a prisoner calls a great assembly of his acquaintances. He ties a rope to one of the prisoner's arms and gives his dearest friend the other arm to hold in the same way, and these two, in the presence of the assembly, kill him with their swords. This done, they roast him and eat him in common and send some pieces to their absent friends.' This is not for nourishment." Richard explains. "Here Montaigne makes it clear. The warfare is not for conquest of new lands. As he says, 'They are still in that happy state of desiring only as much as their natural needs demand; anything beyond that is superfluous.' They fight for valor and virtue. Then, 'They demand of the prisoners no other ransom than that they confess their defeat.

"'Beyond the kindness, the prisoners are entertained with threats. They will have to suffer the cutting up of their limbs, the feast that will be made at their expense. All this is done for the sole purpose of extorting from their lips some weak or base word, so as to gain the advantage of having terrified them and broken down their firmness. For indeed, if you take it the right way, it is in this point alone that true victory lies. But the prisoners do not give in. On the contrary, during the two or three months that they are kept, they wear a gay expression; they insult their captors, reproach them for their cowardice and the number of battles they have lost to the prisoner's own people.

"'The captives sing. They refer to themselves: these muscles, this flesh, and these veins are your own, poor fools that you are. You do not recognize that the substance of your ancestors' limbs is still contained in them. Savor them well; you will find in them the taste of your own flesh.'

"Let me stop here. What do you make of Montaigne's message?"

"I think he admires these people," Lance offers, "but does that mean he thinks cannibalism is—I don't know—acceptable?"

"Smith, what do you think?" Richard asks.

"I'm not sure. At the end there, the prisoners, he thinks they are brave."

"Do you—Erasmus, Fletcher, Skidwarres—want to give us your opinion?"

Erasmus speaks. "I like this Montaigne. I think he's saying it's difficult to judge people who are so different. They have their own ways. He seems to think that living for valor—that's what he calls it—and love for your wife, that these are good things. Basic and honorable."

"Skidwarres?" Richard asks after a few moments of silence following Erasmus' comments.

"Richard, I do not know. Montaigne writes, but he never visited these people. He hears it though a man, another Frenchman, no? Some of these things, they remind me of the Mawooshen. You say he wants us to remain open, but Richard, what is a word for 'willing to believe too much?'"

"Gullible?"

"Yes, I think Montaigne is gullible. He is wise but he is also gullible. That is the correct word? The Mawooshen are good people, but, as you say, 'all noble?' No."

"Well said," offers Fletcher.

"Yes, well said," adds Richard. "You are saying, Skidwarres, be open without being gullible. A good thought to finish by. Now, the book is available. Lance, I want you to find a few sentences you like and copy them. Teach the words, first the easy ones, to the boys here that can't read. When you find a word difficult, ask Fletcher or Erasmus—or me. First lesson over."

CHAPTER 17

July 10, 1607, The South Atlantic
An Unearthly Battle

For the entire month of June and now into the second week of July, the *Gift of God* angles west, as the wind and currents push her southwest into a warmer and gentler climate. Many men and boys now go shirtless, their skin browned and salted, their hair bleached blonder. At four in the afternoon, Fletcher and Lance, with Stow curled up at his feet, stand at the rail after having greased the cannon. The sun is so happy with itself it appears to resist the horizon.

"Lance," Fletcher finally breaks their silence, "you never take off that shirt. Why not give your skin a healthy dose of sun? It's fine medicine. It mends the soul."

At first Lance acts as if he doesn't hear, but then moves a few inches closer and lowers his voice. "You are my friend. I can tell you. I have a large birth mark on my chest. It's ugly, all reddish-purple."

"I'm sorry."

"No, you're my friend. You can ask anything."

The two return their gaze to the curvature of the ocean. As Richard had hoped, the two have become friends, their losses at first providing kinship. Then they began to simply enjoy one another's company.

Something catches Lance's eye off the bow, some hundred or so yards away. A churning in the water, perhaps fish at the surface. He stares and points. "Do you see that?" Fletcher follows Lance's extended finger.

"Yes, I see."

"What is it? Lance asks.

"I don't know. A school of fish feeding, maybe." The excitement in the water roils more feverishly. The *Gift of God*'s course brings them closer.

As the helmsman gazes at the commotion, others come to the rail and watch. All then see a huge black object erupt—a whale, a sperm whale that remains on the surface smacking its huge tail in great agitation.

"There, look!" cries Lance. Fifty yards from the whale, something cuts the surface leaving a fine wake. It travels at remarkable speed and heads directly toward the thrashing whale.

"My god, man, that's no shark, it's a swordfish attacking," Fletcher's mouth hangs open. "Heard about this sort of thing, but never..."

The darting object disappears underwater, and a second later the whale's body lifts partly out of the water. The fish, at least eight feet long with a four-foot sword, has sunk deeply into the beast's mid-section. The whale turns over, flipping the fish over its massive underbelly, but not dislodging it. Both then sink below the surface. The black oily spot churns, turns reddish, and then settles.

Captain Elliot heads the *Gift of God* into the wind so it idles. The deck fills with men and boys. The ship drifts close to where the two disappeared. Stow attempts to place his front paws on the railing, but he's too small. "All right, boy." Lance picks up the dog and points. Stow's nose quivers.

The commotion dies. All wait. Would they learn anything more? Had they seen the last act?

Two, three, four minutes of silence, nothing but the rigging banging and the creaking ship. Then, just off the port bow, the sea breaks open. A black swelling appears over the surface, slides, turns, exposing the great fish still impaled, wriggling back and forth, attempting to free itself. Lance thinks it looks like a strange flag waving. Then, as both sink out of sight, a twenty-foot stream of water and blood shoots into the air— the leviathan's last exhalation. The small section of ocean calms, then covers over with small chop. Except for the expanding redness, the space becomes indecipherable from the ocean around it, as if the spectacle were commonplace.

Nobody talks. Some think his unfathomable event can be nothing but a bad omen, at least that's what many of the superstitious on ship believe and, for the moment, keep to themselves.

Lance and Fletcher remain at the rail. "John," Lance finally asks, "you've heard of that?"

"Lance, my friend, when you sail for years, you hear everything: some of it fanciful, some of it real. I have seen swordfish—remarkable fish, afraid of nothing. Shipmates told me they accomplish great speeds and are incredibly strong. When agitated they attack anything, including ships. That sword can penetrate a ship's hull, six inches of spruce, even bottoms covered by copper, and cause holes big enough to send them back to port. And I've heard how they battle one another, like jousters from the Middle Ages."

"Do you believe all that?"

"Do you believe what you just saw? And if you told it to a landlubbing friend, would he believe it?"

"I see. No. And what else have you heard—and believed?"

"Most sailors dream more about the sea monster with tentacles, nightmares about the giant squid. In their dream, the ship is pulled underwater by this great creature with eyes the size of wagon wheels, a beak like a parrot that can crush a longboat, a blubbery body bigger than a carriage, and those eight tentacles twenty feet long."

"This is real, you think? It could attack us?"

"Yes, but rare. I have never seen one, but I have so heard. I have seen one of their suckers, or so I am told that is what I saw and felt, a dinner-plate-sized rubbery thing encrusted with tiny knives. Their tentacles are covered with them. What I saw and touched was hard to believe."

As Fletcher talks, Lance's eyes scan the water. Once again the *Gift of God* sails slowly, picking up momentum. Again Lance's curiosity and keen young eyes spy something the others don't notice. "Fletcher, look over there." As before, he follows in the direction of Lance's finger. "Another whale, or maybe the same one. It's spouting. No it's smaller."

"I see it, lad. Good eyes. Yes I think it's a baby, a calf. Perhaps that was the mother the swordfish killed. Maybe she agitated the fish by protecting her calf. There she goes." The smaller whale's tail arches into the air and slides under the surface." Probably going in search of her as she sinks."

Fletcher looks down at Lance. He still holds Stow, only now the dog's muzzle rests under Lance's chin and bent head. The dog whimpers softly. He has picked up Lance's mood. Tears slide down Lance's cheeks. Fletcher understands all too well. He places a hand on Lance's shoulder. "I know, boy, another motherless beast in the world."

Softly from Lance, Fletcher hears, "I don't cry. I don't cry. Don't tell anybody. Please. I am stronger than that. I have to be."

"No need to worry, boy. Men cry. Don't let them tell you otherwise. Don't worry. It's between us—and Stow."

Lance raises his head and looks out at the ocean. The afternoon breezes are flagging. The whitecaps are no more. The ocean is calming itself and returning to the breathing of one long roller after another. The ship rocks gently, barely sailing. In an attempt to change the subject,

Lance's voice cracks, then settles into its usual clarity. "So when I have a nightmare about those, what did you call them, giant...?"

"Giant squid."

"Giant squid, you will tell me don't worry. It's only a story bored fishermen and sailor tell."

"No, I will tell you the world has much in store for us we don't know about. Like a battle between a swordfish and a sperm whale."

"So thank you, my friend, now I will have many bad nights ahead."

"And, lad, I will tell you don't bother your head with rare exceptions. Maybe you will be hit by a flying star or a flying fish or thrown overboard by a huge wave or..."

"Thank you, Fletcher, I am much comforted." Lance offers a rueful chuckle.

"What they say of the squid monster is that they live deep, deep in the ocean and don't do well in the warmer water at the surface. But I don't know if anybody really knows. But listen, boy, if any squid gives you trouble, you just let me know. I'll fire off a cannonball down his ugly throat. That make you feel better?"

Lance did feel better. "Yes, I will count on it. But do you think the baby, the calf, will live?"

Fletcher nods. "I do. Whales travel in groups. Others are around out there. And they will protect, I'm sure of it." He gives Lance's shoulder a squeeze under the heavy sleeveless shirt. "I'm sure of it."

CHAPTER 18

August 7, 1607, Off the Coast of Northern Virginia
From the Crow's Nest

After nearly five weeks, the winds began prevailing from the west, and the current, the one emerging from the warm waters of the Caribbean, carried the *Gift of God* north, the preferred direction—though on more than one occasion, a nostalgic George Popham had mused how he'd prefer not to be pressed for time. He longed to take the trade winds from Europe to their natural destination and "vacation" on white sand, enjoying the heat among the natives on the islands. "Very friendly," as he often restated how men without female company for weeks would enjoy themselves and how, in his words, "We might have dined on fresh meat and a wondrous variety of fruit. We should have left sooner and arranged for a merry interlude. It would have been good for morale. The trouble with this voyage is that it is all business."

The shift northward left the New World a few hundred miles to the west. Would it, Popham and others discussed, make sense to first find the Southern Virginia Company settlement, assuming their brethren could be found? The answer came quickly. Two weeks would probably be lost. The *Mary and John*, if all had gone well with the Flemish and weather, would be waiting. No final selection of a site for the fort could be made without President Popham. Already, as the bow nosed its way into colder waters, the evening breezes hinted of fall.

Every day one could feel the anticipation among the crew. The soldiers marched the cramped deck and cleaned their weapons with more purpose. The shipwright, who had enjoyed the respite from his profession, became more diligent with his sketches of the pinnace he soon would build; meanwhile he began assembling the prefabricated section of the shallop, some thirty feet of her. The boys couldn't focus on their studies. Rather, the reality of The New World began to dawn on them and cause both curiosity and trepidation.

On the evening of August 6th, Richard volunteers to keep watch in the tiny crow's nest. He has done so before, enjoying in the dark the sensation of swaying thirty feet above the deck and gazing at the black starry dome which came to life as his eyes adjusted. He will take the midnight-to-six shift and thereby witness the sun's pale watery revival. This morning might also bring an additional delight. According to Captain Elliott, they soon would reach the Northern Virginia coast.

Kind night breezes barely fill the sails of the *Gift of God*, half-asleep on the swells. Richard's eyes close—he dozes, wakes, looks east for a hint of light, and dozes again.

A stray gust snaps a sail. Richard's eyes open. Looking east, toward England, he can distinguish the line between the purple sky and black sea. One multicolored moment slides into another; in fact, he can not determine such a thing as a moment. All is fluid, floating in immeasurable time. While most are sleeping, every clear morning this occurs—the same gaudy theatrics—while the men rest, oblivious to each day's entrance. From a musical standpoint, it is a theme with infinite variations.

He twists his head to the west. "My god!" he exclaims. Land—one small reflected white dot on the horizon. Or did he conjure this? "Land," he says softly to himself. "Land!" he yells.

The helmsman calls back, "Where away?"

Richard points, "Off the port bow at eleven o'clock."

"You're sure, sir? I don't see."

"I'm sure. I'm damn sure."

"Aye, Chaplain." Over the weeks, the crew had accepted the chaplain's use of profanity. They'd even give up shrugging their shoulders and smirking. A few moments later, President Popham opens his cabin door. He and the Captain Elliott stumble on deck. "Ah," the helmsman yells. "Land ho," Popham echoes.

Men pour on deck, half-dressed and groggy, Lance among them with Stow underfoot and barking.

Some minutes later Skidwarres joins Richard at the rail. Both watch while their ship finds more wind and eases forward. The two friends consult a chart, one amended over the decades. Skidwarres concedes, as with writing, that maps provide a superior form of communication. His people's scratchings on bark or sand did not compare—though of course they had no need for charts. For hundreds of years, the island and sea had simply been part of who they were. Before his abduction, his own sea voyages had taken him only a few miles from land. Canoes served better on the plentiful inland waterways between the Sagadahoc and Penobscot and all the estuaries in between. Some canoes over thirty feet in length and high in the bow and sides, manned by eight skilled men, could survive considerable chop and more often than not traveled together for protection.

Skidwarres watches land, his land he's never before seen from this new geographic and emotional perspective.

During the passage, Richard has noticed small changes: Skidwarres now wears his old moccasins, kicked off during his abduction and returned to him, though he'd worn boots since their meeting. Their easy camaraderie has turned more cordial, conversations less spirited and loose-tongued, and humor not so easily available. Skidwarres has recognized his own turning inward and made efforts to reverse this trend. He'd seek out Richard and even start conversations, rather than rely on the Englishman's natural loquacity. But too often, talk died an unnatural death, and the two fell into silence, surprising both of them. Richard at first thought Skidwarres seasick, though neither experienced any symptoms of queasiness. Finally, both recognized it for what it was: uneasy, unidentifiable internal shifts and tears in their friendship.

"Tell me, what can you make out?" Richard asks, as much to break the silence as to learn anything.

What Richard saw shining was a small island a mile or so long, now in full view. "That we call Monhegan," Skidwarres replies. "You English use it for drying fish in the summer. Not far is the Penobscot, the home of Bessabez—that way." He points east. "I have spoken of him, our leader. And that way..." This time he first points to the map and then to the disappearing green to the east, "There lies the Sagadahoc, not far from that other small shining spot, the island of Seguin. Your word is 'turtle.'" Both consult the map again. Skidwarres finds another smaller river on the map and points straight ahead. "That is where my people live. Where Nahanada returned."

The plan, established in Plymouth, envisioned the two ships—in the event they became separated—to rendezvous off the island where Weymouth had planted a Christian cross only a few miles across the water from Skidwarres' village.

Lance finishes with his cleanup duties in the galley and joins Richard and Skidwarres. He carries a small wooden box with wood chips. He tests the wind—it comes from behind them—so tosses overboard the contents, dog turds and saturated urine from the night before.

Richard smiles and bends over to scratch Stow behind the ears. He is now probably five or six months old, his thick black and white hair over an inch long. "Smart dog to learn that trick. Smart owner to teach him. I guess that land will be welcome for both of you."

From above in the crow's nest, the watch shouts, "Ship off the starboard bow, three o'clock."

President Popham joins the captain at the helm. His excitement bubbles. "Can it be the *Mary and John*?"

"Yes, sir, right where she should be."

"Remarkable—no, miraculous. We meet as planned. What an omen. What a wonder this science, this navigation. Indeed, the stars are in perfect alignment." A group of soldiers and unoccupied crew members congregate around the wheel. Popham continues, "Let us give praise to the captain and his navigator and to God. Chaplain Seymour, a few words of praise, here on deck."

Richard, who at first found these spur-of-the-moment requests awkward, used the time at sea to prepare a few short blessings that might be altered, depending on the circumstances. The Book of Common Prayer provided some guidance. A group of forty or so stood, heads bowed. "Lord, we beseech you: accept our gratitude for your beneficence; that we have arrived at this place healthy and unmolested by the might of your ocean and skies. May we honor you in our deeds here in this New World and forevermore. To the Father, Son, and the Holy Ghost. Amen."

"Bravo!" Popham shouts, not caring much if this sounded out of place.

CHAPTER 19

August 7, 1607, Morning
Fishing

Within the hour the two ships lie at anchor a hundred yards from one another. Men yell greetings, some waving hats or shirts. Others furl sails. A few drop fishing lines over the side. Within minutes, large haddock and cod three and four feet long flop on deck. The *Mary and John* slowly lowers a longboat. Admiral Raleigh Gilbert, in full uniform, jumps in and regally positions himself standing in the stern and urges the six rowers ahead of him to "pull hard."

For the past two months, Admiral Raleigh has complained to Sergeant Davies about President Popham's "negligence of duty" for abandoning the *Mary and John* in the face of Flemish harassment. But today he is all good cheer and ready to embrace Popham, to establish his own authority as second-in-command—and more than that, as the younger and more energetic of the two.

Raleigh retires to Popham's cabin. Not long afterwards, the watch yells, "Small ship."

"A shallop," says Fletcher. "Looks to be about twenty feet long." Fletcher, Seymour, and Skidwarres watch the vessel approach under both sail and four oars.

"Looks Spanish to me, but not in the best of care," Fletcher comments. "Eight men and a boy, but not Spanish—natives."

"Not Spanish, correct," agrees Skidwarres. They could see the men were all nearly naked, except for a small loincloth. "Micmacs. They trade with the French and Basques." Skidwarres points east.

The shallop keeps her distance while rowing around both vessels. Popham opens the chartroom door in response to the commotion and then instructs Fletcher to gather a few trinkets before retreating into the cabin. Within moments, men hold up beads and knives; one seaman bangs on an iron pot, another lifts a loaf of bread over his head. The natives maintain their distance and stare upwards, calculating, until they turn and begin sailing away. Popham again appears on the quarterdeck and shouts to Skidwarres, "Call them back!"

"Yes, sir." Hands megaphone style, he calls, "*Chowi, chowi*" (it is safe).

The rowers stop. The small sailing craft bobs about, while its occupants lean over conferring with one another. Then they begin rowing again back to the *Gift of God*. The rope ladder remains over the side so the natives can tie up. All scramble up on deck, wide-eyed.

By the 1600s, contact between Europeans and natives had become seasonal and sporadic. Neither group trusted the other. Fishermen tended to stay on their ships or on offshore islands drying and salting their catch on large wooden racks. Often these islands, such as Monhegan, Damariscove and Matinicus, lay miles from the mainland and a hazardous trip in a small canoe. Each people seemed to the other unpredictable, at one moment smiling and wanting to trade, and at the next ready to pull a knife or raise a musket. The natives had seen or heard told of the huge guns that made a thunderous sound and could kill many.

At first the natives on the *Gift of God* gawk at the bearded aliens, many shirtless, hairy-chested, and wearing greasy pants. They gaze down to the scrubbed wood planking underfoot or up at the furled sails, and then with some circumspection into the face of Skidwarres who now stands before them. A boy who looks about fourteen is the only one who smiles. All including him wear an eagle feather to one side of the head, held in place by a leather band. Their hairless chests are painted with geometric designs in red and yellow.

Popham makes his way down the ladder to the main deck and approaches. "Skidwarres, tell them we will not harm them. Tell them we will trade." Skidwarres' people and the Micmac harbor long-term resentments. Nonetheless, they both speak a similar dialect of the Algonquin language and can clearly understand one another. Skidwarres and the one next to the boy begin conversing.

After a few minutes Skidwarres steps back and smiles at Richard. "My first time speaking their language; it's difficult to find the right words." He then turns to Popham. "They and others are camping on an island not far from here. They fish. Some will leave and return with skins. They say they have but a few but wish to trade. Two and the boy wish to remain. They ask for that pot and a knife. They will return them tomorrow if their friends are safe."

The agreement is struck. Six of the men return to their decrepit Basque shallop and head east. The two remaining men are invited to the chartroom with Skidwarres, Seymour, and a few others to parlay and share grog.

Stow, sitting next to the boys, ears perked, first greets the strangers with soft growls. Then he eyes the native boy and wags his tail. The boy kneels, welcoming the dog. "All right, Stow." says Lance.

The dog bounds up to the boy and licks his face. "*Molsem, mkazawi atsi wabi*" (wolf, black and white).

Lance and the other two boys approach. Lance touches Stow on the head while he continues his enthusiastic greeting. "Dog, this is a dog."

The boy stands. Again Lance points. "Dog. He's a dog."

The boy scrunches up his face and then smiles. "*Molsen*, dug."

Meeks laughs. "A dug. He thinks it's a dug."

"Shut up, Meeks," says Smith.

"Yes, almost. Dog, Dog," Lance repeats slowly.

Slowly the boy answers, "Doog. Dog." The three English clap and Stow barks.

"Brilliant," Lance adds.

Fletcher watches, then asks the three boys to show the newcomer around the ship. Before going below they watch three shipwrights finish assembling an English shallop, one that had been partially assembled and then stored in the hold in sections to save space. Three longboats—"kit boats"—have been similarly constructed. One sits on deck ready to be launched. Paul Meeks has an idea. Usually his half-intelligible comments are disregarded, but not this one. "Fletcher, can we go fishing?"

"Sure, throw a line overboard."

"No, in a boat, this boat." He points to the recently assembled longboat. "Over there." He points to a longboat that had been lashed on deck during the voyage and is now a quarter mile away. Three men can be seen jigging lines. Howls of success are heard coming over the water.

Lance becomes an ally. "Fletcher, why not? We're not headed anywhere soon, are we? Just a few hours, a few of us. We can take the savage boy with us. We'll bring back cod and eat it ourselves."

Fletcher looks out to sea and over the tranquil deck. He nods his head, as if to convey thoughtfulness. "Meeks, good idea. Get rid of the bunch of you devils. I'll ask the first mate. But you'll need to take an experienced sailor. The sea has a mind of its own—now who would that be?" Fletcher scratches his head in mock confusion.

Smith and Lance smile. Even Paul Meeks gets it.

Half an hour later, after introducing the native boy to an oil lamp and leading him to the ship's hold, its bowels, they reappear on the main deck into impossible shards of sun light. They stand in a row, eyes on the deck, momentarily blinded. Fletcher grabs the moment and pushes Lance. He falls into the native boy who in turn topples Meeks into Smith. All end up in a laughing heap. "Mowed down," says Fletcher. "Now get up and climb down that ladder. We'll catch cod with the best of them."

Fletcher instructs the boys to pair up, one to an oar. The native boy, who calls himself Mikowa (squirrel), is the only one of the four who's ever touched an oar. The three English flail about. The oars refuse to hold in their locks. On the stern seat, Fletcher watches, shaking his head. "You three are a sorry lot." Because Mikowa's oar is the only effective one, the eighteen-foot boat turns in a hapless circle and bangs into the *Gift of God*'s hull.

"Stop, you halfwits!" Mikowa catches Fletcher's bemusement and smiles. "Now one at a time. Lance, don't work so hard. Put it in the lock. Good. Now you and Mikowa," Fletcher points to Mikowa's oar. It's at the ready. "Pull, slowly." Fletcher demonstrates pulling an imaginary oar. "Only when I say 'pull.' Jimmy and Paul, just sit, wait, watch. Keep your oars out of the water." Lance and Mikowa follow Fletcher's lead, and in five or six attempts they are pulling slowly in unison. The boat glides away from the *Gift of God* in a straight direction. "All right now," Fletcher says to Jimmy and Paul who sit side by side, "Join them." Both lower their oars into the water. The forward motion kicks Paul's oar out of his hand and it bangs into his chin. Fletcher jumps and grabs the oar before it slides away from the boat. "Keep rowing," he orders to Lance and Mikowa. "Try again, boys."

After a few more unsuccessful attempts, all are able to follow Fletcher's cadence. "All right, boys, I'll make seamen out of you somehow, by god. Now shout with me, Pull, pull, pull!" They do, Mikowa included. A few men who have watched the show from the mother ship whistle their approval—or contempt—it is impossible to tell.

Before long, the boys ship their oars and drop their lines and sinkers. "Let that line out, boys, lots of it. At least thirty arm's length. They like it way down there in the dark and cold." Mikowa watches and copies Lance. With the lines set, all on the longboat settle on the seats. They're within half a mile of the ship. The early summer afternoon bakes.

After a while without a bite, Jimmy suggests maybe this is a bad spot.

"Maybe," answers Fletcher. "We'll give it bit more time."

After more waiting, Paul pipes up, "Got to piss.

"All right then," Fletcher responds, "tie your line around the seat. Anyone else?"

"Me too," says Jimmy.

"Might as well myself," Fletcher adds. "How about everybody, whether you have to or not. Balance the boat. Two off each side, but tie your line." Fletcher begins emptying his bladder off the stern; Lance and Mikowa ready themselves on the port, Jimmy and Paul on the starboard.

"Bet I can piss longer than anyone," pipes up Jimmy. All turn their heads and take note of his healthy arch. Mikowa has picked up the game

"Yea, not better than this." Lance leans back and sends a stream up and out, beating Jimmy by a couple of feet in both height and length. The others are running low, so have lost their competitive advantage.

"Not bad," says Fletcher. "Prize goes to you, Lance. Pisser of the day." All stand focused on their buttoning—excepting Mikowa. It is while in this standing position that the round bottomed longboats lurches over to starboard. Jimmy's line has pulled tight. It's enough to send three boys sprawling to the floor and Paul overboard. Fletcher, seaman that he is, has kept his feet apart and remains upright. The fish on the other end is strong enough to pull the boat's bottom over Paul's head. He is out of sight. Like many seamen, none of the English can swim.

Fletcher quickly takes charge. "Lance, tie this line around you—tight. Get overboard and grab him, wherever he is. Jimmy, use that knife of yours. Cut that line."

"But that's my fish!"

"Cut it now." Fletcher grabs a fallen oar and points it at him.

With the line cut, the boat rights itself. Lance drapes a leg in the water and hesitates. It's freezing, but he doesn't say so. The line is secure around his waist. The other end Fletcher ties in a quick bowline knot around the mid-seat.

"Get in and find him, for god's sake. I'll pull you both in."

Lance drops in, one hand clinging to the gunwale. "I don't see him."

Fletcher and Jimmy look and Jimmy scrambles to the bow. It's been a maddening length of time since Paul's head slid under.

While all are searching, Mikowa has grabbed a line. He ties it, the same as Lance did, around his waist. Mikowa then stands on the fore rowing seat. Fletcher sees him and it dawns, he can swim.

Feet first, Mikowa jumps. The rope plays out, yards a second. The water is dark black–green–blue, with nothing visible below a few feet. Lance continues to hold the boat, feeling useless. Fletcher notices the line become slack. Then it snakes overboard again. "Impossible," Fletcher says watching it snap taut.

Fletcher jumps to the line and begins pulling hand over hand. He's not sure this is what he should do, but he does so with a vengeance. How long can that boy stay under?

Twenty, thirty feet of rope are piled by his feet before the surface breaks. Mikowa spits water and gasps. Both hands are grasping Paul's long blond hair. His head is limp, face down in the water. Fletcher pulls both boys up against the hull. Lance reaches over for a handful of Meeks's hair in order to get his mouth above the surface.

"Jimmy, stay on that side. Don't want to flip over." He leans over and grabs yet another handful of hair. "Lance, get to the other side."

Lance moves in the water, hand on the gunwale, to the other side of the boat in order to provide a counterweight. Mikowa holds Meeks while Fletcher hauls him over the side by the armpits. He flops onto the bottom of the boat, as might a ninety-pound cod, except Paul Meeks is motionless. Pinkish froth drains from his mouth.

Lance and Mikowa move to the middle seat, shivering, Paul at their feet. "He dead?" Lance asks.

"Don't know. Not breathing." Fletcher falls to his knees. He turns Meeks over, stationing himself behind and above, grasping around his waist. He violently jabs both fists into the boy's solar plexus. Again and again, grunting, pulling the dead weight up against his own stomach. "Come on, come on!" Fletcher urges in their eerie intimacy.

"Richard," Lance explains, "Paul was alive and then dead. Just like that. I guess he just sank. Then somehow Mikowa found him. Too late. It's just like that, isn't it? Alive and then dead. And everything else just keeps going on. I mean, it didn't seem to matter much to anyone on board. I mean, it did for only a few moments, when we arrived. They would have paid more attention to a large fish. Fletcher cared, but even he disappeared to his hammock. Is that the way death is, Richard? People just shrug their shoulders. He, Meeks, he told us he didn't have a mother or father. It's like nothing happened. At breakfast he's happy and before dinner he's dead."

"Lance, you are learning things I know little of."

"Richard, it's worse. Even I, I don't know how much I care. This happened only two hours ago. I'm not sure it matters to me, I mean very much, really. Is that a sin?"

Richard and Lance are standing alone at the bow. Fog rolls in off the ocean, a heavy blanket wetting the sails. Above is the blue sky. "It feels wrong, Richard. It feels wrong, I mean, that I can't feel more."

"He was a good boy, a lost boy." Richard doesn't know what else to say. He wishes he did. He feels inadequate.

Lance waits. He wants to hear something, but Richard only stares out at the fog. He wonders how much does life matter, really—whether it's Meeks or hundreds of slaughtered Irish or thousands dead from the Black Plague? Yes, it matters. It should matter, but the heart and mind are so fickle. Finally fed up with the silence, Lance slips away from Richard's limp hand on his shoulder. "You're not a chaplain. You don't know anything."

He runs but he doesn't cry.

During the fishing tragedy, Popham and Gilbert agree that Skidwarres, Robert Davies, and Seymour would go ashore and attempt to find Nahanada. They'd take with them only eleven soldiers. They'd leave early in the morning.

Gilbert took stock of these two unlikely friends, the English gentleman and the savage who knew how to read and write. As a boy, Raleigh had learned to trust his own judgment above all. He maintained this view while in the military, where officers might undermine others for their own advancement, and from the Oxford dons who valued their prissy habits, soft life, and book knowledge above all.

Raleigh Gilbert considered himself to be the embodiment of his father's ambitions. The Virginia Charter had been stolen by John Popham, a conniving businessman, not an adventurer. All this led Raleigh Gilbert to be wary of those around him. However, Seymour might be pivotal, a son of one of a financial backers, evidently a favorite of Sir John Popham. This untested, rather dandyish man who played music and read copiously must be taken seriously. In his capacity as chaplain and friend with that native, Seymour was a potential ally. Besides were they not second cousins? Seymour could be used.

The English intended to initiate good relations, especially with Nahanada. Gilbert and Popham had agreed to spend a few days replenishing their stock of fish and exploring this section of the coast before traveling the half-day journey southwest to the Sagadahoc. Both president and admiral felt the pull to begin building a fort as soon as possible. For only a few days would they dally, catching food and attempting to build good relations.

CHAPTER 20

August 8, 1607, Early Morning
Hospitality

A few hours before dawn, with the winds slight, the air crisp from night, the sky clear, and the moon lighting the way, the crew lowered two longboats, one from each ship. The eleven soldiers eased themselves over the rails and down the rope ladders, clanging about and careful not to fall and sink under the weight of their brass helmets, breastplates, and muskets. Some joked they'd hold on to their weapon as fiercely as if it were their cock. All exhibited the edginess of men who have been cooped up and now face possible battle, though Gilbert insisted hostilities were not expected.

Popham had argued that eleven armor-clad soldiers might appear as an act of aggression. Five or six without armor would more likely convey peaceful intentions. Gilbert countered that they needed to demonstrate strength and power. All negotiations rested on this premise. The English were, after all, a small minority on the edge of a wilderness inhabited by thousands. Skidwarres and Nahanada had been queried about the size of the native population. For centuries groups numbering from a few dozen to four hundred had occupied the region. From Gilbert's reckoning with Nahanada a year before, some thousands now occupied the land between the two major river systems. Of these, hundreds were armed braves, many with fighting experience. Gilbert's position prevailed over Popham's.

Skidwarres directs the longboats during the three-hour row and sail to a small cove beach on the western shore of Pemaquid. It is low tide. Gray, white, and black mottled granite with streaks of orange fortifies both sides of the cove's entrance. The sun rises as they slip by. These outcroppings hang with a dark green beard of seaweed and purplish-red kelp waiting to dry in the sun. Above and beyond lies a thick forest of pine, spruce, and oak.

They row until the longboats run up against a tan mucky bottom. Everyone steps out into knee-deep icy water. Ooze sucks at their ankles. The soldiers grab their weapons in one hand and the boats' gunwales in the other. They haul over dark pebbles, then a band of slimy seaweed and water-soaked logs thrown up by storms, and finally to fine white sand. There they drop the boats. So the incoming tide doesn't set them adrift, they are tethered to a tree. For the first time in nearly two months, the men are standing on solid ground. Except for Skidwarres and another experienced mate who'd sailed with Weymouth, everyone has planted himself on New World soil for the first time.

Skidwarres, with Richard alongside, leads the procession along a narrow path, beginning at the edge of the beach and heading into the woods. The soldiers march shoulder to shoulder, two abreast. "Be alert," instructs Gilbert, an unnecessary command, given the vulnerability felt by all. Open spaces provide visual security. The trees on either side, some standing dead and held up by their neighbors, give the cool forest an eerie feel. The low-angled sun creates shadows over the thick spruce and pine canopy. Loaded muskets are at the ready.

Richard feels no nervousness with the shirtless, erect, and silent Skidwarres at his side. This is his home. The natives mean no harm, Richard is sure. The tension in the column trailing behind does not reach him. Richard hears high-pitched chirping from way overhead. "What is that?"

"Ospreys," explains Skidwarres, almost in a whisper. "Fish hawks."

"Ospreys," Richard repeats.

Skidwarres nods with a slight smile. He does not know what reception awaits him, either from his wife or from Nahanada, nor if his parents, now late in life, are perhaps dead. Would he be received as a man carrying information, even wisdom, or would he be considered tainted and therefore untrustworthy? These thoughts have returned again and again. While on ship, as he had before, off and on—especially during his early months in England—he felt removed from himself, watching himself from afar. Now mind and body are reunited. Now, with these woods and the piercing cry of the ospreys, the past two years recede in an instant.

From behind a massive white pine trunk some twenty paces in front of Skidwarres and Richard, Nahanada steps to the middle of the path. He carries a bow in one hand and an arrow in the other.

"Greetings, Skidwarres. You have returned."

"Halt," barks Gilbert to his men.

"Greetings, Nahanada." Skidwarres does not show any sign of surprise. In fact he has been expecting such an appearance. It was Nahanada's way. But he had not told either Richard or Raleigh Gilbert. From behind trees other braves materialize, thirty of so, with their arrows notched but pointed to the ground.

A few soldiers aim their weapons at whichever brave catches their eye. Gilbert quickly calculates no immediate threat and so orders, "Lower arms."

Silence briefly returns. Wind rustles the upper branches, though none hear it, given the intensity of everyone's concentration.

Nahanada speaks to Skidwarres in their native tongue. "I remember the last time I faced armed soldiers. You and I were captured and removed from our land and people. I do not forget this easily. Do you come in peace, my brother, or are you and your English friends playing tricks?"

Skidwarres responds slowly, gravely, "Nahanada, my sagamore, we are here in peace. I am returning with a glad heart."

"And these men with their muskets and battle gear?"

"They mean no harm. They are only taking precautions. As do you and my brothers."

Gilbert interrupts, "What is your intent, Nahanada? In such a short period have your sentiments changed? You knew we would arrive. Here we are. We bring only good will."

Nahanada nods acknowledgement and then takes five quick paces and greets Skidwarres by placing both hands on his shoulder. "Then come in peace. I much welcome your return."

Gilbert approaches the front of the line and puts out his hand. Nahanada releases Skidwarres and shakes it. This time Nahanada attempts English. "Yes, I watched your arrival. It is true what Skidwarres says, we take precautions. But let us find ourselves where we can offer some food and drink. We will honor your arrival and speak of your plans."

Gilbert relays this to his anxious soldiers who still stand two abreast in a row along the narrow path. Their reply in a ragged unison, "Aye, sir," that carries a lilt of good cheer. Richard looks into the woods. The braves have vanished.

Nahanada and Skidwarres take the lead and speak softly.

"Skidwarres, those English pants. You like them?"

"Do you mean will I begin wearing leggings now that I have returned? And the answer is I do not know. But tell me, Nahanada, how is it with Sokw and Nahnibssat? And my father and mother?"

"They are well, all of them. Some six moons after our capture, English fishermen told our people that we were alive. Most thought we would return. Others, up near the Penobscot, have been taken to France and returned. So they waited, and I returned and again I am in leggings— though I still have my English pants. Sokw, too, has waited. Both your parents will welcome you. But tell me, Skidwarres, what are the English' intentions? Will they settle at the Sagadahoc?"

"That is their plan. Was this not your advice?"

"It was, and I gave it partly from anger. But then, they wished to be there."

"And what does Bessabez say?"

"It is complicated, no? We wish to trade. But a permanent settlement? Some of the elders believe this to be to our advantage. I am not sure. We have seen England. It is not our world, no? They have large ships and ambition. Bessabez has been informed. The elders speak of these things. Some wish to kill them all. Others wait for gifts: shirts, hats, beads, kettles, metal, muskets, alcohol. You will hear of this soon."

"And Sabenoa, does he know of the English plan?"

"We do not think so. But who knows what Sabenoa knows or wishes? Bessabez now wishes to trade and be good neighbors, but he hears my thoughts. He listens. I lived among them, I tell him. Skidwarres, we have much time to talk of this. For now I am hospitable."

The path opens up onto a large clearing. From Richard's immediate calculations, it appears eighty to a hundred birch bark huts encircle a much larger common building, it too made of bark slabs overlapping shingle style. Around this larger building in the open space is a bustle of activity. Many young and adult women are tending the fires and cooking. Others are arriving with baskets of fish, clams, and lobsters. Still others carry berries and corn. Groups of older men, women, and children stand in small groups watching, whispering, pointing, and giggling. The braves have reappeared. They stand at the outskirts of the gathering, the bows and quivers slung over their shoulders.

Nahanada tells Gilbert in English to settle his soldiers in a circle. As they do so, young girls and boys carry from the common building woven reed mats that they present to the soldiers to sit on. Nahanada then ushers Richard and Gilbert toward a small group of elders who are already seated. They rise to greet the two Englishmen.

The soldiers do as they are ordered, while gaping at their surroundings. They settle on the mats but keep their loaded muskets in one hand. They are uncertain about the braves who encircle them.

Women, some playful, curious teenagers, serve with bashful smiles. The young Englishmen are given cod and lobster steaming in piles of seaweed. Wooden bowls of squash, maize, and peas awaken dormant olfactory memory. In order to hold their small baskets full of food, they place their muskets by their sides but touch them occasionally for reassurance. The sergeant, realizing his attention and those of his men has moved from military matters to food and their first sight of women, cautions, "Enjoy yourself, boys, but don't lose track of your arms. Even the admiral there is not sure what is in store for us."

The men became conscious of their heavy clothes and armor, made ridiculous by the light clothing worn by both men and women. The August sun remains bold, though not stultifying, as might be the case with English mugginess. Breezes mollify the heat. But heat it is.

The serving girls, adolescent and young women, wear deerskin smocks and loincloths, flaps in front and back held by leather straps. They carry themselves with modest grace, some with light coquettishness. Not in over two months have the soldiers eyed a woman, and here they are— sunned, reddish-brown skinned, the young ones shapely, their glistening black hair falling to the middle of their backs, some with beads and small shells woven in, most with black and red designs painted on their arms, foreheads, or cheeks.

Anderson, an eighteen-year-old who'd volunteered to join the expedition and never experienced military life before, shoves handfuls of cod into his mouth and gapes. He and the other soldiers eat ravenously, stopping to stare unabashedly at the serving girls. From their position on the ground, they can't help but notice at certain angles, especially when they leaned over to place food on the ground, that the women's loincloths fell open enough for them to catch sight of wispy patches of black pubic hair and shapely bottoms. Most try to avoid staring. But when an especially comely server leans over and drops a basket of maize in front of Anderson, his hand finds itself up under her loincloth and resting on a tight, soft buttock. He gives it a squeeze and she jumps with a soft squeal. She pushes his hand away, but not with a slap, only as if it was a minor nuisance.

Sergeant Green observes Anderson from across the circle. Under his breath he snaps, "What are you trying to do, get us fucking killed?"

"Sorry, sir, wasn't thinking," sputters Anderson.

The other soldiers look up. Green continues, "That hand of yours was thinking. That hand and what you might call your mind—that twig between your legs—are one in the same."

The other soldiers chuckle with their mouths full.

"Sorry, sir."

"Sorry you are," adds the sergeant." But it was unavoidable, instinctive, he thinks after upbraiding Anderson. These boys haven't seen pussy since—when? Some, maybe never.

A few of the staring braves notice the incident and straighten themselves. One begins walking toward the sitting soldier and is called back by another with an "ess" through his teeth.

The young woman does not flee but watches the exchange between these strange men a few feet away. Then Anderson looks up at her and utters softly, sweetly, "Sorry. I shouldn't have."

She returns the utterance with the same chagrinned tone, each ignorant of the other's content. It wasn't until later that Anderson learned her meaning. He heard from Richard who'd heard from Skidwarres who'd picked it up from the braves. Her shy smile masked, "You smell like a rotting fish." The comment appeared to settle the angry braves.

Gilbert, Davies, Seymour, Nahanada, and three elders are sitting a few yards from the soldiers and are similarly eating. Skidwarres, who had left the group to briefly greet his wife, child, and parents, returns relaxed and smiling. He'd noticed Richard eying the serving girls, so offers a small grin.

"Yes, well my friend, it is I who return to my woman and you who must maintain a long abstinence."

The topics of conversation cover trading arrangements, farming practices, and politics with other Mawooshen villages—some twenty along the Aponeg, Damariscotta, Segohquet, and Medomak rivers. Gilbert wants to know more about the terrain of the Sagadahoc, about the natives who live in close proximity to the expected fort site, and if they knew anything about silver and gold mines, or sassafras grasses used to cure syphilis, among others diseases. But on matters of Sabenoa, Lord of the Sagadahoc, of mines and a route to the Orient, Nahanada' answers are vague, though he does promise to contact Bessabez and make arrangements for him to meet Gilbert.

Finally Gilbert, slightly annoyed by Nahanada's evasiveness but pleased with the generous reception which he hopes will portend good relations, states they would soon return to the ship. Skidwarres would return with them.

"Skidwarres has agreed to guide our vessel into the Sagadahoc. It is my understanding the water there runs quick and dangerous with small islands and rocks guarding the river's mouth, like 'unpredictable teeth ready to tear away a ship's bottom,' Skidwarres says."

Skidwarres speaks, "Yes, Admiral Gilbert, my words, but no, I will not return to the ship."

Gilbert is taken aback. He is not accustomed to refusals. "Skidwarres, there is no choice here. I command you join us. After we learn more of the terrain and water, when we select our exact site, you will be allowed to return here, but not before."

Skidwarres looks at Nahanada, who remains silent and offers no sign. Skidwarres then replies, "A command is for your soldiers. Not for me. I do not follow your commands."

Gilbert rises from his position in the circle. He stands and feels his height might offer more authority. "You agreed aboard ship. Are you then a man whose word we cannot trust?"

"I agreed to nothing."

"You nodded your agreement."

"I nodded. I nodded that I heard what you said."

Sergeant Green watches Gilbert stand. He's kept his commander always in sight, if only in the corner of his eye. He, too, rises. The gesture triggers a similar response from his men. They scramble to their feet and pull on their heavy helmets.

Moments after Skidwarres' refusal, eleven English soldiers are standing, muskets at their sides, some with mouths full of fish and lobster. The movement further alerts the braves. Some reach back over their shoulders and withdraw arrows, though none notches one. All stare at Gilbert. As with all young men trained to fight, a few on each side itch and pull against the restraint. The cordial, even festive atmosphere, the soft bubble of female generosity evaporates. The young women fade into the background. In the face of hostilities, all becomes quiet except for the wind softly whooshing the treetops.

The warriors on both sides feel the flow of confidence and fear. Each knows his own form of killing to be superior to the other's. Every Englishman believes that, with muskets, swords, armor and God, the English could not fail in the wilderness at the hands of savages with ancient weaponry. The natives know otherwise. They could down a running deer and re-bow their arrow in a split second. The English went through an awkward loading process, so they were told. By the time the musket could be fired, they could place five arrows in a soldier. They, these pale smelly jokers wrapped and sweating in metal, out-numbered turtles, could be killed at the flick of Nahanada's finger.

Nahanada does not want bloodshed. A slaughter of Englishmen would bring more of them with cannon and retribution. He knows the two peoples, so strange to one another, share at least one compelling sentiment: revenge.

Nahanada rises to near equal Gilbert's height. "This is a matter to be easily resolved, don't you think, Admiral." Skidwarres quickly translates, as Nahanada has spoken in his native Algonquin. He considers his English imprecise.

Gilbert takes a breath. Has he responded too quickly? His adamancy diminishes only slightly. "I am sure."

Richard, still seated, speaks. "My friend has journeyed far and wishes to reunite with those he loves. If I understand correctly, we need assistance navigating back to our ships. If he agreed to join us for one more day, then be returned tomorrow and have Nahanada assign a replacement, would that not suffice? Could you agree to that, my friend?" Richard has been addressing both Skidwarres and Gilbert.

"I will do so for you, Richard, if the promise is that I return by tomorrow afternoon."

Gilbert receives the suggestion stoically. Could he not have said as much? Did he have to rely upon his inexperienced, distant cousin to offer a diplomatic solution? He feels a strange combination of relief and humiliation, though on its heels he also thinks this self-criticism not necessary. Next time he'll find the words. He is still in charge.

"Nahanada, we would welcome navigational assistance. We are glad the mouth of the Sagadahoc holds challenges. We English thrive on challenges."

Gilbert bows slightly. Nahanada returns the gesture. The village relaxes as a whole, as an animal might, no longer sensing danger. Everyone feels relief: native men and women, the soldiers, even a few of the eager braves who moments before were hoping to crush these bugs with their hard-shell bodies and heads.

CHAPTER 21

August, 12 1607, The Coast
Tempest

For four days the two ships remained within the environs of Pemaquid. Because the ninth of August was a Sunday, Popham decided to hold a brief service on the nearby island, where two years before Weymouth had planted a Christian cross. Again Seymour offered a brief homily. He'd wait for the landing on the Sagadahoc to intone something more magisterial. His rather perfunctory service for Paul Meeks's burial at sea originated almost entirely from the Book of Common Prayer. As Lance had observed, Meeks's death felt inconsequential: sewn up in a canvas bag with two cobblestones from the large collection used as ballast and then slipped overboard down a wooden plank. Conversation about other matters had begun among the crew and officers long before he settled on the bottom. Richard had thought to himself, "I'm a fake, just as Lance called me."

Over the past two days many had fished from the longboats, pulling in cod ranging over two hundred pounds.

As promised, the English returned Skidwarres. Both ships sailed and anchored off the western side of the bay. This time over fifty armed men rowed eastward and landed at the river near the village. Before they could disembark, thirty or so braves, again with notched arrows, appeared out of the woods. Nahanada made it clear his people did not wish such a large number of soldiers to land. Then after some discussion, seven were welcomed. Then after yet more talk, he allowed the others to come ashore.

All appeared to be going well. Some of the soldiers handed out trinkets, mostly glass beads or colorful ribbons, but suddenly the natives unexpectedly withdrew into the woods. Skidwarres remained briefly but did not offer any explanation. "Richard, I am home now. I and others will greet you again on the Sagadahoc. That is how it must be."

"Of course."

The two had talked little during the past days. In fact neither could arrive at a useful topic of conversation. Such continued to be the case during Skidwarres' last night on board ship. Events at this point overrode talk. Besides, both were exhausted.

After exploring sections of the Damariscotta and Medomak Rivers, Gilbert and Popham deemed they would sail on August 12th for the Sagadahoc.

Lance's drum and horn belonged to the Virginia Company. His own possessions consisted of a small sack of clothes, his puppy, and a leather instrument case containing an old but serviceable lute. A kindly music teacher at the orphanage had recognized Lance's talent and wheedled the instrument from a wealthy arts patron. Lance had begun lessons at age eleven. At fifteen, he was accomplished.

Lance would practice on deck in the evening, Stow at his feet, not asleep as most dogs would be but eyes fixed on his master, as a border collie's should be. If a stray crew member whom he did not know came too close, perhaps in an effort to hear better, Stow might offer a low, barely audible growl. The dog knew a few ill-spirited men continued to insult the boy, calling him "faggot" and "cunt face." Stow discerned their meanness.

Early in the journey, Richard asked Lance if he would show him how to play. "I miss the harpsichord." Then he corrected himself, "No it's not so much the instrument itself, rather the purposeful time dedicated to it. In fact, Lance, this lute of yours does something for me that no harpsichord does. The harpsichord is wonderful, but it's too prissy, too insubstantial, too mechanical; whereas your lute comes directly from your hands, like a cello. It reminds me of Margaret. The lute, the cello—both are so human, as if you are playing directly from your emotions."

At that time, only days from Plymouth, Richard had found himself longing for Margaret's company. He threw himself into his teaching, reading, and then lute practice, and reveled in the physical activity of hauling sails. That helped, but in the cramped privacy of his cabin, he retrieved her scented handkerchief and buried his nose in it.

Often in the evening, Lance gave up possession of his instrument. Such was the case this night while the *Gift of God* held at anchor at

Pemaquid. "We are both student and instructor," Richard commented, "and your hands seem designed for plucking. They are just the right size. Mine are a bit bigger. God may have ordained them for the keyboard."

Lance, who with adolescent fervor liked plunging into deep subjects, asked, "Richard, does God really ordain things?"

Richard usually welcomed Lance's persistent inquiries. "You mean God's will? Say, that you and I at this moment are meant to be playing music and talking, and that God willed Stow into your life? That at this moment he wills him to look at me and then look at you as we converse?" Richard felt himself in good spirits and answered his own questions. "It does seem so, at least in hindsight. It does seem that when important things happen—even everything in tiny detail—that it was meant to be. If not this, what? Either all is willed or all is haphazard. Don't you think?"

Lance looked at Richard as he often did, with a mixture of bewilderment and awe. "But does that mean God meant my mother to die. Do you think that, Richard? Did he want me to live without her?"

Of course he had read and thought of these matters at Oxford, even more at Middle Temple. Bacon wrote of God's grand design, that science revealed God's majesty. He knew the stock answer, that man is way too feeble to know such things. But Montaigne didn't want to forfeit such interesting questions about destiny

Richard continued, "Yes, and the black plagues that killed so many, his doing, his handiwork? And if so, what kind of God? The church, the English church, the pope, they think so—and then throw up their pink ecclesiastical hands and say 'God's will is a mystery.' They say our minds are not designed for such knowledge. But sometimes, my friend, I think this is a ruse. Maybe this is just another way for them to get us to obey. Maybe they think if we don't, all would be chaos. And maybe they are right. Honestly, Lance, I don't know how to answer your question."

"Richard, sometimes you sound like a heretic, not a chaplain."

"I do not reveal my feelings like this to everyone. Besides, did not God will that we should use our brains? Maybe he gave us brains to drive ourselves crazy. Did he not will that I say what I just said? He also gave us brains to play music. Do you know what I think, Lance?"

In their many hours together, Lance knew that Richard did not mind being kidded. "Chaplin Seymour, you are going to tell me anyway."

"Correct, and what I think is that God does not speak in words. All religions have it wrong. God speaks to us through music. It is his language. So I'd better get to practicing so I can better let God speak to me—or is it through me?"

Lanced giggled. "I think God willed you to be daft."

"Then, praise the Lord, I am doing his work." And Richard took the lute from Lance with one hand and with the other cuffed him gently across the top of his head of dark curls. "My turn." Stow got to his feet, momentarily confused by Richard's movement, but the dog quickly caught the light mood, wagged his tail, and stuck his head in Lance's lap.

That evening they practiced together on deck until the sky darkened, a late summer night, still light past eight o'clock with a refreshing cool breeze. With the break of dawn, they would set sail. A storm was brewing, so the savvy captain predicted. The barometer was falling. Hurricanes formed in the Caribbean this time of year, and some of them blew up the coast and out to sea or headed inland, so the sea lore had it. It was early in the season. The likelihood was low it would carry this far north, but why take chances? At dawn the ships would weigh anchor. The prevailing westerlies would force the ship to tack to their destination, likely almost entirely into the wind. Nonetheless, by mid-afternoon the incoming tide should usher them through the Sagadahoc's mouth and into the safety of the protected bay in front of the potential site of the fort.

During the first few weeks at sea, Richard had lived with an unexpressed distrust of the ship. In his bunk at night, he listened to the sea licking the hull. On other days, with the wind up to twenty knots or from a storm surge miles away, he became accustomed to the large swells, sometimes resembling watery mountain ranges that raised and lowered the *Gift of God*. They swelled, and she rode up and then slid down into yet another of the millions of troughs ahead and behind. It took many hours staring at the horizon where water met sky, and many nights on his bunk, before the Atlantic became, not just the loneliest, most majestic lethal power he could imagine, but a presence he could begin to trust.

During the first month, the wind periodically rose to thirty knots. A small storm jib replaced the hundreds of square feet of sail. He began to trust the wood under his feet, its craftsmanship, and the captain and crew. Richard appreciated the sea's connection with the human soul: the sea as elemental, ineffable. Then he'd chide himself for his romantic notions. How trite. Cold-blooded, that was the sea. It was reassuring how the *Gift of God* had weathered two modest storms with such ease. He knew they were not invulnerable, but he had learned to feel safe. Now within sight of land and just hours after walking on it, another storm should be of little concern.

Richard awoke before sunrise. The ship groaned and creaked in swells that had blown up while he slept. He decided to replenish his energies with a bit more sleep. Though he often joined the crew hauling and straightening lines or mending sails, he was not assigned a specific job. He had voluntarily "learned the ropes," a matter that amused George Popham.

When he arose again and walked, feet wide apart to steady himself, to stand holding onto a bulwark while he pissed, he realized they were sailing under considerable duress. The wind howled outside.

When he opened the hatch to the quarterdeck, a wash of cold salt water and sharp rain hit him in the face. The wind buzzed and whistled, shaking lines and rigging, stronger by far than what he'd experienced before. He held onto the doorway and adjusted his eyes from the dim candlelight below to the menacing gray light all about. A few soaked crew members pushed past and scurried down the ladder. Fletcher looked up as Richard passed him on the ladder. "Turn around, Chaplain. It's a blow."

"Where's Captain Elliott?"

"At the helm."

"Want to speak to him."

"Best wait. Don't want to wash overboard."

"I'll be back soon."

On deck Richard stepped out of the way as more men headed below. The ship strained and lurched further to starboard. Richard's feet slid, and he fell on his backside. Water flowed through the railing and then over the deck. The force of the slosh started him sliding and would have slammed him against or over the railing if he hadn't grabbed the hatchway and then felt himself being hauled to his feet. It was Fletcher again. "Get below." Richard barely made out the words.

"Good advice," he yelled back. "Be there momentarily." This was not true. He did not want to miss this tempest. He would work his way to the helm, only a few yards away. If the ship went under, he didn't want to be below. He could barely make out the captain and helmsman through the rain which came at the ship horizontally and stung his eyes. Richard bent over, ran blind, and looked up just in time to grab the wheel stem as he fell again.

"What the hell?" screamed the captain, who had not seen him until his comic arrival. He clutched the wheel with one hand, and with the other, he handed Richard a line. "Tie this around you." Richard quickly obeyed. He knew the expression "lashed to the mast," but never imagined actually doing so, or at least to the wheelstem.

Without averting his eyes from the dark grey ahead, the captain yelled again, "Is something wrong below?"

Richard held the wheel along with the captain. "No. I wish to ride it out here."

Richard thought he heard, "Damn fool," and then the captain turned and yelled into Richard's ear, "all right, just hold on."

"Captain, how big a blow?"

"She's still working up. Maybe sixty knots, gusts to seventy, eighty.

It was around nine in the morning. At six the wind had turned around to the northeast, thereby pushing them west in their desired direction. They had made great speed, even though they were sailing with only the top main. Then the wind shifted northwest, then again directly from the southwest. By then the crew had reduced the sails to one small storm jib. The captain calculated they were in the vicinity of the Sagadahoc, given their earlier speed. But the storm had come on quicker than expected. If they sailed too close to shore, in all likelihood they'd be smashed against one of the many islands or shoals. Survival depended upon maneuvering out to open sea and riding out the storm into the wind. For the past hour, he had attempted just that, but the tide had changed, so that now it pushed them toward shore, as did the wind.

The tactic in a hard blow requires heading the ship into the wind so that bow meets surf straight on. Taking a sea broadside would likely swamp her and she'd capsize. In a hurricane-strength gale there was no other choice. A storm jib should allow the helmsman to keep the bow headed into the wind—though not an easy task, given the ship's natural tendency to grab the wind and sail. Each time the velocity increased, the small sail created an immense force on the rudder. It took a strong helmsman to hold true. But heading into the wind meant the ship was disconnected from its only source of power and control. By heading into the wind, tide and wind might have their way, in this case pushing the *Gift of God* back toward land and rocks. On the other hand, if the storm jib was allowed to fill for a small angled tack in order to maneuver her out to sea and to relative safety, the mast and spars might blow apart.

These tactics had been explained to Richard by Fletcher. He knew the captain must play the angle of small opportunity, heading directly into the wind when it blew hardest, and then angling off just so when he felt the blow easing off.

A sustained gust hit just as Richard arrived unceremoniously on deck. It seemed to howl forever. The captain had no choice but to head into the wind and hope he'd already progressed seaward enough to make up for the inevitable backsliding. The *Mary and John* was no doubt up against the same, though Admiral Gilbert had chosen to sail a couple of miles south of the *Gift of God's* course. That difference was to their advantage, as it took them further from shore. The captain hoped the intensified blow indicated they were approaching the eye where they might experience relative calm. With sun obliterated by the storm and curtains of rain, it was impossible to identify a landmark. He'd no idea how much ground they'd lost or made. At what moment would he feel—he would never hear or see—the stern crunch into a massive rock formation, disabling the rudder, smashing holes, and tearing away the hull within minutes, sealing their fate?

Soon the light must break through overhead. These thoughts Captain Elliott kept to himself. It was purposeless to attempt a sustained conversation with the crazed chaplain next to him. If anything, the roar of the storm was getting worse. He yelled, "Seymour, your help!" and pointed to the wheel. He and the helmsman had struggled for over two hours. It took a moment for Richard to comprehend, but only a moment. His body and mind were lost in the excitement of the likely destruction of the ship and the dissolution of the world. He grabbed the wheel.

With soaked bodies, they struggled in tandem with the handles of the four-foot-diameter wheel. Whatever adjustment the captain made, Richard copied in an effort to simply add his weight. The captain sailed by feel. She was stressed, an old friend, a lover, this ship. He felt her through the rudder, connected to the stem, translated through the wheel to his hands. He read wind pressure on his face and from the sucking in his ear. They embraced the wheel, their heads forced downwards to avoid the punishing spray and rain. The *Gift of God* kept into the wind, into the abyss of the blow. They waited for fate.

After these moments of eternity, the storm eased. At first they could not accept this possibility. They waited for the roar to return. But no, the wind had let up, even the sea had lost some of its menace. Above a circle of brightening dirty light grew. This was enough for the captain to head off just a bit. Here was the reprieve. From the helm, the entire ship came into view for the first time in two hours. No substantial damage, only a rip in the jib and a tangle of rigging. The ethereal light overhead brightened. "Is this the eye of God?" Richard mused.

While the captain stared straight up at the torn but operative jib and strained to see ahead, Richard turned—and gasped. Less than a quarter-mile behind them, the sun reflected off an expanse of yellowish white rock, a mountain of rock a few hundred feet above sea level. It appeared to levitate. Mist hovered and surrounded what then clearly became an island. And before Richard could collect himself, the mist itself vanished.

"Captain," Richard said pulling on his shoulder to force him to turn.

"By god! By god! A few more minutes of blow and that would be our gravestone."

"Do you know what that is?"

"I should. Been looking at charts for two months. That has to be Seguin, a small island with a little cove. Fishermen have been using it for years. It's a couple of miles from the Sagadahoc. We're right where we should be and a few minutes ago shouldn't have been. Seguin means turtle. That's one turtle."

"Good work, Captain."

"Maybe you mean bad judgment. We should have been running further out to sea, as Gilbert chose. I played it too close. We were lucky."

"She's quite a sight."

"And my job is to get as far away from her as possible before we get knocked down again."

First and second mates emerged from the bow section. "No major damage, Captain."

"Set the upper main and mizzen, but be ready to bring them down." Bells rang, men swarmed on deck. When the sails filled, Richard felt the aft section lift from the water, as a horse might move into a lope. Seguin receded as they headed off on a tack toward the open ocean. In the distance, just a speck on the horizon, the *Mary and John* came into view taking the same course.

A quarter of an hour later, the skies darkened and the wind returned, but this time with less ferocity. Men lowered all but a new storm jib. The wind swung around, so now they flew away from land. The first mate took the wheel so the captain and Richard could retire to the president's quarters. All men were reported accounted for. Within an hour, as Elliott had predicted, both ships turned and headed back toward land. "The tide is still in our favor. If our luck holds, when the last of this moves over land, we'll get the wind behind us again. Then we'll march right up the Sagadahoc, bands a-playing."

CHAPTER 22

August 13, 1607
Hand of God

As Captain Elliott had predicted, the sea had turned from murderous to benign, and then generous. The *Gift of God*—and not far behind, the *Mary and John*—reverse course and head toward land. Richard, Fletcher, and Lance stand together on deck along with many of the expectant crew. They slip past the now innocent Seguin Island. Details of their destination come into view, a mile or so expanse of white beach to the west of the mouth. In the distance, upriver, granite bluffs fall hundreds of feet to the water. To the east of the river entrance, the ubiquitous granite outcroppings are softened with occasional patches of marshland or beach.

"Eight fathoms," calls out the second mate.

"As the chart reads, plenty of depth," Elliot reports to Popham, who stands gazing, speechless.

They don't so much sail in the exhausted weather system; rather they're ushered upriver on the last of the incoming tide. Richard considers how this gentle easing after such a near disastrous blow might be used for the inevitable homily that will be required of him. His thoughts run to what sounds at first original, then quickly, trite: "The *Gift of God* rode on the hands of God." No, he thinks. But then a third appraisal: melodrama is exactly what Popham and the crew want from him. Melodrama inflates the self. Besides, it continuously amuses him how his mental processes find a way to aid him with these odd ecclesiastical responsibilities.

At the narrowest spot at the entrance, the ship passes close by the sandy beach. It curves at a right angle and continues westward. Behind the beach they see for the first time a well-protected bay. All aboard are quiet. It is impossible not to be mesmerized by the radically changed mood, on the one hand the sense of completion, on the other anticipation. The gulls' cries of alarm overhead provide the only sounds. Even the ships have stopped creaking.

Lance pulls on Richard's sleeve, and not wanting to break the quiet, whispers, "Look," and points to a small figure standing where the beach meets a stand of low- growing sumac, already turning light purple with the change of seasons. Richard doesn't see at first. He, too, keeps his voice low.

"What?"

"There. It's a boy, I think. A little savage."

"I see him." The boy stands with his hands at his sides. Perhaps he has seen English or French ships in the distance before, but unlikely one so close.

"Richard, I will never forget this sight." Lance raises his hand and waves at the boy. The figure continues to stand unmoving and then finally raises a tentative arm into the air briefly. Then he disappears into the sumac.

"Nor I, Lance. It's spectacular. And I wager that boy—I suppose it was a boy—won't forget either. Won't he tell his grandchildren how he saw the ship with the English? He saw the beginning."

Both ships drop anchor just past the mouth where the river opens into a shallow bay to the west. A broad stretch of river continues northward.

Two longboats, one from each ship, carry twenty men ashore. The terrain is not a total surprise. The early charts and maps produced by Weymouth and Pring turn out to be quite accurate. But before they can work out the specifics for the design of a fort, Popham, Gilbert, and others need to observe precisely how the land lies. The choice of a site was the subject of much conversation during the voyage. Separately, Popham and Gilbert, along with their principals on board their separate ships, discussed the matter proposed by Sir John Popham and Sir Ferdinando Gorges months before.

Locating at the mouth of the Sagadahoc provided easy access to the sea and exploration both east and south west. Nahanada's recommendation gave further weight to this choice. Other advantages included the protection of the bay, at which they now lay at anchor. A fort at this site would not be seen by French or Spanish ships that might be sailing offshore, be they warships or fishing vessels. Though it was impossible for the Virginia Company to keep their activities in

Jamestown and Sagadahoc a secret—the Flemish already knew—they did not want to advertise them.

When the two longboats hit the small rocky beach, Gilbert hops out into water inches below the top of his boots. He carries the flag of St. George, white with a horizontal red cross. He holds it in the air dramatically and shouts, "I proclaim this land now subject to my Sovereign James, King of our England." He plunges the pole into the soggy beach where it penetrates a few inches. Gilbert lets go and looks back at the others disembarking.

"Admiral!" one of the sailors shouts. Gilbert turns to watch the flag and pole flop to the ground. Gilbert picks it up and shakes off the sand— he doesn't believe in omens—and gives it to Sergeant Davies to place solidly on land.

George Popham, with two soldiers at each elbow, walks gingerly onto shore, his pallor grayish. Gilbert's showy exuberance creates quite a contrast. But once steady with his feet out of water, Popham attempts to regain some of his robust—though never pugnacious—nature. "Even better than hoped. As we expected, water to our north and west, a natural moat." He directs his comment to Hunt, the fort architect, who has worked up to now with only sketchy information.

Popham, Gilbert, Hunt, captain of the fort James Davis, and Sergeant Major Robert Davies, walk up a small incline of grass and low-growing brush. "That rock outcropping there along the shore," Popham says with a gesture. "We can set cannon there pointing to the river's entrance. Then to the west, let us see how amenable the land is." Popham is increasingly animated.

What do you think, Davis?"

"Here, you see some large pine and spruce and beyond that a small bit of grassland. It looks as if it might even have been tilled at one time."

"Tilled?" asks Gilbert. "Who?"

Davis answers, "Nobody but the natives, I'd say, though it looks like some years ago." He kicks the soft ground and then takes a shovel and jams it into the soil. It sinks easily. Quite feverishly he digs eight holes, moving from spot to spot. It is as if he were a doctor palpating his patient. The remainder of the party follows, peering into each hole.

With growing impatience, Gilbert demands, "Well, what is your opinion?"

"Well, sir," reports Davis, "no gold yet. But I can tell you, the land here will form up nicely. Digging a moat from the shore to up there, a hundred paces or so, will not be too difficult. We have topsoil here and sand. Some loose bedrock, and if you look around, no doubt many rocks to aid in building our fortification. A few large trees to cut and many to haul out, but their root systems tend to be on the surface. Shouldn't be too difficult. You can see over there a small stream which suggests a source of drinking water. And the shipwright, Digby, will be pleased at the quality and diversity of the trees. In short, if you give me and my men a few hours, we can tell you more. We can stake out the perimeter, and then I can get to work on a plan, though of course we've already discussed the basics: moat, stone and earthen wall, a location for building the pinnace—over there, I would say, in that area near the shore. Then we have that rise over there, the southern exposure where you see that large granite ledge. We'll need to clear land up there and do a lot of hauling of rock. But you see how it drops on either side. Just as good as any moat. I think we're in luck, sir. I'd suggest this cries out for a fort. And we have no time to waste."

"Very good." Popham is now walking without assistance. "I like your decisiveness. And you, Admiral, your thoughts?"

"President Popham, I say we proceed with all speed. I see this as a defendable location. I suggest I take a shallop—she is about ready to sail—and some men and travel upriver to search for an alternative. I'll be no longer than two days. In the meantime, plan for this spot. In all likelihood we will follow plans. I've delegated a party to search the area for natives."

"Excellent. First, as we have discussed, we will bring the men ashore. It will be good for their morale."

CHAPTER 23

Evening, August 13, 1607
Destiny

By early evening, all but a skeletal crew have clambered over the sides and into the longboats. When they near the beach at the north end of the site, some of the more enthusiastic jump overboard into neck-deep water, then splash, laugh, hoot, and flap their arms like frightened ducks as they stumble ashore. The less experienced, who'd never spent such a long time at sea, fall forward, arms stretched on the ground, and thank God, cry, or quietly lie with their faces buried in the sand.

The four boys, including Lance, run helter-skelter in and out of the woods, around the small field, and across the granite shoreline, where Jimmy pushes Lance in, and soon, still clothed, all hit the water at low tide where it is only few feet deep and splash about. Jimmy attempts to paddle near the shoreline out over his head. He begins spitting cold salt water and is hauled out by Fletcher.

A small contingent of soldiers heads toward the beach in search of natives. Most of the men are given half an hour to wander about and get a feel for the area before President Popham calls them to order. Approximately a hundred of the hundred and forty stand in a semicircle. Those remaining on the two ships watch as they lie at anchor.

Two soldiers roll a log over to where Popham, Gilbert, and Seymour wait. They saw both ends even and stand it on end. Popham ambles up to the makeshift podium. Most of the men stare over his head, up past the ships, beyond the blackish broad river to a bluff a few miles away, sparkling with glassy mica. The afternoon light catches highlights from the multicolored forest just beginning to offer up patches of red and yellow among the predominant green. The blue sky darkens, and the air smells of cedar and funky mud flats

After a dramatic pause, Popham begins. "Men, we are here." They shout, "Aye, sir!" He has a ready audience. "Men, tonight we will eat well. Great servings of cod, potatoes we've saved for this occasion, and corn given us by the savages—the natives." He clears his throat. "Tonight we have double doses of ale."

"Aye, sir!"

Popham continues. "We have sent out one unit to scout the area. Some of you will be given ship duty. We do not know what we can expect from the natives. We are not building a parlor. We're building a fort." Popham is enjoying himself and waits a few beats to emphasize his point. "We are building an English fort."

Another "Aye!"

"Tonight you can choose to stay here on land or return to your quarters on board. We will be manning sentinels—sober sentinels. Speak to your officers and mates. We need to keep order. This is not a picnic, but tonight I want to honor your patience and skill as sailors. And tomorrow we start to build. You know your jobs. Everyone has learned new skills here. The carpenter learned to climb the rigging, the farmer learned carpentry, the soldier pulled the main sheet, and tomorrow the sailor will learn to dig ditches. Admiral Gilbert will spend much time traveling the river, as well as up and down the coast. He will explore and find trading partners among the savages. He will find silver mines and sassafras for the French blight. "Aye," some of the men chuckle. One shouts out, "But where do we find that malady here?"

"Sorry, men," replies Popham, "have you not all sworn to be chaste as virgins?" Before anyone can offer up a snide comment, he continues, "All right, men, we first have serious matters to attend to. Admiral Gilbert, a word to the men?" President Popham steps back and Gilbert moves up to the stump.

"I will be brief. I stand ready to act, not to talk. We seem small on this grand stage. But we are English. This ground will flourish. Your grandchildren will honor your courage. We are destined. On this ground a people will congregate. England is destined, though only a few know this. We are its future."

As intended, his short speech stirs the men in the gut. Many have never seen this gentleman dressed in his admiral's uniform, this young man speaking so eloquently. Their "Aye, sir!" rings true and loud.

Gilbert bows. Popham is again at the stump. "Gentleman, we now will officially designate the leadership and read the Charter of Virginia. Then Chaplain Seymour will offer a benediction, a benediction consecrated by rum."

It takes a half hour for Sergeant-Major Robert Davies to read the formal charter, leaving many to lose interest and shift from one leg to the other. Davies quickens his pace.

Next Richard steps to the half-rotted, makeshift pulpit. A maggot appears from a crevice. He brushes it onto the ground. The men have stood now for an hour. Hushed conversations materialize. This is not good for my first sermon, Richard calculates. Best not read from notes. Their attention is threadbare. Out of fear more than calculation, he begins softly. The muted conversations among his fellow voyagers fade. Richard speaks slowly with less calculation, more insecurity. These men, he thinks, are ravenous for hope.

"On the *Gift of God* we stood together at the rails this morning. We were quiet. We watched. We were tired from a storm, tired of living in the bowels of a ship. And speaking for myself, sometimes fearful it might burst open and disgorge us, leaving us at the bottom of a foreign ocean. Did we think and feel this?" Richard's voice increases in volume as his confidence takes hold. The men murmur their agreement.

"When I stood at the rail, I felt not just the tide but the hand of God under our ship. Those of you arriving on the *Mary and John*, perhaps you felt that too? Are we not fated to stand at the edge of this New World? Did not your courage bring us here?" During the voyage, Richard deemed that representing the Church of England and offering personal counsel to the men was not his only purpose. He, along with the officers, needed to create a positive morale. Creating and maintaining that among a hundred and forty men estranged from their homeland, many rough— and not just around the edges—would not be easy.

"I have met some of you during our voyage, and will do my best to introduce myself to those of you on the *Mary and John*. But I already know who you are. You are soldiers, craftsmen, farmers. You are all brave. Many of you have seen bloodshed in Ireland. Some of you had your land taken from you and faced poverty not of your own making. Some of you have tasted the whip of injustice or the scourge of sickness. All of you, I venture, want to share your skills with others. Like me, you want to create the future—England's future. I speak as a representative of the Church of England and for King James. More basically, most basically, I am here as your friend and counselor."

"But let me return to the hand of God that I am certain lifted us across the ocean, and just hours ago into this wonderment." He stops and raises an arm to sweep it across his body. He turns to take in the Sagadahoc behind him.

"Let us remember, we are only human. Let us remember our friends, the natives are only human. That is what the Lord wishes that we remember."

"Praise the Father, the Son..." Here Richard hesitates, surprised by his oratorical success and by the realization it is the Holy Ghost—and only the Holy Ghost, or so he has said—he believes in, "And the Holy Ghost."

CHAPTER 24

August 14, 1607, Fort St. George
Construction

Most the men opt to return to their ship. The land loses some of its luster when cool fog rolls in off the sea and snakes its way up the river, peeks around the peninsula, and then settles into the small bay. What would they sleep on and under? They also know the heavy labor that awaits them early in the morning. The two rations of rum or ale feel especially warm in their bellies, but it isn't enough to drown reason. A night of little sleep on cold ground would bring a day of exhaustion. The longboats ferry them back to the ship. The cursed hammocks tonight seem the best alternative.

Lance blows his bugle at five o'clock, four brief taps. It is the time of year when all remark on the shortening daylight. As with the rising men, the huge deep orange sun is reluctant as it pushes itself over the horizon. This morning and mornings into the foreseeable future would bring little but labor: felling trees, digging trenches, hauling rocks, pushing boulders, yanking up brush, splitting logs and sawing them into lumber, marching through underbrush, and fetching water. They'd be tending to blisters, scratches, bruises, diarrhea, sprains, itches, broken bones, and crotch rot. At night most would meet loneliness. In their bedrolls, they'd be too tired to masturbate; that would be the night's running joke.

Since their departure from Plymouth, the men had heard about the task ahead. Within a remarkably short period of time, six weeks to two months, they would build an earthen and rock wall around the entire star-shaped perimeter. The nine cannon would aim in all directions—against the natives, against the Spanish or French, against the unknown. Visually, if not in fact, this was a military operation. A storehouse would become the first priority. The ships' holds had to be unloaded—wine, ale, rum, flour, dried and salted beef, salt, lumber, windows, a forge, goats, pigs, rabbits, cannonballs, gunpowder—all needed to come off the ships as soon as possible The *Mary and John* would return to England and then turn around in the spring bearing more supplies.

Officers and men were all glad to know they could leave the claustrophobic, dank ship. But what would take its place? The soldiers who'd been on the Irish campaigns guessed. They'd be left to their own devices to plaster together huts made from saplings, tied together with smaller intertwined limbs, and finally packed with mud and grass. Popham and Gilbert needed a more substantial roof over their heads. And plans called for a chapel.

The final detailed design of the fort took only two days. This involved consultations among draftsman John Hunt, James Davis, Gilbert, and Popham. The essentials had been laid out in Plymouth and on board the *Mary and John*.

The reconnaissance teams sent out the first afternoon returned after a few hours. They reported no contact with the natives except that half a mile away, just on the land side of the sand dunes, they had walked into the remains of a small abandoned village, including five outdoor fireplaces and the ruins of a few huts. Given the still warm coals of the fire, the evacuation must have occurred soon after the ship's arrival.

As the various maps and charts indicated, the fort was to be situated on a small peninsula. About a mile from the fort, over the hill to the south and around to the northwest where the bay became a huge mud flat at low tide, the land narrowed into a small isthmus before it became part of the mainland. The patrol walked the beach until they soon reached a small river which snaked into mudflats, sea grass, and bog. Beyond that, the beach continued around a bend. The land at this point became quite woody and gained elevation. After three more days of investigations, the officers in charge reported no close neighbors.

Fort St. George—named after the patron saint of England—takes on the appearance of an anthill. Axes swing. Small trees fall to be limbed, dragged, and thrown in a pile, most destined to be fence posts, fortifications, and firewood. This leaves room for the medium pine and spruce to be felled. They are then debarked and cut into lumber. Finally, what was a healthy medium-height stand of woods vanishes. Bright sun hits ground accustomed to shade. Delicate lady's slippers, little pink hooded wildflowers, lie exposed. Lance picks a few, only to learn they die quickly when separated from their mother earth.

Human ingenuity and grit triumph over darkness, over a mute and apparently primeval shoreline. The men feel this, even if they do not think it. All stop their labor from time to time and watch. Felled spruce, pine, and oak limbs carpet the ground. A fat hundred-foot white pine stands alone in the new clearing. Everyone knows that this is the prize. Two soldiers cut the lower branches; then experienced lumberjacks alternately sink their axes into the soft wood. The gaping triangle widens. Pitch bleeds onto their hands. Within twenty minutes, the four-foot-diameter trunk displays a wound, leaving only a few inches of spine left. The pine does not complain. All watch, expecting it to fall on its own. Instead, it defies logic and gravity, and holds true. It takes only two swings. The ancient pine teeters, gains momentum, and falls with a whoosh and crash. The ground trembles.

Lance and the other boys stop gathering slash to watch. They join Richard, who is standing with Digby. The shipwright is waiting for his spruce and oak planking which will join the oak keel and sections of oak ribbing that had been cut and dried in England and carried in the *Mary and John*'s hold.

Digby speaks. "It is a curious thing to feel the joy of such enterprise, only to find sadness in the killing of that grand old fellow."

"How old is that tree, do you think?" Lance wonders out loud.

"Hard to say for sure, but we don't have to guess. You can figure that out by counting the rings. Go on, see for yourselves. The wider rings indicate the wetter years."

Lance and his companions run, weaving their way past smaller stumps, and then fall to their knees around the just felled pine. They all begin counting out loud but soon confuse themselves. "Stop," yells Lance, "We need to do this together." Soon they all run back to Richard and Digby on the shore just above the high tide mark, the likely spot for a ship construction. Their sticky fingers smell of pine pitch.

"We counted. It's at least two hundred years old. All those years, and now just a stump?"

Digby smiles. "We've all got our time. Pine doesn't live forever. This one fought its way for light over the others, so it survived. Some of those smaller ones were standing but dead, others nearly so. Just like people. Some still standing but essentially dead, wouldn't you say, Chaplain?"

"Keen observation."

"Still," chimed in Lance, "exciting to watch but sad."

"Yes, I know what you mean," offers Richard. "But I also like light.

Come winter, light will be scarce. Better get back to work, fellows, or you'll catch it."

"We know," they say in unison, then scamper back to the clearing to continue hauling the slash, their enthusiasm still strong.

CHAPTER 25

August 23, 1607, Fort St. George
Savages Arrive

The clear summer weather holds: cool early mornings, wispy clouds, hot dry afternoons with breezes out of the southwest fanning sweating bare torsos. The wind tends to wane in the late afternoon. When the sun falls below the tree line, the feverish pitch of activity continues into dusk, well past seven o'clock. Twelve-hour days of physical labor have replaced the crossing, when little happened but tending to sails and rigging, cleaning weapons, forced exercise, and boredom. Only with the occasional moderate storms and the hurricane did the men have to move fast and truly strain themselves.

For many, the purposefulness of hard work engenders optimism, as does a stunning vista. While resting on their shovels or taking a break to gnaw on bread and fish or slug down water from the stream, the men inevitably stare up the Sagadahoc, the long view north. This grandeur adds to their purpose. Or if one stands on the rocks on the eastern perimeter, the ocean presents another view that makes the men gawk. Over the horizon lies England. Often a sergeant has to bark to get the men out of their reveries.

Gilbert's overnight exploration of the Sagadahoc convinces him the fort's site is, as expected, a natural one.

On their tenth day, during a midday break, one of the boys who has been staring out to sea, yells, "Savages in boats!" A few minutes, later a soldier who'd been posted high on a hill south of the fort runs to offer the same news.

Gilbert strides from the middle of the fort, where he's been conferring with the head carpenter about the location of pilings for the large storehouse. "How many canoes? How many braves? Are they armed?"

"Sir, I saw only four large canoes. Maybe ten in each. Women and children on board. And braves who paddle. I did not see weapons."

Gilbert orders twenty men to muster and stand at the ready. He'd heard many stories from his father and experienced crew members. True, most natives were interested in trade or were simply curious, though one could not always be sure. In 1603 Champlain reported the existence of hostile natives in this region. He certainly didn't expect this of Nahanada, but the visit to his village had not erased his worries. In any event, the armed men standing at attention would impress the visitors, whoever they were.

Fletcher receives Gilbert's second order. On the second day six men had removed one nine-pound cannon from the *Mary and John* and stationed it on the granite shoreline, overlooking the narrow river entrance. "Fletcher, man the cannon." While his three cannoneers run for powder and balls, Gilbert adds, "Load up. Don't aim at them. But when they land, I'll give an order to fire off one shot. Find a tree on the other shore and topple it. This will be a salute to our visitors—and a warning."

The few men guarding and maintaining the two ships stand with their muskets and watch below as long canoes with eight paddlers each strain in synchrony, jabbing paddles, raising, jabbing into the water. Passengers include five women and three adolescent boys. They sit erect and quiet. All wear deerskin sleeves attached to leather vests, leggings, and loincloths. They carry with them a restrained formality.

All three canoes pull up onto the beach in unison. By then the men have stopped their work and moved down toward the water to stand at a distance, allowing the members of the council to congregate at the shore.

Nahanada, at the bow of one canoe, steps out into shin-deep water, followed by Skidwarres. Gilbert walks forward and solemnly puts out a hand. While in England, the captured sagamore kept his pride by never relinquishing his resentment. Gilbert had learned to keep a remove, even with his fellow officers, while in the military. Some thought this arrogance, others simply self-possession. But he could also be charming.

Seymour and Skidwarres nod and smile at one another from a short distance, but wait to speak until Nahanada formally greets Popham— who, buoyed by the good cheer of the past few days, has regained yet more of his energy. His time out-of-doors has replaced his grey pallor with a pink complexion. After shaking hands with Nahanada and Skidwarres, an effervescent Popham wades into the water and offers a hand to a woman who is probably in her late thirties or early forties. She is Nolka, the eldest of Nahanada's three wives. At first she does not respond. Instead, she looks at Nahanada for guidance. Aware of English social graces, he knows Popham to be friendly, though the action would have been interpreted as forward in his culture. In his native tongue he tells his wife, "Take his hand. He is their sagamore."

When all are ashore on the beach, Gilbert signals Fletcher to ignite the cannon. The boom startles nearly everyone, especially the women who shriek. The native boys' mouths gape. A moment later, across the river, the upper branches of a large spruce fall into the limbs below.

"A salute to you, Nahanada and your people," announces Gilbert. "Fine marksmanship, Fletcher," he yells over his shoulder. The men put up a cheer.

Skidwarres looks at Nahanada and comments in English with a slight tone of sarcasm recognizable only to Richard, "A powerful greeting, Admiral."

Gilbert responds with a broad smile. "Thank you, sir, and good to have a visit." They shake hands. "President Popham, shall we show them around?

"Indeed, Admiral. Will you instruct the cooks to prepare a sturdy meal of cod for our guests, and the carpenters to build more tables and benches? And before the meal, should we not hold a service, Chaplain Seymour, in honor of our guests?"

"I'll make preparations, President Popham. Shall they share the Eucharist with us?"

"Excellent idea," Popham answers, as he, Gilbert, and Nahanada, followed by his braves and the women and boys, head toward the construction site.

Skidwarres and Seymour remain momentarily on the beach. Richard looks down at his friend's leggings. "I see you have traded in your English pants?"

"Richard, I had become accustomed to them. But on my return I was, I think you say, ridiculed? Some did—do—not trust me. Some think they have made me part English. Besides, consider the advantages. Here we do not sit on toilets."

"Yes, squat. So it is at our rustic fort. Now I recognize this advantage." And they both chuckle and feel their previous friendship that had cooled on ship begin to warm tentatively. By simply having land under their feet, they feel more familiar and comfortable in their roles.

"And my friend, are you not part English?"

"It is true, Richard, I am changed. And this I must keep to myself. Even my talking alone with you may make my job as a diplomat difficult. Some in my village strongly distrust me—and all of you."

Richard takes note of a young woman and her small daughter standing a few paces behind Skidwarres, staring at the two of them. She returns Richard's smile and Skidwarres turns.

"Ah, you will now meet Sokw, my wife, and my daughter, Nahnibssat. She waited, as you see, cared for by my parents. On the second day, Nahnibssat, she poked me in the stomach with her finger and asked, 'You are not a ghost?'"

"Not a ghost of yourself, I hope. And you make me lovesick for Margaret."

Skidwarres translates Richard's words to his wife, who listens intently and then shifts her eyes to the Englishman. They are large and dark brown, nearly black. She smiles again, looks at Richard, and quietly says in Algonquin, "It is difficult to wait, especially when you don't know if he is alive. Your woman, she, too, must worry as I did." And feeling with these words she might have become too bold, she drops her eyes to the ground. Skidwarres translates.

"Yes, thank you. What you suggest is probably true. It is more difficult for her. I am so busy. She does not face uncertainties except for sickness." They begin walking up to the beginnings of the storehouse. There, to the already assembled visitors, one of the carpenters is explaining the large building that will stand on the pilings now under construction. He points to the holes, three filled with lumber and slopped with tar.

In what will become the central area of the fort, but is now stumps and pockets of dried mud, another group of natives stand in front of sketches of a completed fort, with the buildings drawn three-dimensionally. They point and talk excitedly. When they leave, Richard, Skidwarres, Sokw, and Nahnibssat stand together looking at the rendition. Richard explains while Skidwarres translates: here the battlements, the brook dissecting the area, there Gilbert and Popham's houses, and highest on the hill, the chapel and Richard's home to be.

Skidwarres listens without comment. He wishes not to convey his thoughts, so similar to many he had while in England. He has to admit his wonderment. First, for the sketches themselves, so precise and comprehensible, even beautiful, but even more, here on this spit of land, the English were building larger, more durable buildings than had ever stood on these shores. He knows about English ingenuity, but here on his own land this organized commotion, this productivity strikes him deeply. The storehouse, the admiral's house, the gardens, the cannon, and Richard's chapel: England, as Nahanada had portended, was transplanting itself.

The four head up the rise to the site of the chapel. Richard and Skidwarres bend their head close together in conversation as they walk. "Richard, a fort, nine cannon, a moat? I had not considered this much before, but looking at those sketches and hearing that cannon—why? We live in small villages, fifteen in this part of the Mawooshen and usually not more than a hundred small huts, usually less. No cannon. No firearms except a few rusty muskets you French and English sell us, and then usually no powder or balls. Who will attack you?" Skidwarres' tone is more plaintive than Richard has ever heard.

"I, too, hold these reservations. And I believe the answer can only be fear. But then, my wise friend, it is the fear of the unknown more than fear of the French or Spanish. We do not know our neighbors. You made it clear to me, the Mawooshen are as different as the character of their sagamores. Besides, you know the English have been fighting, building ships and armies for centuries. That is what we do well." Richard smiles and shrugs his shoulders. They stop at the chapel site. "That, Skidwarres, is my best diplomatic answer."

"Yes, this is where you will build your church, where your men will worship your god and your king." His plaintiveness has turned to mild sarcasm. This was not new between the two of them. Their friendship allowed this and, in fact, thrived on it.

"Friend," answers Richard, "you are putting me on the defensive."

"I'm sorry. I don't mean to be disrespectful. But your position—I think of your English saying—is it not 'fear breeds fear?'"

"Correct, except it is our friend the Frenchman, Montaigne."

They stand looking at the ground. Richard points out wooden stakes and rock cairns that define the footprint of the structure. He walks over to a twelve-by-twelve section jutting off the main building. "This is where I will live. A fireplace there," he points. "By the way, your comment about fear, thank you. I will try to use it in my service. Please. Allow me a few moments over there, my outside desk, to write some notes. Please be tolerant. I am new to this job. Afterwards we will share food."

CHAPTER 26

August 28, 1607, Afternoon
A Eucharist of a Different Sort

It is a curious gathering that fills the nave with its dirt and rock floor. Afternoon breezes substitute for walls and a clear blue sky for a ceiling. In what would be a small chancel, Richard stands behind a crude wooden lectern on which lie the Book of Common Prayer and notes he's just hastily written. Near him sits Lance on a stool, cradling his lute and playing a pensive fantasy in C major by William Byrd. A loaf of bread, large jugs of wine, and a silver chalice have been placed on a piece of linen on the ground. In front of Richard and to his right, the native visitors stand with the same dignity they demonstrated when they paddled upriver and onto the beach two hours before.

Nahanada has carefully considered who would join him. The inclusion of women and children would convey peaceful intentions. When his eldest wife, Nolka, heard of this, she insisted on joining him. After her husband was captured, she convinced the two younger wives and a majority of the elders that he would return. She would not believe otherwise, and given her stature as the eldest wife of the sagamore and one known for her implacable nature, her belief became widespread. Where before the three wives often found reason for petty jealousy, especially Nolka—Nahanada tended to share his time equally in the huts of the two youngest and only occasionally joined the eldest—his absence created a sisterly camaraderie. The village tended to treat them with equal amounts of respect, and behind their backs, affectionate amusement. Everyone knew of the previous squabbling.

Nahanada also wished to include three elders, two of whom were sympathetic to Nahanada's efforts to create harmony and a third, Kasko, who represented a small but influential group which opposed him on matters English. The English, even without a permanent settlement, had already sown disharmony among those living in the Mawooshen territory. Though the beaver and bear were still plentiful, they were harder to find since the English, French, and Spanish traders had arrived in greater numbers during the past years. The English were known to steal and cheat. They would bring no good. Some, even in Nahanada's village, believed they should be attacked immediately. Woboz, the son of Kasko, expressed this sentiment most strongly. If Woboz and Kasko met the English and experienced their hospitality, maybe they'd change—so thought Nahanada. Familiarity might lead to acceptance. Nahanada had received promises that the elder and the brave would not stir up trouble.

The anti-English brave, Woboz, had also spread rumors that Skidwarres could not be trusted. Most in the village saw Woboz' perspective as tainted. For during Skidwarres' absence, Woboz had designs on Sokw, Skidwarres' wife. Once he was bold enough to propose that she needed him, a man; that her womanliness needed to be replenished by him or she'd go dry. In response she had pushed him away with a laugh. It stung. As with most small communities, Nahanada's village held contrary views, jealousies, and trans-generational resentments.

Another elder's daughter, Sipsis, had pestered Nahanada for space in one of the three canoes. He agreed. She had stature due to her father's position, as well as a growing reputation at age eighteen for her intelligence, beauty, and wit. Additionally, Sipsis possessed a unique heritage: a French trapper had fathered Sipsis' mother. Therefore, Sipsis' paler skin and the red highlights in her hair reminded the villagers daily of her different blood. Nonetheless, Nahanada believed she would one day be an influential member of his clan. It was she, among others, who had served the English food, and she in particular who had received a squeeze from young Anderson. The incident had not embarrassed her as much as it incited her curiosity to know more about these men. Was her grandfather not like them? Most in the village agreed, Sipsis was the most likely to receive a pinch. Had she encouraged it? Some young women gossiped so. Additionally, Sipsis, two years before, had also spurned the self-assured Woboz after their adolescent coupling.

To Richard's left, the imaginary nave filled with soldiers and craftsmen. Popham and Gilbert disagreed whether such a service should even take place. Popham argued that work must halt and all should attend the ceremony. A religious event would establish a respectful tone.

Gilbert, with no strong feelings for the Church as anything other than a binding English institution, felt the slippage of time. Fall advanced daily. Every moment must be devoted to building, especially in such good weather. They amicably compromised: sixty or so men would attend. If they crammed themselves together, they could stand within the confines of the footprint on the left side. The remainder of the men would be tending to the ships, fishing, cooking, acting as sentinels, and working on projects such as digging trenches, hauling logs, and collecting material for huts—work that would more or less be out of sight and sound of the airy chapel.

As Richard gazes at his parishioners, he's reminded of weddings. On one side the groom's family, on the other the bride's, but in front of him today are peoples from different worlds separated by a dirt aisle. It is certainly an extraordinary event, even historic. It is also just odd.

Lance finishes his third piece. The natives watch and listen with keen interest. Richard speaks after the last notes fade. "Welcome to those who have been working so diligently, and to our guests. First, may I ask Skidwarres to stand and provide translation so that all can fully take part." Just prior to the service the two had agreed to this procedure. "May I say as an introduction that we have been friends for more than two years." At this he stops and allows Skidwarres to speak to his people. Richard continues, looking to his left and right and back again, taking in the contrast. "It is our job to spread this friendship between those of you on my right and on my left. Let us remember, fear but feeds fear. Happily, friendship encourages friendship." Again Richard allows time for the translation, as he will continue to do throughout his short sermon and the truncated Eucharist.

"It is tiring that we stand, so to save time, I will move to the Communion, our moveable feast." Lance moves his stool to the center of the chancellery, takes the loaf of bread under his arm, and places the linen on the stool. While Lance is doing this, Richard reads from the Book of Common Prayer, "The Holy table shall have upon it a fair white linen cloth and the Priest, standing reverently before it." Richard has decided to omit the Lord's Prayer and move onto the Collect. "Almighty God, unto whom all hearts are open, all desires known, and from whom no secrets are hid; cleanse the thoughts of our hearts by the inspiration of thy Holy Spirit."

Richard realizes he's forgotten to give room for translation. He stops. "Skidwarres, I'll repeat what I just said in sections." After each short translation, the native parishioners repeat Skidwarres' words.

Having planned a much-reduced version of the Eucharist, Richard continues parsing out small sections: "Love thy God with all thy heart, and with all thy soul, and with all thy might. This is the first and great commandment. And the second is like unto it; thou shalt love thy neighbor as thyself."

During the translations, the Englishmen stare at their guests as they attentively repeat Skidwarres. Hearing the well-known scripture repeated twice in a foreign tongue has the strange effect of enhancing its meaning.

Richard continues, "Now if you will repeat after me only a section of the Nicene Creed and the Confession: "I believe in the Holy Ghost, the Lord, and the Giver of Life." With the translation of "ghost," a few natives smile. The Mawooshen religion, it seems, holds similar notions. The Englishmen speak in unison, and then the Mawooshen repeat Skidwarres' words. And so it continues, "And I look for the Resurrection of the dead, and the life of the world to come." Without making the distinction, they slide into the Confession, "We acknowledge and bewail our manifold sins and wickedness, which we, from time to time, most grievously have committed. By thought word and deed..."

While the English listen to their guests, Anderson, the young soldier who touched Sipsis, realizes he is at this very time grievously committing a sin by thought. He is watching and thinking of her, or more precisely of her loins under her deerskin. At the moment, she is entirely caught up in the recitation, but earlier she walked by him as he was digging the endless trench. They recognized one another, and she smiled modestly. Anderson wonders if they might actually speak afterwards. But if he tried, what could he say? She wouldn't understand a word.

"...Against thy Divine majesty, provoking most justly thy wrath and indignation...We do earnestly repent, and are heartily sorry for these our misdoings." Along with his fellow parishioners, Anderson repeats these words.

Richard jumps to the end, "Hear what comfortable words our Savior Christ saith unto all who truly turn to Him, Come unto me, all ye that travail and are heavy laden, and I will refresh you..."

Richard then briefly explains he will offer bread and wine, first to the Englishmen, hoping they will set an example for the natives who will follow. Seymour continues with Communion, "Grant us, therefore, gracious Lord, so to eat the flesh of thy dear Son, Jesus Christ." At this point he stops for the translation. While in England, Skidwarres attended a few church services. The translation allowed him a different perspective. Would they not be confused by this cannibalism? He hesitates. Richard, thinking Skidwarres needed help repeats, "Grant us therefore, gracious Lord, so to eat the flesh of they dear Son, Jesus Christ."

"Yes, Chaplain." Concluding he had no other choice, Skidwarres offers up his translation.

Richard continues with less assurance "...and to drink His blood that our sinful bodies may be made clean by His body..." Again the translation. He watches. A few of the natives look at one another quizzically. One smirks.

Richard concludes, "...and our soul washed through his most previous blood and that we may evermore dwell in Him, and He in us. Amen."

Skidwarres' translations have taken on an air of incredulity. Both native and English hear this. Amusement simmers below the surface. Seymour ushers the first group of English to the front where they kneel and offer up cupped hands into which Lance places a small piece of bread torn from the loaf. Richard follows with the chalice for each supplicant.

While the English receive the Sacrament, Skidwarres quietly informs his people they will follow. And so it is with considerable dignity, even in the face of the recent unease over the chaplain's words, that the guests file to the front and kneel, as did their hosts before them. They lift up their hands for the bread, the body. Then their darker faces reach upward for the wine that has miraculously turned to blood. Many of the natives have taken the minister's words literally. Magic, after all, fills their own stories and spiritual understanding.

The ceremony goes smoothly until nearly the end. Nahanada, in his attempts to appease, had told Woboz he could bring another young brave to join him. Woboz chose a friend Nahanada knew had a reputation for antics. But he was good-hearted, if not the brightest of his age group. When Richard places the chalice to Woboz' friend's lips to sip, the young brave tips the bottom upwards. The sip becomes a gulp. The stomach receives its warm gift and the brave responds with a resounding belch which, in Mawooshen culture, is considered a compliment to the host.

Compliment or gaff, Lance, who has been lightly strumming his lute, stops without thinking. From the Englishmen come a few muffled chuckles and then giggles from the boys. As if to punctuate the entire indelicate incident, cannoneer Hodgkins fires off a sonorous fart. Many know it is he. All on the *Gift of God* had adjusted to his daily practice of what Hodgkins considered an art form. On the surface the mood had remained serious enough, but an underlying lighter mood grew, partly from the incongruity of the entire affair, and then by the implied cannibalism of the Eucharist. The belch and fart pushes the levity up to the surface. First, a few Englishmen begin swallowing uncontrollable laughs. The Mawooshen watch. Hearty laughter is contagious. So when it arrives, they join in, adding fuel to the fire, especially since the native's high-pitched version strikes many English as additionally outrageous. Soon most are caught up in the contagion. Richard looks at Skidwarres, who smiles broadly. The chaplain's head turns left to right in hopeless acknowledgment. He then joins in the laughter.

It takes a few moments before the commotion settles. The few natives who had yet to receive Communion are herded back to their previous standing positions. And then, in place of hilarity, all become quiet, suggesting the chaplain's—or even God's—wrath might smite them. The Mawooshen, having regained their composure, look and wait, delighted by the entertainment, but by now unsure what might happen to a ceremony gone awry.

Richard surveys the unlikely assembly. "Well," he says finally, and then grins, "On the seventh day when God rested, I suppose he sat down and had himself a good laugh. After all, when he blew life into man, among other things he created something amusing. No harm done. Skidwarres, please translate."

When he finishes, the guests murmur to themselves. They are not sure what to make of Skidwarres' words. They will have to ask later. He simply translated, "Their god laughs."

The chaplain needs to regain some semblance of solemnity. While the two peoples wait quietly, he picks up the prayer book and peruses the table of contents, settling on a prayer of thanksgiving: "Almighty God, who hast blessed the earth that it should be fruitful and bring forth whatsoever is needful for the life of man..." At this he gives room for translation. These sentiments all peoples could appreciate. "...Bless the labors of the husbandman, and grant such seasonable weather that we may gather in the fruits of the earth, and ever rejoice in thy goodness. Amen." As hoped, the words fell well on the English, some of whom felt mildly repentant. The Mawooshen, too, had regained an attitude of respect.

With a good deal of relief, Richard announces that a meal will be offered within an hour or so. "May we all then rejoice in the goodness of life and in God's abundant wisdom..."—and at the end adds with a smile "...and humor. Amen."

And so ended the first Thanksgiving service in the New World between the English and Native Americans.

CHAPTER 27

August 28, Evening, Fort St. George and Beach
Translations

The grounds within the confines of the newly-dug trenches and some two hundred feet of earthen-rock wall are filled with activity. In what will be the central common of the fort, twenty crudely-built benches encircle various cooking fires. Recently gutted sturgeon, some seven and eight feet long, lie on canvas ready to be broiled. Baskets full of clams and crawling lobsters wait by their pots for boiling. As a gift, the Mawooshen have offered baskets of corn, squash, and blueberries. The day before English hunters shot four reddish-brown deer. Now they hang upside down, bled out, dressed, and ready for a spit. Around the fires small groups of English and natives communicate by hand over cooking preparations. To the side men fill their cups from barrels of ale. As with any such event, conversations and laughter increase with time. Near the fires and benches, two men with fiddles begin playing dance tunes.

To the west, on the outside of the trench and partially-built rock wall, on an open piece of ground, Lance and his three English companions play lacrosse with three native boys who brought extra sticks made of wood and rawhide. A bare chested sixteen-year-old helps Lance with the basics of throwing, catching, and cradling. The absence of a shared language doesn't impede instruction; all is demonstration, plus trial and error.

The young Mawooshen demonstrates by standing behind Lance. Two left hands hold the bottom of the stick, two right hands cradle the head in unison. The others boys watch and copy. Within half an hour, the English master the basics. They run around, catching and falling and laughing and butting each other with the ends of their sticks. Smith bleeds from a fat lip; another trips on a root and limps a bit. As the neophytes gain a little skill, the Mawooshen begin playing rougher. Lance takes a fast throw and misses. The ball smacks his chest hard, crumpling him onto the ground. He rolls over to his knees, forehead to the ground, and stays there whimpering softly. The boys play on for a few moments and then stop. They hadn't expected such a response. It was as if he'd been hit in the testicles, though they'd seen the mishap and knew otherwise.

Smith leaned over Lance. "You hurt Lance? Or you just a pussy?

"Fuck you, Smith."

The native who'd been teaching Lance puts a hand on his shoulder and says something softly. Lance lifts his head off the ground and turns to see his new friend's smile. The native boy points to himself and says, "Moskwa," and then points to Lance. Still in pain Lance returns his head to the ground, repeats the boy's name, and then offers, "Lance."

"Lance," says Moskwa. His hand continues to rest on Lance's shoulder. "Lance," he says again.

"Moskwa," Lance says, still facing the ground. Then with a sigh, he raises himself to his knees. "It's better. Thank you. You're kinder than my idiot friend over there."

The boys decide they have had enough, so they wander over to the cooking area, draw ale, and sit by the fire to rest. The cool evening arrives. Lance and Moskwa sit together and look into their cups while occasionally lifting their heads that bubble inside a bit from the alcohol. They smile shyly but don't attempt conversation.

Gilbert, Popham, Skidwarres, Nahanada, and Robert Davies occupy one table. Gilbert explains that within a week here, on this ground, will be the main section of his house. Nahanada and Popham exchange gifts. Popham offers the usual: glass beads, copper bracelets, cloth, and an iron pot. Nahanada receives these with feigned appreciation. He knows these items to be near worthless from an Englishman's perspective. Nonetheless, it is important not to be rude. Besides, he has to admit, his gift of five paltry beaver skins is equally valueless. Popham, not so dull to the transactions, demonstrates equal grace.

Men well into their second cup of rum or ale begin dancing by themselves and with one another on a dirt and grass dance floor, as the Mawooshen watch. One retrieves a small drum he'd left in the canoe and begins tapping it softly. A fiddler beckons him to join them. Another young brave moves to the music and sings. Native and English loosened by grog gravitate to the dance area.

Other men line up to fill their plates and squeeze themselves together on the benches.

Anderson was not the only English to gaze at Sipsis during the church service. Fletcher watched how she carried her lithe self with a slight aloofness. He managed to catch her grayish-green eyes, unusual for a native, as far as he could tell. After the service he decided to exchange work clothes for his red, white, and blue cannoneer uniform, thinking it would provide a bit of status the young woman might appreciate.

Fortified by an additional gulp of rum, Fletcher approaches the head table. "Skidwarres, sir, might I dance with a young woman in your group?" He points to the girl standing with three friends along the perimeter of the dancing.

Skidwarres smiles. "Why the 'sir,' sir?"

"Not sure what protocol, ah...under the circumstances."

"I see no problem." Skidwarres looks over at Nahanada, who hears the request and shrugs. In the absence of the girl's father, Nahanada speaks. With this lukewarm approval, Skidwarres stands and takes Fletcher by the shoulder. Amidst the commotion only a few notice, including Anderson, who—outranked and out-maneuvered by Fletcher—begins a night of sulking that will end in a drunken stupor.

Sipsis watches Skidwarres and Fletcher approach. She was hoping to meet one of the English, perhaps the one who touched her rump. She thought about the braves who vied for her attention; her skin, hair and eyes, different and so compelling. The teasing she'd received as a young girl from other girls and the boys, she'd learned to interpret as jealousy and desire. When she reached adolescence, young braves fought over her. A marriage proposal from another Mawooshen village churned up inter-village hostilities, but not much had come of it. Meanwhile, Sipsis flirted and even lay with a few, but without truly giving of herself. She bided her time. Nahanada and Skidwarres' abduction and return had awakened a longing to know more of the white men whom, like her paternal grandfather, she had never met.

Sipsis greets Skidwarres and then Fletcher. She knows of the European custom of shaking hands. Nahanada had taught her.

"I know this man. His name is Fletcher. He would like to dance with you. You have Nahanada's permission."

She nods her assent and Skidwarres slips away. Fletcher smiles, Sipsis's two friends move back a step. He takes her hand and they step into the opening where men are attempting a ragged country line dance.

Fletcher decides to simply lock arms, right elbow to right elbow and slowly turn. They do so quite modestly with their eyes to the ground, entirely deaf to the growing clamor about them. Each finds pleasure in their little patch of earth. Then he stops and unlocks their arms, turns her quarter around and re-engages, right forearm hooked under her left arm just below her shoulder. He offers his left hand. Sipsis clasps it. Again they circle, more quickly. They began catching one another's eye with fleeting smiles and, as they do, their circling becomes a larger swirl. Fletcher's grip stiffens. Sipsis' two friends look on in amazement. The young brave, Woboz, stares at them scornfully from a distance.

When the fiddlers take a short break, Fletcher leads Sipsis to the rum barrel. He fills two mugs and picks up a section of venison leg off a large pewter platter. They wander fifty yards or so to sit on the eastern granite outcropping. They settle down and watch the water gurgling in and out of the crevices at near high tide.

Behind them the volume of music and excitement picks up again. In the dying light, they watch the water curl around the rock under their feet. It swishes the seaweed gently back and forth, before withdrawing, receding, then collecting itself and returning slowly, voluptuously. They watch and sip.

Fletcher attempts to say her name.

She corrects him with a smile. Then he says, "Fletcher," pointing to himself.

"Fetcher," is her first try.

He repeats stressing the "L." On her second try he hears it. Then he holds up the mug. "Mug," he instructs."

"Mug."

"Perfect."

Sipsis repeats, "Perfect."

Fletcher raises his index finger. "Finger."

Sipsis repeats with her finger, "Finger."

"Good," Fletcher says with a smile.

"Good," she answers with an equally warm smile.

Fletcher sticks his finger in the rum, swishes it around. Sipsis repeats his actions.

Next Fletcher withdraws his finger and sucks on it. "Rum, good rum," he says, smacking his lips.

Again Sipsis takes his lead, but instead of sucking her own finger, she offers it to Fletcher. "Rum," she says, "good rum." He sucks on her small finger until she withdraws it. They stare at one another, both surprised by the sudden intimacy. It has been months since Fletcher lay with a woman, the last in a cheap brothel, leaving him with a monstrous headache in the morning. It has been six years since his wife died giving birth to his stillborn son. While serving in the Queen's Navy, he frequented many a whorehouse—English, Dutch, French, Spanish, Portuguese, even African women—he'd bedded them all. Tonight though, he felt almost chaste, Sipsis was so sweet-smelling— of what flower scent he could not tell—and her manner both girlish and seductive. Her rum, half-gone, must be taking effect.

Fletcher, somewhat nonplussed, points to his mouth. "Mouth."

Sipsis returns with "Mouth," then mouth in Algonquin, "*Wdon.*"

Fletcher picks up this variation and continues with eyes, nose, hand, leg, first in English, followed by her native tongue. They laugh. He then holds up his mug. "Cheers."

Sipsis copies him. "Cheers." Sipsis has tasted ale and wine, gifts from the occasional French or Basque trader, but never has it so warmed her stomach or softened her skin and loosened her thoughts.

Fletcher picks up the deer shank and passes it to her. Back and forth it goes, until they end up gnawing on the remains, nose to nose. Fletcher finds a thumb-sized piece of meat and makes an offering. "*Wilwni*" (thank you), she says.

Then she makes a similar offering. He nibbles it off her fingers. His attempted "*Wilwni*" produces giggles.

With meat, gristle, and fat gone, he stands and throws the bone as far as he can into the water, his pronouncement that the meal is over. He offers his hand, and she allows herself to be pulled up. The crest of an orange, oversized, full moon splashes across the water. Fletcher retrieves both mugs and slugs down what remains in his. She sips and offers the last swallow to him.

"*Wilwni*," Fletcher manages with some improvement.

"Cheers," says Sipsis.

An easy surf flops on the beach, a ten-minute walk away. They head in that direction, away from the commotion, moonlight on a clear night allowing for easy vision. Fletcher points to his nose. He is testing her.

"Nose," she says."

"Ah, so quick to learn."

"Quick to learn," Sipsis repeats with a satisfied smile. In fact, over the years she has learned some French and English from traders and more recently from Nahanada.

Soon they are at the beach, then the water's edge where the ocean meets the Sagadahoc. In the declining light they watch the receding tide churn up where it meets the oncoming ocean waves.

As the moon rises, phosphorescent sparkles appear on the watery moonbeams. They multiply while the two watch in silence. They shimmer, creating a molten surface that works its way across the water toward their feet. It appears so substantial that they might step onto the water and run toward the source. For minutes it holds.

"Gold," says Fletcher. Sipsis remains silent.

The orange oversized disc begins to shrink and yellow as it climbs. The gold twinkles become scattered fireflies and disappear, leaving the sea black. They have been watching for nearly half an hour.

The mesmerized couple turns wordlessly and begins walking down the beach that broadens by inches with every wavelet. Soon the low, twelve-foot tide will leave nearly a hundred yards of exposed sand from dunes to waterline.

Fletcher again takes her hand. He is not sure what they are doing, though he knows he hasn't been happier in years, perhaps his entire life. The so-called New World, this exotic woman who seems to know him, even though they have just met. He brushes his hand across her cheek. "Cheek," Sipsis repeats.

In less than half an hour they arrive at the small river dividing the beach, the same one the soldiers found on their first reconnaissance. They stop on the bank and turn toward one another, bathing in the moonlight.

Years before Sipsis' grandmother and French grandfather had left her mother with relatives. Most thought they had journeyed to his country across the ocean. Sipsis grew to believe it would be her destiny to be carried away, to follow them. Her grayish-green eyes and pinkish skin, did they not signify this? Someday she would live in her grandfather's world.

They face one another on the sandy banks of the shallow stream. They take off their shoes and moccasins. Hand in hand they wade into water warmer than expected, cooked by the afternoon sun in the shallows upstream. They turn, knee-deep, and face one another. Fletcher takes her face in his hands. He bends down and lightly kisses one cheek, then the other.

"Kiss," he whispers. "Kiss."

"Kiss," Sipsis answers. "Kiss."

He kisses her on the lips, softly at first, and then with pressure. She responds with a sigh that carries a question, but she doesn't pull away. Fletcher drops his right hand to her rounded hip, just above the water.

They hold one another, his lips moving from mouth to nose to cheek until his right hand slips down and then under her loincloth. She feels his open palm, his light stroking fingers.

The quick-moving outgoing tide causes them to sink into the muddy sand, so the water now circles almost waist high. They scramble out of the water and sit on the sand above the high water line, a section that hasn't entirely lost all its warmth. Their love making progresses horizontally.

She feels him against her stomach. Her right hand seeks him over his heavy wool pants. Her fingers touch something unfamiliar, buttons. She utters something.

From her tone he gathers she is asking a question. "Button," he answers.

"Button?"

"Four buttons," Fletcher takes her finger and lets it touch each one. He doesn't want her hand to withdraw. With his fingers and hers intertwined, he shows her how to undo one button after another. Sipsis does the last two on her own, while with the back of his hand he brushes the soft hair under the front of her loincloth.

Her hand slips in and encircles him. His entire body stiffens with pleasure. She extracts him and continues her attentions. Unexpectedly, with a groan, his pleasure trips into its headlong course. He pulls her up against him. His right hand returns to her bottom, this time deep into the crevice. His finger finds her warm dampness just as he climaxes.

While he holds her tightly and she him, his pleasure recedes, replaced by a mixture of contentment and embarrassment. The air is now cooler. His hand caresses her sandy buttocks.

"I'm sorry. It has been a long time. I suppose I was nervous." The contrite tone is clear, the words meaningless to Sipsis.

In her own tongue Fletcher hears, "No, don't worry. I am happy." And so he hears consolation. That conferred, Fletcher loosens his grip, kisses her on the nose and whispers, "Thank you." He chuckles and she imitates him good-naturedly. "Thank you," she says in English.

Fletcher sits and—as if Sipsis will fully understand—suggests, "We had better return. I understand you will camp across the river. We should not be late. I might catch hell." Again she comprehends the gist, so rises to her knees. Fletcher gets to his feet, buttons his fly, and helps her up.

While they amble back looking for their shoes, the couple is unaware they are being watched from the edge of the grassy dunes. Woboz has kept an eye on them while they ate and then followed. It gave him proof that the English take what they want. Why not attack him, or at least, threaten? But on second thought, what of Nahanada's wrath, as well as his father Kasko's. Nahanada's opinions of the English are not easy to fathom. Besides, both elders are capable of inventive, verbal abuse— Sipsis even more so. Action might undermine whatever chances he had for her. He, Woboz, should not lose face. He uncharacteristically checks his impulsiveness and watches, even as his anger grows.

CHAPTER 28

August 28, Night Across the River
Parlay

During Fletcher and Sipsis' absence, Popham, Gilbert, Nahanada, Skidwarres, and Seymour sat at the same table. Due to the high spirits and noise, the principals have given up trying to conduct business. That could wait. President Popham feels energized. Urged by the men, Gilbert and Seymour periodically join them in line dances. At one point George Popham and Nahanada sit alone facing one another on either side of the pine slab table. Popham leans over to ask a confidential question. "Nahanada, I've heard some of your men trade their women— if the deal is profitable. Is this so?"

"It is so, President. Some men do. One or two in our village, depending on how many wives or daughters they have. But it is not common. In other villages, more."

"Well, let me tell you my friend, this old body needs rejuvenation. I'd be very appreciative if you might consider my situation."

"I understand. It was a long journey. It will be a cold winter. Warmth under the blanket is a great gift."

"Yes." The prospect further cheers Popham as he pries open a clam with a knife, plucks out the soft meat, barely chews, swallows, and washes it down with more ale. "Yes, glad you see it that way. But tell me, what is the arrangement? Is it a sale or more like a lease?"

Nahanada understands the difference. "When to another village, the woman tends to remain. The French, they want wives too. The English fishermen, so I'm told, prefer to rent, something less permanent.

Popham rises with some effort and lumbers over to fill his cup. He returns breathing heavily and sits with a thud. His cheeks are especially pink and his breathing short. "Glad you see it that way. See what you can do."

Gilbert, winded and merry, returns from dancing. "What do you say, sirs, not a bad party. But what are you doing, President, sitting here, when I hear you are a fine dancer? You bring with you your reputation."

"Years ago, Admiral, years ago."

"Nonsense; let me help you up. We can find a fine native woman for you." Gilbert makes a point of speaking so others might hear. With a nod of Gilbert's head, two soldiers nearby assist Popham and escort him to the dance area. Others part to allow clear passage. Still more clap and call out encouragement, "President Popham, President Popham!" Nahanada follows the near abduction. Gilbert turns to him and asks the sagamore to choose a good woman for our president. "Is that not a fine idea?"

"Well, gentlemen," Popham momentarily regains some composure and breath, "I am here and it would be a great honor, Nahanada."

Nahanada bows. Men clap and shout their approval. He crosses the matted grass, slippery and muddied with spilled drink, and puts out a hand to his wife, Nolka, the woman Popham had so gallantly escorted out of the canoe. She offers a broad smile. It is an obvious choice. Though probably twenty years younger than Popham, she is the eldest woman in the group, but still strong and handsome with only some strands of white in her long hair that falls nearly to her waist and is intertwined with small sea shells. Being the center of attention pleases her.

The musicians chin their fiddles and strike up a jig. Popham is not only an experienced dancer, he is a patient teacher, inebriated or not. Before long the two are circling gracefully about, while all clap to the beat tapped out by the young brave on his small drum.

While Nahanada watches in approval, a thought occurs: what might the old man be willing to trade for a woman—his woman, for instance? He will think about this.

Skidwarres appears with his wife, Sokw, and puts her hand in Richard's.

"My friend, Richard, would you teach my wife to dance?"

"Indeed." Richard smiles at Sokw and slowly walks hand in hand to the open space. He turns and says over his shoulder. "But you, Skid, you know this dance as well as I." As she relaxes, the couple is caught up in the tempo. Men hoot their approval. Skidwarres decides to introduce a couple of Englishmen to the remaining three women. The festivities reach a fever pitch; even Popham maintains a vigorous pace.

Late in the evening, Gilbert notices Fletcher standing with Sipsis. He approaches and offers a hand to dance, staring at her with his slight, wry smile. She knows the look, even at her young age. It is that of a desirous, proud man. "Fletcher, that is your name, is it not?" he asks.

"Yes, sir."

"Would you mind?"

"Of course not, Admiral."

Sipsis looks quizzically at Fletcher. "It's all right. Dance." He takes her hand and gives it to Gilbert.

"Thank you, Fletcher. Much obliged." Gilbert intends to make an impression, no more. After only a short period, he stops and steps back. The fiddling continues. He bows just a bit, turns, and leaves her standing alone. She looks about a bit before finding Fletcher's dejected face.

After nearly five hours of festivity, at ten at night, Gilbert calls off the music and shuts down the barrels of grog. Tomorrow morning, like every morning including Sunday, work will begin at daybreak. Some men put their blanket rolls in the partially-roofed storehouse. Others crawl into wattle huts erected on the eastern portion of the fort. A few still prefer the hammocks on the ship. The Mawooshen push off in their canoes for the other side of the river, only a few minutes' paddle. There they will stay in some old but usable bark huts. Mammoth sturgeon brought previous generations to this site periodically.

An exhausted George Popham, aided by his orderly, retires to his partially-built small timber house.

Gilbert asks Seymour to join him across the river to continue conversation. They row across behind the natives. Raleigh wants to make arrangements to visit Bessabez on the Penobscot River, but he wishes to do so without Popham's oversight, and there is no telling if the natives might disappear early in the morning. Though each sagamore governs his own group, Bessabez holds moral and political influence for all Mawooshen villages.

Around a roaring fire, English and native sit smoking, and drinking tobacco from empty lobster claws, an indulgence Gilbert and Seymour try only once, cough, spit, and then offer their apologies. Nahanada explains in his native tongue, "The English only smoke." The offering was something of a practical joke.

Exploration of the Sagadahoc and nearby coast is, for Gilbert, the first order of business. He plans to row and sail the thirty-foot shallop upriver, along with ten men. He wishes for Skidwarres' help navigating and translating, if necessary. Would Nahanada also arrange a meeting with Bessabez? Gilbert has other questions to raise. Months ago, and then more recently at Pemaquid, he'd spoken to Nahanada about a route to the Orient, about the location of silver mines, the abundance of sassafras and, of course, of pelts. On these issues he had continually received vague reports. In fact, while in captivity Nahanada had exaggerated the bounty of the land and kept alive the long- standing rumor of a river leading to a huge ocean. Besides, many Mawooshen believed that beyond the sunset lay a fantastic world. This or that river might lead to it. Some held that after death the purified souls lived at the eastern horizon, the tarnished ones in the west. In any case, Nahanada thought it more likely he'd return from his abduction if he kept the prospects high.

With persistence on Gilbert's part, they reached agreement. Skidwarres and one other brave would remain and assist in the exploration of the Sagadahoc. He knew the inland waterway, though he'd never traveled far beyond the Quabacook. The unpredictable Sabenoa occupied this land. Skidwarres had met him as a young brave, but not since. Some years before, Skidwarres, Nahanada, and others were involved in a skirmish. Sabenoa's son was a casualty. In retaliation a year later, Sabenoa captured and married a Mawooshen. Relations between the two groups waxed and waned. Skidwarres would act as translator, if—as likely—they met the Lord of the Sagadahoc. Meanwhile, Nahanada would send word to Bessabez of Gilbert's wish.

Gilbert also wanted to know if Nahanada's village and other groups on the Sagadahoc and Aponeg would trade their food. The farmers among the colony had started seedlings aboard ship, including squash, onions, and turnips. On arrival they realized nothing would grow to fruition. Already the nights had turned cold, and the soil around the fort was sandy and shallow. Nahanada could not offer much. The Mawooshen grew no more than could be consumed. They planted for survival, not trade. Traditionally Mawooshen men fished and hunted; the women gathered. Within the last couple of generations they'd begun modest plantings.

A groggy Gilbert felt more or less satisfied. Nahanada held out the promise of many beaver pelts. And nowhere had he seen such majestic forests. What would his father think if he were alive? Would he, his third son, not be glorified?

As the men rose, Skidwarres and Seymour agreed to talk later. For now, Skidwarres wished to join his family.

Gilbert took Nahanada's elbow and drew him aside. "Nahanada, I wonder if you might be of help. I danced with a beauty. I cannot pronounce her name."

"Sipsis, Admiral."

"Yes, and would she, I wonder—would she welcome some company tonight? Or am I being too forward, Nahanada? I mean to insult no one."

"No insult." Nahanada showed no emotion. "She is old enough. I ask. You wish?"

"Indeed."

Nahanada walked past the fire's glow to a hut in the shadows.

Gilbert turns to Richard, "Are you not in the mood for a woman?"

Seymour nods with a serious face. "I am but a man." Gilbert thought it best to push no further. In fact, the presence of the young women had stirred Seymour as much as it had the other Englishmen. It was not just the rum that gave the dancing such energy.

Nahanada returned moments later. "Admiral, Sipsis is pleased by your interest." Nahanada looks to Skidwarres. "How do I translate this?" The two conferred softly in their native tongue, smiling.

Nahanada turned to Gilbert. "She says at some other time you meet. Tonight, she says, one handful of English was enough."

CHAPTER 29

September 8, 1607, Fort St. George
Construction

With the dawn and the sound of Lance's bugle, men, like burrowing animals, stick their heads out from wattle huts or blanket rolls laid out on the newly-floored storehouse. They blink at the dull sun. Others roll out of their canvas hammocks on the ship and drop into the longboats waiting to ferry them to the hours of work awaiting them. They line up for the morning rations of tea, biscuits, and dried fish. Others line up in front of Surgeon Thayer who applies ointment on blisters, offers tinctures for the pain from sprained ankles, and sets the occasional broken bone. At one point or another they stand at the shore to piss into the bay and gaze upriver. Others find their way to trenches, as outhouse construction is not yet a priority. By the third week, the adventure and novelty have worn thin. The warm tea helps, but it won't be until after the sun burns off the mist and chill that humor and optimism spring up.

First conversations include the inevitable: Fish again for dinner? How do we construct these wattle huts? In the morning men keep their thoughts mostly to themselves. What would their sweethearts or wives be doing at this very instant? Had they been lying with another man? How long would the clear weather hold? The rain had come only a few times at night, but that would change. Should they eventually bring their family or a woman to the New World? Would they be offered free land, or should they return? Return to what? Poverty? What would winter be like? Would they be warm enough? Who was really in charge, Popham or Gilbert? How friendly were the savages? Not all seemed so during the festivities. A few strong-looking braves never smiled. Images of the native women flicker across their consciousness. Sexual matters come to mind. With the sun, the men's backs sweat and tongues loosen. How do the savage women like to fuck, from behind like dogs? The Virginia Company investors plan to get rich. How much will end in our pockets, the ones doing the real work? I don't even get stiff at night, too tired. Erasmus and his goats, he's the only one getting laid—unless you count those two fairy farmers.

Soldier, sailors, onetime vagrants are now hardworking men all far from home—discipline remained strong, attitudes generally positive. By midday, or at least after the daily rations of ale or rum, conviviality and antagonisms spread. Arguments and fisticuffs sometimes break out over food, territory around huts, work orders, and favoritism. Unintended slights were inevitable. A soldier on a moonlit night mistook a sleeping comrade for a rock and pissed on his head. As is typical in any large gathering without women, some men found themselves attracted to one another. They acted upon this or not, and when done they faced the consequences of their own moral twinges, mixed with fear of exposure, ridicule, or even harsh punishment. Buggery could lead to the gallows. Nonetheless, a few exercised this flexibility, brought about by necessity. But usually a long day of work, followed by food and drink, led to early sleep.

With time, the meanness of some men, having been kept under wraps in the tight living quarters of the ship, erupted. Alliances formed and rumors flew. The most pernicious, beyond the jokes about body parts, odor, and lack of intelligence, came from the mouth of the soldier who nearly threw the puppy, Stow, overboard. On board the ship, Hawkes had subtly harassed Lance, muttering under his breath, "Soon I will have your little ass." In the relatively expansive grounds of the fort and around its outskirts, Lance felt more threatened. Within any large male population, sexual assault against boys was not uncommon. The four between the ages of thirteen and sixteen tended to band together for safety, though none of them talked of their fear. From his years at sea, Fletcher knew of the Hawkeses of the world. He let it be known that any harm to the boys would bring retaliation. Fletcher and a few friends became the boys' protectors on ship and remained so on land.

Each evening all took pride in the fort that was being built by their heavy labor. The twenty-foot-wide trench, along with the stone and mud wall, arose out of the land, impressive and ugly. Nine nine-pound cannon pointed separately in all directions. The storehouse, approximately twenty by seventy feet, became a grand presence, even before completion. Here English craftsmanship planted itself firmly. Why should the white man not claim all lands that were not previously held by Christians? Yes, all knew that meant all the land, as no European settlement yet existed on what the Virginia Company had usurped. Was it not inevitable that a superior race and culture should settle this raw land? Like King James, all his subjects assumed this. Besides, plenty of wild land existed for all, including savages. Many of the soldiers, craftsmen, and especially the farmers or their ancestors had tasted the bitterness of being removed from "common land," land now under the control of large landholding gentry and royalty. As the fort took shape, many saw it as a sign of long overdue prosperity, or at least potentially so.

Richard stood regarding the footprint of his chapel. It would be the second largest structure. He slept under some boards offered to him by the shipwright, Digby. Gilbert told him he'd soon have a place to worship and live. First a wooden storehouse, followed by a wooden home for Popham and himself. Repeatedly Gilbert commented, "This, the first church in the New World." But it sounded shallow to Seymour. None of the principals were especially religious, not even he—the representative of the Bishop of Exeter. Nonetheless, Richard had sworn to uphold the Church's presence. He dutifully reminded both Popham and Gilbert that a chapel was important for the men's morale.

After the second week, a few men were assigned to the task. The five young boys camped nearby. When it rained, their poorly constructed twig and mud roof dripped. Early one rainy morning Richard awoke to find the boys huddled under his board roof. The next day Richard insisted to Gilbert that the boys be able to salvage a few battered canvas sails and create a cover for themselves. The idea took hold, and yards of old sail became makeshift roofs for many.

Today Richard would join Gilbert and several soldiers on the shallop, along with Skidwarres and another brave in their canoe, for the first exploration of the Sagadahoc. Often Richard felt both exhilarated and disoriented in equal portions. He would awaken and stare from his vantage point on the small hill overlooking the fort and the river beyond. This morning he felt two contrary thoughts. The first: this is where I must be. It is fated. It is so and therefore must be so. I can't imagine myself elsewhere, strange as it seems. Yet, the alternating—or rather simultaneous—sense was just as strong: who am I? I am really standing on this rock, looking up a river in this wild part of the world surrounded by lost men, commanded by an ailing adventurer and a young man, his cousin, hell bent for—well, Richard wasn't sure. Wealth and prominence, he assumed. Richard considered this odd amalgamation: fully sure of his present existence and momentarily not living in his own body or mind.

At these moments he'd shake his head and walk toward the men lined up for breakfast. He'd hear a voice or feel the warmth of tea in his stomach, and the ambiguity faded. Sometimes he felt inauthentic as their religious leader, but for the most part he'd come to grips with this. He'd uphold his agreement with Sir John Popham. He'd simply do his best. He'd conduct a weekly service. Seymour's days involved counseling men who came to him with their loneliness or sinful thoughts. Mostly they wanted to talk—or rather, they wanted to be heard. It wasn't really confession; it was counsel or something in between. And somewhat to his surprise, after simply listening and not making judgments, just asking questions for the purpose of clarification, the men nearly always told him they felt much better. The need to be heard, the chaplain concluded, was as important as food.

Seymour oversaw the construction of the chapel—slow as it was— and continued to insist the boys maintain their reading and writing instruction, if only for an hour or so each day. When not occupied by church matters or teaching, he joined Digby, the shipwright. It captured his imagination, the fifty-foot pinnace that would ply the sea, built from the English oak with New World pine and spruce, shaped by English craftsmanship. Shipbuilding seemed to him more holy than the construction of a chapel. A ship was alive. She was given a name. He'd considered the symbolism of a ship under sail many times during the voyage. We all need a keel, otherwise circumstances control us. Without a rudder we are aimless. Without a mast to hold the sail, we are powerless. Yet we must abide by the wind's rules. We cannot sail straight into it. The helmsman must have a purpose and knowledge.

These thoughts amused him. Sometimes he thought of himself as a ship under construction. Might he be reconstructing himself here in the wilderness? Was that his purpose in the New World? Was Sir John correct that one only finds oneself by getting lost? Richard also reminded himself what a dilettante he was at everything he did. But was he not learning and improving? Even his lute-playing showed progress. His daily practice provided moments of continuity with his prior self. And while he was playing, Margaret seemed a bit closer, her scent on the handkerchief still detectable. Or perhaps it was simply his olfactory memory. In either case, he cherished the subtle, warm stirring.

CHAPTER 30

September 8, 1607, Later in the Morning
Upriver in the Shallop

By nine in the morning, the thirty-foot shallop has begun following the canoe upriver. Six soldiers wearing metal breastplates and helmets accompany four experienced rowers. They strain at their oars, as the wind and tide do not cooperate. Gilbert decides to include the head farmer and the mining expert, Carew. Muskets, powder, and shot have been stowed. A small three-pound cannon perches on the bow. Gilbert has ordered bean-sized grapeshot. It would wound, kill, or simply frighten more effectively than a single large ball. The English might well be outnumbered. However, gunpowder tips the scale, especially with a backward opponent. For cannon and cooking fires, a soldier keeps a fire alive in a small metal box. Gilbert expects at least a two-day journey. When the wind shifts to the prevailing westerlies, he'll set the sails.

The siting of the fort on the Sagadahoc made sense in part because it allowed access to the vast interior. On this foray into the land, they hoped to identify large stands of pine and oak that could be used for future construction, as well as for export. Many of the trees in the vicinity of the fort were not large, given the thin sandy soil and wind off the ocean. However, it took only minutes before huge white pine, spruce, oak, cedar, birch, and walnut came into view. They expressed autumn in yellow, red, purple, green, brown, and shades in between. Trees lined the river and continued as far as they could see. It would not be difficult to fell and then float them downriver.

While they prepared to disembark, Gilbert and Carew ask Skidwarres what he knows about silver mines. Skidwarres knows of a multicolored stone he's seen worn for ornamentation, but as for silver—he shakes his head and shrugs his shoulders. As to their present route, Skidwarres knows of an open bay, the Quabacook, where the Androscoggin meets the Sagadahoc. Sabenoa lives there on fertile land. As Gilbert expressed it to George Popham and the other principals, "We must know the countryside in which we will eventually settle. If it offers immediate riches, that will be fortuitous. In any case, we must survey it, as no reliable charts or descriptions exist."

Seymour stands in the stern next to Gilbert, whose hand rests on the tiller. A high bald bluff, perhaps three hundred feet, identifies the northern entrance to a river running east. Seen from the fort, sunsets turned the rock a light gold that sparkled with mica. Paddling alongside the shallop, Skidwarres explains this river leads to yet another bay. Beyond lies an extensive inland waterway he knows well.

Seymour stares ahead. The broad Sagadahoc narrows, though still more than a hundred yards wide. Then it tunnels in the distance. And wildlife: ducks paddle about dunking for food, fish jump and slap, lone herons stand in the shallows stoically waiting to stab a small fish with their long thin beaks, or they skittishly lift off with annoyed guttural squawks that are nearly growls. Eddies and tides meet and swirl. Black cormorants in a V-formation fly thirty feet over the water, straining toward their destination. Gulls and hawks lollygag in the thermals, alert to any source of fish on the surface. Way above comes honking a black cloud of geese, their urgent communication amplified in the crisp air. Fish, fowl, and humans are on a mission. This river is unlike any Richard has seen in England. The Thames, the Exe are docile, long ago tamed, mostly murky and slow-moving with soft banks and human traffic. The Sagadahoc runs wild.

By midday the river has narrowed to fifty yards. The tide in this gut works against the shallop. The weak wind is useless as the four oarsmen strain. All watch the water stream by, giving the false impression they are making excellent headway, while the shore creeps by inch by inch in the wrong direction. Skidwarres directs his canoe to the shore. Taking his cue, Gilbert orders the crew to join him and wait for the tide to change.

Along the banks, on an expanse of flat rock, English and native crew share beef jerky and sip ale. They watch the tide fall a few more inches. For a while it slackens, about to make up its mind.

The rested rowers and the elements are soon in alignment. The new incoming tide sweeps them through the gut and into a broad stretch of river half a mile wide. And as they slide into the open, an invigorated wind appears from behind and snaps the sail full.

A half hour later the river narrows again, this time into even swifter and more turbulent water. Gilbert watches the current at the surface. Occasionally the water either boils or smoothes, in both cases indicating rocks below. Gilbert follows Skidwarres' course. It is still low tide. The shallop doesn't draw more than two feet. At one point they can nearly touch the shore. Though it might be counterintuitive, the channel often runs close to land.

Canoe and shallop, a hundred feet or so apart, pick up speed. The river squeezes between two outcroppings. They rush forward and shoot through at the river's mercy, the shallop's rudder at this point only marginally useful. Then the water underneath loses its grip as they are delivered into in a wide bay. They come to a near standstill. The wind weakens, the sails flutter. The shallop seems to say, "Where next?"

"Well done," says Richard.

"Luck came along for the ride—and Skidwarres." This is the first modest comment anyone has heard from Raleigh Gilbert, who seems himself a bit surprised that all has gone well.

The canoe comes alongside. "Skidwarres," says Gilbert, "from my reckoning in that direction, another river, the Androscoggin, runs northwest and there," he points northeast, "the Sagadahoc continues." Skidwarres agrees. He is impressed by Gilbert's knowledge, gained from crude charts and conversation. The man is no fool.

As Gilbert, Carew, and the farmer consider their options, Seymour notices four canoes heading in their direction. The tranquil mood produced by their safe arrival at the bay turns tense. Gilbert orders the muskets and cannon be loaded. "Listen, do not appear hostile. Keep your weapons out of sight. Be ready to act quickly, but not until I give orders. We are not here to make trouble."

"Who are they?" Gilbert turns to Skidwarres.

"Sabenoa's people, as expected"

Richard notices the shoreline is less rocky, behind it meadowland and trees marginally reminiscent of home. If it were not for the unknown motives of the natives energetically paddling in their direction, he would feel serene. The air and water have warmed. The bay is more like a lake. The tide is taking its time, barely noticeable this far upriver.

When the canoes come within fifty yards, the English discern faces painted blue and hair spiked like a porcupine's.

"What do they intend, Skidwarres?" Gilbert asks.

"One can never be sure. It is Sabenoa in the lead canoe, their sagamore you've heard about. He is unpredictable, and also one to make much noise and show."

"He would be stupid to attack us."

"Sabenoa thinks much of himself—but stupid, no. I don't think he will attack."

"Steady men. Ship oars. Let them come to us."

Sabenoa and the twelve braves stop paddling. The four canoes bob in the calm water. The two groups stare at one another. Finally, the one in the lead canoe stands and shouts in Algonquin, "I am Sabenoa, Lord of the Sagadahoc. What do the English want?" Skidwarres translates.

Gilbert, who is already standing at the tiller, shouts back, "I am Admiral Gilbert. I come as a friend."

The Lord of the Sagadahoc remains standing but does not respond. He is a stout man, not young. His face is painted with red and black streaks beginning at the corners of his mouth and fanning out over his cheeks. Another broad black band bisects his forehead and travels down his nose, across his mouth and chin, ending on his hairless upper chest. His men, similarly painted, continue resting their paddles on the gunwales.

"Skidwarres," says Gilbert, "tell them we wish to trade. Tell them we are armed but come in peace."

In the middle of the translation, Sabenoa shouts, "Ah, the English—referring to Skidwarres—from the village of Nahanada—the one with those who murdered my son." Skidwarres has heard insults from his own people and the accusation, true enough, from others in Sabenoa's village.

"Hello, brother. Nahanada has already offered his sympathy, explained how it was a mistake. And will you not talk with my friends? They are armed, but would you not be armed if you had paddled across the sea and up their river?"

Sabenoa laughs and is echoed by a similar chorus from his braves. The death of his son occurred five years before, and even his own braves spoke of the young man's foolhardy charge into the group of Mawooshen, who were then forced to defend themselves. He tells three canoes to remain; then, still standing in his own canoe, approaches the shallop. "I will board your large canoe and one of your men will take my place here." He points to his seat.

Skidwarres translates. The request surprises Gilbert. It seems impetuous but friendly. Was not Sabenoa risking his life? Gilbert quickly agrees. "Which of you boys wants to do something you can tell your grandchildren?" All the young soldiers' eyes focus on the bottom of the boat.

"I'll be your man, Admiral." The voice comes from the farmer, a man in his mid-thirties who'd proved himself hardworking and intelligent. Early in the ocean voyage he had raised concerns to Gilbert about the food supply. Popham took it for granted they could grow and harvest before winter and the natives would trade. "Admiral," the farmer had said the day they arrived, "this is a fine place for a fort, but a piss-poor place for a farm. Little is tillable. And not enough time to grow." Skidwarres had conveyed to Richard, who passed it on to Gilbert, that Sabenoa's villages were known for growing surpluses, or at least more so than the Mawooshen villages to the east.

As the canoe slides alongside, Sabenoa, a man probably in his early fifties, nimbly climbs aboard the shallop, while the farmer eases himself onto the empty canoe seat. Before saying a word to Skidwarres or Gilbert, Sabenoa shouts to his men. In response the braves snap to and begin feverishly paddling toward the shore.

All the English are taken aback, especially the farmer, who looks over his shoulder from his seat. He watches as the space between canoe and shallop grows.

Sabenoa plasters his face with a grin that looks especially diabolical, given the paint. "You see how quick are my men?" Skidwarres translates and then adds, "It is his way of playing a game. He expects to race you."

"Ah, tell him yes, he is quick, but we are more powerful. Tell him we will race him across the sea. Ask him which vessel travels farther and carries more? Which does more damage, the arrow or cannon shot?"

Sabenoa listens to the translation with a growing scowl. He looks at Gilbert, then laughs, this time with a higher, crazed pitch, and adds, "Those fat ugly ducks with the big sails. They are afloat only because we have not burned them, sunk them. Burned your escape from our land!" His grin reappears during the translation.

"Ah," Gilbert says again, "the Lord of the Sagadahoc has a sense of humor."

This revives Sabenoa's good nature after the translation.

"Row boys!" shouts Gilbert." But the distance between the two parties grows. Wind in the sails might have made a difference. Within minutes and from a few hundred yards, they watch the canoes being pulled onto a beach. Its occupants disappear into the undergrowth. The farmer, a brave at each elbow, looks back in dismay.

Gilbert doesn't know what to make of either Sabenoa's taunting or the farmer's possible abduction. In an effort to reverse the turn of events, he asks Skidwarres to ask Sabenoa about trade. "Ask him if he is aware of silver mines in his area. Ask him about beaver pelts and food. Will he trade food?"

The conversation between the two natives continues until the party reaches the mud and sand shoreline. The rowers jump out and haul the boat in close enough so the remaining occupants can jump to shallow water.

Gilbert presses, "Lord of the Sagadahoc, where have you gone with the Englishman?"

Skidwarres translates, "You should not worry. He will not be harmed. We follow. My people, most of them have not seen an English close up. I told my braves I would give them one."

To Gilbert, Skidwarres explains, "I don't think your farmer will be hurt."

Gilbert orders one soldier and the four armed rowers to remain and guard the shallop. "If they try to take it, use force. You men," he points to the five remaining soldiers, "bring your loaded weapons. And you too, Chaplain, bring a musket. You know how to use it?"

"I do."

"Skidwarres, take a weapon."

"Admiral, that I won't do. It is wrong for them to see me with an English weapon. It would bring more distrust."

"All right, I see that. Let's go. Sabenoa, lead us to your village."

Sabenoa adopts a slow pace and continues an intent conversation with Skidwarres at his side. Later Seymour and Gilbert learn the self-proclaimed lord was less interested in trade than in the construction at the mouth of his river. Never before had the whites planted themselves. He was well aware of their arrival. He had heard so from a small contingent of his people, the group that had abandoned their temporary summer camp when they saw the ship entering the harbor and the men disembarking. Sabenoa himself had gazed down on the English from one of the nearby bluffs. Would they be attacking? Since Nahanada appeared to be friendly, why was it the English didn't settle nearer his village? Would the English ally with Nahanada against him?

Skidwarres realizes this maverick sagamore has asked reasonable questions, regardless of their paranoid flavor. He tries to mollify: The English had no interest in forming alliances against Sabenoa. He also offers a warning, one made by Nahanada to other sagamores. Their numbers may be small, but I can tell you, across the seas live many more. They have boats, more than can be counted, and guns. These aliens can not be taken lightly.

Sabenoa listens without interruption. As they enter the village, he simply mutters, "These are my lands and river; they were my father's and my forefathers' before time began. But right now, Skidwarres, you have carried yourself well. Tell them I will trade."

In what is more or less the central area of the village, a group of men, women, and children stand in a circle, talking loudly. Laughter breaks out. The approaching English realize the farmer is standing in the middle, surrounded and naked, his hands covering his genitals. He calls out when he sees Gilbert and company, "Admiral, call these idiots off. Tell them to give me my clothes."

"Skidwarres," Gilbert looks astounded. "Tell this son of a whore to do the honorable thing."

In mid-translation Sabenoa calmly orders a brave to pick up the clothes and hand them back. "They are only curious. No harm done."

With his pants hauled up and his shirt unbuttoned, the red-faced farmer walks over to where Skidwarres, Gilbert, and Sabenoa stand. He spits on the ground two feet away. The gesture seems directed at all of them. "Fucking, ignorant savages! One of those older bitches—she actually came up and touched me—touched me! Next time, Admiral, you want a pawn, remind me." He buttons his shirt halfway and clears his throat to spit again, this time nearly hitting Sabenoa's moccasin. Then he storms off to stand next to the soldiers as Gilbert says, "My apologies. Let me consider how to make this right."

One of the soldiers leans over and suggests, "Tell him to give you that one over there for half an hour." He points to a native girl standing with thirty or so others, watching. The still mortified and outraged farmer utters under his breath, "Christ, no."

Another soldier offers up, "Then tell him I'll be a good soldier and step in for my fallen comrade." The farmer offers a sardonic chuckle, and the matter is dropped.

Gilbert tells the farmer, this time with two soldiers in accompaniment, to visit the village garden. Sabenoa orders a brave to fetch beaver pelts for Gilbert to inspect. To Gilbert they look scruffy. He makes no offer, leaving Sabenoa annoyed. "You come in the wrong season and then offend us?"

Gilbert realizes this is not the time to haggle. "My apologies."

Sabenoa remains irritated. "And what of this trading for food?" he snaps. "We feed ourselves, as does Nahanada. If you cannot feed yourself, you deserve to starve."

Gilbert listens to the translation, though he barely needs one, given the defiant tone. Six braves standing behind their sagamore with their blue spiked hair and bluish tattoos, plus the thirty or so others in the vicinity, reflect their leader's pugnacity.

Gilbert rises and prepares to leave before someone in either party makes things worse. "Lord of the Sagadahoc, I meant no offense. I am sure at a later time we can find reason to trade. I'm sure your hunters are skilled, your planters skilled. I thank you for your hospitality."

The words in translation have the desired mollifying effect. Sabenoa's face is expressive and constantly moving. To Richard, who has been listening and watching in silence, this face is a showcase, a fascinating mixture of real and feigned. He wishes to threaten, to woo, to placate.

Farmer and soldiers return. All are escorted back to the shallop. There they find a group of young braves armed only with sheaved knives taunting the four sailors and soldiers. Muskets in hand and anxious, they stand at the ready. Just as the rowers begin pushing the shallop further into the shallow water, one of the braves jumps in and snatches the fire box, throws it into the shallow water, and scrambles out to the gleeful whooping of his friends.

A soldier takes aim.

"Hold your fire," Gilbert shouts.

"Yes, sir."

Gilbert walks into the shin deep water and retrieves the doused box. "Skidwarres, tell that boy, good idea—and I might have killed him." While the English re-board the shallop, the braves try to make sense of Skidwarres' translation. At first they laugh out of semi-comprehension and then, after conferring with one another, let fly more insults.

With Gilbert at the tiller, the oarsmen begin pulling. "Good day, Lord of the Sagadahoc. Thank you for your hospitality and entertainment."

After the translation, the sagamore offers no words. In fact he appears to be contemplating. He stares, expressionless.

"When we're out of view, we'll figure where to make camp for tonight. Somewhere on the other side of the bay. This is good land here, is that right?" Gilbert asks the farmer.

"Yes, sir, those bastards have ample gardens, maize, squash, and the sea grasses here include some kind of rice they harvest. And many a duck, as you can see."

"Sir," gestures one rower, whose line of sight is toward shore.

All turn. On the shore the braves, twenty or so in a row, have reached under their front flaps and are waving their members at the English.

"Well," says Richard, after a few moments of taking in the scene, "I suppose that proves our boys and theirs speak some kind of universal nonsense. Maybe that's promising, Admiral."

They watch six braves launch three canoes. They appear to be heading after the shallop. Sabenoa, it must be him, though they are too far away to be sure, gestures for them to turn around.

Gilbert offers a big smile. The mood tumbles into giddiness and chuckling.

"What do you say, Skidwarres? What do you make of the Lord of the Sagadahoc?"

"Admiral, I think he is worried."

"And so he should be, that strange bird, for I covet his fair land."

From this point to their arrival back at the fort the following afternoon, the expedition becomes an outing. They shoot duck and catch bass for dinner, and quench their thirst with ale. Gilbert considers following the Androscoggin River but resolves otherwise after learning that falls made the river impassable after a few miles.

Beginning early the next morning, the journey back takes them through an intricate inland waterway of bays and estuaries, past seals sunning on rocks. All look up. Some hump themselves into the water and disappear, others bark and stare, still others return to their sleep. Eagles circling high above come and go. The outgoing tide offers a carefree ride in a cloudless day that feels much more like summer than fall. They glide by more high bluffs, are turned by small whirlpools, and then must row across a shallow bay, the Hockomock, studded with a few islands. Eventually the air cools from ocean breezes. By midday, with Skidwarres navigating, they again approach open ocean. They pass through a small gut to three-foot swells produced by the outgoing tide and the incoming rollers. They have played it perfectly. When the tide turns, they will have rowed and sailed to the mouth of the Aponeg River, Seguin in full view, the Sagadahoc just a short two hours to their west. The following tide will take them back.

CHAPTER 31

September 12, 1607, Fort St. George
Internal Discoveries

A native messenger arrives to announce that Nahanada would meet with Gilbert, and then together they would travel to the upper reaches of the Penobscot where Bessabez resided. Gilbert asks Seymour to join him, but Popham decides his presence at the fort is too valuable. The chaplain fills his days counseling the men and helping the illiterate and semi-literate write letters that the *Mary and John* would soon deliver to Plymouth. He mediates minor disputes and, when possible, assists Digby on the beginning stages of the construction of the *Virginia*, the name given to the pinnace. Seymour also continues tutoring the four boys, sometimes accompanied by Fletcher, Erasmus, and a stray or two. Finally, Popham, only recently moved to his newly constructed house in place of his cabin on the *Gift of God*, looks forward to Seymour's company. Gilbert, who demands so much of Popham's time, would be gone at least a week.

"I am a convivial man," he says to Seymour, as they converse and sip claret in front of a crude mud and stone fireplace. Popham and Gilbert are gentlemen. In every fashion possible, with the cutlery, the porcelain dishes, pewter mugs, and linen, they live with the transplanted trappings of their station.

"I suppose you've heard the scuttlebutt. The fact is, I'd like to talk to you about it, inasmuch as you're a priest."

"President Popham, you know I am not ordained."

"Ah, of course. No matter. I'm a tired man. In any case, call me George. I'm tired of the inane formalities and details every day. Not enough nails, not enough board feet of lumber, too many men complaining—

everything. I'm cooped up in here listening hour after hour and day after day. Give me the simple privateering days. Find a vulnerable ship, a Spanish, Dutch, or French galleon, and take her. Loot her. Give the Queen her cut. Some blood on your hands, maybe. So be it. That is the game. Here, it is all drudgery and future plans, a future—if it's more than a few years—I'll never see. While Gilbert, the admiral, flits about having a fine time, off here and there to whatever island or new river. Oh, Chaplain, I complain. Perhaps that is why I invited you. Do I need to confess? At least I have no shortage of reasons." He raises his glass.

Richard hears himself speaking in the measured, rather optimistic words of his position. "I, too, wonder of this grand venture. It is difficult to imagine where our day-to-day, our small steps might lead. I, too, may be dead before that is answered. But the possibilities? Such possibilities, I think you will admit."

"Seymour, do not I hear John Popham's voice in yours, from across the sea?"

The chaplain takes another sip. A warm, sad glow builds in his stomach and chest. If he walked out the door, could it not be into the Dorset night, sweet and soft, not sand, granite, mud, and pine.

"But I repeat. You have heard the scuttlebutt?"

"Sir?" Richard is aware of the drift.

"Damn, Chaplain. I don't want to confess. If sin leads to Hell, I will be at the head of the line. I simply want to talk about it. I haven't been able to talk to anybody. Gilbert has a dead ear for the heart, at least mine. When you get to my age, talking and remembering is the pleasure you get. Memories ferment, do they not? Bottled up for years and then you savor them, mix them with the present. But it is not long-term memory that excites me." He fills his glass and Richard's.

"I traded with Nahanada. For blankets, beads, brass ornamentation, linen—he bargains well, that educated savage. But I don't complain. I got to lie with his eldest wife, Nolka, she's called. Twice. Twice I met her and stayed the night in one of those bark huts. Quite sufficient, really. A fire in the middle, not unlike this one. I bring a blanket. She puts it over a woven mat, and under that the fresh spruce boughs. It smells cleaner than I can remember, and she is clean, too—and cooperative. Damn, Seymour, I didn't consider she might enjoy this arrangement. But I swear she does. I am a gentleman. She, on her part, is helpful and does not appear to resent that I am twenty years her senior, perhaps more. I am nearly sixty, you know. I give her respect and tenderness. She smiles and coos. Such camaraderie, I just didn't expect it."

Popham takes stock of the chaplain. "Seymour, you are offended?"

"No, sir, do I look it?"

"No, you look interested. Maybe even envious?" With that Popham gives a hearty laugh. Richard smiles. Popham, for all his beefy bravado, is good company.

"I have to confess—well not confess in a religious sense—but admit I expected a simple uncomplicated fuck. Instead I found myself lying with a real woman. You know, the light was low from the fire. Her skin was warm, her hair long. It comes down to her navel. She was a woman. A good one. A generous one. Instead of wanting to leave afterwards, I wanted to stay. So what do you think, Seymour?"

"You were correct. I am envious."

"Hah. Well you should be. And do you know what? I don't know if this is also scuttlebutt. That cannoneer, Fletcher? He joined me on the trip across. He rowed, and he somehow arranged his own tryst with a magnificent girl. I'll be damned if that row across didn't make me a quarter of a century younger. The two of us, young bucks rutting together."

Popham appears to have come to an end. He gets up, throws another stick on the coals. He sits and stares as the flames lick around the piece of wood and then begin to consume it.

Richard finds himself in his new position: the listener. The man essentially wants to be heard. But to say nothing? No. If he doesn't want dispensation, perhaps insight? It happens with the soldiers, the craftsmen, whoever comes to talk. They will say their piece and then look at you— expectant. Sometimes they just want recognition that you've heard, so he often attempts to state in his own words the gist of what he's heard, but with a twist. They want something reflected back, something reassuring or even insightful. Seymour has come to think of it as a second order of listening. How does one imagine another's existence and then say something that not only recognizes its reality, but adds to it? In these matters, Montaigne, sometimes Bacon, even the Bible come to mind.

"It appears to me, George, that you have made a discovery." Richard wants to say more, but decides not to.

"Hmm? What do you mean?"

"I'm not sure, but that is the tone of your story. You expected—well as you say, a fuck—but received something else."

"All right, Seymour? Yes, she was a good woman—and a good fuck— and what else?"

"Perhaps 'discovery' is the wrong word."

"No, damn it, it's the word I used. What do you think I discovered?"

"What do you think?"

"No, goddam it, you're here to tell me, not ask me questions." He hears his own pugnacity and apologizes. "I sound too harsh. I make too many demands, full of demands from morning to night."

"All right, then, so let me take a stab. Let me guess that the discovery is that she is extremely human, and at a level beyond your reasoning. We know Skidwarres and Nahanada are human. But until you lay with this savage, or maybe it was her kindness or her smell, I don't know, but not until then did you realize we are faced with a human new world." This interpretation of Popham's lusting comes more glibly than expected. Richard thinks he's consumed too much claret.

Popham pulls himself up, throws in another stick, lowers himself slowly, and groans. "Not a bad sermon, Chaplain. Not bad. Maybe more your thinking than mine, but not bad. But what do you make of trading your wife—well one of your wives—for two blankets, ten beads, and a brass kettle?"

"I have enough trouble imagining one wife, and the one I have in mind I wouldn't trade for gold."

"Nonsense, it's just a matter of how much gold. Anyway, anyway..."

"Sir, I have to say there is much I don't understand about the Mawooshen. But then, there is much I don't understand about the English."

Popham coughs and spits into the fire. "To be honest, my friend, I should be back in a soft bed and tended to by my disagreeable wife and overseeing my modest estate. Instead, well, to be honest, I sweat too much. My hearts pounds and I'm short of breath. I am here because Sir John is a force to be reckoned with. Since his childhood, he has gotten what he wants. I sit here managing this muddy mess because essentially I do what I'm told." He tosses the last of his claret into a wide open mouth. "Come talk to me again. It has done me good. Now, though, my aged bones must get their sleep."

"Thank you, sir. I shall take my leave. The gift of sleep, it is what we all receive most nights. You know of the playwright, Shakespeare? I have been teaching the boys *Midsummer Night's Dream*. I met him at Middle Temple, Shakespeare. In it he mentions dreams. He writes, 'I have an exposition of sleep come upon me.' That's what I look forward to, 'an exposition past my wit.' Those are his other words. So, President Popham—George—sleep deeply and dream well."

"Deep sleep? Rarely. Uncanny dreams, every night."

CHAPTER 32

September 20, 1607, Mouth of the Aponeg River
Encounter at Sea

Whales tend to stay offshore on their migration between the Arctic and southern waters. Occasionally, though, they follow food within sight of land or even into the broad mouth of the Aponeg. When they spot one, the younger braves might take to their larger sea canoes or dugouts and make for a kill. Whale is not a major source of food or material, but they offer an exciting, dangerous hunt, undertaken as much for daring as for meat and oil.

Early fall of 1607 brings an unusual number of sightings. Woboz and four other braves had, in August, prepared a canoe with harpoons, extra-powerful bows, and large knives. On this September morning, an excited ten-year-old boy runs into the village. He'd been standing on shore watching. And then not too far away, less than a mile, a whale breached and spouted. The braves, all between the ages of seventeen and twenty-five, run to the beach, launch their armed sea canoe, and paddle wildly.

They follow in the directions given by the boy. Two miles out into open sea, a whale finally breaches. This time they get close enough to paddle through its oily slick just after it dives. Again, fifty yards off, it surfaces and raises its head high enough to see the oncoming canoe. Again it dives, leaving its tail momentarily visible and waving back and forth, almost as if to taunt the braves. Woboz in the bow throws his harpoon way off the mark. They wait for a resurfacing. And wait longer until, "There!" the youngest shouts and points a hundred yards off. "Quietly," instructs Woboz. When they arrive at the spot, only the oily surface remains.

Fletcher awakes on the same warm day feeling lucky. President Popham has tried to find ways to keep his men happy. This is the way he'd captained his privateers: extra rum for extra work, time off when earned and possible, a chance for the men to vary their assignments, thereby relieving the inevitable monotony of ship's life. Over the years Popham had gained a reputation as a genial scalawag and a fair captain.

From the outset, catching, drying, and salting fish was an essential activity. Fish would be the primary source of nourishment. Now, three weeks after their arrival, it became a top priority. Every day one or two longboats headed upriver for bass and sturgeon or out into the gulf for cod. Since most days continued to be warm and clear, many men relished the job. A few of the sailors became regulars. They were experienced fishermen, but Popham made sure others—soldiers, craftsmen, cooks, lumberman, all who wanted to throw over hand lines and spend a day at sea—would get their chance. Today was Fletcher's day.

One of the experienced fishermen had found good luck over a ledge, a two-hour row or sail from the fort, depending on the wind, out past Seguin and the mouth of the Aponeg. It meant leaving with the sunrise and returning as it set, or even later. They were far enough offshore so that it took awhile before sea gulls caught wind and grouped overhead, kiting in the breeze, squawking, screeching, then diving and grabbing a morsel, flapping their wings once they'd settled in the water. They seemed to act as much out of pride as dominance. Finished, they'd bob and wait, opportunists all.

Fletcher considered himself the luckiest man at the fort. He, and only he—if one discounted Popham—had a love at hand. Twice he'd rowed the aging but apparently randy president to meet Nahanada's wife, Nolka. He and the president. He and Sipsis. He marveled that this beautiful, vivacious native girl agreed to lie with him, a poorly educated nobody. Not since his wife, dead now so many years, had he felt such peace. These thoughts came to him as he fished in the hot morning sun. He'd throw over the many-hooked line and wait, but it was not long before he felt the tugs. During those quiet moments he thought of her. His nose touching hers, rubbing the tips and then more vigorously sweeping back and forth, nose kissing. He thought of his nose exploring her breast or buried in her stomach until she giggled; and he thought of the heat on his back and the lolling about, the drift with no conversation, and then noisy camaraderie when they hauled in the flopping, ugly cod.

Near noon, the fishing English notice a canoe coming into view. The men have little reason to be anxious. The festivities at the fort a few weeks before, and especially Sipsis, have given Fletcher a sense of equanimity. The New World feels like her. Neither he, nor the sailor at the tiller, nor the other three are worried. They look over their shoulders, return to their work, then check again.

They can now see five braves. Two small insignificant vessels, land a few miles off, a thin line between sea and sky. Fletcher knows how ships making an ocean passage often stop to gather information. The vacancy of the ocean makes friends out of strangers, even adversaries.

Within fifty yards the strenuous paddling stops. The brave in the bow stands. At this Fletcher feels a stirring of fear. He's heard about the natives' unpredictability. Was the tightening his chest based on ignorance? Except for knives, how could they defend themselves? All stop fishing. Fletcher wraps his line around the seat so he won't lose it. The seaman at the tiller shades his eyes with his hands. He has to look directly into the sun and sparkling water. Have they chosen this course intentionally? Fletcher stands and stares, half-blinded.

They watch as the braves paddle cautiously, narrowing the gap to within thirty yards. Again they cease paddling. "All right lads, says the older seaman at the tiller, "let's see what they want. I'm not sure." His calm voice allows all aboard a faint exhale, a release of tension. The afternoon wind begins throwing up chop. The longboat, weighted down by its catch, rocks. Most of the gulls have lifted off the water and are circling high above.

Standing in the bow, Woboz utters a high-pitched scream. He's noticed Fletcher. With a one-syllable bark, an order, the four paddles dig deeply into the water. It becomes obvious to all the English that this is an attack. The braves are skilled paddlers and on the heels of whaling frustration. Woboz picks up the harpoon, cocks it back over his shoulder and, jettisons it toward Fletcher's chest. The swift throw lands low. Fletcher looks down to see the wooden shaft just below his navel. He becomes aware the object has just inflicted a mortal wound before he feels the searing pain, before he topples over backward, over his seat and onto the fish, some of which are taking their last shallow breaths. He looks up at the cumulous clouds building high above. His vision narrows. He hears screams, some in English, others otherworldly. He isn't aware Woboz has jumped aboard and slit his throat. The pain subsides. His eyes close. *I am dying*, he thinks again. His parents appear. He runs toward them with his arms outstretched. He runs past them, or rather they disappear. He keeps running. He slows. The ground falls away, his arms still reaching, the shadowy figure of his wife far away, and then everything disappears.

In the first few seconds of astonishment, the four English watch Fletcher impaled and fallen. The large canoe bumps alongside. With knives in hand, three braves follow Woboz into the longboat, nearly capsizing the canoe. The sun-blinded English are too stunned to defend themselves. The braves fall on them, grab their hair and pull their heads back, exposing the vulnerable jugular. Two barely struggle before it is over. One fisherman manages to brandish his knife and swipes a gash in his murderer's thigh. The older seaman at the tiller holds a shaking fishing knife out in front of him, as he watches this last rower struck in the stomach and then swiped across the throat with such ease and rapidity, it is almost beautiful. He'd seen knife fights on ships and the streets of Plymouth, but never actually fought in one himself. While the four slain men gurgle and gush blood, their attackers stand facing the man at the tiller. It is only a brief standoff. The remaining brave in the canoe releases an arrow, a large one intended for a whale. It finds its mark. Wide-eyed and with only a slight grunt, the seaman falls off the stern, propelled by the arrow sticking out of his bare chest.

The braves in the boat raise their stained knives and whoop in triumph. When they first set out toward the English, they were not sure what action they might take. The four young men venerate Woboz. They believe his stories about English stealing hundreds of pelts from a village on the Penobscot. The English soldiers all fornicated with each other and the strange four-legged beasts they brought along. They ate children. Obviously they abducted men, cheated on their trade. Their fort of stone and wood was a stain on the native countryside. Its very existence was a hostile act. Nahanada, who had traded his wife for blankets; Skidwarres, who had that Englishman as a friend—they were not to be trusted. They told lies.

Disappointed by their failure at whaling, perhaps they could at least intimidate the vulnerable English. As they approached, Woboz recognized Fletcher. He remembered this man and Sipsis, eating, drinking together, walking on the beach, touching, lying together. He had heard the rumor she now fornicated with him. "Kill them," he had said under his breath, "attack." After the harpoon pierced Fletcher, they did not need to be told what to do. They had never killed before, not in the two skirmishes against other villages. Over the past weeks they'd talked of taking action. Negotiations, eating, and dancing with the English was for cowards, for women. But once they sprang into action, every muscle, every section of the mind had its purpose.

Now though, with no life left in the heap of men and fish, Woboz and his followers hesitate.

Chols, the next oldest brave cautiously speaks, "This will bring us trouble."

"Yes, who else dares to fight? They will say that. No?" is Woboz' reply.

"What do we do now?" Chols continues, his body still quivering.

Another speaks, "Nahanada will be very angry. He will say the English will come and kill us with their guns, big and little. Will we not be punished?"

"No," answers Woboz, "No one will know. We will throw them in the water and destroy the boat."

"Will they not wash ashore?" asks Chols.

Woboz' answers come quickly. He knows a leader must think clearly and quickly. "We will cut them out like deer. Then they will sink. And the sharks will help us. We are far out. We will leave the boat on that island, in the woods. It is a useless small island. Nobody goes there. Later, when we are ready, we will tell and show them."

The other braves look at one another. Their eyes suggest approval or at least a course of action in a desperate situation.

"Woboz, I have never dressed out a man," Chols protests.

"Then this will be your first, and you may hope not your last. Take the man you killed and finish him. Throw out the fish. They are soiled with the white ghost's blood. Do it. I will show you how."

Standing in human blood and fish slime, Woboz takes one step, slips, regains his balance, and bends on one knee over Fletcher. His knife rips open the shirt, revealing a tanned chest. He reverses direction. He rams the knife under the top of the pants and yanks upwards and pushes down tearing one entire trouser leg. Woboz looks down at his dead adversary's exposed genitals. With one hand he grabs Fletcher's penis and testicles and with the other slices them off. His four young followers stare in amazement. Briefly he holds his prize aloft, and pronounces, "One less English *askoks*" (penis), and throws the handful at the seagulls who've settled on the water not far off, apparently sensing opportunity. As the body parts hit the water, three lift and dive for the morsel. The knife point next enters just above the groin. Woboz pulls up his shirt, up to the rib cage. In a frenzy he gouges the man's insides and scoops out mangled internal organs, dumping them overboard. This was not a man. He was a beast. No different from a deer or a large fish. This he screams at the others. "Do what I do—now! Do it. Clean out these *adias*" (dogs).

They do as he demands, but more hesitantly. One young brave, having opened up his victim, falls to the boat's gunwale and vomits overboard.

Nonetheless, within minutes the English have been disemboweled, their slimy innards pulled, hoisted, and dropped into the water. Yards and yards of intestines float momentarily around the boat, then begin sinking. The fifth brave, still in the canoe, his hands clean, looks at his bare-skinned companions, covered in blood and bits of flesh. They have turned feverish with primal fear, disgust, and blood lust. He watches while his friends howl like the village's domesticated wolf-dogs. The fish arrive and nibble around the edges of the offal. More gulls with their mean yellow eyes and tainted blood-like red tips on their beaks arrive, screeching their scavenger chant. Soon, no doubt, the sharks would come. Woboz pulls the harpoon from the remaining sinew and jumps back into the canoe. "I will find the other with the arrow in him."

When he returns fifteen minutes later, the men have emptied the boat of fish and human body parts—the body of the fifth Englishman, missing. One of the dead men's shirts becomes a bandage for the native's gashed thigh. The four filthy, slimy braves are ordered to row, an activity they'd never attempted. It takes awhile before they reach the pebble beach of the small wooded island and drag the heavy boat into the brush. The exhausted and traumatized young men wade into the icy water and do their best to clean body and mind. A whaling hunt might take two or three days. It was not unusual for men to sleep in their canoes or take refuge on an outer island. They would remain here and consider the consequences of their acts. They would build a fire on the back side of the island where it would not be seen from the mainland, and they would drink from deer bladders and sleep. None eats either the berries or the dried fish from their leather pouches. And finally when sleep comes, it is irregular and disquieting.

Woboz wakes before dawn. The coals have lost most of their heat. He is sure the seaman with the arrow in him has washed ashore. Half-asleep, he hears the English crawling up the beach for revenge. Woboz gets up with knife in hand. In the early dawn light, he cautiously investigates the beach. He finds in the gentle wash a small log bumping up against the pebbles.

CHAPTER 33

September 25, 1607, Fort St. George
Letter to Margaret

After an early morning of reading and lute practice, Seymour reads the second act of Midsummer Night's Dream to the boys, as he'd been doing for the past week. He helps two soldiers write letters, and adds to his own many-paged correspondence to Margaret. His afternoon routine—though often interrupted by Gilbert or Popham or by needy soldiers—takes him to the fifty-foot pinnace, Virginia. After three weeks, two ribs stick up from her keel like the skeleton of a beached leviathan.

In the dwindling light after dinner, Richard, Lance, and Stow walk the beach where it follows the Sagadahoc's contour past the mouth and west, the same walk taken by Fletcher and Sipsis weeks ago. Stow darts about, ears cocked, eager for anything new, while visually maintaining contact with Lance and Richard. On their way back, they might follow an ancient native trail through woods and up the hill behind the fort, where the view offers miles of coastline. Or they might simply turn around and return the way they came.

The fort still teems with activity: twenty future masts, tall pine trees, straight and true, limbed and barked and lashed together before being floated downriver with an outgoing tide. They rest next to the *Mary and John*, waiting to be hoisted with block and tackle onto the deck for its upcoming return to Plymouth. These are prizes for His Majesty's growing Royal Navy, trees not easily found in England.

As yet they have no gold or silver and only a small number of beaver pelts. It was not the season. Surely, the backers in England would understand; the colonists so little time, especially given that construction was the first priority. Optimism still holds sway. A superb sketch of the fort, drawn by draftsman, John Hunt, would be sent home. It showed in detail over twenty-five buildings now in various stages of construction, some still imagined.

On the walk Richard feels closer to Margaret, now that he knows she will receive word of him within two months.

"Dearest Margaret,

"Yet again I write. When yesterday I sat on a hill overlooking the ocean, I imagined my sight—that is, some particles of energy, whatever sight must be—could carry over the curvature of the earth and continue to you. I honed this invisible force, my energy, into your endearing green eyes. How I long to look into them. These thoughts and so many others bring me close to you. All those miles are for naught. I am by your side. I feel your warmth—and not incidentally take in your scent that lingers still on your gift and is kept in my trunk, dry and safe. Is it not so that I am as close to you here in the New World as I would be if I were in my father's study and you only a few hours ride away? What is the difference? In both cases, do I not imagine you next to me?

"As I've told you, I am reading Shakespeare's *Midsummer Night's Dream*, as I did for you last spring. But now as I write, I feel so much the opposite of my sentiments just offered. I am fickle. Was it not a millennium ago when we sat on the couch reading and warming our shoeless feet at the fire? How love knocks one about in its shifting breezes! Here summer hangs on by the skin of its teeth. Skidwarres tells me it will be very cold. 'England,' he says, 'doesn't know what cold is.'

"Ah, Margaret, my dear, I hope you read my offering here, knowing each day I think of you as I rise in the morning and then when I lay myself on the hard board bed at night. And in my dreams you appear in guises. Last night...but should I tell you? I've told you about the tiny river that flows in and out with the tides. Incoming it is icy cold. Then after basking on the shallows, it exits warmer with the outgoing tide. In my dream I am standing, watching where the river flows through a cut in the beach and into the ocean. There I see you floating past me. You are on your back. Yes, you are naked. You smile, contented. And I don't know what to do. You pass by. You smile at me, still floating, as if you don't want to be bothered. Past me you drift. I expect you to stand and join me, but you don't. You keep going with the tide, further and further, smaller and smaller. You make no effort to swim. It is then I awake, and I am—I am bereft.

"I'm sorry. Perhaps that sounds too morbid. But that is not what I think. I don't know what I think. I simply make this nocturnal offering. Bereft is not morbid. I suppose I worry about you slipping away, that you have found someone nearer by.

"What more do I have to convey? With this comes more than fifty pages of what is more journal than letter. Please know when you read about the crossing, about Lance and Stow and Fletcher—Fletcher, by the way, and a fishing party did not return. We assume at this point that he and the others were lost at sea, terrible. When you read about the storm, Gilbert, President Popham, the ludicrous Eucharist, my journey up the Sagadahoc, about the glorious land, about daily work—please know all is written for your eyes. I wrote it for you. If fate allows these pages to be held by you, then I am at least partially fulfilled. To touch—does not one have to be touched to be known?—that will come.

"Your loving Richard"

CHAPTER 34

October 8, 1607, Fort St. George
A Walk on the Beach

Late September holds onto summer, even as the hundreds of sumac bushes that grew back from the beach turn from orange to regal purple, and the maple's incandescent bright yellow fade. The view up the Sagadahoc turns from its summer monochrome green to multicolored, as if everything is in bloom rather than dying. The oak is burnished oily bronze, then turns a somber faded brown and stubbornly holds on while most other leaves have begun their letting go.

The *Mary and John* sets sail on a pewter ocean, under a tarnished silver sky with little distinction between heaven and earth at the horizon. It is early morning. Richard, Lance, and Stow watch from the beach, as the chilly northwestern breeze takes her into the vast gloom, then to be swallowed by mist. "You can almost drink it," Lance says, and to prove it sticks out his tongue.

"Better put that back in your face," Richard warns. "That osprey winging up there might consider it a tasty morsel."

"Richard, you think me an idiot? Can we just walk? You've heard? I mean about Stow biting that shit last evening."

"I heard at breakfast. That is why I asked you to walk with me."

"Yes, I thought so. That fuck finally tried to grab me—while I was carrying firewood, came up behind me, but Stow—he's always had his eye out for him. Stow was on him like lightning. Went right through his shirt. I saw the blood. He cursed and tried to kick Stow, so he bit him in the thigh. More blood."

"And you? Nothing happened to you?"

"Yes, I laughed. I told Stow 'that'll do.' Hawkes held his thigh, cursed, and I just walked off."

"Do you want me to speak to President Popham? I think I should."

"So what will happen?"

"I'm not sure. A whipping probably, or a few days in the stocks."

"Richard, he's a mean bastard. They should have put him on the *Mary and John*. Be done with him."

"That's true, but he's also a hell of a worker."

"I know. He's got the body and brain of an ox."

"I'd speak to Hawkes myself, but he's beyond reason. He needs to be acted upon. It's his language. I will speak to Popham, if he hasn't already gotten word."

As they walk further down the beach, the conversation shifts to the machinations of the fort. For some days the disappearance of the five fishermen has dominated conversations. At the chapel President Popham offered officially, "We have no basis to conclude foul play. We must assume at this point they were simply lost at sea. We have sent out two longboats for two days and found nothing. When I next contact Nahanada's people, I will, of course, make inquires. As of now, we have heard nothing." The chaplain offered a simple prayer. But the lack of closure only fostered rumors, nearly all of which were based on ignorance and fear of the "savages."

Gilbert returned from his trip to meet Bessabez on the Penobscot. The meeting with Nahanada at the mouth of the Penobscot never transpired. After a day of waiting, the shallop ventured upriver a day and then returned without seeing any sign of human life. This snub or miscommunication left Gilbert edgy and annoyed by the waste of time. Had either Nahanada or Bessabez changed his mind? When Raleigh Gilbert queried Seymour, the chaplain had no answer except to say that decisions made by the elders could change. Most villages were not governed by a dictatorial ruler, and even if they had been, opinions among the villagers could be quixotic. As with the councilors to kings and queens, native elders were known to hold contrary views.

The presence of Englishmen, Richard had no doubt, caused some friction. Nor was there unity between villages. The fur trading over the past decades had reduced the beaver populations and strained territorial agreements between groups, adding to the perennial spats based on long-standing family quarrels and jealousies. Skirmishes occurred. Also a perpetual animosity between the Mawooshen and the tribes to the east, the Micmac, periodically erupted. The most serious warfare had occurred only a month before the English landed, though in this case the hostilities by the Micmac were directed toward the villages on the Sakohki River, fifty miles to the southwest. A large war party, armed with French and Spanish musketry, had paddled in canoes and sailed in European shallops, two hundred miles. There the Sakohkian were surprised and overpowered. Many died. It was the first such raid with firearms in the northeast.

Seymour reminded Gilbert of the obvious: they had not wandered into the wilderness. The land between the Sagadahoc and Penobscot, the land of the Mawooshen, had been occupied for hundreds of years in scores of villages by thousands of inhabitants. Other groups occupied the land west and south of the Sagadahoc. These groups, as with Sabenoa's people, existed on agriculture as well as hunting and gathering. Just as Skidwarres had learned of the English and their ways, Seymour has learned bits and pieces of an old and probably extensive civilization. "I have no idea why Gilbert didn't find Nahanada, nor do I know if the fishermen might have been captured—or killed." After thinking he wished to hold out for more hope in Lance's presence, Richard adds, "But I doubt it."

Fletcher's disappearance had touched a hollow fear in Lance. Here was yet another adult protector, this time not turned evil, but vanished.

"Best we turn around," Richard finally says as they near the tidal river. "They'll be looking for you."

When Lance and Richard reverse course, they notice Stow has wandered into the shallow surf so that he nearly floats. A small wave curls and breaks over his ears, then lifts and drops him, before it spreads over the sand. He is attending to something floating, half-submerged.

"Stow, come," Lance calls. "That'll do." Stow looks up in recognition, shakes the water off his head and returns to the object, this time grabbing and pulling. Another larger wave breaks over Stow, submerging him; but he comes to the surface, still attached to the object.

"Damn," says Richard. "Stay here. Let me look." He trots thirty yards or so into the salty broth and confirms his fear. The grotesque remains of a seaman, an empty abdomen, with only one arm and a nearly severed head, rest on the sand, face up and blanketed in water. Most of the flesh has been nibbled away. Two lobsters are living in his near empty stomach cavity. Cheekbones protrude below hollow eyeball sockets. His long brown hair swirls about like seaweed. The skin under it remains unscathed, except for a large pink crab that clings to the crown, looking like a small absurd hat one might wear at a costume ball.

"Enough," Richard tells Stow, who lets go and backs off, then barks, still intent and curious over his find.

Lance comes closer. "Lance, don't look," Richard warns, but it is too late. They both stare at something both human and not. This disconnect provides some objectivity. Something is in the rib cage. Richard bends down, lifts. He looks at a section of arrow shaft, four inches, with a flint tip, the feathered ends broken off.

"It's not Fletcher, is it Richard?"

"No, I think it's Mason, the sailor."

Richard and Lance back up and stand on dry beach. Stow retreats to their side and stares at the object meandering this way and that with the capricious tide.

"Richard?" Lance finally asks. "He was killed by the savages?"

"Yes, that's what it looks like."

Stow sits and waits.

"Richard, what do we do?"

"That's what I'm wondering. If we report this, we have possible outrage and revenge on our hands. If we don't, we keep important information from Popham and Gilbert, who ought to know. Keeping secrets is a form of power. I'm not sure what to do."

"Don't we have to do something?"

"A fine question. We always have to do something, even if it is to do nothing." Richard's mind is racing. He turns and looks up toward the beach grass in the distance. He takes a few steps in that direction and turns again. "So here's what I'm going to do. I'm going to drag this carcass up over the beach and into the grass. I don't want anybody finding him. Not until I know what to do."

"I'll help you."

"Good, but I don't think he's...it's heavy. Lance, I'll grab under the arm. You grab the hair. We'll go slowly." The grey half-eaten arm is rubbery and nearly frozen. Richard's hands jump back reflexively on first touch. Before handling the body again, Richard grabs the lobsters and throws them as far as he can back into the water. The crab, having sensed human presence, lets go, drops into the shallows, and scuttles seaward.

"I'm never going to eat one of those again," Lance offers up.

"All right, I can do this," Richard says to himself out loud. But he needs both hands. He will walk backward and drag. Lance will hold up the head. Otherwise Richard is sure it will separate from the skeletal shoulders. Huddled together they drag it for over fifty yards to the three-foot-high grasses.

"I'll come back and bury him and hope some animal doesn't find him first."

As Richard drops the body, his instructions to Lance come too late. The remains flop to the ground, leaving Lance holding the hair and head. In horror he drops it. The head rolls almost into place, but impossibly askew. Lance turns and bends over. His stomach heaves. He groans, but nothing comes up.

Richard averts his eyes and backs off. "We need to leave—now. Don't look back."

Without willing it, the two jog away, allowing distance to lessen their repugnance. Stow enthusiastically runs ahead, doubles back, and runs ahead again.

When they arrive where the beach turns a right angle north at the river's entrance, they finally slow to a walk. "Lance, of course you know you must not tell a soul. I know I will have to confer with Popham and Gilbert, but I also need time to think. You must not say a word, understand? I will speak to them about your tangle with Hawkes, but not a word about this."

"Yes."

"Good, I know I can trust you, but I also know how difficult it will be to not talk of this."

"Don't worry, I won't."

"All right, you'd better get to work. Just tell your foreman you've been with me. If that's a problem, have him talk to me."

It was not unusual to see the chaplain with a shovel, so no one questioned Richard. The hour it took him to bury the remains allowed him time to think. His first impulse—that he must share the information with the two leaders—still made sense. But should he not first confer with Skidwarres? He might then have more information to offer. Was he not, as implied by Sir John, an ambassador? Though perhaps when the Chief Justice said as much, it was mostly flattery and seduction. The botched meeting with Nahanada had soured Gilbert. His tone had become more bellicose since his return from the Penobscot. He'd instructed the cannoneer unit to fire one shot each morning and evening. "Remember, he'd told them, this is a damn fort, not a monastery." The message was clear. Five villages within earshot and probably Sabenoa's miles upriver would be reminded of English power. On foggy days, even Nahanada's village might awaken to a muffled thump. Popham and Gilbert's dislike for one another grew. "Goddamn it, Popham," Richard heard during a meeting of the principals, "power doesn't come from force. How many soldiers do we have here? Sixty at best. If they wanted to overrun us, they could. Power comes from fear. You know that as well as I."

Gilbert's adamancy often won over the other council members.

CHAPTER 35

October 15, 1607, Fort St. George
Family

D ay by day the heavens squeeze out the extended summer light and warmth. On the path leading up the hill behind and above the fort, the maple leaves layer a soggy carpet of moribund yellows, orange, and reds. Through the remaining denuded trees, Richard looks down from the nearly-roofed chapel onto the scattering of buildings, a village—a strange one for sure, but a village—a marvel, really. In approximately two months, a completed storehouse, as well as Gilbert and Popham's smaller houses. The kitchen, the munitions house, the cooper's house, the forge, the bake house, the iron smith's house, and the court of the guardhouse in the middle of the fort—much of it crude and unadorned, but still a marvel.

The intensity of the work continues while the sun weakens. In addition to construction, men cut firewood and lumber, hunt, fish, march, send out patrols, cook, clean, forge nails and musket balls, and fortify with stone, mud, and wood. The overall population of Fort St. George was reduced to ninety after the sailing of the *Mary and John*. Included in those who left were Sergeant Robert Davies, who captained the ship; John Hunt, the draftsman; the surgeon, Turner; the furrier; Carew, the inspector of mines; as well as seamen and a few soldiers.

Dwindling food supplies have become the central concern of Popham and Gilbert. Trade with the natives for corn, nuts, dried berries, fish, rabbit, and venison has amounted to little. Gilbert's requests both to Nahanada and to other villages were met with vagueness or outright ridicule. Though food is always a subject of rumor, few men are aware of a possible long-term crisis.

The mood remains positive for most. Increased leisure time comes with earlier dark and later sunrise, allowing more time for sleep and brewing beer. Even conversation about the vanished fishermen dwindles. Many of the men know of death through the vagaries of misfortune. Seamen and soldiers tend to be fatalists. Furthermore, the existence of a native population is easy to forget. Weeks pass without a visit or sighting. To Seymour's relief no other remains appear, and Lance keeps their secret. When sun sets, with dinner completed, the men return to their huts, talk in small groups, play cards, and drink draft after draft of ale, only to arise hours later from sleep to piss in pots or stumble in the dark and chill to the privies.

Gilbert and Seymour have yet to get acquainted beyond their trip upriver and running across one another during the frenzy of development, as well as the occasional suppers held for the members of the council in Gilbert's house. The second-in-command spends many days and nights exploring the coast. To the south he finds sassafras, as hoped. He's made contact with villages on the Aponeg and arranged with a remaining English fishing vessel to drop off cod before they return to England. And when not attempting to establish trading partners with the elusive sagamores, he throws himself into fortification work and joins hunting parties. His exuberance impresses Seymour, as well as everyone else.

That evening Gilbert asks Richard if he'd join him after dinner. "We have much to talk about, Cousin," was how he had phrased the invitation. The familial tone sometimes used by Gilbert appears ambiguous to Richard. On the one hand, it suggests the two share a common lineage. But it sometimes comes with a mocking ring, as if to say "this could hardly be." Richard wonders if Gilbert doubts his masculinity, what with his lute playing, reading, and teaching. His new identity has stripped him of horseback riding, his favorite form of male exercise. Or does he question his loyalty, given Richard's ties to Skidwarres?

"Why of course." Richard welcomes the invitation. He is more than curious about this "cousin" who teems with confidence.

Gilbert resides in a post and beam house, the third largest structure after the storehouse and the chapel. It contains three rooms, with a fire pit and chimney at one end. It is the preferred meeting place because of its size and warmth. He had persuaded Popham that the arrangement made sense. Meetings would not disturb the president. Popham could have his privacy in his smaller residence. Besides, this difference reinforced Gilbert's higher social status. George Popham, the brother of a chief justice, an ex-privateer, and administrator of the Port of Bridgewater, was gentry, but not of Gilbert's more noble blood.

Gilbert greets Richard profusely, his two Mastiffs, Dumb and Dumber, at his side. They move to the section where the fire blazes, overheating the room. Gilbert immediately sticks a glass of Bordeaux in Richard's hand and pours himself another. His face is flushed, his smile slightly too eager. "Sit, sit, Cousin," comes with a tiny slur. He's a bit rushed. "How goes it with you? I am anxious to know of your impressions. In your position, you learn much from conversations, no? You seem, I must say, both with us and above us, up there in the chapel. Reading, teaching, conferring with your friend, Skidwarres." The emphasis on "friend" suggests the friendship might be illicit. Seymour sips his wine and listens. Gilbert's rapid-fire greeting and excellent wine do, in fact, put him at ease. Behind the volubility, Richard believes the admiral genuinely wants his company.

Gilbert points to a piece of paper on a table in front of the fire pit. "You see, I have something I want to show you. It's about our families. I am related to you through the Champernownes. I believe that is correct. You see this circle I've drawn. I have a circle for you, the Seymours. It intersects the Champernowne family, but what is more interesting, so does the Popham family intersect with the Champernownes, as does my family, the Gilberts, and beyond that the Raleighs, Uncle Walter's family, and even Gorges' family. Is this not interesting? Here we are across the sea in a wilderness of savages and you, I, Popham, and even Gorges, we are all related. Even Uncle Raleigh. Maybe even Robert Davies and James Davis."

Gilbert is pleased with himself and empties his glass.

"It is indeed. Maria Champernowne is my great-grandmother," Richard says.

"Mine as well. So what does that make us, second cousins, no?"

"That is so."

"And it gets even thicker: Carew is related to the Raleighs. You remember Carew, the disappointed mine inspector who sailed home believing he'd been duped?

"And as I understand you were named for him, Sir Walter Raleigh?"

"You are entirely correct. My father, the famous seafarer and explorer, was his half-brother. They were very devoted to one another."

Gilbert continues as if he had prepared his conversation. "You might say one big happy extended family, all of us connected to the Champernownes. But then that would be a lie. As you are well aware,

I'm sure, it was that weasel John Popham who presided over Raleigh's trumped-up trial for treason. It was Popham who condemned him to be drawn and quartered. That old bastard, the well-known hanging judge— and now his wreck of a cousin presides here over Sir John's affairs. But I'll get to that later. First, let me introduce you to someone." Gilbert pulls himself up, pours wine into the two empty glasses, takes another half-full one off a shelf, and pours from it. He then goes to the inner door, opens it, and disappears for few moments.

He reappears, hand in hand with Sipsis, Fletcher's lover. She wears a man's silk robe with the sleeves turned way up. It is wrapped around her petite body and drags on the floor. She clasps it together in the front with one hand and off the floor with the other.

"You have met?"

"We have not." Richard rises from his chair and offers a courteous bow. Sipsis curtsies.

"My god, man, isn't she marvelous? And damn smart! I've taught her a few words and some of our customs. Her grandfather was French. You see it, don't you?" I managed through Popham, and with Nahanada's assistance, to sneak her in here. I suppose for that I should be thankful to the old man. I've kept her out of sight and myself next to her as much as possible. I just had to share this incredible find with someone, and you came to mind—a family member, someone who knows how to keep a secret. And, my pretty bird, can you say hello to our guest?"

"Hello, Chaplain Seymour." She does not lower her eyes as many native women do.

"I taught her to say that. Not only is she smart, she's well I'm not sure what the word is? Uninhibited? Or perhaps exuberant? And she is a beauty."

Gilbert reaches for the third glass of wine and puts it into Sipsis' hand. She immediately tips it up and swallows half the glass. Gilbert, still standing in front of her, unties and unwinds the sash. He opens the robe, tucking the upper portion behind her shoulders so to expose her fully. She is naked. He steps to her side allowing Seymour to see. "Have you ever seen anything as beautiful? A European-native mix. Can't be many."

Richard's eyes cannot help but take her in from the delicate light brown legs, up over her black wispy patch, past full breasts, to her grey-green eyes that catch his. She smiles and apparently is not embarrassed.

"I don't blame you, man, stare. A feast for you, as she has been for me. In fact, as I hear it, in the savages' culture, a woman may be offered to a guest. I have asked my sweet here if she would be so kind to you. So she is yours, if you wish—Chaplain. You are a man, as well as a man of God, no?"

"If I am a man of God, it is no different from you or anybody. I am also engaged."

"She is a long way away. What of it? You don't want to be rude."

"No, Gilbert, I don't wish to be rude. I wish to be loyal. Though I must say, you are straining it to the point of breaking." Gilbert laughs merrily and coughs at the same time.

Richard walks up to Sipsis, takes the corners of the robe, wraps it back around her, and gives her the sash that lies at her side. "Indeed, miraculous." He kisses her on the forehead and steps back. "Not tonight, in any case, Cousin. But I will give it thought. How can I not?"

"I take you to be a fool or a saint, Seymour. I can tell you she is eager to try anything. Of course, if you change your mind in the next minutes..."

"I mean not to offend, of course," he says to her in broken Algonquin. "You are beautiful. Thank you."

Sipsis smiles and utters a "thank you," in English.

"Do you mind, Cousin, if she stays? It is warmer here by the fire, boring for her in bed alone."

Sipsis sits on a woolen blanket near the fire pit staring into it while sipping from her glass. Richard is offered his third and he accepts.

"She is one reason I invited you, to share her—at least for your eyes. The other is to share another secret. Because we are related, I hope you will have sympathy for my grievance. My position. You do realize the original charter for the New World was given to my father and Walter Raleigh by Queen Elizabeth. My father lost at sea and Uncle Raleigh thrown in prison, the Tower. For treason! Never! Popham and his slimy council members, all eager to amass more wealth, wanted him out of the way and his charter stripped from him. John Popham is treacherous, but he is no fool. Do you realize the Virginia Company controls more land and riches than can be imagined? And in whose hands, the knave Gorges and now my arch rival, President—President Popham! Do you not see that the company is my legacy? It is rightfully Raleigh's and mine, and if you wish, it could be extended to the Seymour family. I know your father has invested funds. George Popham here is but the titular president. All can see that. Am I not the energy and brains? He is old, and John Popham even older. His son Edward has no imagination or balls. The sooner they are gone, the better."

Both Gilbert and Seymour have remained standing. They now sit, pulling themselves near the fire. Sipsis gets up and adds three small logs, then sits on the blanket between the two. Gilbert strokes her hair. "So, Chaplain, do I sound mad?"

"As you say, aggrieved. And I much appreciate your confidence—and your offer. Offers. Though of the particulars? You speak of your desires to take charge of the Virginia Company, at least the northern part, not the London group that controls Jamestown?"

"Correct."

Seymour continues, "It seems a reasonable long-term plan. We can speak more of this. I sent a letter to my father and spoke of you highly. With the coming spring and new supplies, we can reassess, no? Like you, I believe, I am not the eldest son. We will inherit little. That is our plight. We must live by our wits. We can speak more of this later. What else would you have me do?"

"Good. Then I ask you to tell me everything you know. I believe Popham keeps information from me. I have been gone many days."

"I have to tell you, Raleigh, you missed little of import. You have heard that Hawkes tried to attack Lance. His dog bit him. I convinced Popham to have Hawkes thrashed. This occurred in your absence."

"Yes. I would have been harsher. Hawkes is a good worker—but a fool and a pervert. But Popham knows nothing of estimating food supplies. I should not have trusted him in those matters. And he is often too lenient with the men. I know some bugger one another. That's worth a hanging—to show some discipline. I'm sure there is thievery. Let me know what you know."

"You are probably correct. But I know of nothing specific."

"Ah, I ramble. Just think about what I've said. We will talk more." Gilbert appears to have lost interest. He leans over and lets a hand slip into Sipsis' robe while kissing her lips.

"It is late, Cousin. Thank you for your wine and your generosity. I will let myself out." Richard stands and swallows the last of his wine. Not until he reaches the door to the next room does Gilbert release Sipsis and rise.

"Yes, farewell for tonight." The bulge in Gilbert's pants tells Richard he will not be offered a second opportunity with Sipsis tonight, nor is he sure what his answer might be if he were. Gilbert is indeed persuasive. In a little more than an hour, had he not begun to collude with the admiral? And was his refusal to lie with Sipsis more decorum than honest response? As he walks up to his anteroom off the chapel proper, Montaigne's words came to him, or at least a version: "There is no man so good that if he placed all his thoughts under the scrutiny of the law, he'd not deserve a hanging ten times in his life." Richard chuckles and says to himself out loud, "True enough." He also thinks of his tutor, Bacon. Seymour tries to remember, but it only arrives in dribs and drabs: "We humans are like false mirrors that..." That what? His recollection is fuzzy. He offers a goodnight to a soldier ducking into his hut. Ah yes, "...like a false mirror that distorts," that was it. "That distorts things by mingling its own nature with it." That was it, more or less. "When do we not fool ourselves?" One of his favorite Bacon quotes was similar: "Be careful when interpreting the nature of things; it's more likely to be one's own conception of things." He'd enjoyed putting these to memory during the long hours on the *Gift of God*—and there they were.

CHAPTER 36

October 20, 1607, Fort St. George
Bestiality

Now that Gilbert spends more time at the fort, due to the cold rough seas, he attempts to enforce more discipline. He and Popham usually oppose one another on these matters. Gilbert argues that strict application of punishment may create resentments, but respect as well. Popham's believes his laissez-faire policy, established in Gilbert's absence, works well. If a worker or soldier sleeps past revelry, pilfers here and there, if his drunkenness interferes with work—generally Popham preferred that James Davis, captain of the fort, have a word with the offender, or Popham might address the man himself, perhaps dock his pay. Though he had the power invested by the Virginia Compact to mete out corporal punishment, Popham chose rarely to do so. At times he'd asked Richard to intervene and provide counsel.

A recent case referred to the chaplain by Popham had perplexed Seymour. Yes, the charges involved moral issues. More than that, if not handled well, Erasmus Bean would be executed. It was a serous matter, so why, thought Richard, was it also so ludicrous? In fact, that was the perfect word for it. Yet here he was, representing the Church of England in this matter.

Rumor had it that Bean fornicated with members of his small goat herd. It was only a rumor until one night Corporal Peterson, the one in charge of organizing the food supply, unexpectedly visited the small goat barn and found the shepherd astride a goat in a dark corner. Someone else might have turned away, but not Peterson, one of the few Puritans to make the voyage. When he reported the act to President Popham, he did so quoting Leviticus: "And if a man lie with a beast, he shall surely be put to death: and ye shall slay the beast." Popham, who cared little for church doctrine, did his best to respond in a stern fashion and told Peterson he'd see to the matter immediately. "Hang him, hang him in the name of the King. Hang him for fouling our fort," implored Peterson. "If not, I will broadcast to everyone that I know what a vile place this fort has become."

Richard greeted Erasmus Bean the first thing in the morning. Other rumors had it that Bean not only practiced bestiality, but pandered the animals as well. Given his dwarfish size and preference for goat's company over human, most considered him a mentally deficient deviant and left it at that. Because of limited bathing at the fort, Bean carried the pungent, virile stench of billy goat. To make matters worse, he displayed a scruffy goatee that drooped three inches under his chin. Without saying much about it, the men had allied the shepherd with his goats. The possibility that he copulated with them mattered little. After two months, nobody thought about it much—except two soldiers who, when full of drink and desperate, periodically offered money or bartered with Bean. They knew him to be no fool but kept it to themselves.

"Sit down, why don't you," Richard offers.

Wisely, Erasmus has washed. Except for the blond goatee, he is clean-shaven, his hair combed. From the occasional times Erasmus joined the boys and others on ship during teaching session, Richard found the man both curious and intelligent. Since arriving at the fort, their paths have crossed little.

"Erasmus, I've missed you at our discussions."

"Aye, I enjoyed them, but I am not much for company."

"Yes, well, I'm sorry we meet under these circumstances. Perhaps you could tell me a bit about yourself."

"Not much to know, sir. Like so many of the lads, down on my luck. Run off my plot in Ireland. Lived in London for less than a year. My family done in by the Black Plague of 1603. Worked on the docks. Hated it. Can't tell you how many times they beat me. Come from a line of shepherds. Living in the city not right, really. Coming here was better than starving. No complaints, though. Except, guess they have some with me."

"Yes, that's why the president wanted us to have a talk."

"Yes, have a talk. I don't mean to sound disrespectful, Chaplain Seymour. But I haven't done anything to anybody."

"That may be true, but the act is punishable in England—by death. I assume you know that?"

"Lots of things will end you on the gallows or the chopping block, from stealing food you can't pay for to just being poor. Or, if you're gentry, they'll find something you said treasonous and next you'll find yourself without arms or legs and some fellow pulling out your liver. I've seen it done."

Richard decides to back off for a moment. "Have you any family left?"

"A brother. Small like me. In prison. Couldn't get work. Maybe he'll join me here. I sent him a letter on the *Mary and John.*"

"Yes, you are well-read."

"Had some schooling. Mostly taught myself. Brought a few books with me. Otherwise my brain would shrivel. Chaplain, as I said, I do no harm. I take good care of my flock. What I do is harmless. I prefer goats and books to people. Attachments only bring sadness. Tell you the truth, those little things seem to like the attention. I don't hurt them none. How about them, the other men, have they been charged?"

"I don't think so. Don't think President Popham has that information."

"I'm not telling."

"Could you tell me how many have...used your services?"

"Two, Chaplain. You know, I've read the Bible. The Old Testament, Leviticus, Genesis. Did you know, Chaplain, it is a sin to eat shellfish? Should we not hang one another for eating lobsters and clams? And what about fellows that diddle with each other? A sin, even in the New Testament. Not a word there about animals. And a sin, tattoos. And if you pull out of a woman so not to leave your seed in her: again a sin. My favorite, Chaplain, you could bring this up with President Popham. Do you think that might help my situation? If your wife defends your life in a fight by grabbing the attacker's genitals: a sin. Punishment: her hands get cut off. Maybe you'll mention this to the president?"

"Well, I suppose that's why we're having this conversation, to see if I might add any information."

"Thank you, sir. If it wasn't for that Peterson, his holiness, do you think they'd have just let me alone?"

"I don't know. But once it's out in the open, the authorities find it difficult to ignore."

"Then I might be in serious trouble."

"Yes, I think so."

"And you, Chaplain, what do you think?"

At that moment Richard doesn't know what to think. His role as chaplain requires that he daily try to imagine the perspectives of those who come for counsel. He tries to imagine himself in their place, with their problems, background, personal hardships, and character. This is what he automatically does with Bean. And he is successful, up to this point, in removing his own unreflected aversion to bestiality and buggery. He knew men and even women practiced sex with non-humans. In rural England men fornicated with sheep. He knew of Leda with the swan between her legs. He'd been told things by school friends and peasants at his father's estate. And he knew from Skidwarres that native men and women might have sexual relations with same-sex friends as an expression of friendship. He knew sexual boundaries to be more fluid in some cultures than were accepted by the Church of England. But where did he stand with this surprisingly sympathetic individual?

"Mr. Bean, I can say I'm sure I don't know."

"I'll be hanged? Burned?"

"I hope not."

"Nor do I, but what's going to happen now?"

"I'm not entirely sure. I will report to President Popham our meeting, and..."

"And, sir, may I ask what you will report?"

"As I said, I'm not sure. Certainly I will report what you've told me. I will try to be your advocate. And somehow I cannot forget I represent the Church of England?"

"You mean you will represent the teaching of Jesus?"

Richard is not quite sure if Bean says this in jest. He assumes so. "Mr. Bean, you are aware the two are not exactly the same. But yes, I will try to consider forgiveness."

"I do not think I have sinned."

"Then that is what I will tell Popham and the council."

The two are quiet for a long moment, until Richard breaks the silence. "I am not sure what to say about the two others."

"Best you not mention them. Only get me and them into more trouble."

"That is probably the case, but I believe it is my obligation to inform."

"Then so be it." Bean's tone is not hostile; rather it appears he is taking Richard's perspective: that he understands the chaplain needs to consider more than a shepherd's behavior. Richard reads this demeanor, and in so doing cannot help but like this odd, if troubling, man.

In Gilbert's house that evening, members of the council congregate, including Popham, Gilbert, James Davis, Richard, and Digby, who's taken the place of Robert Davies, the latter having sailed back to England in October.

"You gentlemen understand the problem here," Popham begins. "Bean, the herder, caught with his pants down with a goat. Bestiality is a sin condemned by the church and by our own charter. We have a duty to bring this man to justice. Bad for morale." From the sound of Popham, it seems to Richard that he and Gilbert have already spoken. As a result the president is taking a hard line. "So I sent the bugger to talk to the chaplain. He's damn well going to need the help of the Lord. What can you tell us, Chaplain?"

"Thank you, sir. I have assumed responsibility, in this case, to listen. In one sense I will attempt to be his advocate."

"Advocate?" barks Gilbert. He has been sitting glowering. "You're a priest. You offer the Eucharist. Now you want to advocate for fucking goats? My cousin is soft in the head."

Richard is momentarily taken aback. This is the first time he's tasted Gilbert's well-known wrath. "Sir Cousin Gilbert." Richard uses "cousin" with the same ambiguity the admiral has used before, familial but ironic. "By advocate, I mean I wish to tell you what he thinks."

"Do I care what he thinks?" continues Gilbert. "Are you going to tell me he's fallen in love and wants you to bring them together in holy matrimony?" James Davis grunts a chuckle.

"Gentlemen, Erasmus Bean simply told me he does no harm to his animals or anyone else. That is his argument."

Gilbert continues his pugnacious line, "That is no argument. He does harm. Those Puritans are looking for him to hang or burn. They say this place is a rat's nest, a sacrilege. They've written back to their people. They scream to everyone. We are an English outpost. We represent the King. And if I hear my cousin correctly, he condones bestiality. I'm sure the Archbishop of Canterbury would be pleased."

Digby speaks. "Oh yes, Bishops know something about sodomy." Popham laughs heartily, welcoming the lighter touch. Richard smiles, then intercedes.

"Admiral, you know I am not ordained. But you are correct, I try to represent the Church, and part of that responsibility is to be fair to this man."

Gilbert sighs. "Put him out of his misery. That would be fair to him and us."

Popham says, "Well, Seymour, do you have a recommendation, given your role?"

"I'm not sure that is my place, but I do have more information."

"Speak," says Gilbert.

"Other men are involved. Two others have sodomized the goats. Bean made them available."

"Good god, I don't want to know about this. Procuring goats." Popham pushes himself back from the rough hewn table, but doesn't get up. "Not that I'm surprised. I've been sailing with men. I know what men do. But this will not look good, not with the King's Council, not with our investors."

"Exactly. We need to act. Who are these scum?" Gilbert turns to Richard.

"I have no idea."

"Did you ask?"

"I did not. Nor do I think Bean will divulge the information."

"I might think of a few ways to get him to talk. I didn't spend six months in Ireland and not learn how to get information from those trolls." Now turning his attention to James Davis, he asks, "What are your thoughts?"

"You have already stated my opinion, Admiral. Sodomy is blasphemy. It is punishable by death, simple as that. We make an example of him. We strike fear into the other bastards who can't keep their puds in their pants."

Popham pulls himself back up to the table. "What if we flog him? I find hanging... well...distasteful, especially if I'm giving the order."

Gilbert slams his fist on the table. "And then send him back with his four-legged lovers to continue his mockery? Flogging, it's a gutless response." Everyone in the room, including Gilbert, realizes this insult goes beyond propriety.

"Gutless, am I?" Popham's chair is shoved back again. Except for his dancing, it's the most energetic move Seymour has seen from the president. This time he rises and points at Gilbert. "You are ignorant and trumped up. Your father and I were cool to one another, but we showed respect. A privateer in those days, gutless? Never! And you the instant, puppy admiral." Their smoldering antipathy finally breaks open. "I demand your apology, Raleigh Gilbert. Now!"

Except for Digby, who clears his throat nervously, the room is silent.

"Now!" repeats Popham. The phlegmatic president has summoned up his old self.

Gilbert raises himself slowly from his seat, as calculated as Popham was impulsive. Popham's finger is still pointing, quivering. The younger man points back. "Not now, not ever. You were never the man my father was. And now you are a gutless old woman." Gilbert turns and walks out of the room into his private quarters.

Popham, red-faced and short of breath, slumps back heavily on his chair. Richard gets up and pours ale into his glass. "Sir, drink this." He then turns to Davis, "Do you think you might talk some sense into Gilbert?"

"I suppose. I know him better than anyone else. I can only try."

Those remaining stare at the table and keep silent. They listen to the conversation through the plank walls without making out the words.

Within five minutes Davis returns, followed by Gilbert. They take their seats. "Gentlemen," Gilbert begins, subdued but still with a confident voice, as if speaking for someone else. "I let my passions run away with me; that was unprofessional for a military officer. For that, gentlemen, I hope you will accept my apology." He scans those at the table eye to eye, even Popham. Each knows the insult remains in the room, hanging more insidiously than before in the face of his insincerity.

Popham decides to act as if he's heard something else. The man exasperates him. Nonetheless, they've both had their say. In his report to the King, Popham vows to sink Gilbert's ambition. "Then I accept your apology, and we will continue. Does anybody have another alternative, or shall we vote on this?

"Does this need to be unanimous?" asks Richard.

"It does not," offers Gilbert, under his breath. And then with more force, "This is a matter the president can decide on his own."

"You are correct, but I am not going to hang a man, even this sad sod, without a vote. Chaplain, do you have more to add?"

"Yes, I have given this thought since this morning. There are two positions. Indeed the church finds sodomy a crime punishable by death. Yet the church rests on the teaching of Jesus. And we know he taught forgiveness for sins. Forgiveness is paramount."

Gilbert breaks in. "Jesus did not command an army or a colony. He spoke of an ideal. He said we should love one another. That ideal you can preach. That's what makes you a chaplain and me an admiral. You are against hanging?

"I am for forgiveness."

"A vote then. For hanging," Gilbert commands. He raises his hands. So gentlemen, those with me..." Davis and two other members' hands rise immediately, Digby's slowly. Richard and Popham's hands remain on the table.

Gilbert looks at Popham. Again, the air begins to thicken with tension.

"I will vote with the majority," Popham finally speaks. "I am responsible for discipline."

Richard follows quickly, "Before you act on this, a final vote, I ask that Bean be allowed to speak for himself. Should he not face the council? Is that not an English tradition? Do we not owe him that?"

"We own him a hanging," states Gilbert.

Popham now finds an opportunity to override this man. "I agree. Usher him in."

Bean is escorted by two soldiers from the brig. He wears chains around his legs, though they were made for a much larger man. He is told to stand at one end of the table. Richard decides to stand next to him.

Popham speaks first. "You understand the reason for your arrest?

"I do, sir." Bean stands straight, all four foot eleven inches of him. His voice does not break.

Popham continues. "Do you then plead guilty to bestiality?"

"President Popham, the papers served to me use the word 'sodomy.' I plead guilty to sodomy."

Gilbert cannot contain himself, sitting at the other end of the table from the two standing. "Ah, you not only sodomize goats, you trifle with us?"

"Sir Gilbert, I do not trifle. I am not a beast. I act human..."

"Shut your hole!" Gilbert's anger is stirred again.

"Gentlemen," interjects Popham, "we have asked Bean here to explain his actions. Should we not listen?"

"I've heard enough," Gilbert growls.

Popham continues, "Gentlemen, gentlemen, let us proceed. Let us get this over with. Bean, we understand others have, ah, have used your goats with your knowledge. Is that so?"

"That question I choose not to answer."

"Sir," Popham continues, "the answer to that question might have some bearing on the verdict and punishment."

"I understand."

"So you would rather hang than divulge?" Popham knew giving names would not save Bean, so his question was more an entreaty.

"President Popham, my position is quite simple. I do not fear death. Before I arrived on these shores, my parents and all but one brother died from malnutrition, from a broken heart for being cast off their land, from the plague. My brother is in prison for vagrancy. I do not believe in Hell. And if there is one, and sodomy sends me there, then I believe many in this fort will follow me, for the definition is broad. Consider your own actions, gentlemen. When you put me to death, either I will enjoy eternal sleep, without dreaming or ever waking, or, as many believe, my spirit will greet all those who have come before me. In either case I welcome death."

"I see," says Popham, who tries one more time. "You leave us little choice. Might you reconsider your position?"

"If, for argument's sake, I were to expose others who may have sodomized, would they not beat or kill me? I have had enough of that. Do you see this scar?" Bean opens his collar and pulls down his undergarment to displays a six-inch line on his neck. "In London they missed my jugular, but not by much. You look upon my pocked face, my stature. What woman would lie with me except the ones I pay, and even they have scorned me. So I do not fear the noose. Only a few moments of agony, and then a bliss I've never known."

Popham stares. "Tell me, Bean, what schooling did you have?"

"Very little, but I do read. It is all that I have."

"I've heard enough. I call for another formal vote." Gilbert looks at the others around the table, wondering if Erasmus Bean's words might change the outcome.

"Chaplain Seymour," Popham asks, "do you have anything to add?"

Richard looks down at Bean, who shakes his head to indicate he is done. The small man looks at peace. Not so Seymour, who is awash with emotions he's never experienced, something between fear and shame and helplessness. Should he not be able to mount a defense based on the teachings of the church or some other non-ecclesiastical argument? Has he not failed? Seymour's knees quiver. He hopes the table blocks any view. "Like all individuals, the Church of England is complicated. It is of two minds, at least. Yes sodomy is a sin, punishable in some cases by death. But like so many laws, not of Christ, but of humans who establish institutions, this law is overbearing. Oral sex, gentlemen, is sodomy, and yet we know it is practiced widely, enthusiastically."

Gilbert is again unable to contain his silence. "For god's sake, do you equate fucking goats with the French way? What kind of idiocy are you offering, Chaplain?"

Popham interrupts again, "Let him finish."

"It is not I who make this equation, it is Church doctrine. And as I said before, the Church is of many minds. Above all, as a chaplain, I speak for the gospels, and they teach of love and forgiveness. Therefore, it is forgiveness that I ask again. No, I implore you all to consider before you inflict the ultimate power invested in you." Richard's knees have stopped shaking.

"You are finished, Chaplain?" asks Popham softly."

"Yes."

"Then I call for the vote again," Gilbert repeats.

Popham's voice is weary, "Those voting for guilty of sodomy, punishable by death?" The vote does not change. Popham raises his hand barely off the table and then utters, "Guilty, to be hanged until dead tomorrow morning at daybreak. This council is adjourned."

The soldiers approach Bean, who puts up a hand and sits on one of the vacated chairs. The two soldiers are momentarily dumbstruck. They watch as the small man removes his shoes and wriggles out of the chain collars. He holds the shackles up and hands them to one of the guards. "Where would I run?"

The men look to Popham. "Let him be."

CHAPTER 37

October 21, 1607, Fort St. George
Dispirited

Bean's small body hangs in the main square from a hastily constructed gallows built by the shipwrights. Gilbert would not allow a hood to be placed over his head. Those who choose to venture by comment how unlike the contorted gruesome faces of the hanged he looks. His mouth does not gape open with a purple bloated tongue. He seems at peace.

The night before Richard remained with Bean in the stockade until dawn. At first they talked. Mostly Bean reminisced about his family. Then, around two in the morning, Bean excused himself after explaining that he was determined to place himself in a trance in which he hoped he could remain until death. Richard learned how Bean had become aware of this capacity while being beaten nearly to death a few years before. "Without trying I simply removed myself from myself. I think it is something natural the mind does when reality becomes too overwhelming. I could see myself set upon, but I didn't feel anything. While I healed—in a convent by the way—I read about mystics who taught themselves something very similar. And after a while I, too, could go deep into myself and remain there for hours. Being a shepherd isn't a bad job to practice that sort of thing."

"Do you want me to leave?" Richard asked.

"No, your presence is comforting. I'll know you're here with me, only I will be focusing inward. You will remain with me to the end, correct?"

"Yes, of course."

"Good. Goodbye then."

"Goodbye, Erasmus. I will see to that. You are the bravest man I have ever met."

"Thank you, but it is simply the way it must be." Bean settled himself on his wooden bunk and placed a dirty woolen blanket around him. Quietly he hummed what sounded like a chant. It became softer and softer until finally it was inaudible.

When the guard arrived at six in the morning, Richard found he'd fallen asleep sitting against the wall. He rose and took Bean's elbow. The three walked silently.

Around the gallows nearly all the men of the fort are huddled groggy in the cold fog. They, too, remain silent. Richard has expected some jeering from the cruder ones, but none disturb the still of the morning. Lance has placed himself near the small stairway leading to the platform with the hole in the middle. Instead of a bugle, he strums his lute softly. From Bean's lips comes the flutter of a smile. His eyes remain nearly closed. It is his bearing and the lute that engender respect, make him both vulnerable and dignified. Popham, Gilbert, and the other members of the council stand together with identical grim faces masking whatever they might be feeling. Everyone stares at Bean. The mystery of death descends on the ragged crowd. The guard places the noose around Erasmus' neck, exposing his knife scar, and tightens it.

Richard, his shoulder nearly touching Bean's, says quietly, "May God have mercy on your soul—on your gentle soul."

"Step forward," orders the guard. Only those within a few feet hear. The voice holds no malice.

Erasmus steps briskly. He drops four feet through the opening. All hear the crack. And from the men comes a communal release of breath. Bean's body twitches. His head has fallen askew. Those who are nearby smell excrement. The viewers begin leaving. They head for the mess for tea, but few take food. Nearly all return to their huts for solitude.

Later in the day Richard oversees the slaughter of the six goats. The cook decides to turn the meat into jerky. Later in the winter the men will have forgotten. Originally, Popham decreed that Bean's corpse hang for three days as a grim reminder that lack of discipline leads to death. Crows begin congregating in the afternoon, first on the overhead beam holding the rope; later they hop on Erasmus' shoulder, where they begin pecking his neck. Popham can't stomach this and what is to come, so he orders Bean cut down. Richard, Lance, and Digby carry him on a board. Two soldiers dig a grave in a far corner of the open space to the west of the fort, throwing off the frosty thin topsoil. Richard excuses the grave diggers after a while, allowing the two men and the boy to complete the job. They lower Bean down and shovel the dirt back. Lance had spent the morning building a small wooden cross, using the shipwright's tools to carve a line from Shakespeare's *Julius Caesar*: "This Was a Man."

It seems to Richard that afterwards the weather and mood of the colony changes nearly overnight. Starting on October 22, a northeast storm blows for three days, bringing with it rain and cold. The large, dark brown oak leaves give up and fall to the ground. A thickening carpet of slimy half-decayed leaves covers the paths. The skeletal trees now let in the anemic yet strangely sharp light from the sun, and night brings a dominant moon. The dampness of earlier October that tended to dry by noon now holds incessantly and settles under the skin. Fires remain burning. Men awake are shivering. Warm dry clothing becomes the central topic of conversation. The heavy work of building becomes a reprieve from the chilly damp.

With the season's turn, with the insidious, penetrating dampness, with what a week ago felt like a miraculous accomplishment, this English outpost—the fruit of so much numbing labor—the men can't shake off death. It hangs in the collective consciousness of soldier, sailor, craftsmen, and officer. Few speak of Bean's image, appearing in dreams at night and in nagging flashes during the day, or of the funereal crows squawking their raspy voices in the morning. Soldiers begin firing at them in the trees with little effect. The fort transforms itself into a muddy absurdity. For what purpose is all this? Where are the riches, the gold and silver, the river leading to the Indies, the wanton native women? Is this all about fish and beaver and self-serving gentlemen? So the grousing goes. Gilbert and Popham still spout homilies about a foothold, a beachhead, the beginning of English world domination. Mostly the men are tired. They want to smell the hearth at home or in a tavern, to lie with a soft, warm, accepting woman. What is to sustain them? Even Gilbert, the most dedicated to the grandeur of their efforts, even he sounds dispirited. And the chaplain, after holding one Communion on the Sunday after Bean's execution, busies himself with building the *Virginia* and has little interest in Church matters.

The death of five fishermen at sea could be accepted as fate, but the murder of a shepherd feels ominous. Even the most hardened men, those who might have jeered during the execution—even they can't entirely avoid their nagging consciences.

CHAPTER 38

November 1, 1607, Fort St. George
Rude Awakening

Before the sun rose, the temperature just above freezing, the sleeping fort awoke to the cries from a guard on the ramparts, "Fire, fire, the smokehouse! Fire!" Men pulled on their trousers and shoes—those who didn't sleep in them. Depending on the type of construction, they pushed open a flimsy door flap made of canvas or opened a crude wooden one on leather hinges, or in the case of some officers and gentlemen, a door on iron hinges forged at the fort. All stuck their heads out to see the smokehouse engulfed in a blaze.

Captain of the Fort Davis took immediate charge. The twenty buckets of water kept in the storehouse for just such an emergency became the first line of defense. The smokehouse was a fifteen-by-fifteen-foot structure with a thatched roof and wattle siding, much like many of the huts only larger. Apparently, the fire had begun on the roof. One wall had already caught. Wispy embers swirled upward into the dark morning breezes and spread overhead like a mass of giant fireflies. This became Davis's immediate concern: half the buckets would be emptied on the roofs of the adjacent structures, the remainder on the smokehouse. A bucket brigade that had practiced once every two weeks began slinging the empties to the shore, where they were immersed, pulled out, and given to men to carry—the theory being one carrier would spill less. Embers settled on a corner of Gilbert's roof and began to burn. A contingent of water carriers quickly doused them before they spread.

Within fifteen minutes the smokehouse was smoldering. Two of the four walls still stood, but on the ground were the charred remains of cod, sturgeon, venison, moose, and goat, all burnt to a crisp—in all, enough food to feed the men for over a month.

Though the eastern horizon remained dark, the cook decided to boil water for tea. He'd serve an early breakfast. It felt to him the day would bring fair weather. A blurry-eyed President Popham agreed, no point returning to sleep. Shortly the men began warming their guts. Some commented how even disaster could be welcome in the face of boredom. They speculated on what had caused the fire. The obvious answer, most agreed, involved the fire pit. A spark had ignited the ceiling. This pointed to the three men who tended the fire around the clock. The man responsible for that night argued he had banked the fire around two in the morning. The construction was similar to the other fire pits, only safer, as the chimney was larger and more likely to collect sparks. Most didn't believe him. They needed someone or something to blame.

Gilbert decided to convene the members of the council, with the exception of President Popham who reported feeling out of sorts. They would review the situation and inspect the remains after they cooled. The three responsible for the smokehouse and three other guards were called in and interrogated. They were adamant: they had seen and heard nothing. They did not convince Davis. It was common knowledge men would sleep, play cards, and drink on duty. Even the officers were lax about oversight, finding it a chore to get up in the middle of a cold night to check on their men. Just the week before Captain Davis had caught the guards huddled together in the northeast corner, next to a cannon, under a tarp protecting them from the cold drizzle. They spent three days in the brig and received lashes.

Two other logical explanations existed: sabotage from within or an attack by the savages. Sabotage was unlikely but not to be ruled out. One of the men might be in the employ of the Spanish or French. Or one malcontent might have his own twisted reasons. But no obvious culprit came to anyone's minds.

An attack by natives might be more plausible. But the guards swore they had seen nothing. Could they have climbed walls? Perhaps. In the morning, Gilbert inspected the perimeter for tracks or other evidence. Could they, Gilbert wondered, have ignited the roof with an arrow? Surely the guards would have noticed—if they weren't asleep or indisposed. And how would the natives know which building would be most strategic? And if savages, which ones? Might Nahanada be the crafty dog Gilbert occasionally suspected? Or was Sabenoa the culprit? Other villages on the Aponeg and to the west could not be ruled out.

What did Seymour know? All at the council meeting finally looked to him. What was his opinion? Gilbert and Davis considered privately. Could Seymour be holding out on information, or even be responsible for sabotage? Was he not a rather odd duck? Did he not preach compassion? Was he not the most unpredictable and unknown among the leaders of the colony? What were his loyalties to Skidwarres?

"Chaplain," Gilbert directed his gaze and his questions, "tell us what you know. What do you think? Were we attacked?"

Richard attempted to ignore the suspicion he heard in Gilbert's tone, though of course he realized there was some basis for suspicion. Did he not hold secrets? He wondered if this knowledge showed somehow on his face. He knew guilt could leak out around the eyes and mouth.

"Gentlemen," Richard decided to talk slowly and to re-hash the matter as he evaluated his situation, "I follow the line of argument here, and it does appear either this was simply an accident, or it was an attempt on the natives' part to make life more trying for us. As to a saboteur, like you, I think it unlikely. I have heard no such underground sentiment." In making this statement Richard lent credence to a native attack. By endorsing this view, he found mild relief. "I find a native attack likely."

Gilbert appeared to be content with his answer. He adjourned the group, with orders that all officers keep their ears close to the ground, and that they reassemble in the evening after a thorough inspection of the fort perimeter and smokehouse. Gilbert was reinvigorated by this crisis. The possibility of military action awakened him.

As the council members exit, Gilbert touches Richard's forearm. "Cousin, hold for a minute."

"Very well," Seymour replies. Though he hopes he sounds confident, his stomach is sour with his deceit, his withheld knowledge.

Alone, Gilbert asks Richard to sit again. "Tell me, Richard, you know better than anyone here what those heathens think. You know as well as I, they could overrun us. I know. I know. Fear is our weapon. But it is I, Cousin Richard, who am fearful at night—while everybody else sleeps—or while our president snores or wallows with his savage. It is I who wonder when we will be overrun. This morning when I awoke to the alarm, for just a moment—perhaps it was from my dream—I was underwater. And then I put my pants on before I knew what I was doing." Gilbert looks at the table. "I'm not making sense." He gets up and paces around the table. "Maybe it was an accident. Hell, I don't know if I can count on you. You appear above it all. You don't command this goddam forlorn outpost. You have no responsibility. You act as if you know it all."

He stops his pacing and sits down. Richard watches and listens. It is not only he who broils inside.

"Raleigh, Cousin, I try to appreciate your command here. I wish to help."

"A commander is helpless without information. We are low in food supplies. The winter is approaching. Should we attack, before we are attacked? Should we demand food from Nahanada's village or Sabenoa's? His fields are abundant. They even have stores of rice. Are we in peril? Or am I just...? Look man, I want to take action. Help me know what action."

CHAPTER 39

October 1st, 1607, Pemaquid
Skidwarres' Return

Skidwarres did not easily readapt to Mawooshen life. At first he and Sokw treated one another shyly. She and their daughter stayed close as Skidwarres greeted the elders, he still wearing English trousers and shirt, though he quickly took off the latter in the August heat. Besides, many of the braves stared at him warily. Nahnibssat held his hand, but she also confided to her mother, "I don't remember him."

Finally, that first day, the three took refuge in their hut. Newly-woven grass mats covered fresh cedar boughs. In the middle a small fire chased away the evening chill. Two large black bear pelts served as mattress and cover. Skidwarres, wife, and daughter shed their clothes and settled on top of the soft fur. Sokw, on her side facing Nahnibssat, sang softly and rubbed warm seal oil onto her daughter's skin. Skidwarres did the same to his wife's back. All day he'd taken in the changes: the enlargement to the community lodge, the additional huts set up by young men and women who had married, the new births, the enlarged garden and additional storage huts. His mother and father had aged. His eyes and ears had darted, consuming all. Now he lay quietly in the confined space. This allowed his senses to attend to the immediate: the odor of cedar and smoke, of his wife's skin, a sweet earthy smell, some of it from the oil he rubbed onto her shoulder, down over the muscles on either side of the spine. Here he pushed with his fingertips. Then he reapplied more oil to his palm and rubbed it onto and around her left buttock while she continued to sing.

After a time Nahnibssat's eyes fell permanently shut—at one point when she appeared to be sleeping, her eyes popped open and she got to her knees and peered over her mother to Skidwarres lying on the other side. *"N'mitougues"* (father), she said, confirming his existence. Skidwarres answered, *"Unh-honh"* (yes). She settled and moments later slept.

Sokw turned and embraced her husband. They said nothing but lay feeling the skin and heat of the other, their warm cheeks touching, noses resting alongside, her breasts flattened against his chest, his hand against the small of her back as he pulled her to him gently, stomachs touching softly. Their knees touched, their toes wiggled, reacquainting themselves. Each was the other's center of existence. They lay nearly motionless and silent for a long time, both near sleep in a mutual, exclusive arousal. Then Sokw, her hands still soft and slippery with oil, touched Skidwarres. He instantly became fully erect. Carefully he rolled his wife onto her back and entered her, she making small bodily arrangements that snapped cedar twigs beneath, but without waking their child. Skidwarres moved slowly until soon he fully felt himself softly explode, as a shooting star might arch across the sky, and disappear. Sokw's breath quickened. Like a child, she offered a nearly inaudible whimper, soon accompanied by a few sniffles and small convulsions in her stomach.

The aftermath for Skidwarres was like no other he'd experienced. He began to shiver—not from the cold, though that is what Sokw thought as she reached around her husband and placed the bearskin over his exposed legs and torso. Tremors came in waves. They originated from some overwhelming recognition: he was now back in the arms of his wife. His right hand grasped her left lying inches from her ear, their fingers knitting together; his other hand reached for their sleeping daughter's small forearm. How could he not feel entirely present? Yet this was not a new sensation. Often in England, his existence felt insubstantial. Here again, even in his wife's arms, this altered sense of himself. He watched himself, a stranger from afar, a foreigner on his native soil, in warm, conjugal union.

Since returning, Skidwarres had thrown himself into a routine of hunting, fishing, and keeping close to his wife and child. When asked to become an elder, due in part to his expanded perspective, he accepted and then explained that, for the immediate future, he wished as much as possible to be alone or with his family. He needed to readjust. Nothing seemed quite real to him, not yet. Nahanada said he understood. It had been the same for him but had not lasted long.

In fact, the two had experienced their abduction quite differently.

Nahanada had held onto his anger. It had been his shield and his means of maintaining his dignity. He had made no close friendships, only acquaintances. He had learned to speak English, but not well. On the other hand, Skidwarres had welcomed his indoctrination. He relished the sheer amount of information—historical, scientific, cultural, technical, and athletic. This absorption came within the milieu of mutual trust between himself and Richard. His dignity remained intact, in part because Richard assumed its existence, even in the face of English condescension, even when Richard himself offered subtle, unintentional dismissals. Skidwarres weathered these as displays of ignorance. Richard knew nothing of what they called the New World. Skidwarres realized his violent coupling with Emily had been a form of retaliation for her toying with him, for the indignity of the abduction, and for the English blind spots. Nonetheless, he did not hate. In this sense he did not protect himself.

His father, cousins, friends all asked about his adventure, but Skidwarres wasn't eager to talk, not yet. He answered in less detail than his questioners wished, so they eventually stopped asking. During the long quiet periods on their bearskin pallets, the opposite occurred with Sokw. She did not ask, but Skidwarres wished to convey details of England. He tried to explain what it felt like to ride full-gallop on a horse, an animal he compared to a moose, but much more elegant and with the speed of a deer. She laughed at him as she imagined him riding a moose as graceful as a deer. And he tried to explain the act of reading. He had with him four books—Montaigne, Plato, Bacon, and Shakespeare—that he kept away from the others, thinking they might consider them magic, and he tainted with it. He explained how words came from sounds, not pictures. This Sokw found odd and amusing, but she remained interested and patient. He even recounted his experience in the brothel, how curious the girl was that he, a savage, looked much like her other clientele. At first, Sokw wore a grave face as she tried to understand the circumstances. When she thought she understood, she put her hands to her mouth and giggled.

Skidwarres' time with her during his first week back helped heal his internal disconnect, his insubstantial sense of reality. The trip up the Sagadahoc with Gilbert and Seymour, the meeting with the shifty Sabenoa, and the tour of the early stages of the fort followed by the religious service gone awry, plus the dancing—all, in hindsight, pushed him back into a state of confusion, much of which he could not identify. Away from the English and Richard, he could put aside his two-year transformation. In their company, he could not—especially with Richard. There at the Sagadahoc, Richard appeared as his friend again. Was their friendship to survive? It seemed easier to simply repudiate the two years in England. To further this cause—or at least cleanse his dispiritedness—Skidwarres asked Nahanada if he might absent himself from the village for some days and nights to travel, to fast and seek truth. This form of purification, long a tradition of the Mawooshen, did not make Sokw happy, but she quickly relented.

He would travel on an ancient path to a lake where he could drink and bathe in water that held still some warmth from summer. He would apply himself to simple tasks. Mostly he would sit quietly and seek clarity.

One could not rush. The mind, like a disturbed and muddied pond after the winds churn up the bottom, must lie quietly before it clears. Only then could one see the bottom. He would attend to the ways of his grandfather and to the many generations before. He would occupy a bark hut built some years before, and he would repair a small canoe built by his father. He'd fast for a few days and then hunt, fish, and gather food. His mind would join his hands. Neither idle chatter nor village or family matters would preoccupy him.

When Skidwarres arrives at the lake after five hours of walking, he slips off his moose hide satchel with food and tools, strips off his leggings and deerskin smock, and walks groin-deep into the pond. There he scans the shoreline. At the far end, a family of deer take their evening water. Ducks scuttle away. A great blue heron lifts into the air with its six-foot wing span and prehistoric rasping squawk. The deer look up, startled, spy Skidwarres, and then return to their refreshment. His grandfather had shown Skidwarres how to plunge under the surface and fly underwater like the cormorant.

He dives deeply and propels himself with frog kicks and breast strokes. He counts to thirty and surfaces. He sucks in air, then descends again and resurfaces in the middle of the pond. The deer have vanished. On his return Skidwarres keeps his head above water but continues the frog kick and breast strokes. He thinks, "My grandfather is dead and I am a man—and the water is cold." But the pond holds the spirit of his grandfather. He feels at home. Here he is not divided.

The hut needs repair. He will begin by choosing birch trees from which he will cut strips of bark. With these he will replace damaged pieces. This hut is small and light, Skidwarres observes. The English homes of wood, stone, and cement lie heavily on the land. They appear permanent where the hut is temporary, even transportable. The hut is simple, the wealthy structure of the English complex. True, many English lived in dirty huts made of mud and rock and toiled for others and smelled bad, and in the cities were strangers to one another. Richard had read from the Bible about Hell. Was London not hell, at least the poorer districts? The grand cathedrals were, of course, another matter— English heavens. How could they not consider themselves superior? What was it that gnawed at him as the beaver does a tree? Here he was again, his mind like the duck, flapping about when disturbed. Skidwarres had not anticipated anything other than solitude; and now his two years in England emerge, flooding him. So be it, he thinks. It is time to let my thoughts take their own course.

Skidwarres' grandfather and father had taught him to hunt and build. After the fast, he will kill a deer for food and hide, so he can cut straps to replace the ones on the hut that hold together the bark. Tonight he'll eat from the small food sack—berries, corn, roots, and dried fish. Tomorrow morning he will begin fasting.

In the brush beyond the clearing, Skidwarres finds the small canoe covered by deerskins and evergreen branches. He pulls it out into the opening, uncovers it, and wipes it clean. It has been over ten years—a time concept, years, he's adopted and hasn't yet dropped—since his father introduced him to the complex craft of canoe building. Like the hut, the canoe requires attention. Through his hands, he'll reorient himself.

His father had suggested burning the old one and beginning with new raw materials: large rolls of birch bark, many arms' length of spruce roots for lacing, beech for pegs, cedar for ribs and planking. But no, Skidwarres insisted he'd repair what he treasured, what he wished to offer the next generation, to his daughter. Besides, building a new canoe would take too long. He looked forward to the hard work of digging, cutting, and then splitting the roots. Some inside planks that give the canoe a solid floor and ribs that give it strength and shape needed replacing, as did a section of gunwale. He hopes he hasn't forgotten the exacting tasks of splitting, cutting to size, pulling the roots just so though the holes, shaping the planking to fit. He would then scrape the outside bark clean, boil spruce pitch, and add animal fat so to make the mixture pliable in order to fill holes punched out for the lacing and for the birch bark seams. With him he'd brought an English saw, knife, and planer, all metal, all an improvement on his native bone and rock instruments. Yes, even in this ancient activity, he'd rely on the white man's inventions.

Skidwarres sits that first night, eating and staring into the fire, his mind gathering events from recent years. Life in England returns, a phantom self he can not escape. Thoughts, voices, and images sort themselves and then run together: the power of Richard's horse at full gallop; the countryside of roads, fields, and estates; the carriages and ships and guns; but mostly the strength, the power of that horse and the immensity of the cathedrals. Even the garbage and excrement in London had its hellish power. Thousands of people, teeming. He remembers how his excitement and wonder quickly overpowered his initial fear.

The return to quiet, to the smallness of his village and the confines of the hut, had initiated a feeling that slowly overrode the others. But what was it? Like the deer and the grey heron, the Mawooshen lived lightly off the land. Not like the English, who dug, burnt, cleared, and built to last for generations. They dominated the land. Skidwarres thought of his people's ignorance. He did not want to call it that. His grandfather and the ones before, how could he think of them as ignorant? They had taught him so much and told such tales. It was not just the horse and the interminable massiveness of London and Exeter, or their lavish and sometimes preposterous dress, or the spiritual grandeur of the cathedral that made the English so powerful. It was their language. It was the written word. It was their books. Hundreds of books lined the shelves in the Seymour estate library. Predominately it was this that made Skidwarres feel small and childlike in the presence of the English, standing in the library surrounded by books. From these assessments and feelings of weakness came a more troubling emotion: shame, and not just for himself, but for his people, even his father and grandfather. This shame held a sinister effect, for when one felt shame, it devoured itself with further shame—the shame of shame. Skidwarres believed that awareness of the source of one's feelings increased one's capacity to control or even change those feeling. But what of shame? What was he to do with this knowledge? Shame stemming from ignorance, was this not a fact? How could such self-knowledge assist him? How might he convince himself that it was wrong-headed? Should it be his mission to destroy these insidious thoughts? The English could write what they thought and felt, and in so doing make obscure thoughts clearer and capable of communication, even across generations. This was their power. Yes, he, a Mawooshen, could read. He was even learning to write. But he, the Mawooshen, did not even possess paper or parchment. His mind began to wander as he imagined writing on deerskin, something his grandfather did not teach him. Nor could his people read what he wrote—if ever he might untangle this confusion.

During the first few days, his mind falls deep into a morass. These thoughts are not new. In England, though, excitement had vanquished them. Back in his village he'd chase these thoughts away, as if they were pesky mosquitoes, and retreat to his hut and his small family. But even there he could not escape the distant rumble of the cannon set off every night at sunset, miles away. So many things English—yes, even the explosions—fascinate him.

From a distance and now deep in the woods away from all, watching the embers and hearing the rustle of wind and occasional owl hoots, Skidwarres begins to imagine the meaning of these reverberations: it is doom. This shame and powerlessness can only lead to doom. His grandfather, his old father, they considered the English, Basque, and French settlers—many with white skins, blue eyes and blond hair—strangers from another world. Did he, Skidwarres, the traveler to this other world, know better? Skidwarres had walked through cathedrals and gazed at the light shining through stained glass. He had listened to the chants, to the thunder of the organ, the delicacy of the harpsichord and violin together. The English were a different people. The Mawooshen were insignificant and expendable to their world.

The English build and create. They are always thinking of the future and how to improve everything from food to ships to guns. For the Mawooshen, there is no word for future. For the English, life moves forward on a straight line. But where forward? For the Mawooshen, whose life follows the seasons and who live life in circles, would they not devour themselves like the snake eating its tail?

The English are killers. Skidwarres had witnessed hangings, even drawing and quartering. Richard read to him of the thousands cut down in Ireland and of the Spanish who burned and drowned during the Armada. Skidwarres is no stranger to killing, either of animals of humans. But for the English, it is a form of art, praised in their songs, their stained glass windows, their books, the Bible, and their plays. They slaughter in the name of honor, for their God and for their future.

Skidwarres decides to build a large fire in his hut. He will sit and sweat out this poisonous thinking. Then he will again plunge himself into the lake. Finally, sleep might diminish his melancholy.

The next morning and the ten that followed, whether they came with sun, fog, or rain, saw Skidwarres follow the same ritual. He walked into the pond, dove, swam underwater to midway and then returned, as he had the first time, head above water. He then dried himself, standing next to the warm hearth. After his three-day fast, he began his day by heating a pot of cornmeal, fat, and venison or fish that he ate in the hut. If the sun shone, he sat outside on the ground on his blanket for hours. He hummed. He treated his thoughts like clouds passing by. He watched them with detached interest. He knew these were his thoughts, his images and feelings, but as time passed they appeared more like the clouds themselves, distant and ephemeral. So when thoughts of his own or his people's insubstantiality arose, he watched them, too, in his mind's eye. It was not like before when he felt unreal, when he was lying with his wife, united yet detached. Sitting on the ground and attending to this cloud-thought formation was not unreal at all. It was most real. Or rather, he recognized that the observing part of himself was the most substantial— while also being entirely non-material. When he considered shame, and even felt its dull burn midway between stomach and heart, he watched this pass as well. These thoughts and feelings were real, as real as the hard ground under his half-numb bottom. But it was the observer—his self of selves— that maintained continuity.

At these moments, moments that might extend for long minutes, he felt no urgency or anxiety about shame. It was like the deer he had killed three mornings after his arrival, the buck with his family watering at the end of the pond. It was an easy shot. He simply waited. They arrived and he pulled back and let go. The buck lived and then didn't. Of course his family fled, no doubt to join the herd. The female would mate with another. He dressed the dear, keeping the liver. All was warm, his hands dripped with the buck's sticky blood. That animal, Skidwarres knew, shared the same insubstantial life as his own. He was a beautiful animal in his prime with six points. Skidwarres could feel sadness—it was there, so why not recognize it? It, like his other concerns, would fade. He also felt hunger and needed the hide.

Every morning Skidwarres found it easier to transcend his very existence, if only for moments. Or rather, for moments he occupied his true existence. Perhaps, he thought, I am with my own spirit that is not so insubstantial. The ducks came in low over the pond for their landings, the grey heron on his stick legs fished with its stabbing beak, flipping the small fish in the air and catching them. Nearby a bear browsed, too shy to show itself. They were all part of this place. In a few years all of them would die, though their ancestors might return. That grey heron was preceded by hundreds of generations, he the present representative, perhaps making the claim for heron substantiality. No, it was different for the heron. He was not aware, nor were the ducks, the deer, or that bear who would eat the deer's entrails. They were not aware, and so were they less substantial? Perhaps, but all had a place in the universe. We do not chastise the bear for not reading Shakespeare. But the Mawooshen? That was his next insidious thought: they cannot read.

Richard had told Skidwarres of the Greeks, the Romans—entire civilizations grander than the English. How the stone Coliseum and temples and homes had crumbled over time. About the Aztec civilization reported by Cortez and then destroyed by him. Richard insisted these people and the Mawooshen were related.

Skidwarres tired of sitting. It was time to finish the canoe. Today he would apply the pitch. Tomorrow he would float it on the lake.

On his final day, after the morning swim, Skidwarres collects his light possessions. Soon he will join the elders for their daily conference. This will involve all matters, though the most vexing was the growing spectacle of the English fort. Nothing so threatening had existed before. He knows of the disagreements within his own village, and he was told the same had occurred in villages from the Aponeg to the Penobscot, as well as Sabenoa's people on the Sagadahoc where it meets the Androscoggin. Talk of war was carried in the breezes, along with competition for trade, primarily between the Mawooshen and the Micmac.

Was not warfare entered into with a foolish mix of enthusiasm and fear? Were they not like the English? The legends of the Iroquois and the Mohawk, hatreds originating before his great-grandfather's days? The great nation of Iroquois on the biggest river of them all to the north, and the entanglement with the French? During Skidwarres' lifetime, battles with the Micmacs and skirmishes among the Mawooshen dominated the elders' conferences. Only weeks before, Bessabez had been attacked. Yet how stupid it was that typically they fought over trivial matters: metal pots, cloth, guns, gunpowder, sugar, women, competing commerce with the English, French, and Basques.

Skidwarres' canoe sits evenly in the water. He strokes to the middle of the pond. A midday autumn sun arcs its way to the south, leaving the air crisp and light. Skidwarres considers how he must apply his thinking to the needs of his people. But what might he advise? To attack? His friendship with Richard pales in significance, compared with his obligations to Sokw, Nahnibssat, his people, and his land. Seymour's friendship has been uprooted. It lives in the past. Skidwarres amuses himself with his definitiveness, especially since he also feels it just as likely they should learn to live with the English. If they were destined to occupy the land—as Popham, Gilbert, and Seymour often preached—was not a fight futile? Besides, thinks Skidwarres, Richard and he remain true friends. He has never felt such camaraderie or learned so much or laughed so openly and often.

As an elder, Skidwarres would offer his opinions. He is at peace, but with no course of action. With the elders he would listen and talk, and when action became necessary—be it war or peace—he would become one with them.

CHAPTER 40

November 11, 1607, Pemaquid
Renewing Ties

Richard and Skidwarres had last met before the fishermen's murders. As Gilbert's ire grew after watching the provisions diminish and a large portion of venison, goat, and hog go up in flames, the likelihood of retaliation grew. He had no proof natives killed the fishermen or set the fire. Nor could confirming evidence be found in the smokehouse remains. Some of the footprints in and around the fort did not look to be made by English boots, but this was hardly conclusive. Gilbert tired of his house, of the interminable meetings with Popham. Sipsis had not visited in weeks. Mostly he itched for action.

So it was decided that he and Seymour would travel to Pemaquid to confer with Nahanada and Skidwarres about trade, food, and information. Lance would join them. He'd pestered Richard for weeks about visiting Skidwarres' village and reacquainting himself with the boys he'd met when the natives journeyed to the fort. Stow could come, but on a leash, and Lance would carry a club against the domesticated wolves that might rip him to pieces.

Though the wind from the west and north produce impressive wave action, Captain John Elliot of the *Gift of God* chooses to sail the shallop in the sea rather than take the extra time navigating the inland waterways, a route which would require waiting for tides to change and probably an overnight. If the wind held, they could sail to Pemaquid in a few hours, well before sunset.

"This will be like taking a sleigh ride," Elliot shouts as the thirty-foot open craft leaves the protection of the river. As promised, they outrun the wave action, down the trough and up again, the wind to their backs, running with it, past the wide Aponeg, leaving Damariscove and other small, bald rocky islands to the north and Monhegan to the south. The wind, often this time of year a careless murderer, becomes their enthusiastic friend. Within three hours Elliot veers northeast where the yellowish rocks of Pemaquid come into view. Just a little under two months ago, it had taken them ten hours and a hurricane to make the trip in the other direction.

As is usually the case, sails from a European ship, even a small one, are caught by native eyes. Word quickly passes to Nahanada. By the time the shallop finds the protection of the small Pemaquid River, three canoes have put in to greet them. Skidwarres stands in the bow of the first. When he sees Richard he shouts, "Tally ho!"

Richard manages a "*Kwai*," (hello). They anchor and paddle ashore. There he and Skidwarres embrace, hands on one another's shoulders. After introductions and small gifts of trinkets and food are exchanged, they step aside.

"My friend," Richard speaks first, "how strange that in this vast country we are always in the close proximity of others. The fort and your village are so crowded. We huddle together with so much space all around us."

"My thinking as well. In your country, there are so many people all about, yet so many rooms in your father's house to be alone. So much inside space. The English are a solitary people. Now, though, you and I must talk together. If you had not come to visit, I soon would have come to you."

"Shall we walk," suggests Richard. "What I have to say and ask is for your ears only."

"Yes." The two face the English, who are awaiting instructions. "Tell your men they are welcome at the village. We have food and a hut for them. Nahanada will be glad to see you and the admiral again. And Lance, Moskwas speaks of you often and looks for your company. He can introduce Stow to some wolf pups."

Captain Elliott, the three seamen, and Lance have never visited a native village, so their curiosity is mixed with trepidation. "All is well, you are welcome," Skidwarres repeats.

"Very good," adds Gilbert. "I will confer with Nahanada."

"Yes, Admiral," responds Skidwarres. Gilbert has nearly been forgotten while Skidwarres, Lance, and Seymour are becoming reacquainted.

Down a path at the edge of the shore and out of earshot, Skidwarres begins speaking in a more serious tone. "I believe I know what brings you here."

"I am here for more than one reason, one of which is our friendship."

"I am pleased. But I suspect another purpose might be heavier than friendship."

"Yes, and tell me what that might be."

"This is a dangerous matter, Richard. I considered keeping it from you. Silence is often the best course. But I have a strong belief this truth might come to you somehow. Like fire, some truths spread with the wind."

"Skidwarres, let us be open. We must assist one another with whatever difficulty faces us."

"Nahanada knows we are speaking, but agrees I am not forced to tell him your thoughts."

"That is how it is with Popham and Gilbert." Though Richard knows they never said as much, this is how he plans to conduct himself. He also decides to put aside the vagueness. "Skidwarres, I have strong reason to believe five fishermen were killed by natives. I do not know which village. I would guess Sabenoa's people."

"And Gilbert, what does he know?"

"I found a corpse with an arrow in it. This information I have kept to myself. Lance also knows. I have told only you. Fletcher, too, was killed. Now I ask you, what do you know?"

"Fletcher...I am sad to hear so. But I can tell you, it was not Sabenoa. Five braves from this village killed them. It took two days before *moji* (shit) stopped coming from their mouths." Richard nodded. He hadn't expected to be jolted by this news. What, he thought, could be more disturbing than a rotted corpse?

"Yes," said Richard. He finds a large flat rock and sits. "Tell me more."

"At first they lied. The fishermen shot at them, they said. They pointed to the brave's wounded leg as proof. But it was a lie, an obvious knife wound. When brought before the elders and questioned, Woboz, one of our hot-headed braves—I have that right, hot-headed?"

"Yes, you have it right."

"He, Woboz, became angry. He began to shout, 'The English will kill us all if we don't kill them first.' There are many who are fearful. It does not help that we hear your cannon from so far away."

"Friend, you are sure my men are safe in the village?"

"I am sure. Nahanada has given his word. It is a difficult matter for him. Some in the village think Woboz a hero. Most do not. Most listen to Nahanada. He and I want peace. I must be honest. I wonder—you, Richard, you are an honorable man—but I know you are not the fort."

"And this Woboz, he's at the village now?"

"No, he and fifteen braves and some family left to go north. They said they would hunt. It was what you English call a compromise. Nahanada wanted to punish them, but two elders persuaded Nahanada to let them leave. One, Woboz' father, is an elder, Kasko. At this season young men go on hunts up rivers where bear, fox, beaver, deer, and elk live in more abundance. They are gone for a long time. Their families join them. Others remain here. Our gardens are here. It is complicated. Our ways change."

Richard interrupts. "What do you mean, 'they say?'"

Skidwarres smiles. "You listen well. I should not be surprised. Hunting is what they said they'd do. I think they may be more interested in hunting English. They enjoy the kill." Skidwarres tries to correct himself. "They have given Nahanada their word. Kasko, the father, is with them. He will control Woboz. For now, until spring, they will be a three days' journey away."

"I know you are attempting to comfort me—and my people. But we English, too, enjoy the kill. If Gilbert hears what I know, even Popham— and for certain the soldiers—will demand revenge. To kill. I am supposed to be a chaplain. I would be required to bless the kill. If I report what I know, a seaman killed by an arrow—I found him washed up on the shore, the reason I'm here, and now what you have told me—killing will happen. I am sure." The conversation falls into something the two men created over two years ago, and now they are stuck with it—honesty.

"Skidwarres, there is more. One of our houses burned. Gilbert strongly suspects natives. What do you know of this?"

"I know nothing of a fire, though Sabenoa and Woboz are capable of such."

"And it could have been an accident. I am not sure what to do. I am here for your help. And what if I keep this secret and more sailors or hunters are killed? Will not their blood be on my hands for not warning Popham and Gilbert? And what if I tell them the truth? Then the blood of your people or some other village—any native blood will probably do—is my doing."

"Richard, I do not think they will attack again."

"That is easier for you to believe. Could they not have started the fire? What do you have to lose? I know you are not pleased by our fort. I know you and I are friends, but I believe your warm feelings end there."

"It is true, what you say. I am not of one mind. And you, what do you foresee?"

"I do not begrudge your mixed feelings, even your animosity. The English are also settling way south of here in Jamestown. You know this. Walter Raleigh's Roanoke settlement failed largely because of the resistance of the natives. If we fail here, if Jamestown fails, we English will only try again. A toehold, this fort or another, will become a settlement, then more, and soon there will be many wooden houses like our storehouse and church. We will build roads. We will bring, pigs, horses, and cattle, and grow large gardens. It is inevitable. We are less brutal than the Spanish. But I am not sure."

While Richard offers this small oration, it sounds as much a threat as a possibility. Skidwarres looks out over the water to Monhegan in the distance. "Richard, no one knows what you know? You mentioned Lance."

"Lance saw the body. He has promised not to utter a word, but he is a fifteen-year-old. And what if other bodies wash ashore? It could happen, though not likely after these weeks."

"Yes, but if not, or if they do, your secret is safe."

"Yes, that is a good point. But if Lance is unable to keep his word, I will have lost all credibility."

"Yes, that is a risk. And do not Popham or Gilbert at least have suspicions? Do they not think it possible your fishermen were murdered? Might they take action?"

"Yes, they have suspicions. And I see where you are leading. You think it best I remain silent."

"And you think my reasons are selfish?"

"No, that is too strong. They involve self-interest, but I don't think they are selfish."

"Ah, as always Richard, you play with words. I learned to be a diplomat from you."

"No, I am not playing, the difference is real. And in this case your self-interest— saving lives—is mine as well."

"Good, then Nahanada will be pleased with our talk."

"All right, I suppose that is our decision. And now I must get Lance to promise again with his life to hold his tongue—if it hasn't already wagged. And you, Skidwarres, do you promise to keep me informed about your hostile braves?"

"Yes, I promise, and from my observations Lance is an unusual boy. He has seen much of life. He is both delicate and strong."

"Yes, you are correct. But another question: what of Bessabez? Gilbert wishes to know his thinking.

"Yes, he—we—face many pressures. The Micmacs from the east are always troublesome. Skirmishes occur often. It was not a good time to meet with the English, when Gilbert traveled. Besides—though your Gilbert need not know of this—it is up to you. Many do not want to meet with the English. Some trade with the French. They and their priests are kind. Many villages to the north follow their god. Some Frenchmen marry our women. And the French say bad things of the English."

"Gilbert knows this."

"But the Mawooshen, we have less contact with the French. Nahanada will tell Gilbert we appreciate English hospitality at the fort. In return we will have many beaver and some bear for you in the early spring. Nahanada has already spoken of this with Popham. They have, as you know, already made agreements."

Richard cannot help but laugh. "Indeed, and all are pleased, as I hear it?"

"I believe so."

"And you, Skidwarres, only one wife and you now an elder?"

"Only one. Besides, there are not many extra women. And do you remember our talk of the English 'love?' I am not sure I understand, but what we talked about and what I read—your Shakespeare, remember? It has, as you English say, 'opened my eyes.' Sometimes I see Sokw through the eyes of the English. I have told her this and she laughs. I tell her she has my heart, that has always been so; but you and your Margaret— she appears to require your respect, if that is the best word. I tell Sokw this and she laughs, and then so do I."

"That is curious, my friend—respect? I suppose that is so, if by respect you mean a certain—I don't know—regard? Maybe fear? Or esteem? I have read that we English have given up God and replaced him with woman, womanhood. In any case, it is of some consequence that queens have ruled us, especially Elizabeth."

"You sound like Emily. She said much the same. We say here, '*bloti kikas*,' something like, 'the vagina confuses men.' So, I ask you Richard, would you not like a woman for company? To be confused tonight?"

"Again I refuse. Gilbert offered Sipsis. I will not last long with such generosity. But Skidwarres, I never asked you about Emily, not in the carriage or in Plymouth or on ship. You didn't appear to want to speak of her."

"Ah, this English woman who burrowed herself into my mind like a worm. And Richard, before we return and feast on duck, I must say Woboz made a mistake, a bad one. But he and many others say we must exterminate the English before they exterminate us. You are my friend. But I must say, if I thought we could eliminate the white man, I would help. It is a strange thing to say to my English friend. Not kill you, but send you away. Only I and Nahanada know how determined a people you English are."

"And here I must speak, if not for the Church of England, at least for its founder: 'Love one another.'" Then Richard laughs. "I believe this, but coming out of my mouth, it sounds hollow."

"Chaplain, our stories, the Mawooshen, they, too, speak of respect, of sharing."

"Elder, we are full of ourselves, but now let us be full of duck."

CHAPTER 41

November 11 1607, Pemaquid
Dissimulation

Gilbert, Seymour, Nahanada, Skidwarres—even Elliott, Davis, and the seamen—considered the diplomatic visit a success. Over dinner in the communal lodge, with the elders in the inner circle along with Gilbert, Seymour, and Elliott, Nahanada soothed Gilbert's feathers over the botched meeting with Bessabez. The Pemaquid sagamore insisted that when spring arrived they would again make the journey, this time leaving together.

Within the communal lodge, perhaps seventy adult and teenage natives sat quietly in an outer circle. Nahanada's prior attempts to clarify matters with Gilbert had ended in confusion and antagonism, in part due to the barrier of language. In the lodge, with the assistance of Seymour and Skidwarres, their deliberation turned in a more positive direction. In his earlier attempt at conversation Gilbert had mistaken Nahanada to say Bessabez was preparing for war against the English, when in fact it was against the tribes to the east, the Micmac. The more he'd queried Nahanada, the deeper their confusion, until they'd broken off talks in favor of discussions over food and clearer translation. Later Gilbert accepted Nahanada's assurance that the more eastern villages, many miles up the Penobscot, had access to beaver pelts. Nahanada welcomed trade, especially if the English could offer guns, so they could defend themselves against their adversaries who increasingly wielded French and Spanish muskets.

Regarding food, Nahanada directed Gilbert to Sabenoa's villages, where he suggested they might be willing to trade for maize, rice, and squash. Nahanada also spoke of precious stones far to the north. In a variety of ways, Nahanada angled for the protection of his people—and himself. His eldest wife remained happy. From George Popham she had collected many fine beads, silver jewelry—even a china plate and glassware were offered as presents—besides his kindness and attentiveness. Nahanada's attentions to his two younger wives no longer riled her. Sipsis' eagerness to couple with Gilbert not only fed her ambition, it made it additionally unlikely Gilbert would turn on her village. Besides, Sipsis pilfered information about the English. She quickly picked up words and phrases and questioned Gilbert during the long nights, assisted by his favorite Bordeaux. Nahanada made sure she and Gilbert would occupy their own hut after they had eaten, smoked, and talked into the night.

When Gilbert asked what Nahanada knew of the five fishermen's disappearance and of arson, the sagamore lifted both palms up and shrugged his shoulders. He did not know. And would it be possible that Sabenoa was responsible? Again Nahanada responded with a gesture: he nodded his large head, with its graying long black hair, back and forth and shrugged again. The message appeared to be "possible, maybe possible." With this answer, the attending elders and villagers seemed content. The two tribes had been squabbling for generations. Why not point Gilbert in their direction. As with so many successful deliberations between adversaries, everything simmered in the soothing oil of dissimulation.

As Gilbert listened, he thought offering guns in trade for beaver pelts made sense, especially if most of the gunpowder was so mixed with finely ground grain as to be ineffectual, thereby lessening the chance they'd be used against the English. He wasn't convinced Nahanada's village or the others in the area didn't have food to spare. But now was not the time to press that case. As the hours of talk passed, the strong physical sensation of Sipsis took over. Gilbert finally stood up and ended the proceeding, thereby snubbing the native tradition that the sagamore should rise first. But Nahanada did not mind. His knowledge of the English was far greater than Gilbert's of native culture. Gilbert was a young man. Every day was rutting season.

Gilbert left the lodge and headed for his guest hut, knowing he was about to take action on another front. Nahanada had almost told him that it was Sabenoa who had food. It was Sabenoa who might have murdered the fishermen and committed arson. He didn't need more information. He understood Nahanada must be subtle, that was his nature. When he ascended the Sagadahoc next time, it would be in the *Gift of God* with cannon and much greater armed manpower.

When he opened the deerskin flap and ducked underneath, he felt the heat of the fire in the center. Sipsis arose from her bearskin pallet. She wore the silk robe he'd given her. Images of the *Gift of God* anchored near Sabenoa's village, her cannon able to deliver terror if not real damage, quickly dissolved when Sipsis untied the sash and offered up an immediate and gentler engagement.

Seymour and Skidwarres remained in the lodge after the others had retired to their huts. All the English, excepting Gilbert, would sleep under this thatched roof. Lance was exhausted from hours of lacrosse. He'd reacquainted himself with Moskwas. As a present Lance had received two sticks and a ball. Elliott and the seamen fell asleep, languid from food and drink they'd brought, and filled with the uncanniness of their host's world.

Before leaving for his family, Skidwarres underscored Nahanada's insinuations about Sabenoa. One hand rested on Richard's shoulder. "You are a wise man to keep full knowledge from Popham and Gilbert. For that you demonstrate your friendship to me and my village. Though Nahanada has no proof, his intuition is strong. Sabenoa cannot be trusted, and it is true his fields and storehouses are bigger, much bigger."

"Yes, but Nahanada also misleads. We both know."

"My friend, I think Sabenoa a likely enemy."

In truth Skidwarres thought Sabenoa more a jokester than a warrior. But he had heard the rumor of Woboz and his braves living nearby Sabenoa, further north on the Sagadahoc. What might that portend? His insinuations to Richard were real enough. Besides, as he had already made clear to Richard, might it not be better if the English were squeezed out of this land—at least for the short term—by Sabenoa taking up arms, especially if he was provoked? Would it not be gratifying for the English to taste some of the fear they so happily generated?

Diplomacy, Skidwarres thought as he settled next to his wife Sokw, how seductive this business, seductive for its feel of control—of power. Nahanada's nurtured anger served his people well. "I have much to learn from Nahanada," he said unintentionally out loud. Sokw, half-asleep, grunted her approval while pulling her warm body next to his. As he was lulled into sleep, he thought, half-dreaming, half-consciously, "Nothing is inevitable. The English are not inevitable."

CHAPTER 42

November 12, 1607, Return to Fort St. George
Plans to Intimidate

The shallop set sail early, an hour or so before low tide turned, before the stiff November wind woke up and churned the black sea. This time Elliott and Gilbert set a course that would take them up through the complex, more protected inland waterway, up past a bay, then an estuary, another small bay, and across the Aponeg where it begins to narrow. They passed by an island to the south through the fast moving tides, up through Knubble Bay, and again through even more determined tidal rips, to shallow Hockomock Bay. Here three estuaries connected, one heading northeast to reconnect with the Aponeg River, another northwest, the Sasanoa, the section Skidwarres used with Gilbert when they returned from their visit to Sabenoa's village, approximately six weeks previously. The third estuary snaked west for a few miles and at one point narrowed to less than thirty yards before it finally broadened and connected with the Sagadahoc, only two miles north of the fort. This was the obvious route. With the luck of the wind, plus all six adult males rowing, they might have managed it in one long day. Instead, it took them two, the wind having spent most of the time blowing at twenty knots from the northwest, leaving them at various twists and turns in the route heading directly into it.

Gilbert remained buoyant. His two extra passengers, Sipsis and Nolka, huddled in their blankets. His upcoming nights held promise. And Popham would be delighted and more agreeable to his plans. The women would remain as guests for two weeks before a native canoe would come to retrieve them.

The trip allowed time for Gilbert to work out some of the details of his plan with Captain Elliott. They would transfer four nine-pound cannon back onto the *Gift of God*'s deck. He'd travel with forty soldiers, enough to provide substantial intimidation, plus he'd include a crew of ten. Enough cannoneers would remain to man the heavy guns. The remaining artisans, cooks, shipwrights, iron workers, and others were all trained to use muskets. Besides, to date no attack had been launched.

What did Elliott think of the waters? How shallow did it get in the Quabacook Bay? Exactly how far was the village from the water? On the previous visit Elliott had calculated the depth. At low tide it was not possible to get very close to shore, but close enough, he estimated, to put the fear of God into the savages. The nine-pound cannon had a range of half a mile. That would reach their village. So far as anyone knew, including Nahanada, Sabenoa did not possess firearms. Skidwarres declined Gilbert's request that he be the interpreter, thereby disassociating himself from potential bloodshed. The few other braves who spoke very limited English shared Skidwarres' views. Then Sipsis offered her services. Gilbert wasn't sure her English was sufficient, but as usual her enthusiasm and charm won him over.

Popham's cheerfulness over Nolka's arrival for an extended stay did, in fact, help lay the groundwork for his approval of an expedition upriver. He knew as well as Gilbert the necessity for more food, especially vegetables. Daily hunting parties left in search of deer, moose, and duck. Nonetheless, even with a reduction in rations for the ninety men and four boys, in two months most of the barrels would be empty. Though the officers did not share this worry with their men, rumors spread from those whose job it was to stock and guard the storehouse.

Since the hanging, spirits had turned morose. The cold, wet earth, the elongating dark, the less-than-fever-pitch work schedule had eclipsed any grand vision Popham or Gilbert tried to conjure up during their weekly speeches. The chaplain's services lacked commitment. Fewer attended, choosing to remain burrowed in their blankets on Sunday mornings. Except for the undiminished rations of rum and the occasionally tasty meal, life had little to offer. Only those working on the *Virginia* maintained optimism. By late November they'd planked her hull and laid her deck. Every day most men would straggle down to the shore and watch for a few minutes. They'd gaze at their symbol of industry and escape, even though she could carry no more than thirty or so men. She represented their ingenuity. It simply made them proud, if for only a few moments.

Though willing to support Gilbert's plan to intimidate Sabenoa in the hopes of bargaining for food, Popham cautioned the admiral. "What we don't need is a hornet's nest of angry braves twenty miles upriver, especially if Sabenoa is as unhinged as rumored. Use restraint. We need the damn food, but I don't want to be looking revenge in the face."

Since his visits to Nahanada's village, Gilbert appeared to have mitigated his resentment for Popham. Besides, his admonition rang true. In addition, Popham did appreciate the emotional appeal of an attack. The soldiers and sailors and craftsmen tended to believe the fishermen had been murdered at sea; the fire, too, probably set by the savages. They wanted a scapegoat for their growing restlessness and apprehension. With little evidence to back it up, Gilbert believed the fire had begun on top of the roof, not inside. Sabenoa's village on the Quabacook became the most convenient target—a source of food, and a chance to demonstrate English firepower.

CHAPTER 43

November 28, 1607, At Quabacook
Chaos

The dulled occupants of Fort St. George came to life with the news of an armed expedition. The soldiers had for weeks been merely laborers: felling trees for firewood, digging trenches, cleaning latrines, hauling rock on wooden sleds, cutting monster oak and pine, dragging them to the shore, and sending them with the tide downriver to the *Gift of God*. Most took orders from their corporals and sergeants, as the operations followed military command. At other times they were assigned to farmers, carpenters, lumbermen, and cooks. Many groused about the lack of military objectives. Many had vague notions of Cortez and his glorious bloodshed and riches. Now, with the mosquitoes and greenflies gone, they battled mostly the cold, the damp, the toe fungus, and the aching backs, necks, and shoulders. With no aggressor to fight, each man's body became the enemy.

With the news of "action," men shined their breastplates and helmets and cleaned their muskets, knowing it wasn't just useless protocol. Teams ferried four cannon from the ramparts, and with block and tackle hoisted them off the barge and onto the deck of the *Gift of God*—never a man-of-war, but impressive nonetheless, especially with a fifth bow cannon, a six-pounder, that had remained onboard. Gilbert barked full-throated orders as men rolled barrels of food and drink for a possible four-day adventure. Officers oversaw marching to Lance's fife or drum. Stow occasionally barked his approval while he darted about. Dumb and Dumber sat, watched, and drooled. As a puppy Stow had shown no fear of the two Mastiffs, then at least ten times his weight. Yapping and nipping, he'd herd them here and there. The potentially ferocious dogs nonchalantly obeyed, apparently happy for the attention. Eventually the three curled up together quietly, more or less friends.

Spirits pulled themselves out of the cold mud. Nearly all walked up the hill to the chapel where Popham reminded the congregation their actions were for the glory of God and King. Seymour delivered a tepid homily and led everyone in singing. He had decided to remain at the fort where he'd continue work as a shipwright's assistant, read, educate the boys, and practice his lute. He knew Gilbert's growing enthusiasm for revenge to be at least partially misplaced, but to divulge the truth made little sense. He understood the need for food and a reinvigorated fort population. Nonetheless, instead of cheer he felt an anxious gloom. And he felt removed. Better to read Montaigne, Bacon, and Shakespeare—to put his head in the freezing sand.

That night's dinner included venison, the last of the salted pork, plus two rations of rum. It wasn't until later that evening that spirits dampened. The officers were briefed by Gilbert and Popham. This was not to be a raid, at least not a violent one. Over dinner the soldiers' and seamen's spirits had risen over expectations of battle. Some of the more experienced, especially those who'd served in the Irish campaigns, talked of plunder, of catching women by the hair, throwing them to the ground, and having their way. One known braggart told how "some not only didn't complain but screamed with pleasure and held on afterwards, insisting they be taken along. They wanted to have you forever. Strange, something about the power of it all." The younger, inexperienced boys and men listened. They'd heard it all before, but not with such immediacy. And kill? "It's easy. Nothing more commonplace—still, you'll never forget. It gets more complicated afterwards. In the moment, it's just what it is. You get it or they get it."

When the officers fanned out to inform their troops about the purpose of the engagement—solely securing food—the men sobered. Bloodshed would occur only in self defense. "No plunder. No fucking. Got it? Strict orders! Remember they outnumber us, just the braves, at least three to one. That doesn't count all their skinny-assed friends who live out their in the woods. In truth, we don't know what to expect. So we keep our discipline. Listen to orders and you'll come out alive. If this becomes a fight, you know what to do. The maneuvers we've practiced. You do them in your sleep. Listen to orders and nothing else. The purpose is to procure food, to save your skinny sorry asses from starving."

At ten in the morning, forty soldiers and ten sailors scrambled up over the sides of the *Gift of God*, along with Captain Elliott. The ship burst into purposeful action. With the anchor cranked up, a generous southwesterly—warm for late fall—swept them northward against a tide that would soon shift and quicken their pace. Gilbert emerged from the captain's quarters where he and Sipsis had spent the night. To his delight she was fascinated by all the details of the ship and insisted on a tour. When he offered her his favorite Burgundy, she downed the first glass in one gulp and ran to the bottle for another. Gilbert marveled at her, more in admiration than titillation. The weak cabin stove had yet to warm the room. After flinging off her leggings, she dove into his bed, covered her head, poked it out, and ducked in again.

Instead of joining her lightheartedness, Gilbert sat on the side of the bunk where he practiced with her again what he intended to say to Sabenoa. Translations, he knew, could easily go awry. Remarkably, Sipsis' vocabulary had increased exponentially with Gilbert and Skidwarres' teaching. Someday, Sipsis insisted, she would travel to England and France. Her girlish coquettishness was mixed in equal proportion with ambition.

Within two hours, traveling at six knots, they entered the wide stretch of river where one of the estuaries led to the inland waterway. No native canoe came into sight. Two miles north the waters narrowed at the place where the shallop had shot through on the tide. Captain Elliott shouted for a depth reading. The tide was still low, but at this part of the river the difference between low and high ran only five feet, rather than the twelve-foot differential at the fort. Elliott navigated midway between the western shore and an island, and without any menacing grind, the ship slid into the expansive Quabacook, as through the neck of a bottle. It was early afternoon. The sharp yellow light bore little resemblance to the hot summer sun of two months ago.

Gilbert and Elliott stood at the helm, Sipsis at the bow, her feathery headdress and hair blowing behind her. A few mentioned how if she were bare-breasted, she might be attached to the bow, thereby becoming the ship's living nautical figurehead. Men stationed on port and starboard sides called out the depth—now at eight fathoms, moments later at six.

At five fathoms Gilbert ordered the anchor lowered: enough depth and within range. Up till now no human forms had appeared on the shore. The chain scurried through the hawsepipe and stopped. The shore was at some places sandy beach, at others marshland or granite. It was mid-tide. If they waited, they could move closer, but dusk came quickly in late November. Gilbert needed to act. The *Gift of God* swung into the fifteen-mile-an-hour wind. "Lower the longboats." Over the past month the shipwrights had built two additional longboats. Two were in tow, two on deck. Six men dropped into one of the boats, tied a line to the stern and began pulling the ship so her starboard side lay facing the shore. All six strained at their oars against the wind. With the adjustment completed, Gilbert ordered the second anchor to be dropped.

The two starboard cannon now pointed directly toward shore. The bow cannon, smaller and more maneuverable on a swivel, had a one-hundred-eighty-degree range.

On shore Gilbert now saw men and women watching, waiting. They did not have to wait long.

In the twenty minutes it took to align the *Gift of God*, the gunnery crews readied themselves, applying the powder bags and the nine-pound balls. Gilbert's voice was steady and slow, "Ready, boys." Silence for a moment. "Fire!" The two balls erupted within a split second of one another, sounding like a single elongated explosion, accompanied by an orange flash and smoke that quickly blew back over the gunners' heads.

The steaming balls cut threw the damp air over the trees and into what Gilbert hoped to be uninhabited woods. The cannon recoiled with a clatter. Sipsis shrieked.

The few observers who had appeared on the shore disappeared into the woods.

"I think they know we've arrived," offered Gilbert, serious and nonplused. "But let's give them another salute." The well-practiced men had already cleaned the barrels, reloaded, and pushed the cannon and their casing into place, all within thirty seconds. "Aim a few degrees higher. We'll fire separately this time, Ready, fire one! Ready, fire two!" This time with hand over her ears, Sipsis' eyes remained wide opened, fascinated with the high trajectory and then its steaming decent nearly out of sight.

The forty armed soldiers who'd been standing at attention, weapons on their shoulders, were ordered into the four longboats floating at the ready. Gilbert, with Sipsis at his side, dropped into the first boat, quickly followed by the first ten soldiers. They would wait for the other three to fill before rowing four abreast. The soldiers held their muskets loaded and pointed to shore, shields at their side. It was certainly possible they would be met with a slew of arrows, even though each of the boats flew a white pendant. As Gilbert had restated before disembarking, "Remember, the cannon is our intimidation calling card. The flags mean we are not here to kill. Do you all understand?"

"Sir!" they responded, loudly and in unison.

Within ten minutes the party of forty men and officers, along with Sipsis, stand on dry ground, unmolested, at the same spot where they had landed before. Neither Sabenoa nor his men are in sight, though Gilbert expects they are not far off, somewhere only a few yards into the thick underbrush or in the dark pine woods with many trees large enough to hide two men.

On their previous visit, Sabenoa had led the men through the woods on a narrow path to the village less than a quarter of a mile away. Gilbert remembers most of the braves had taken a shorter route, as they had reappeared in the village before the English. Discussions with Nahanada had substantiated this hunch. Gilbert orders his men to spread out and be ready to quickly take cover in the bushes along the sand and mud beach that they would travel for a few hundred yards before it opened up onto a broad sandy path leading to the hundred and fifty or so huts and lodges.

Two skinny domesticated wolf pups bark as the group approaches the central area. Either the population has concealed themselves well in their huts, or they have retreated to the woods. Of course it could be a trap. The well-practiced defensive maneuver involves forming a circle with shields at the perimeter. The English musket fire established a huge advantage, at least in the first few minutes of a skirmish. Sabenoa knows this. Besides, they are marching with four white flags and a cart carrying items to be traded. This is topped with a ten-gallon copper pot, plus a specially-constructed chair with a red cushion, an item Gilbert hopes will speak to Sabenoa's vanity—he, the Lord of the Sagadahoc.

As Gilbert, Sipsis, and four soldiers who lead the column turn into the open center of the village, Sabenoa comes into view. He stands with a royal headdress of eagle feathers, one hand on a spear, his face expressionless, his head nodding recognition. Gilbert notices his eyes dart toward the cart with its offerings and return with its straight-on unperturbed gaze.

Davis orders the men to halt and take a defensive position facing outwards, thereby creating a semicircle with Sabenoa and the main lodge at their backs.

"Lord of the Sagadahoc, we return to honor you and to do trade." Sipsis begins translating this line, which she has already practiced, before Gilbert finishes."

"You come to make a great noise." Sipsis translates Sabenoa's reply as, "You make big nose."

"We do this in your honor," Gilbert responds.

Prior to this moment of facing one another, each has made many calculations, some recently, some over the past weeks. Sabenoa knows about Woboz and his band separating from Nahanada. And he knows the English need food. That was the case a month ago. It would be more so now. Rumor has it that a few young, unruly braves from his own village had unleashed ignited arrows into the English fort and started a fire. Anticipating the English would return for food, Sabenoa has removed most of the baskets of produce from the main storehouse and hidden them a good distance away. Furthermore, once the bombardment began, he ordered fifty braves to remain in the woods surrounding the village and more to hide in the huts to wait for instructions to attack or at least present themselves in force, if need be. Another group of twenty was assigned to launch their canoes. Their mission was to capture the landing boats and hold them as bargaining chips. Sabenoa considered capturing a few soldiers as well.

Gilbert had also schemed. He had ordered the sailors to row the longboats back within the protective cover of the *Gift of God*. There the gunners and twenty armed sailors were at the ready. With grapeshot and musket fire, the ship sat like a tiny fort surrounded by its natural moat. Additionally, various signals would initiate different action. Three shots in quick succession from the soldiers in the village meant an immediate alarm. The ship would provide a cannon broadside to the village. The soldiers would be ordered to retreat down the path toward the water, thereby hopefully getting out of the line of fire. The longboats would quickly return to retrieve them with cannon and musket cover.

Two shots in quick succession would indicate that Gilbert had consummated a deal. The longboats would return, but the cannoneers would remain alert ready to provide cover.

Sabenoa did not intend to be generous with food. Because he produced more than required to feed his people during the winter and spring, the Lord of the Sagadahoc could be generous toward other villages that might turn to him, typically in the early spring. This gained Sabenoa respect. But he did not want to be generous toward the English. They were a sacrilege in the land of his forefathers. Unlike Nahanada and Skidwarres, he could not even imagine an England across the water. Sabenoa was crafty, but he was not curious.

Woboz had visited some days before. To him and his followers,

Sabenoa had offered baskets of food in exchange for one woman, arrowheads, venison, bearskins, and a few muskets that Woboz had traded from villages which cooperated with the French. One French musket hung on a post next to where Sabenoa stood. It suggested greater firepower than he could muster. Only two others existed in the village, along with a minuscule amount of gunpowder and a dozen or so balls.

Sabenoa did not want loss of life. All life was precious. In a village the death of one warrior would mean backbiting, especially if brought about by recklessness. He wanted to get rid of the English, give them little while gaining something through trade. Gilbert might be desperate or rash and belligerent. Had he not already frightened Sabenoa's people with his barrage? But Sabenoa refused to lose face. That would be to lose everything. He considered his pride essential to his people's wellbeing.

Gilbert wanted food—and he intended not to be made a fool. And he did not want to create any more hostility than he judged already existed. His firepower and the soldiers were the trump cards—best unused, but once actual hostilities began, one had to hedge all bets.

The two men face one another, each aware of the other's deviousness, though not of the details. Sipsis begins, as practiced, by asking to trade for food and by offering the chair and pots. Sabenoa eyes the chair, especially the velvet tasseled cushion, an adornment suggested by Sipsis, a woman's touch. He approaches the cart. At Gilbert's orders, a soldier places the would-be throne on the ground. Sabenoa turns, bends over, holds this position while testing the alignment of his backside and the chair behind his legs, and finally, ceremoniously lowers himself squarely in the middle.

"Excellent," says Gilbert. "Fit for a lord." Sipsis translates this after conferring with Gilbert some. Then Sabenoa rises, approaches the cart, and peeks under the linen which covers various trinkets, beads, and a few woolen blankets.

"Guns?" Sabenoa asks in English.

"Tell him we have only enough for ourselves." This translation had been anticipated and practiced.

"Huh," Sabenoa mutters. Clearly he does not believe the admiral. "The same for food," is Sipsis' translation to English. At this the sagamore calls out a command. Twenty or so warriors appear from within a number of nearby huts. The soldiers immediately raise their muskets. Gilbert sees the bows are at the natives' side, arrows in their quivers. "At ease men. No harm yet."

Sipsis informs Gilbert that they have been told to proceed to the store lodge. The procession begins, led by Sabenoa carrying his spear, followed by Gilbert who walks abreast with Sipsis, and behind them the soldiers. The braves follow on either side. As they pass other huts more braves appear, doubling their numbers by the time they reach the store lodge at the edge of the village. Like most native buildings, this is constructed of bark covering a skeleton of saplings. Only Sabenoa, Gilbert and, Sipsis enter. Bushel-sized reed baskets filled with root vegetables and maize are stacked to the ceiling, filling less than a quarter of the space. A row of fifteen or so baskets of smoked fish occupies the other side of the hut.

Sabenoa announces, "You see, not much."

Gilbert looks at the open, firmly-packed ground between the stacks of food, suggesting at one point the lodge has been more fully stocked. "We need all of this for the winter." He says, more or less to himself, and Sipsis translates.

Sabenoa walks to the stacks of vegetables and touches ten baskets, turns, walks to the opposite side and puts his hand on five baskets of fish.

"That isn't enough for two weeks, let alone two months. Tell this liar I know he has more. Do you understand? More!"

"Yes, Admiral." She turns to Sabenoa and their conversation goes back and forth, heating up.

Outside the soldiers stand in formation, ten in a row, four deep. The braves wander around or stand watching in small groups. Men and women are covered by deerskin smocks, leggings, and moccasins. The men have shaved the sides of their heads. Their remaining hair in the middle is thickened with bear grease and propped up, giving the appearance of a rooster's comb. Their tattoos are uniformly black and blue. The two groups eye one another with wonderment and fear. They can hear Sipsis and Sabenoa as their voices rise. Some of the women giggle. They can't hear all the words, nor are they used to hearing a woman speak with such authority.

Sipsis' voice has become angry, her face reddens. Finally she turns abruptly in frustration and faces Gilbert.

"What is it? What did he say?" insists Gilbert.

"He says he will give you twice that, but I must stay with him. He needs a new wife."

Gilbert asks Sipsis to repeat herself. He isn't sure he has understood. But he has. Sabenoa stands there with a grin he can't contain. He shrugs and says, "You came to trade for food. The blanket, beads, the pots, and the chair—I take them and this woman. You take this food."

Sipsis translates. What at first seemed absurd to Gilbert begins to appear plausible. "How much food? For that I want all that is here and more."

Sipsis looks at Gilbert with surprise. She looks at him and then at the sagamore who leers at her, his grin still immobilized on his face. She doesn't translate.

Sabenoa asks her, "What did the white fool say?"

Gilbert asks her, "What is that bastard saying?"

"You trade me? You trade me?" Her voice goes from a question to an accusation.

Gilbert responds quickly, "I don't know. No, I was just thinking, calculating. Tell him I don't believe him. Tell him if he wants peace, then he must be more generous." Sipsis doesn't fully grasp his words. They haven't practiced this. He repeats himself, "Tell him our guns talk when we get hungry." This she translates.

Outside soldiers and braves each catch a one-sided interpretation of the talk going on inside the lodge. The words become clearer as the tension rises. The potential combatants continue to eye one another. They talk under their breaths in English and in Algonquin dialect. The two wolf puppies who'd greeted the soldiers earlier pick up on the tension and raise their hackles. One advances on the column of soldiers from the rear. The closer he gets, the more emboldened he becomes. Finally, the year-old wolf lunges at one soldier's calf. Taken by surprise, the man yelps, then swings around and punches the animal's muzzle hard with the butt end of his musket. Blood gushes from the wolf's mouth where an incisor hangs loose. He makes a wobbly retreat and drops to the ground to nurse his wound.

From the edge of the group watching, a ten-year-old boy runs to the dog. He falls on his knees and examines the smashed face. Two other children, a boy and girl about his age, rush over to join him. As they kneel, the first boy bolts up. He dashes headlong into the offending soldier, punching his fists into the man's stomach. The soldier, nearly as surprised by this second attacker, puts out a stiff arm to defend himself. Out of nervousness and pain from the bite, he laughs. One of the aimless flying fists catches the eighteen-year-old Englishman in the testicles. Now he joins the dog ten feet away on the ground, on his knees. The soldier next to him in line takes one step toward the boy and with the other foot delivers a kick that lands in the boy's stomach. Now three lie on the ground, the boy gasping for air. For the first few moments everyone watches in silent amazement. Then a stream of bilingual complaints and threats erupt.

Next, the boy's mother arrives, screaming, "*Wkeji! wkeji!*" (asshole). From somewhere behind one of the huts, a group of adolescent boys begins hurling whatever they can find—small stones, pieces of half-eaten squash, a couple of fish heads, and wolf turds. These objects begin hitting the agitated English. One of the braves, the older brother of the boy on the ground, joins the screaming woman.

Captain Davis orders his men to form up twenty in the front row with their rifles held in front. As they arrange themselves, a brave swings his bow and clips the kicker across the head. He, too, lands on the ground.

Sabenoa and Gilbert, in their bargaining impasse, hear the commotion. Sabenoa pushes the door flap open. The three step out to noisy, danger-fraught chaos. The natives offer equal portions of mockery and threat. He sees two soldiers being steadied by others. A native boy is carrying away his puppy. Everyone senses the hostility in the air. "Order!" Gilbert shouts, not knowing for the moment what else to do. A large root vegetable passes by his ear and hits the lodge behind him.

Sergeant Gross, who's been instructed to signal for cannon fire in the event of an emergency, yells to his three riflemen, each with their loaded musket. "Fire, one, two, three!" The rapid consecutive fire of three muskets will alert the *Gift of God*. Sergeant Gross has mistaken "Order!" for "Order cannon!"

With the three musket blasts, everyone stops. At the same instant Gilbert realizes the mistake. In the moment of quiet he announces with a steady voice, "Men, we have ordered a barrage." His wits quickly calculate the mistake might be to their advantage. From less than a half-mile they hear a two-syllable ka-boom, then another. Three seconds later one ball whooshes overhead clipping treetops and vanishing in the woods beyond the village. Another with a lower trajectory smashes through the top of one hut, then ricochets into three pine trees before burying itself in the ground. A young native woman with her baby in arms stands paralyzed in the ruins, with pieces of bark draped over her head. She and the child appear to be in shock, but uninjured.

Never before had the natives witnessed a cannon bombardment. Stories they'd heard made it something of a mythical threat. They had heard the muted thump of the cannon shot from the fort some twenty miles to the south and, in the last hour, the booms set off before the English arrived on foot. Now the braves begin to panic. Some rush to their huts or into the woods, looking for their family members. Others, out of obedience or fear, congregate around Sabenoa. Expressionless, he watches as if it were now a bizarre military parade gone awry.

"Men! Each of you, two to a basket, in there, get as much food as you can. Now!" Gilbert decides to use the pandemonium to his advantage. There is another resounding blast. This time a ball flies way over their heads. Another round falls short. Soldiers file past Gilbert, Sipsis, and Sabenoa and into the lodge, double up, and grab the fifty-to-sixty-pound baskets.

Sabenoa watches, not sure what to say to his braves. Gilbert turns to Sipsis, who at the beginning of the blasts grabbed onto his sleeve. "Tell him the chair is his, the pots, everything." He says this three times before she collects her wits and passes on the information. Sabenoa watches as the English emerged from the lodge, scurrying as fast as they can with their awkward loads. Gilbert orders the three appointed musket signalers to reload and keep them at the ready.

The next series of cannon shot lands in the middle of the village. By then most all the inhabitants, including the braves, have run into the woods. One ball blows apart three huts, another two, the third sinks into soft earth with a sucking sound. The master works his ballistics from a crude map he and Gilbert drew. They'd decided if this maneuver were necessary, it would be best to scatter the shots, as they had no visual validation of their accuracy.

Before the signal to begin the barrage, those on the *Gift of God* watched as eight long canoes set out to attack, or at least intimidate, the ship. This Sabenoa had planned with his elders. He had expected they'd be able to capture the landing boats, but instead, they had returned to the *Gift of God* for protection.

The sailors on the ship were ready to pick off the oncoming canoes with rifle fire, or if need be by grapeshot from the bow cannon. But before the natives were within decent range, the cannoneers heard the three rifle shots. The cannon barrage began. The oncoming paddlers turned immediately and headed toward a small river past the landing beach. The four longboats, now safe to retrieve Gilbert's party—assuming they'd soon appear on the beach—head back.

Gilbert, Sabenoa, and Sipsis continue to stand together. Soldiers carrying baskets of food hold their loaded weapons in their other hand. The natives hear Sabenoa say, "Let the English go. We will have another day." Sipsis translates this for Gilbert. He nods his approval. Sabenoa and Gilbert each know the other has gained something. Gilbert orders the riflemen to fire two shots. He then turns to Sabenoa. "Thank you for your food, Lord of the Sagadahoc." Sipsis translates. "Enjoy your throne—your chair," he amends, realizing "throne" could not be translated. She stares at Gilbert with a hardness he hasn't seen before. Sipsis, though relieved he did not include her with pots and chair, remains outraged that he'd seriously considered such a deal.

The exodus from the village to the beach and the portage of the foodstuffs and men to the ship bring on only a few stray arrows. The eight native canoes hold their position more than a mile away. The chaos of screaming, gunfire, shouts, threats, anxiety, fear—it all dissipates as the sun falls behind the tree line.

Night will fall quickly, along with the cold. Elliott tells Gilbert they can catch the last of the outgoing tide, allowing an anchorage before the tide turns, and far enough away a night attack would be unlikely.

Nonetheless, the still-angry braves persuade Sabenoa to allow them to harass the ship as it lies at anchor that night in the half moon. Gilbert expected as much. The canoes come in sight, small specks on a dark sea, before they unleash arrows wrapped in burning cloth soaked in bear oil. All but one falls short. It sticks to the deck, there to be immediately doused. One blast from a cannon, intentionally aimed to bounce toward the canoes like a skipping stone, tears off the bow of one, sending six braves into the cold Sagadahoc. The would-be battle turns into a war of insults neither recipient understands. With the soaked natives pulled aboard the remaining canoes, the small flotilla turns upriver. So ended the ineffectual coda to a day of marginal gains and hurt pride.

CHAPTER 44

December 13, 1607, Fort St. George
The *Gift of God* Sails Back To England

Gilbert returned with twenty baskets of vegetables and dried fish, his reputation enhanced. He had carried himself well, albeit it with luck. As far as he knew, no deaths had occurred on either side. A wolf pup had inflicted the most serious English injury. Gilbert's reward included laudatory words from President Popham and a cold shoulder from Sipsis, who continued her refusal to lie with the admiral. Three days later, earlier than expected, during a relatively warm spell, she and Nolka had returned to their village, escorted by Nahanada's braves.

At the meeting of the council, it became clear the food stocks could not sustain a group of ninety until spring. They had to act now before sea travel became even more dangerous. It did not take long to decide. Approximately half the population of the fort would sail back to Plymouth on the *Gift of God*, taking the southerly route. The bulk of the passengers would be the farmers and craftsmen, excepting the shipwrights, leaving the fort with a contingent of fifty-eight, until they could be re-supplied with material and manpower in the spring of 1608.

Popham set to writing a letter to the King. It must be positive. Popham wrote half to bolster his own flagging spirits, half to impress his sovereign. He chose the official language for such communication, Latin.

"13 December, 1607. George Popham, President of the Second Virginia Colony, does humble obeisance at the feet of his most illustrious Sovereign. If Your Divine Majesty's indulgence may be pleased to accept a few words from the most diligent and devoted, albeit unworthy, servant, I consider that they will far from detract from Your Highness's fame, since they seem to be conducive to the glory of God, to the scale of your eminence, and to the advantage of the British people.

"I have, therefore, deemed it perfectly proper to inform Your Majesty that nobody in the world is more admired by the people of Virginia and the Mawooshen than the Lord King James, Emperor of the British, because of his wonderful sense of justice and his scarcely credible constancy, which brings great happiness to the natives of your provinces. For they say, moreover, that no god is truly worthy of worship except the Lord King James's, and that they would willingly give military service under his authority and command. Nahanada, a native who has been to Britain, has broadcast your praise and your fine qualities to them here.

"What good I might do, and how much, in undertaking this enterprise and in consolidating these feelings, is for those to judge who have given it informed consideration at home; for I recognize that all personal endeavors are as nothing when compared with my obligations toward the King. I am firmly convinced that the glory of God is beginning to shine out freely in this region, that Your Majesty's empire is being enlarged, and that the common welfare of the British settlers has been increased in a short time. As regards commercial resources, all the native inhabitants repeatedly assert that there are nutmegs and cinnamon in these parts; furthermore Brazil wood and ambergris, along with many other important and valuable things, all very plentiful at that.

"Moreover, they impress upon me that, in the opposite or western part of this province, no more than seven days' journey from our Fort St. George at Sagadahoc, there is some sea which is extensive, wide, and deep; but they have no idea how far it extends. This can be none other than the Southern Ocean, stretching toward the land of China which doubtless cannot be far away from this region.

"Therefore, if it may please you to take divine notice of the subject of my testimony, I have no doubt that Your Highness will accomplish a task which is most acceptable to God, which brings honor to Your Majesty, and which is of great advantage to your kingdom; and this with fervent entreaties I earnestly implore you to do. I pray also to God, the good and the great, that he will long preserve the glorious Majesty of my Sovereign Lord James.

"At Fort St. George, Sagadahoc, Virginia. Your Majesty's devoted servant in all things. George Popham."

Popham read his letter over twice and considered tearing it up and reducing its hyperbole. He wished it were true but knew or guessed otherwise. Most of his claims were based on Nahanada's earlier reports. Now they seemed highly suspect. However, he knew—or hoped anyway—the main value of the colony remained political.

The ship would sail in three days. The temperature had dropped into the twenties. He heard the wind whipping about the tall pines and spruce. They creaked in the cold. He wished Nolka was lying in his bed, waiting. He swallowed another large mouthful of port and signed his name. Tomorrow he would write a more forthright letters to Gorges and Cousin John. They, too, must remain inspired; but both would be discussing the matter with the returning men, so would need to know of the soldiers lost at sea and of the flagging spirits during the past weeks, since posting letters with the *Mary and John*. He couldn't persuade himself to mention the hanged goatherder. In fact, he so little liked thinking of the matter, he'd nearly forgotten.

Richard took the opportunity to write to Margaret. As before, he looked to his journal and copied many of his entries and, like Popham, Richard decided to omit the murders—as they remained a secret—and the hanging. And like Popham, he imbued the letter with optimism. Following the journal entries he added, "We, the boys and I, huddle close to the crude fireplace burning log after huge log. It is a different cold from that in Dorset. It pierces the bone. Less and less are we outside. It is difficult to imagine the warm breezes and hot sun of August, or that they will ever return. However, the cold is good for the boys' education— though only two will remain—what with all this time inside. And I read much and practice the lute with Lance's assistance.

"I ache for you at night. Though I've kept busy lately helping many to write letters, with the sailing of the *Gift of God*, my responsibilities tending to the men will be reduced. Simply, there will be fewer of them.

"My spirits remain high most of the time, knowing how vital our existence here is to the future of England. I often feel part of destiny. I even imagine we might both inhabit this extraordinary New World, you and your cello, I and my horse and harpsichord—though I must say, I am becoming partial to the lute.

"You know of the adventuring part of me, that part that liked riding off for three or four days at a time, not knowing where I would end up at night. That is the part of me who is here—some of the time. At other times, many times, I wish for comforts, a warm bath and warm library full of books; and I miss English architecture, the sound of your cello, and delicately prepared food. Salted fish has its limits. Oh, you see, I am not so much the hardy explorer. Perhaps I am hankering for domestication, your sweet domestication—be it on either side of the Atlantic.

"Your constant, Richard."

After reading the final paragraphs he focused on the word "destiny." The word had come to him unexpectedly, though not as a new concept. He and Skidwarres had bumped up against this notion more than once. Here, though, the word had arrived on paper as a confirmed position.

When Richard suggested that Lance write a letter, he declined. Richard pushed. "I am sure someone would greatly appreciate news from you. What of your music teacher?"

"Richard, understand. I want to forget England. It is only here that I have been happy." Lance's decisiveness ended the matter, but when the ship sailed on December 16th, a letter to Lance's teacher joined the others in the mail sack. "I told him I have been your teacher. I think he will appreciate that."

The *Gift of God* would sail far south before she headed east, thereby avoiding the worst of the North Atlantic weather. A few days after her departure, the temperature dropped yet again, precipitously. Within days the ice froze on the Sagadahoc, miraculous given her swift tides. It would be, as it turned out, the coldest winter on record for both the New World and the Old. A few days' delay and the *Gift of God* might have been immobilized, and then with the melt crushed by boulders of ice. With her leaving, the men felt an extra sense of isolation. Now no ship lay in the bay, a sight that suggested escape was no longer possible. They looked at the shallop and the incomplete *Virginia* grounded high up on the beach above the high water mark and felt forlorn.

CHAPTER 45

December 30, 1607, Fort St. George
Birthmark

During a spell when the temperature didn't rise above fifteen degrees, Richard found himself again enjoying Montaigne while huddled in a blanket next to the fire. Lance and Jimmy had finished their lessons and were helping prepare the noon meal.

The solitude ended with Lance's high-pitched voice from some distance away. "I'll kill him, kill him." His voice gets louder. Then the door flies open. Panting through his crying and gasping, Lance sputters, "Stow! Those bastards cut off his tail. Stow's tail. I can't find him." Lance raised his fist. In it he holds Stow's black tail with the small white tip on the end. "He always stays outside the cook house door waiting for me. Today only this. I know who, that bastard Hawkes, tied this to a stick. Blood on the snow. I don't know where, where the rest of him is. Help me find him. Help, help me kill that bastard. You have to, Richard." And at that Lance runs across the room and into Richard's arms. At age fifteen he still barely comes up to Richard's chin.

After allowing the worst of the sobs to fade, Richard releases Lance in his bulky clothes. "All right then, let's see if we can find him."

Snow has now covered the ground for nearly a month. Unlike snow in England that often melted within a short period of time, here one storm builds upon another, so the overall accumulation in late December topped two feet. The soldiers' major task has become that of snow removal. This involved pushing it aside with two-man wooden shovels or packing it with their feet. Few ventured beyond the fort, given the difficulty walking. The snow cover did, however, provide a huge asset: a much reduced chance of attack, or so was the assumption.

Richard and Lance walk down the path between the four-foot snow banks to the cleared center, to Gilbert's house across from the large storage building. He was inside taking lunch alone and reading.

Gilbert listens patiently to Lance's story and finally sighs. "Sorry to hear that. It was—or is—a fine dog." Gilbert's tone holds some compassion; he is after all the devoted owner of two giant Mastiffs who lie by the fire asleep. "But..." And then rather than continue with that thought he shifts, "I will confront those men. It's not the first time."

"And they'll just lie to your face," Lance blurts out.

"So they might. But you have no evidence. Not even a body. Your dog might still be alive, only tailless."

"No, he would come to me. He would find me. He always does. They've killed him."

"Listen, Lance." Now the admiral shifts back to the tone he began with. "That dog was not invited. Some found him a nuisance."

"No, only those imbeciles."

"Silence. This is the way it is. I will ask questions. I will bring these men in. If I have evidence, I will punish them. Do you understand?"

"I understand, Admiral." What Lance understands is that the world has not changed. Beyond his music teacher and Richard, justice does not exist.

Richard breaks in. "I, too, will ask around. But it is a great pity."

"Yes, a pity. Now if you please, I will return to my work. I will let you know, Seymour, what I learn."

"Of course, Gilbert." Richard usually used his title in response to Gilbert's referring to him as Seymour. But this occasion feels different.

When Richard and Lance approach the main chapel door, simultaneously they see the black object curled around itself and licking its bloody stub of a tail.

Lance runs and drops to his knees. "It's Stow, he's alive." Stow lifts his blood- soaked nuzzle, licks Lance's face, and wags the remainder of his tail.

"Let's get him inside and tend to him. Clean him. And you."

Lance, sniffling with streaks of red across his cheeks and forehead, burbles, "Richard, he's not dead. Do you think he'll live? Does it hurt a lot?"

"He looks unhurt otherwise. He'll live. It's mostly cartilage. But, yes, it must hurt. I'll pick him up. You fetch some water. Warm it a bit. Looks like the snow staunched most of the bleeding."

They feed the fire. After kitchen duty, Jimmy is assigned to the sailmaker who taught him to stitch the new sails for the *Virginia*. She would be commissioned in early spring. For a while Richard and Lance would be alone.

On their return to the chapel, they pick up bread, cheese, and beer. After attending to Stow, who lies on an old blanket asleep in front of the fire, they nibble and sip in silence, Richard on the chair designed for him by the shipwright, and Lance on a low stool. Finally Richard says, "That was a scare."

"He really loves me. I know dogs can love. You can see it in his eyes. He trusts me and I trust him."

"Of course he loves you. You are everything, his friend and God."

Lance buries his face in his hands and begins sobbing. It comes from deep down and Richard knows it isn't just for the near loss of the dog. Richard rises to stand behind the boy, hands on his shoulders. When some minutes later the sobbing subsides, he squeezes, releases him, pokes the fire with the iron, adds two logs, pushes them into place to allow air between, then sits again with the book across his lap and watches Lance for a few moments.

Then Richard picks up reading where he'd left off. Lance remains on the stool, quiet, his knees propped up on the highest rung, his forehead in his hands, staring at the fire. It is a calm, cold day, with nothing but occasional calls from one man to another or a gull screeching or laughing overhead. Finally Lance raises his head. "Richard?"

"Yes?"

"Do you know why I never take my shirt off, even when it was so hot, or why you never see me wash?"

Richard had not thought about this quirk of Lance's in quite a while. "Well, only what you told me. You don't want people seeing your birthmark. I thought it a bit overly...well I don't know, overly sensitive, but it is your business. The boys use to tease you, but no more, correct?"

"Correct. That's because I handed out two bloody noses. Anyway, I'm ready to show you, if you wish."

"If it would make you feel more comfortable." Richard puts the book on the near table. "More comfortable with yourself, of course. Is that it?"

"Exactly." Lance slides off the stool and stands with his back to Richard. First he removes a heavy woolen shirt and then unbuttons the lighter cotton one, revealing what looks to Richard like a modified corset. Before he can make any sense of this, Lance turns while unhooking the lacing. Two small breasts reveal themselves, two adolescent, female breasts.

"Here are my birthmarks. They're getting bigger. I won't be able to hide them much longer."

Lance has to laugh. He's never seen Richard so dumbfounded, blinking, mouth dropped. She—as it was now obvious—feels emboldened. "Do you want to touch them?"

All Richard can utter during the first few moments of this revelation, while his eyes remain on her naked torso covered in goose bumps, with the tiny pink nipples erect in the cold and the corset now on the floor is, "Do I want to touch?" The answer he realizes later is "yes," but this he does not utter.

"What is your real name?" Their eyes meet.

"Lillian, or Lilly. Call me Lilly."

"Well then, Lilly, how about putting on a shirt before you tell me more." Richard is relieved to regain his composure.

"Are you sure you don't want to touch me or see the rest, just to prove it. Richard, really, I love you. I wouldn't tell. I want to be touched by you. I've wanted that for a long time. I was sure you knew."

In spite of his self-possession, even in the face of such an unsettling transformation, Richard feels the stir of arousal. "Lance—Lilly—put on a shirt." The voice is stern, a great lie. "You are beautiful. But you are still mostly Lance to me. Besides..." This sentence trails off, while Lilly does as requested. She picks up the corset, wriggles into it, begins lacing it and then reverses herself. Lilly throws it into a corner. Stow, awake, stares as well. Lilly grabs her shirts, hurriedly puts them on without buttoning and plunks herself back on the bench. She looks down at her still-exposed breasts. "I'm not wearing that thing anymore. It hurts."

"Please explain." Richard lets out a sigh that speaks for his own sexual awakening, as well as for his perplexity. "And button."

"Nobody's ever given a damn about me. My parents were too young and poor and stupid and drunk most the time, until they died— starvation, the plague eventually—and I was taken by my uncle, who liked me only because he could paw me and later fuck me."

Richard stares, taking in what now appear obvious: Lilly's delicate features. He'd been hoodwinked by her boldness, her overcompensation in the form of bravado. He realizes his head is slightly nodding in recognition of her tale, one he'd heard before, in part.

"So I ran away. Then and there I decided I couldn't be a girl. Too dangerous, too humiliating. I didn't have to wear a corset then. I was only twelve. Even back then, nobody saw me without clothes. Nobody really cared anyway. You know the rest more or less. The orphanage. That's where I learned to piss standing up, using this little wooden pipe." She fishes in her pocket and pulls it out. "See. It takes a little practice. Fooled everybody including you, right? I got accomplished at being a boy. It felt good, especially when I broke a nose in a fight, or a finger. I carried a knife. You know, I still do." Lilly puts the pipe back in her pocket with one hand and displays the knife in the other.

"Pretty remarkable. And you did have me fooled, though like most people, I considered you effeminate in some basic way. A sweetness you couldn't hide—but tough as nails."

"That is what I was counting on. I was successful, wasn't I?"

"You were pretty successful, yes."

Lilly smiles. She's even put on her heavy overcoat and her hat in order to get warm. "Richard, do you want to know what I think?"

Richard chuckles, shakes his head. "I'm not sure."

"Too bad. I'm thinking I have two choices. You take me as your woman. Then nobody here will hurt me. You can help me learn to be a woman. You could do that. I can learn. You know I am smart. I don't think I can pretend much longer. I'm changing. But I don't want to be a girl, a woman in this freezing dungeon around all those men. But if I'm your woman I'll spend most of my time here. Anyway, they won't bother me if they know that. Then I can do it."

"Lance...Lilly. Hold on."

"You could teach me. You know you could. Not just to be a woman, but like the Margaret you talk about."

For the moment, rather than resist this request, Richard asks, "And your second choice?"

"I want to stay here, I mean in the New World. England is a nightmare. When I played lacrosse with Moskwas, we ended up wrestling after the game. We were alone. I never let the boys here touch me, but this felt different. I didn't worry. I think I just wanted him to touch me and hold me. I didn't really think about it. Just did it, by accident he held me from behind around the chest. He felt me for a moment and then dropped his hand and spun me around. I know the word for girl, *behanem*. That's what he said, and I said yes. He smiled and then laughed and touched me again, and then we both laughed. Later that day we kissed. That's all. It was my idea. I wasn't ready for anything else. But I think he likes me. I think he would marry me. So that's my second choice."

"From the day I met you on ship I've been impressed. Now, Lilly, I'm dumbstruck," Richard admits. She sits across from him, still on the stool, again with her feet on the top rung huddled in her winter coat, a small, black-curly-haired creature peering out at him from under her hat with huge expectant blue eyes. How could he have not known?

"So, Chaplain, what am I to do?"

"Lilly, you're right. I'm the chaplain and what are you, fifteen?"

"Sixteen."

"You told me fifteen a few months ago."

"That was a few months ago. Richard. I'm old enough."

"For what? I'm engaged. I'm your teacher."

"And I'm your teacher."

"Lance, Lilly, it's out of the question."

"Why?"

"You're a child."

"I'm no child."

"I'm...well, I'm the representative of the Church of England. I am engaged to be married. We are betrothed. It's wrong."

"Betrothed! You are thousands of miles away. We might all die in the cold or be shipwrecked or killed. What are you afraid of? What's wrong? You don't think I'm really a woman?"

"Enough, Lilly. No more talk of this."

"But you'll think about it."

"I guess I can't help but think about it. But change my mind? No. As to your second choice, you need to think more about that. Then we can talk to Skidwarres, though I don't expect to see him soon in this weather."

"Just think about it then." At this Lilly jumps off the stool, takes two quick steps, and kisses Richard sweetly on the cheek. His hands do not rise to ward her off, he thinks in hindsight.

Richard coughs and stands. Stow, stiff-legged, rises and stretches, then walks slowly to Lilly who greets him on one knee.

"He's all I've ever really had—except for you."

Outside they can hear Jimmy approaching, jabbering away with a young man who has joined their tutorial group. They are scheduled to write an essay on lying, based on Montaigne's essays and discussion. Then they would all have tea.

Lilly grabs her corset and stuffs it under the covers of Richard's bed. She goes to the door to let them in. "I will now miraculously change myself into a boy. Black magic." She pulls it open, "Come on in, you filthy toads."

CHAPTER 46

January 15th, 1608, Fort St. George
Hippocratic Oath

January begins with a thaw. For the first time in nearly a month, the temperature rises into the high 30s during the day. The sun sparkles brightly off the ubiquitous snow cover. Day by day it angles higher. The recent high tide has upended the frozen Sagadahoc channel, sending shallop-size chunks of ice floating out to sea or jammed a mile or so upriver, carried by the incoming tide. The men, like the landscape, lighten. They emerge from their huts like the black bear and raise their faces to catch the warmth and to stir their brains. Heat, blessed heat, saturates their long beards and even penetrates clothing that hasn't been removed in weeks.

Three concerns become topics for the council: first, the growing indifference of the men. Punishments—brief stints in the stockade, lashings, wages docked—are increasingly meted out for insolence and slothful reactions to orders. This only fuels the disgruntlement. Second, adding to the stupefying cold, the men constantly complain about the small portions of food and its lack of variety. By halving the population and purloining the twenty baskets of food from Sabenoa, Gilbert and the others have calculated they can manage until April—but only with strict management. Firewood becomes the third potentially deadly necessity.

The firewood close to the fort has already been harvested. Beyond the nearby clear cut to the west of the fort, the men have created paths allowing access to favorable trees. But the amalgamated snow cover, some of it frozen ice, makes travel painstaking. Hauling logs hundreds of yards on crudely-built sleds chews up time and energy. Across the river on a low stretch, Gilbert has spotted a large stand of pine and birch. Green pine burns better, hotter than hard birch, oak, or maple. It would be best to ferry the barge across the river. If the weather allowed, they might cut twenty cords. They could be delivered to the water's edge by the fort—that is if longboats, six men to a vessel, could tug the weight and manage the tides. More than three-quarters of the remaining regiment would be detailed. At the cutting yard a small contingent would maintain a fire all night, providing for cooking and warmth. The light of the fire would also allow cutting, limbing, and stacking to continue after dark. The warm spell would not last forever. If all went well, the activity might enliven the men. At least they could discontinue rationing firewood. "An army decays without some kind of purpose," proclaims Gilbert.

The next day a heavy snows blows in and out, leaving another six inches. Yet again the men clear out the fort's grounds. Afterwards, most are detailed across the river. Richard stands in the chapel doorway with a cup of tea. Lilly, still Lance to all but himself, works in the kitchen. Richard takes note of the muffled near silence brought about by the recent snow. In particular, he watches recently accumulated patches on the limbs of white pine, white on green. The wind stirs the branches. He continues to watch. With the exact calculation of wind and gravity, just so, the snow silently explodes in slow motion, sparkling in the sun—miniature bursts of silent fireworks, each a small revelation, occurring how many times across the woods, across thousands of square miles?

Breaking this silence come the muted sounds of axes thumping into trees across the river and two-man saws, back and forth. The sky turns a brilliant baby blue. That is what Richard is remembering as he crawls into his cold bed that evening. Lilly, who has at least temporarily returned to her life as Lance, remains with him alone in the chapel, he in his study-bedroom, she in the nave. Tonight Jimmy is across the river. Lilly has complained of a recurring headache, an ailment she has reported enduring periodically since childhood; therefore she didn't join Jimmy. For over a week, neither she nor Richard has mentioned her incognito life. To Richard, day by day, the gender transformation has taken on aspects of a delusion. Has the blinding snow altered his vision and mind? Only out of the corner of his eye does he see Lance looking at him as a Lilly.

In bed he tries to see again in his mind's eye the soothing, exploding snow. For some reason it reminds him of the expression, "the mind of God." That tiny moment of such sheer simplicity and exquisite beauty proves the existence of God. Was everything God's mind? Not that God knew us personally, anymore than he knew of exploding clumps of snow.

So do the beautiful and the base, the tiny snow bursts and the shooting stars, make up the mind of God—along with the buckets of shit hauled from the men's huts every morning? The beautiful and the base? No, he's not making any sense.

No matter, Richard tries to explore these images and thoughts. It might take the form of a sermon. As the weather turns bitter, he's been preaching to fewer parishioners, so he's requested large urns of tea be set up and music played by Lance. Consequently attendance has increased. But tonight these thoughts seem unformed, even ridiculous.

An unordained chaplain, nonetheless Richard feels responsibility—for what? His "flock?" Helpless sheep? Rather, he considers the Hippocratic Oath, something he'd learned from the surgeon, a man who had kept to his drink more than his fellow man, before he left on the *Gift of God.* "Above all, one should not do harm." That made sense as a kind of ethical standard. But would it, he wonders, be harmful to lie with Lilly? Or would it simply be fornication? At age sixteen, she was no child. Many married at that age, even before. She wished to be treated kindly. Could he not be kind and lie with her? Was that not what she wished? But what was her motive? Or his own, for that matter? Was it anything beyond desire? Might she not gain from their intimacies? Would they not make one another happy, at least for a period of time? Is he bound to Margaret? He thinks so. Why then does he feel so tested? Could he be assured of Margaret's fidelity? For how long? Was Lilly not a beautiful offering, as with the snow burst, a tiny infinitesimal moment in time and place? Who cared, anyway? Was not God part of love, however it manifested itself?

"Time," the word on the tongue so often, time came to him—most of the time—as something elongated, stretching from his early childhood to the far horizon of the future, to death, even beyond, so history taught him. He thought of "the ages of man" and even visualized himself as many persons, each at a different stage in life, each with a life of his own, a period of time with a continuum, but separate as well—infancy, childhood, youth, middle age, old age, infirmity, death. And within these periods, smaller periods. Certainly this first year at the fort would be one of those segments. In the future, he would sit as an old man, if he were lucky enough to endure, and look back on this unique period. Time seems both a flowing essence of life, and then in a twinkle of an eye, time becomes encapsulated units. Some people, perhaps including Lilly, lived life in disconnected eras, each apparently uprooted from the other. His own life has never felt that way—until now. These thoughts have dominated his thinking during the past week.

As he lies near sleep, more thoughts trickle in. Do most of us walk forward into our futures, looking only a few steps in front, while paying more attention to a mirror we hold that allows access to the past? This, Richard thinks, is how many appear to live—dumb to a long-term future—while others cut off their pasts, as with a gangrenous leg. But who can know the future? What of fate? Or accident? Or unseized opportunity? We might plan for a future, but what would be the point?

With the bed warming from his own heat, Richard begins to stretch out from his fetal position and shuck these puzzling, disorganized thoughts, as fascinating as they are. Time could also present itself as simply "now." Everything was simply now. Now expanding like a balloon in a room, expanding until the past and future disappear for lack of space. At the edge of sleep, he recognizes sleep itself is like falling into the expansive now. It is a fine feeling.

He doesn't hear her open and shut the door. She first appears as a cold draft of air immediately followed by the warmth of her small body. He lies on his side, she behind. Lilly whispers, "Please don't make me leave."

Immediately wide awake, Richard feels paralyzed and wordless. She begins rubbing his back over his flannel nightshirt.

"Please don't make me leave. More than anything I want to lie here. I'm cold. Please."

Richard feels compelled to say something, "You can stay," arrives before he wills it. "To get warm," he adds, "then back."

They lie quietly together in the immense blackness, with only the embers of the fire suggesting anything existed beyond them, or ever would. Richard finds himself returning to his thoughts of a few minutes ago, only now the expanded moment centers on Lilly's fingers as they move slowly up and down his back. In this space the two are invisible. They don't even exist in time. One hand now slips around to his stomach and little by little she inches up the nightshirt until her palms and fingers touch the flesh of his stomach. Richard does not protest. Beyond the intense focus on her fingers and of her small legs pulled up against his, he simultaneously feels miles away or nonexistent. Yet another recognition: he is being seduced.

Then Richard turns over—as one might think about getting out of bed and then without knowing, find oneself standing—with the vague notion of protesting. Instead, he now realizes Lilly is fully naked, that his nightshirt rests around his waist, and that he can not hide his arousal. She reaches down and touches him. In response he offers a low sigh that turns into a quiet groan. He pulls her close.

"Please don't ask me to stop," Lilly whispers.

"I won't," Richard mumbles. The expanded world of touch, the warmth of her breast, the hot curve of her hip crowd all else out. Reservations evaporate. Lilly begins to whimper and sniffle and then silently cry. His hands cup her wet cheeks. He adjusts his body a little and finds her lips in the dark with his thumb. Their kissing is gentle and tentative. After a little while she pulls back, and sounding a bit like Lance, says, "My headache is gone."

"I don't want to do harm."

"What?" Lilly asks.

"I don't want to harm you. That is the last thing I want."

"Richard, I think the first thing you want is me." With this comment and a little chuckle, Lilly pulls herself up so she is astride. He completes the needed adjustments.

It is not long before Richard lies spent and in a timeless, deep sleep. Lilly remains atop him, feeling him finally retreat. She, too, falls into a lighter nap, full of happiness, as if embarking on a long-wished-for trip. Her capacity for full pleasure is stymied by the past, but she is certain Richard can awaken her in the future.

CHAPTER 47

January 16, 1608, Fort St. George
Lilly's Project

Richard awoke to find himself living a life substantially dislocated from the day before. Perhaps his meandering about time was his way of preparing for the inevitable merger, once Lilly had revealed herself. His life back in England now took on the feeling of an old dream. He felt emboldened after they made love three more times before the sun rose. He dressed to present himself to Popham—Gilbert being on the other side of the river directing operations—and announce the metamorphosis within the chapel. The man's response, first a stupefied expression—the dropped mouth and wide eyes equaling Richard's a week before—was followed by a great guffaw and a slap on Richard's back. "If a few other fellows could do such magic, we could make some officers happy men like yourself, I can plainly see." Popham cheerily offered his permission to take her as his woman. "When you get back, you and the bishop can have it out. As for me, I only wish I had such warmth between my blankets. Nolka's visit is overdue."

"And Gilbert, what do you suspect his reading on this matter?" asked Richard."

"Chaplain, I'm the president here. Beside, he's a worse wencher than I. Yes, he's very impressed by probity. He might grumble, but it will be out of jealousy, mark you."

"Then, sir, I hope you will announce this news to him and the men without my presence. I will try to explain once I have figured out how." At this Richard comprehended for the first time the full foolishness of his situation.

Whereas Richard and Lilly's lives head off in new multi-emotional directions, the life of the fort drags on day by frozen day in the same direction. Cramped lives led in their torpid, linear track toward an imagined spring at least two months away, though nobody is sure. Late January into early February becomes even more frigid, a circumstance unimaginable to everyone. The thermometer falls to thirty below at night and then doesn't rise above zero for a week; and after that, during the first few days in February, not above twenty.

The sentries' rotations become impossible after two hours. Gilbert begrudgingly discontinues the daily cannon salute soon after his return from Sabenoa's village. The council finally agrees such provocation isn't necessary. The men rarely raise their voices. Marching, food preparation, and firewood splitting occupy the lives of the soldiers and the few remaining craftsmen. Work on the *Virginia* ceases. Men huddle by fireplaces, sleep twelve and fourteen hours a day. Beyond the members of the council, few can read—those who can read to others. Urinating and defecating becomes nearly impossible outside. Men swear their piss freezes before it hits the ground. Fifteen buckets are lined up in one bay of the storehouse.

After the sailing of the *Gift of God*, all had happily abandoned the wattle houses for ones made of wood. Each has at least one fireplace, crude holes lined with stones and an equally makeshift stone chimney. The cold nearly eliminates arguments and dampens most sexual fantasies— except in dreams. Men report them becoming more bizarre and colorful, apparently replacing the frozen white of their waking hours.

Lance's alteration felt uncomfortable to Jimmy, so he joined Digby, the shipwright, in his small structure, leaving the chapel for the couple. Lilly remains indoors, and Richard only ventures out for food, wood and to care for their "thunder bucket," as Lilly puts it, a term she picked up from her abusive uncle, the only thing she cares to remember about him. "That connection fits," she tells Richard, "that I should remember him and shit together."

Their lovemaking consumes hours at a stretch. They often get up only to tend the fire or relieve themselves. Lilly encourages Richard to experiment with his affections. As a child, she confided, the "nasty bastard" taught her things she now insists she repeat little by little with Richard. "I want to replace my memories of him with memories of you." She takes this project on as she did her music and studies, with consciousness and good humor. Nonetheless, as ardent as Lilly is, her deeper sexual interior can not yet open up. "I know I have to learn how to trust you. I know I can. I already do, it's just that some other part of me doesn't."

Richard listens. He tries to understand. Trust for him comes easily, and when occasionally betrayed—say by a greedy shopkeeper, an adolescent girl who won his heart and then made fun of his too-quick love making, a lying soldier—Richard tended to take it in stride. No trauma had blackened his past beyond the death of a young friend in a horseback accident, or a dog crushed by a wagon wheel when he was six, or the passing of his kindly grandparents. At sixteen, his loss of virginity to the older maid had given him confidence with his sexual self. At eighteen, he had witnessed a beheading and then a burning at the stake, both more or less by accident during his ventures in London alone. The images had stayed with him for months, then faded, still available to him but now with a more objective perspective. His father and mother had been kind. One young sibling had died before the age of three. He had been fond of her, only a year younger than he. He held this sadness. The sight of a young child often brought it to consciousness. He pictured these sadnesses and small betrayals in his own life, and what it might be like to multiply their seriousness by ten. He tried to imagine how it might be to have been Lilly and treated like a thing, worse than your domesticated animals. As a child he had read—and stared at the woodcuts in Fox's *Book of Martyrs*—of Queen Bloody Mary's torture of Protestants, the burning at the stake, the strangulations, the stretching apart of the bodies by rope, the flames encircling naked women. Later he had seen it with his own eyes, smelled the flesh. Perhaps imagining another's existence, especially their pain, was ultimately a futile game. In any case, he couldn't begrudge her transformation. Richard became a happy ally.

In the middle of the deep cold spell, the two remain in bed late one morning, their backs against the headboard, heavy blankets up just over their waists. The bright weak sun shines through the one window directly onto them, enough that Lilly goes shirtless, one breast resting on her lute as she demonstrates a piece for Richard. He listens with eyes shut. When she finishes he opens one eye. She smiles her little coy smile of satisfaction. "Are you cold?" he asks.

"A little, but it feels good to have the sun right on me. I haven't felt that in years. Never on my breast."

"Play that again would you?"

"Certainly, Chaplain.

Now Richard offers up a smile, one he can't remember having before, a kind of sweet ironic smile, flavored with a smirk that concludes with a tiny nod.

Lilly reaches for her shirt, buttons it up, and repeats the andante movement. Again Richard closes his eyes. It brings an aching, a sweet aching, with the flavor of loss. But he fathoms this isn't what he was feeling. He is not yearning for Margaret or England, of that he is sure. Deep under the covers, his lover's toes beat a slow rhythm against his. It is the music itself that prompts this feeling. This is what music does. It can elicit the pure feeling without the human associations, though of course the music can only be music as created and interpreted by humans. Is the pure feeling part of God's mind what the lute captures? He likes that notion, along with the exploding snow of a few weeks before. And he loves her toes—so much that he burrows under the blanket to kiss all five that tapped his. His head reemerges. "I'll get the other five later."

Mid-February finally brings another break in the weather. Never have the men been so delighted with the existence of slush and mud over which they are ordered to place boards and sawdust. The temperature rises into the forties. One day after lunch a group of soldiers sits on the ramparts sunbathing, their systems having been so radically recalibrated they could enjoy forty degrees in the sun half-naked. Large chunks of ice again float past the neck where river meets ocean. It is from that position that they notice three canoes approaching from upriver. They watch as the canoes avoid the larger pieces. "Savages arriving," one yells.

Much to the approval of Popham and Gilbert, Skidwarres and six other braves have arrived on the shore next to the nearly completed *Virginia*. Sipsis and Nolka step out onto the sand and reveal their faces, nearly hidden under their bearskin blankets. Richard, who has been preparing a sermon while Lilly removed buckets of ash and swept the chancellery, hears the sentry's announcement. He puts down his quill and asks Lilly to join him.

"No, I'll wait. You explain, and then I'll meet them. I wonder if Moskwas is among them." Richard goes to the door and peers out. "I can't tell from here. I'll return soon. Would you put on some tea?"

"Cleaning churches and making tea, is that what I will do when I'm married to you?"

The comment doesn't quite register as he trots down the slight hill. Then it does: "Married?" He shakes the thought off, as he might a mosquito buzzing around his head. Skidwarres heads in his direction carrying three pairs of snowshoes.

CHAPTER 48

February 3, 1608, On the Banks of the Androscoggin
Camaraderie

The nearing solstice offers an edge of hope. The sun holds into the early evening, even while winter persists with its three-foot snow cover and bitter cold nights. Skidwarres insists the worst weather lay behind. He, Richard, and Lilly are sitting in a bark hut around a fire, twenty-five miles northwest of the fort and a mile south of the Androscoggin Falls. They have canoed and then snow-shoed, along with three braves, in order to hunt moose and deer in this area of frozen freshwater swamps. Fresh meat for the fort—Skidwarres thinks it a useful gesture of goodwill. It's also a time to parlay with Richard.

The conversation crackles with the enthusiasm of renewed friendship from men entering the prime of their lives and invigorated by female company, plus three bottles of Bordeaux, a present from Gilbert. The conversation picks up from bits and pieces of information shared en route.

"What does it mean, Richard," Skidwarres asks, "that your ship and so many men have returned to Plymouth?"

"Food—the lack of it. But my friend, they will return in the spring, they and others, with supplies. It is only a temporary matter." Beyond the truth of their friendship lies another fact: each represents his own people. Richard doesn't wish to give the impression of weakness.

"So, the inevitable—that is the word, that is correct? They will return. It is inevitable?"

"What is inevitable?" Lilly asks.

"It is something of an amusement between us," answers Richard. "Do you think it is our destiny, we English are to be here and to settle here? Is that what you think, Lilly?" The conversation has taken on the playfulness Richard and Skidwarres shared in Dorset.

"Yes, yes, I think so. Don't you, Richard? I think it is my destiny to be here and to be right here in this hut with the two of you. I think it could have been no other way. I don't know why I think that. It is just what I feel. I know it doesn't fully make sense. And when the snow melts and the ships return, more people will come. I've heard Gilbert talk. You've said yourself, how you sometimes feel this—you know being with me and being in this big, lonely, wild land feels like you. You've said that."

"I have. I think that sometimes."

"Sometimes. Why do you always say 'sometimes' or 'maybe' or, 'I don't know' or 'that could be?'"

"Because sometimes I'm not sure. Besides, I don't always sound so unsure." Over the month they'd been occupying the chapel together, Richard has begun to find himself a bit hesitant with Lilly's definitiveness, her sexual determination.

"You," Skidwarres looks at Lilly. "You are sometimes a boy and sometimes a girl."

The comment carries with it affection. Lilly picks up a piece of jerky and throws it, hitting Skidwarres on the forehead. "I am who I have always been. I did what I had to do."

Skidwarres picks up the thrown jerky and takes a bite. "You are a fine woman. And I think I knew before Richard that Lance had no testicles."

"Moskwas told you?"

"He did."

"Does he like me?"

"He likes you."

Lilly smiles. Then she gives Skidwarres a blank look. "But I have my man. Richard, don't I have my man?" Her insecurity materialized off and on. Richard wasn't sure what to make of it. It had its side touch, her eyes, those of a puppy. But behind it, he sensed something much deeper and compelling: her need.

Richard reaches over and places a hand on her knee and smiles.

"Richard, what is that smile. You are not my chaplain. You are my man. You're not going to say 'sometimes' or 'maybe?'"

Skidwarres' laugh sparks a similar good natured one from Richard, but not Lilly. She stares at Richard.

He feels obliged to say, "I am your love. I am your man. It is ordained— it is our destiny." The slight irony attached, though not intended, is taken in by Lilly and dismissed.

"And this he—now she—is a very pretty destiny, Richard." Skidwarres reaches over and pinches her cheek. Lilly grabs Skidwarres' hand and nips it—then kisses it.

Richard groans and rises to grab two small logs outside the worn leather door. He adds them to the fire, then settles himself so he is sitting behind Lilly with his arms around her, she resting against his chest, he with his bootless feet warming next to the fire.

"I came to deliver the women to Gilbert and Popham, and to hunt, but I am also here as a diplomat."

"Ah," answers Richard, more interested in the smell of Lilly's hair, still flower- scented from the last piece of soap he'd saved.

"Richard, Nahanada wishes I speak to you. Sagamores from other villages within the Mawooshen have talked much. When the weather allows, we will travel to meet again with Bessabez. This winter has been very cold, one of the coldest people can remember."

"That is good to hear," adds Lilly. "I like the cold. There is nothing to do but eat, piss, and—you know—be in bed."

Richard smiles and tousles her hair, but his attentions shift to Skidwarres, who continues, "With the winter comes talk. Not new, but it is growing. The winter is like a dream. And when some dream, they see spring and summertime battles—victory over the Micmac with our English guns, and more important, victory over the English."

"Yes," Richard offers, letting him know he's listening, even though his face remains buried in Lilly's hair.

"Richard, we have talked of this: the differences, the growing anger. The Micmac became more hostile just before we landed. You know of this. When we made friends with you—the English—the Micmac complained. They deal with the French and Spanish. They insist they are masters of trade with the whites, including the English. Our friendship, the Mawooshen and the English, it disturbs their order."

"If we are diplomats," Richard remarks, "then we should consider long-term peace. How do we bind our peoples together? Perhaps we are your allies against the Micmac. Is it not possible? You already have a few of our rifles. Gilbert will be asking for supplies and men, this time including families, to venture here. He believes thousands of English will choose the clean New World over the diseased old one. Do you know, Skidwarres, not one of us has been sick during all this cold? Like myself, Gilbert is not first-born. Already his brother rules the family estate. This land is his fortune."

"Yes, I am not surprised at what you say."

"Where I think of some kind of vague destiny for England or myself, Gilbert lives with raw ambition."

"I've also seen this about Gilbert, Richard, even since I heard him speak in Plymouth. And if you were first-born, perhaps you would not be a chaplain among the savages."

Lilly breaks in. "I find him despicable. If it weren't for you, Richard, he'd be trying to seduce me. He's slimy. He might even succeed."

Richard kisses the top of her head and ruffles her hair. Stow lies exhausted next to the fire. "Only after both you and Stow have bitten him. And now you, Skidwarres, I have not made a diplomatic offering. I offer the truth, an undisguised truth, if that is possible."

Skidwarres looks at Richard, and at Lilly leaning back against him. Is this the time to profess strength? It is not what he feels. These visitors from another world appear quite comfortable. They are adapting as he did. Might he find this tiny quiet moment a time to plant the seed of fear? No. Not now.

As the men talk into the night, Lilly's eyes close. Finally she wraps herself in a blanket and rests her head on Richard's thigh. She feels safe, safer perhaps than she's ever felt. This thought settles in her hazy mind—away from all potential harm, cocooned in a warm hut, and in the protection of two men who would never harm her. For a while she wonders if she should offer to make love to both of them. She feels generosity and love for the two soft earnest voices that float over her. She would be happy giving them pleasure. Her image of the three of them together is innocent, but she keeps her eyes shut and her voice silent.

Richard is not a prude. He willingly accepted Lilly's challenge to rehabilitate her. He will touch and kiss her anywhere. His hands are gentle. He is patient and even combines laughter with his obvious passion for her. But she also senses a reserve. It is perhaps his aristocratic upbringing, a prudence or propriety, even when naked and sweaty. If she really wanted to have the two of them, he might agree. But she wasn't ready to disturb this warmth of trust that occupies the space between her skin and the bear pelt. Natives, she'd been told, at least those with more than one wife, might often have the two together. But here, too, she wasn't sure about Skidwarres. Lilly happily accepts inaction. She falls asleep with the embers cooling and male voices fading.

When she opens her eyes, the early diffuse morning light is working its way through the snow and cracks between the bark slabs. Skidwarres and Richard stand, bent over, arranging their packs. Hot water boils in their one pot. Richard throws in tea. Lilly, half-lost in her universe of sleep, remembers they will hunt.

The bull moose, standing with his cow and calf fifty yards away, does not see the human party at the woods' edge. He stands on the ice, pawing it, breaking through where grassy nutrients float below.

It is too easy, Lilly thinks. The braves move stealthily. The bull raises his huge floppy snout, revealing long silly legs under his bulky body. He appears unperturbed. He focuses on the puny men. The braves move a few paces closer. The bull recalculates and begins to paw the ice, this time not to break it, but as a warning sign. He lowers his massive rack, at least five feet wide, lowers it and raises it again. Fear comes slowly to such an animal. Lilly notices the cow and calf have disappeared.

Simultaneously three arrows whistle into the bull's side. The bull responds with surprise and then a huge grunt. He begins lumbering in the direction of Richard, Skidwarres, and Lilly. His hooves smash through the icy marsh. His slowness allows the braves to prepare for a second barrage. But before they release their arrows, Skidwarres moves forward, cocks his arm, and throws his spear with his entire calculated weight. It finds its mark just beyond the front hip bone and sinks in at least six inches. The bull stops and looks at Skidwarres, as if to say, "You too?" This time, his snort splatters blood on the clean snow. He stands, moving his head back and forth between the men. The braves lower their arrows as the bull begins losing balance. He drops to his knees, his heavy rack resting on the ground. One of the braves runs up and reaches under his snout. With a flourish, he slits the beast's throat.

"I didn't realize they were so huge," Richard comments. "They are both grand and comical at the same time." Skidwarres orders the three braves to spread out and find the cow and her calf; meanwhile, he will dress out the bull.

Lilly watches Skidwarres' knife move down the length of the belly and behind it; the skin opens up like a mouth, the lips parted, then gapes open to the purple entrails. He slits open the sack where so neatly and intimately the liver, kidneys, stomach, and lungs—the mechanisms of life—fall obscenely on the ground.

They hear shouts from the woods. Skidwarres informs Lilly and Richard the cow, too, was killed. The calf they spared, too small, not worth the effort.

"Skidwarres, what will happen to it? Won't it die? Wolves?" They could see it now on the edge of the woods staring at them.

"It is possible. It is also possible the herd will take it in, similar to the whale calf."

When the two moose have been fully dressed and loaded onto sleds, along with the small amount of gear and a third sled stacked with the meat of four deer, they strike out for the Androscoggin. It is still only mid-morning. The trek back to the canoes will be arduous, with Richard, Skidwarres, and Lilly tethered to one sled and three braves to the other two sleds. The meat would be parceled out in stews and might stretch for weeks for the English.

When they return to the canoes, the tide has a time before it reaches its height. The hungry party builds a fire to roast one moose and two deer livers. After some hesitancy, Lilly agrees that it's a delicacy worthy of her ravenous hunger.

For five hours the party travels down both rivers and finally to the small bay with the fort on its shore. It is dusk with just light enough to see the fort's white flag with its red cross, the flag of St. George, flying at half-staff. They learn from the nearest sentry, even before disembarking, that President Popham is dead.

Minutes later all learn from Gilbert that it was a heart attack. "The president briefly regained consciousness before dying. He smiled while the makeshift doctor, a man trained as a veterinarian, attempted to make the recently pink and at times crimson gentlemen comfortable by applying warm washcloths to his now pallid forehead. His last words were "no complaints."

Soon a weeping Nolka tells Skidwarres more of the story. He, in turn tells Richard. "I killed him," she had told Skidwarres. "He insisted I not stop. He breathing, like he was running, out of breath. No, he said, don't stop. I didn't. On and on, I riding him. He called himself a horse. He and Nahanada, they told me about horses. Then he grabbed his heart and pushed himself up at me. He finished down there, his man thing, the same time his heart broke."

Later in the evening Gilbert requests Seymour's company. They meet alone. Sipsis keeps to their private quarters.

"You know, Seymour, I was even getting to tolerate the old bastard. Should we put him on ice? Bury him in the spring? Not cremation?"

Richard agrees.

"By the way, Cousin Seymour, how does President Gilbert sound? Are not the muses on our side?"

CHAPTER 49

March 10, 1608, Fort St. George
Adoration

The next day Skidwarres and the braves paddled upriver through the inland waterway, back to Pemaquid. Nolka joined them, now bereft over the loss of her gentle if buffoonish Englishman. Sipsis stayed with Gilbert. She withdrew her resentment in exchange for his promise to bring her to England.

George Popham's death changed little. The fort continued its moribund daily life. Like the trees and the hibernating bear, the men waited for the land to warm. A week of rising temperature in late February was deceptive. Even with the growing light, severe winter settled in again, as if for the kill. The screeching gulls overhead sounded more petulant and urgent. Crows by the thousands roosted in a stand of white pines, cackling fiendishly, waiting for the mating season, when they would separate and establish their own domains. All were waiting.

By early March the dirty snow began to melt. Small patches of corpse-like ground were exposed. Then there came another cold blast from the north. Great winds ushered in twenty inches of snow, large flakes of miniature interlocking ice crystals, some the size of a baby's hand. Again the men awoke to the pristine, shining shroud and to the unending distant rumble of the sea throwing itself against the land.

Richard didn't know what to think as he lay in bed. It was a Sunday. He would not preach. The day before, he'd reported to Gilbert that he felt ill, but he had lied. In fact, few even complained of a fever. It seemed every infirmity known to England froze in the New World. He told Gilbert of his fatigue—that was true enough. More to the point, he'd lost his ambition to preach. His role as chaplain felt as dead as the land around him.

The sun filters through the single multicolored stained glass window. The shaft of light bathes their end of the bed. Lilly sleeps naked. The heat from the recently-stoked fire and the morning sun allow both to kick off the heavy wool blankets. She lies entirely exposed on her back. Over the past few months Richard has become preoccupied—that was his word to himself—with her body. How had he not known Lance was female? What had been "his" curly black hair at Plymouth now rests on her shoulders, full and extravagantly feminine. Her skin is darker than his, her breasts seem to grow daily. He stares at the gorgeous plumage around her sex, an extraordinary thick display. How could one so young present with such lush maturity? He strokes her apparently sleeping, soft, and muscular belly. Then her eyes open. She takes in a long breath of satisfaction, releases it, and closes her eyes again. His hands rest below her navel. He lightly massages and gazes at the curly black patch. Within the hair he notices for the first time four small swirls the size of his thumbnail, a design, delicate as on a butterfly wing—four tiny perfections, not symmetrical, rather off-center and more appealing for this. How wondrous these details. Had he not read—was it in Plato—that beauty contains not perfect symmetry but something less predictable? Were not women meant to be adored, men to venerate and savor them?

With the winter extending into early April, they often lay reading and luxuriating. The few hours spent working on the *Virginia*, holding lessons, and conferring with the men feel extraneous compared with the essential matter: himself.

Their lovemaking had evolved. At first Lilly had urged Richard to experiment, replaying what her abusive uncle had demanded of her. Lately she'd become more urgent, even aggressive. Richard, at first a little abashed, accepted his task. "At your service," he had told her once, and before she could take offense he nuzzled her between the breasts and offered up, "My love." Full pleasure came easily for him, less so for Lilly. After two months of what felt like a lovely, if peculiar, form of therapy, Lilly reported that she had nearly banished the memories of her past. Yet she berated herself for not reaching full satisfaction. She had not experienced a climax. It galled her. Lilly enjoyed herself immensely, so if she tried harder then maybe she'd achieve success. "I've come so close."

One night, after they have indulged one another, he reaches his own satisfaction and lies in and over her, his head resting on a makeshift pillow of clothes. She is quiet. Minutes pass. He senses her disappointment and finally speaks. "I think this, my Lilly. It reminds me of practicing the harpsichord or lute. First, you have to know where to put your fingers, get the timing, the basics. But after that, at least at some point, you have to not try so hard. You have to let the music find you. Sometimes the more you exert, the less available you are. You know what I mean?"

Lilly would often find humor in the pontifications that Richard routinely offered, but not this night. "I think so."

"The moon over my shoulder, take it in. And when your mind wanders, gently return to the moon. Try."

"Yes," Lilly replies. She is dreamy, half-asleep.

Richard begins to move slowly. "Of course you can think about how good you are feeling. You are feeling good?"

"Yes." Her voice has a slight distance.

"But return to the moon, only the moon, and feel wonderful." His own movement is slow, andante. "Whisper to me, tell me when you are thinking of the moon, and when concentrating on your wonderful feeling."

Lilly doesn't respond right away. Richard thinks she is lost in concentration. But no, quietly she begins languidly to murmur, "Moon... moon... wonderful us, moon... moon." Then quiet for a while till she begins again, "Moon, wonderful us, wonderful, wonderful, moonlight, moon." After an extended period, her breathing quickens. It overtakes his slow beat, and finally she responds as never before, with a high-pitched release of breath followed by soft whimpering pants. She catches her breath, as a child might after crying and being comforted. Richard, who has been restraining himself, gives up and joins in the wake of her full pleasure.

After that night, with nothing to prove, their lovemaking becomes easier. No longer does Lilly strive.

And then slowly, nearly imperceptibly, entirely unexpectedly, tension grew between them. The supply ship would come in the spring, and with it correspondence. Richard could not help but look forward to Margaret's letters, confirmation of his other world. Richard realized he had grown comfortable with the present as well as his past. They simply existed unfettered by each other. But might Margaret be on that ship? Such an unorthodox move was not beyond her. In any case, his and Lilly's relationship faced a challenge.

Lilly began speaking of their future in the New World. She even goaded him about his lack of primogeniture. She reminded him of his cousin, Gilbert, the opportunity for owning vast amounts of land and becoming wealthy, more than he could ever be in "corrupt England." Occasionally she talked of their both retuning to England. As to either trajectory, Richard listened but did not add much to her hopes or fears.

As their lovemaking settled into a lusty, more relaxed friendship, he found himself backing away slightly, so negligibly; he wasn't even sure that is what it was, or if she was aware. Her project to reconstruct her sexual past had succeeded, but Richard felt something new come between them. She watched him more often, wanted his touch. Her need at times felt overbearing. This once feisty boy ready to defend his dog or himself tooth and nail, had learned as a young woman the most elemental of capacities: to trust. As a child she convinced herself that survival required strength. Others were not reliable. People were basically out for themselves. Should she be no different? Yet she had allowed Richard to enter her life, herself. In pursuing him, she hadn't expected to lose herself. Yet she had momentarily lowered her guard. She had let go. She loved without maintaining defenses. Trust had tricked her. How could she have been so stupid? Richard remained kind, even passionate. But she could feel him slipping away. Of course, she, Lilly, a common orphan, how could she compete against a well-educated woman of the gentry? Lilly was a crude girl, Margaret a sophisticated woman. No matter how Richard denied this—for she had begun expressing her doubts—Lilly knew better.

And yet, she didn't always feel this gnawing desperation, not on those nights when the two of them read next to the fire, sharing sections of Shakespeare and Montaigne, feeling the warmth; when he'd get up to add a log and then bend over to kiss her forehead before returning to his chair; or when in bed he stroked her hair and said, "How beautiful you are, my Lilly," while the wind howled all about, and in the distance the sea thumped onto the beach. Then she felt safe. She even began to identify within herself how that feeling of safety in his presence had melted her old resolve of independence. Briefly she could observe it without panic creeping around the edges.

CHAPTER 50

April 14, 1608, Fort St. George
Exposure

By mid-April, while patches of snow lay on the frozen duff in the evergreen-shaded woods, the men's spirits, like the maple sap, began to run. Again small parties traveled into the swamps to dig iron ore for smelting, and hunting parties sailed upriver in the shallop to disembark near a lake, where they'd learned from Skidwarres that deer, moose, and bear watered in the early morning. Fishing parties returned offshore in longboats. Fresh fish and game helped enliven their prospects. At the water's edge, the cradled *Virginia* neared her christening.

One afternoon the boyish energies of the men came to a halt. Instead, many began to feel their blood boil. With the snow cover nearly melted, Gilbert's two Mastiffs began roaming the area beyond the immediate fort. On one occasion they chased down a fawn and killed it. They returned, their faces soaked in blood, each with a small leg in their massive jaws. It was clear they were proud of their accomplishment. Late in April they returned with another prize: Dumb with a skeletal torso and Dumber with a decapitated head, still with strands of blond hair. They dropped their find at Gilbert's doorway. Soldiers spotted them. By the time Gilbert got to the entrance, a silent group had congregated to stare. One observer pointed to the four-inch arrow shaft still lodged between the ribs. Richard, who was only yards away at the *Virginia*, joined the silent vigil.

During the many winter storms, the high tides had battered the dunes. No doubt the erosion had gone on for eons. Richard had wondered if the burial site might be too close to the beach and subject to exposure. He had considered returning to investigate but had no stomach for it. He wasn't even sure where along the mile-long expanse he'd hastily dug the shallow grave. Besides, he told himself, until very recently the dunes had been covered in snow. Now his pondering could stop.

Richard offered to return with the dogs and a few men to retrieve whatever might remain. He'd then give the man, who was apparently MacDougal, the fisherman, a proper burial along with George Popham. Until the ground thawed they'd remain in a small structure surrounded by sawdust and ice. Three of MacDougal's friends talked together; then one confronted Gilbert before he returned to his study. "President, we want heathen heads on a post. We want to give those savages a message. When, President?"

Gilbert turned. "Do not take me as weak, Corporal. In time." With that he entered his house and slammed the door.

That evening the council met to discuss the consequences, if any, of what Gilbert argued was clear evidence the fishermen had been murdered. Davis argued for swift retaliation. But against whom—or did it matter? Would not brutality, wherever aimed, make the point and satisfy the soldiers? The arrow fragment, small and weathered, without feathers, didn't allow for identification. Weren't these people called the Mawooshen? Did it matter which Mawooshen they killed?

From the moment Richard saw the skeletal remains in front of Gilbert's door, he considered exposing his long kept secret. But no, he quickly concluded, he would ride out this situation. Admission might ruin his position. And what was to be gained?

Around the council table, Gilbert turned to Richard and squinted in what Seymour perceived as a flicker of suspicion. "When we traveled to Pemaquid after the disappearances—murders—what is it that Skidwarres actually said—to you alone?"

"The same as he and Nahanada told us together." Richard felt secure. His voice did not betray him. In the New World he had learned, among many things, to be a convincing liar. He drew confidence from the greater good derived from dissimulation—what all diplomats must learn.

"And if my memory serves," continued Gilbert, "Nahanada hinted Sabenoa might be behind whatever happened."

"Yes," added Richard, "but we traveled to Pemaquid only a few days after the men's disappearance. Would it not be possible that whatever was kept secret in that short time might now be known to many? Might another trip to Pemaquid be prudent?"

"In February you spent much time with Skidwarres. Did you not converse on these matters?"

"We did not."

Gilbert looked at Richard. Has he found a chink in my armor, Richard wondered. Perhaps, but nothing else was said between the two.

Now that the weather had improved, all agreed that Richard should return to Pemaquid and interrogate Skidwarres and Nahanada again. This decision relieved Richard. The passage of time would allow tempers to cool. If he admitted what he'd known all along—even if he explained his motivation, that of maintaining peace—he would lose all trust. Better to strategize with Skidwarres. They could maintain ignorance—though the council was correct, it was likely Skidwarres and Nahanada knew who the guilty party was.

Gilbert, always eager to travel, argued that he, too, should make the trip. Others on the council, especially Captain Davis, insisted the men were on edge. Discipline might flag with Gilbert's departure. He had earned the respect of most of the men, albeit respect laced with fear. Unlike George Popham, Gilbert inflicted punishment for minor infringements. Recently two men received lashes delivered by the new president with vigor leaning toward viciousness. They'd been caught sleeping at their posts.

The next morning, April 15th, with the clearest of blue skies and hardy but safe westerlies, the shallop, with five fully armed soldiers, the copper three-pound cannon on the bow, oarsmen, an experienced seaman skipper, and Richard headed east to Pemaquid on the open ocean.

CHAPTER 51

April 15, 1608, A Beach East of Fort St. George
Run Amok

On the same morning Seymour set sail, three soldiers, two carpenters, and an iron worker began rowing a longboat out of the Sagadahoc's mouth, just as the sun was slipping out of the water. Gilbert maintained President Popham's policy of rewarding diligent work with fishing outings. One of the soldiers, the oldest, had served during the various Irish campaigns. This time, all went armed.

They worked the eastern coastal area while staying close to shore. An hour later they watched the shallop work its way out of the river and leave Seguin to the south, heading down east. By midday the warmest air since September, seven months ago, arrived. The men shed their shirts.

As so often was the case, the conversation returned to the exploits of the more seasoned soldiers who'd participated in the bloody Irish campaigns, and the sailors who had been among the crew of the English privateers. Nothing pleased the younger men more than stories of plunder, rape, and pillage, the burning of Irish villages, the murder of all habitants—men, women, and children. A favorite involved Raleigh Gilbert's father, Humphrey. He had the habit of placing the heads of the slaughtered Irish on stakes that lined the path leading to his tent and then inviting their relatives for negotiations. The same fate fell to the Spanish towns in the Caribbean. The privateers' crews lived for gold, gems, wine, plus the heady sense of power that goes with instilling fear.

Around noon the men come upon a large beach, much like the one to the west of the Sagadahoc's entrance. They know how lobsters might be plucked from the shallows as the tide receded, as it was doing now, though none has ever tried. They decide to eat their hardtack and drink their rations of beer on land.

Having beached the longboat, the carpenters and iron worker take off their boots and roll up their trousers. They yelp when the forty-degree water numbs their ankles. They splash around like children, thrusting an arm into the foot-high water and shouting to one another. When they catch a lobster and hold it into the air, it wiggles and snaps. They wing them onto the beach. Soon the water churns up with sand, obstructing their vision. The iron worker steps on a five-pounder. Its pincer-claw latches onto the soldier's small toe. He grabs for it, loses balance, and falls into the gentle surf. He quickly regains his footing and hobbles ashore with the lobster still clamped on. The other two follow onto the beach in convolutions of laughter. One regains his wits enough to smash the determined beast with a stick of driftwood. It joins seven others in a barrel.

The three soldiers walk approximately half a mile to a granite outcropping that allows a better vantage point to survey the surroundings. As they near the top, Edwards, the oldest and a seasoned yarn-teller, puts his finger to his lips and stops. They work their way down a few feet to where they can peer around the ledge. A few hundred yards down the beach, a small group of women are wading at the water's edge, evidently doing exactly what the men were doing: collecting lobsters. Ethan, the youngest at seventeen, counts six in all.

"Women, by god," says Edwards. "By god, I'd like to have myself a woman. What do you say, boys, you ready for a ripe woman?"

Ethan wonders out loud, "What do you mean?" He knows the answer while the question forms.

"Pussy! What do you say, Maxwell?" Edwards address the eighteen-year-old. Edwards' eyes don't leave their prey. Maxwell answers more out of deference to the seasoned soldier. Stories of rape are one thing. He is less sure of the act itself. "I'm with you."

"Ethan, you too?" Edwards' tone sounds more a command than a question.

"Yes, sir."

Edwards points to grassy dunes that run the entire length of the beach. "We'll go there. Keep ourselves low. Surprise them, corner them." He turns, not interested in a response.

The six women all face the ocean. The constant whistle of the wind and commotion of the small waves meeting the sand hide the sounds of the men's approach. Ethan finally raises the courage to ask, "How do we do this?"

Edwards, nonplused, stops for a moment and looks at his two younger, inexperienced men. "What you do is grab the first one you can get your hands on. You slam her to the ground, smack her hard on the head. Daze her, and then you fuck her good and hard. Hell, you don't even have to tear her clothes off. They're about naked. Just that simple." He turns, walking, bent over in the grass. Ethan follows, but the distance between him and the other two grows. He's never had a woman, not even a girl. He wants one very badly—but he isn't sure. What else can he do?

When they are directly behind the women, Edwards stands and begins to walk through the grass and onto the sand. He drops his helmet and peels off his breastplate. Maxwell and Ethan follow suit. When they have narrowed the distance to within fifty yards, the youngest girl— perhaps an eleven-year-old—turns to carry two lobsters to a basket. She stops and stares. Ghosts? Three white men? She has never seen one, but they are walking quickly toward her. She drops her lobsters, becomes briefly paralyzed, and then screams. The three men pick up the pace, trudging in their boots through the heavy sand. Three women, knee-deep in water, the other two at the edge, turn their heads simultaneously. The young girl runs to her elder sister and clings to her arm. All walk out of the water, only half-believing what they are seeing. "We must run. They will hurt us," says the oldest. It is a statement of fact, not hysteria.

By the time the women begin to run, Edwards, only yards away, picks up his pace. The women, like a frightened pack of deer, run along the edge where the packed sand allows them an initial advantage, especially since they are barefooted, healthy, and young. Soon they would reach a large granite outcropping. They either have to scramble over the rocks, in places difficult or impossible, or they can cut across the beach to a path leading to their village a mile away.

The woman in the lead chooses to head for the path. The English calculate that this makes it easier to cut them off. Ethan, the fastest, is the first to be within arm's reach. The very action of pursuit—part game, part adrenalin, part fear—overrides his earlier misgivings. He lunges for her flowing black hair. To his surprise he catches a handful. He yanks, pulling her feet out from under her. There she is, lying at his feet on her back, his hands still grasping her hair. She looks up with no expression, not even fear. For a moment their eyes meet. Then, with the determination of a small wild animal, the woman twists her body and lunges to sink her teeth into the fleshy part between Ethan' thumb and finger. He screams and instinctively kicks her in the stomach, freeing his hand as she doubles up, breathless. With the pain comes a sense of injustice; he has been bitten. She looks about his age, eyes wide open, fear now showing, gasping. Under the tunic, her breasts heave. As ordered, he smacks her hard on the temple with the fleshy portion of his palm. Her eyes dull.

The experienced soldier, Edwards, angles with surprising speed and bowls over another young woman. He falls on her before she can react. He grabs her throat, reaches back with his other arm and swings with a large open hand. She doesn't make a noise. He begins with an outburst of profanity aimed at women and heathen savages in particular. It's understood, rape is a reward for putting up with the hardships and danger of soldiering, especially true when the victim is alien. He and his comrades had convinced themselves that slaves, the Irish, and these natives weren't fully human anyway, so it isn't a true rape. He is between her dead-weight legs, his pants yanked down to his knees. He's accomplished this maneuver in seconds. This will be his tenth. He's kept count.

Maxwell runs faster as he watches. Two girls are beyond his reach, only the one with her young sister, hand in hand, has slowed a bit and is a possible target. Out of the corner of his eye he sees Ethan on the ground. He grabs the arm of the elder sister and pulls. But her resistance keeps her on her feet. She yanks herself free and begins running backward. In so doing she lets go of her little sister, who now runs ahead of her. Her maneuvering allows Maxwell to pounce. He grabs her shoulders. Instinctively he uses an old wrestling move. He puts his foot behind her and pushes. She falls on her back and he lands on her as he had his wrestling opponents, knees on her shoulders, his weight on her chest. He hesitates. Hitting her doesn't feel right. For a stupid moment he considers maybe this rather beautiful young thing might like him. Her dark brown eyes stare at him. He even hears himself saying, "I won't hurt you."

That was all he remembered. In that moment of inaction, when a glimmer of sanity and kindness arrived, a piece of heavy driftwood connected with his temple, the little sister holding the other end.

When moments later he regains semi-consciousness, he notices Ethan on his knees watching his woman running toward the path. It would be a month before Ethan admitted to Maxwell what happened. While on top of the woman, apparently still stunned by his slap, Ethan shoves his pants down and begins fumbling between her legs. It is then she grabs his member, at first gently. She is going to help him find the spot, he thinks for a brief second. He has heard stories of such things. It feels wonderful at first, her hands. The pleasure is brief. She opens her palms and grabs his testicles. She yanks. Ethan rolls off and doubles over on the sand while the girl bolts to her feet and escapes.

Edwards completes his fornicating and beating, his profanity unabated. He next takes the knife from his sheath and with a wide arc, swings to slit her throat. Neither of the younger soldiers sees this. Instead they are watching the remaining four women and girl reach the edge of the beach and disappear down the path.

When they do turn, they watch Edwards at the shore dipping his knife in the water and cleaning it between his fingers and on his pants. He sheaves it and walks toward a basket of lobsters. The two others join him. A few yards away, under the woman's neck, a crimson stain in the sand continues to expand.

"You killed her?" Ethan asks quite incredulously.

"I killed her."

"But...why?"

"I killed her because I could. I fucked her and killed her because I could.

"Why?" Ethan mutters again."

"Listen you fool, we did what we did because we can. Because it felt good. Very good." The two boys continue looking at the dead woman on her back, her flap raised over her stomach and leaving her exposed. "Now you two pick up that basket of lobsters and we'll fetch our gear and head back—before those fucking savages start coming down that path."

"But Gilbert, he'll hang us," Ethan protest.

"Not Gilbert—his father, maybe. You need to listen to your history lessons. Besides, nobody knows, including those buggers on the other section of beach. Nothing. You keep your months shut. Or maybe you will hang."

The three soldiers retrieve their weapons from where they had dropped them and quickly walk back along the rim of the dunes. They see the three other men sitting on the sand sipping beer.

"We are leaving now," Edwards commands. "We stole these from a bunch of women. How many lobsters did you catch?"

"Twelve," answers one of the carpenters.

"Then we must have nearly thirty," Ethan adds, trying to be nonchalant.

The outgoing tide has stranded the longboat twenty yards up on the beach, requiring all six to grab the gunwales and drag it into the shallows. They begin rowing against the wind. "Pull hard, boys," orders Edwards. He stands with the tiller in one hand.

Not more than ten minutes later, Maxwell sees four canoes coming into sight as they round the granite outcropping, perhaps two miles away. Without altering his strokes, he calls out, "Savages!" Four braves in each canoe are paddling furiously, one in each bow ready to let arrows fly. Within a few minutes it is clear they are gaining.

"Just keep pulling, boys. We don't have a problem here. When they get a little closer, I'll remind them who we are. Besides, their arrows will go against the wind."

Fifteen minutes later the longboat has traveled about half the distance to the mouth of the Sagadahoc. The canoes continue to gain.

"Another five minutes and we'll be in range," offers an increasingly tired carpenter."

"Won't happen," says Edwards. He picks up his musket, turns, and straddles the tiller so to keep the boat on course. The rocking and jerking of the boat from the waves and oarsmen make accuracy impossible, especially at such a range. That, however, isn't the point. The shot lands between the boats. "Another loaded rifle." Ethan unwraps his from the canvas that kept it dry. Edwards shoots again. This time he may have hit one of the canoes. In any case, it is enough for the braves to stop their paddling. Clearly they might be picked off or sunk before their arrows become a threat. Instead, the natives begin shouting and screaming. Soon the wind and sea smother their outrage.

The older soldier faces his rowers. He begins laughing. "All right, boys, a successful outing, what do you say, Ethan? The best day I've had in this fucking New World."

"Yes, sir." And Ethan, indeed, finds himself pleased. He has followed orders. His first woman. She was a fighter. A pretty fighter. His spirits had never felt so strong, and when for that brief moment she touched him, what he first felt as a friendly stroking had been enough for him to empty himself. It didn't matter if this rush of pleasure ended with sickening pain. It was gone now. Ethan considered himself a man. "Yes, sir," he repeats.

CHAPTER 52

May 10, 1608, Pemaquid
Weighing Consequences

Again the steady spring westerlies quickly push the shallop to Pemaquid. Lilly has persuaded Richard to bring her along. As before, young boys fishing on shore spot the small ship. Skidwarres and Nahanada are in their canoes waiting when the English drop anchor in a protective cove.

All are ferried ashore and offered food and drink. Lilly's friend, Moskwas, watches Lilly in wonderment. He touches her homemade dress and bonnet. Lilly begins laughing at Moskwas' dumbfound face. Soon he joins her. Then he stops and seriously gazes at her, looking up and down, ending at her bust—mesmerized—a bit of cleavage showing above the scooped line. He points. His finger a yard away comes closer. Just before he touches her, Lilly grabs his arm, twists, ducks under, leaving her behind him, he moaning in pain.

Nahanada allows Richard and Skidwarres to speak in private. After a meal of eel and squash, they wander down the path that leads to the spot where six months ago they'd discussed murdered fishermen. This matter, as Richard soon informs his friend, remains alive.

"The skeletal remains with the arrow—Gilbert's dogs found it. There is no question, the blond hair. Gilbert sent me for more information. I upheld our diplomatic lie. But he rightly assumes you and Nahanada would know about a murder. So we must now conjure up something."

"Richard, since the snow melted, we have heard that Bessabez' people are more and more troubled. The Micmac are like ravens, armed with French muskets. They run raids on Bessabez' villages, stealing beaver pelts, food, abducting women. Their sagamore has threatened Bessabez.

The Micmac say only they, no one else, can trade with the whites. They know Nahanada has made friends with the English. For safety Bessabez is considering moving his people closer to us, the heart of the Mawooshen. I don't think he will. For many, many generations, they have lived on the Penobscot."

"And Nahanada and Bessabez, they still intend to trade directly with us?"

"We are not cowards. We are not, as you say, lackeys of the Micmac. We have many beaver pelts. Bessabez delivered them here. They are yours. Gilbert will be pleased."

"Your news sounds promising. What else has transpired during the winter and early spring? My countrymen, they want blood."

"The rest is not good for you, the English." The two have been resting on a flat smooth rock, again overlooking Monhegan on the horizon. Skidwarres gets up and begins pacing back and forth in front of Richard. "Things are complicated, just as you tell me they are back in England. Nahanada is a friend to the English. He and I know of your people. We wish to trade and to remain friends. But the young men who killed your fishermen have gone north, as you know. Others have joined them. Nahanada, he is the most respected Mawooshen here at the Pemaquid and on the Aponeg. In the past they have given bear, beaver, mink, and deer pelt to Nahanada to trade, and in turn Nahanada gives them to the to the Micmac who trade with the French and the Basques. But to the English, no. The English and the Mawooshen need no Micmacs."

Skidwarres continues, "Braves from the Aponeg villages, and from others to the north and west of the Mawooshen, some have joined Woboz. Two hundred—a few from our village. Some say Woboz talks to Sabenoa. Young braves, often foolish. But their bragging of war is not without intelligence." Skidwarres believes his statement of Woboz' power is an exaggeration, but Nahanada has insisted he present this case.

"You mean, Skidwarres, rid us while we are few, that is your point?"

"Yes, that makes sense to many. Nahanada, who knows of English cannon, considers anger as something he must join someday—if he cannot stop it."

"And you, Skidwarres?"

"Few die in our battles. They are not even battles. You have taught me of English warfare, where thousands lie in their blood without arms or heads, their insides spilling out. You have read this to me. Mawooshen fight for honor or food, or to settle old grudges. You English kill, and then kill and kill. That I have learned. Our arrows and spears usually wound. Your cannon, so—what? What do the English say?"

"Mincemeat."

"Yes, that. I know this. Nahanada knows. Most others do not. But if we must fight, we will, even if many die.

"What of the Micmacs? Do they not aim to eliminate Bessabez.

"That is clear."

"And what of Nahanada's council? About peace with English? Do they listen?"

"Some laugh, wanting to show their bravery. Others listen quietly. No one has attacked you. Maybe it is words; or maybe they are waiting for summer, the season to fight."

Richard rises and picks up a few small stones. He throws them, one by one, into the agitated ocean. Skidwarres follows his lead. For a few silent moments, while assimilating their thoughts, they compete for the longest throw.

Richard finds a smooth black rock the size of a plum and hurls it high and long. "And if I had my lacrosse stick, I could double that length," Skidwarres says and laughs.

"Skid, I think I need to return with the news that Woboz and others are the murderers. I will say that you learned this only recently. I cannot return offering ignorance."

"Yes, Richard, that is clear."

"And if I can return with Sipsis, Gilbert's mood will brighten."

"That becomes complicated. She is now with Woboz?"

"With Woboz? Why? Where?"

"Nahanada has much confidence in Sipsis. While with Gilbert, she learned English—and other information."

"A spy? Her idea?"

"Yes, but Nahanada told Sipsis that Woboz would be a danger to her. She has lain with Gilbert."

"Yes, that makes sense."

"But Sipsis laughed. She said she knows Woboz. He is like all men. My words, she said, my smell, my hand make him a wolf pup."

"Where?"

"Near Sabenoa."

Richard nods his head. "One last matter, Skid. I was told to return with pelts. Soon a ship will arrive with all manner of material and manpower." In much the same manner as Skidwarres before, he finds himself exaggerating. "When she sets sail for England, Gilbert wants a full hold."

"Yes, pelts, but for muskets, balls, and powder. Bessabez is clear. We must protect ourselves from the Micmac. Muskets the Micmac respect."

"And how do we know these will not be turned on us, Skidwarres?"

"As you point out, my friend, Gilbert must send back prizes from the New World, or your hold on our land will slip. Because you are a fine teacher, I have begun to understand the English. They do not need these pelts or long trees or sassafras. No, they want them. And for the English, a want grows stronger than a need."

"So the Mawooshen need firearms to kill their brothers? That is how the English can help."

"Yes, you and I stand here saying such things."

"Skid, I cannot promise. I must return with your demands. Then we will see."

They begin walking back on the narrow path, through the bayberry and scrub pine, sumac, grasses, blueberry bushes, over granite and bog. "Skidwarres, might our children and grandchildren live together in harmony on this land, hunting, fishing, growing gardens? Or will we on either side of the fort wall be aiming muskets, cannon, and arrows at one another?"

"It is possible both, no?"

"Nothing destined, my savage friend?"

CHAPTER 53

May 12, 1608, Fort St. George
Replenished

While Richard is at Pemaquid, knowledge of the rape and murder soon spreads throughout the fort. The cooks boil and pick out the lobster meat and add it to corn gruel, thereby allowing all men a portion. With extra beer rations, tongues loosen. Rape—Maxwell's own made-up version—and then the murder tumble out of his mouth. News spreads, as only salacious gossip can. By the next morning, Gilbert knows.

In the morning the two youngest provide accurate details. When Edwards alters the facts as he has heard them, Gilbert rises from his chair behind the large table, walks around to stand within inches of Edwards' face. "You are lying. You lie to my face. Admit it." Spittle lands on Edwards' cheek and nose.

"Yes, sir," the grizzled man admits. Though brutish, he remains cowed by authority, in this case authority that isn't at all sure of the facts.

Without warning Gilbert backhands the older soldier. "Throw him in the brig. Throw them all in. We'll hang them. Dammit, I don't need this. We've had good relations with those fucking savages on the Aponeg. Get them out of here."

The council confers. They have the authority, but what of the consequences of more hangings? Quickly all agree that the younger two essentially followed orders. They would remain in the brig for a week, their wages garnished. But the older soldier? Would a hanging be wise? Five English murdered by natives near the mouth of the Aponeg. Might this murder be—well, reasonable, or at least retribution?

Gilbert listens. Any severe punishment, certainly hanging or handing over the man to the savages, would cause much grumbling and low morale. After all, license to pilfer, rape, and kill drew men to the military. Punishment for such acts rarely called for the death penalty.

The council sits, quietly stymied.

Outside a few muffled shouts become louder. Gilbert rises and shoves the door open in the face of a soldier with a hand in the air ready to knock. Bloody-nosed he offers, "Sir, sails, just off Seguin, flying the flag of St. George. The *Gift of God* and the *Mary and John*, we think."

By the time Gilbert and the council members reach the top of the ramparts, nearly all the men are either standing there or are running to the beach where soon the ships would pass within a few hundred feet. Nearly a year since these men set sail from Plymouth, here is the first sign that they exist—that is, beyond their own sense of themselves—and that in the bleakest months of winter had become nearly frozen.

By the time the *Gift of God* drops anchor, all four longboats are waiting in the water to ferry men and goods. Gilbert stands in the bow of one.

Captain Robert Davies is the first to lower himself over the ship's side. Gilbert's previously morose mood turns exultant. "By god, man, never have I been so glad to see sails or shake hands!" His enthusiasm nearly capsizes the boat. By the time they row to shore, Gilbert has learned the ship carries thirty men who will remain, a welcome addition, though he would be shipping a few disabled and disconsolate men back. Most of the new arrivals are artisans, along with a handful of soldiers. The cargo includes gunpowder, new muskets, salted beef, wine, live chickens, sheep, goats, pigs, barrels of barley, wheat, molasses, seed for planting, and—most precious—letters.

Someone on the Plymouth Council, the party responsible for financing the venture, had the dubious foresight to include six whores as part of the cargo. They are sternly supervised by Gertrude, an otherwise jovial madam in her forties. The seven are standing at the ship's railing, waving and blowing kisses. Three wildly happy men jump out of a longboat and swim for the rope ladders, until an officer with an oar not so tenderly strikes the head of the first fellow, just as his hand reaches for the rope. "Wait your turn, son."

While joyous pandemonium infects everyone on shore, as well as those who have been at sea for two months, Captains Davies insists he speak in private with President Gilbert. With him, he comes right to the point.

"Sir John Popham is dead."

"Popham is dead?" Gilbert isn't sure he's heard rightly or, if so, how he should respond.

"Sir John Popham died last June, the 10th."

"June 10th, 1607? How can that be? Only—what —days after we left Plymouth?"

"That is true. The nature of his death is quite mysterious."

Gilbert wants to calibrate his response. Sir John Popham dead. George Popham dead. "Then besides Gorges, who...who is...in charge?"

"Nobody has taken his place, sir. His son, Francis, he and his mother—John's wife—they take an interest. But no one has taken his place."

"Yes, he was a man of some force," Gilbert admits.

"The *Gift of God*, sir, had a very rough voyage last winter. Over two months. Food near ran out. And the ship herself took a beating. At least one man died, and many others sick. When they landed in the Azores in order to make repairs and purchase victuals, they had to sell much of the cargo—pine masts, most of the fur. When finally they arrived in Plymouth, some of the investors, including the Pophams, took offense and attempted to sue. Nasty business."

Gilbert listens, wishing, waiting for a conclusion to the story that would offer more hope.

Captain Davies, following his optimistic bent, continues. "But, you see, we are here. With Sir John gone, our financial resources have dwindled. The hold of the ship might be fuller. We might have recruited more men. But we are here. Fort St. George is alive."

"And the settlement to the south, Jamestown, I believe they call it?" interjects Gilbert. "How do they fare?"

"Not well, sir. Many lives lost, trouble with the savages, sickness. But they, too, are surviving."

The bland look on his face a facade, inwardly Gilbert sees himself anew.

Before the sun sets, there is more commotion from the ramparts. The shallop from Pemaquid has entered the Sagadahoc.

CHAPTER 54

May 14, 1608, Fort St. George
A Grand Scheme

On his desk Richard finds a foot-long box made of cherry. It's wrapped in parchment and sealed with Margaret's father's mark. He unwraps it and slides the top off. Inside Margaret has tied a pink ribbon around a stack of letters, the first written the day of his sailing from Plymouth, the most recent, the 1st of March 1608, the day before she shipped the box by stagecoach to Plymouth.

As with Richard's letters, she presents many journal-like entries, most describing her daily routine: helping her mother manage domestic matters for the estate, assisting the tutor with her three younger siblings, cello practice, and reading. She also made monthly visits to London with Emily for music lessons and shopping. She affirms, "With every breath I wait your return," or, "As with the tulip bulb, my heart waits the spring of your warm touch," and more pleadingly, "Please, find whatever excuse to venture home, then don't let me out of your sight."

The last letter comes in a larger, soft envelope. From it he retrieves a white handkerchief. He smiles. After two months, Margaret's scent remains potent. He realizes he's not tested her original gift, not since Lilly revealed her "birthmark." The last letter mentions that her mother is well, but her father's heart is weak. "He is ailing."

He places the box under his Bible and prayer book. For the next few days he does his best busying himself painting, oiling, and assisting with the final carpentry work on the *Virginia*.

Two days after the shallop's arrival, Gilbert and Richard are seated at one end of the council table in Gilbert's quarters.

"I have matters to discuss, Seymour. As do you, I'm sure. But let us begin with the least pleasant. I want your opinion. It's a matter of the bloke, Edwards, who raped and murdered the savage woman. He's in the brig. I flogged the bastard good and hard. Don't know what to do with him, though. If I hang him—or worse, hand him over to the savages—it would seriously disgruntle the troops.

"When are the ships returning, soon?

"Yes, now that we have goods for the hold, as you suggest Nahanada has promised."

"Why not send him back for a court martial?"

"We're empowered to discharge justice here. Don't you think handing him over makes me look weak?"

"Admiral, you know the military better than I. But I think it judicious."

"Well, good then. Davis had the same thought. It's done. Now to change the topic. What, if anything, from your friend, from Skidwarres and Nahanada, what did you learn that is beyond trade?"

"I learned what I feared. The fishermen were killed by braves, Woboz and his friends from Nahanada's village. Neither Skidwarres nor Nahanada knew until quite recently. Soon after the incident, the renegade group moved north for the winter hunt. There is growing concern over our presence. The long winter has brought interminable talk—same as here."

"You think they will attack? Nahanada, we give him firearms, then what?

"I can tell you, Nahanada prefers peace."

"Exactly, right up until they cut our throats. Beginning tonight, I'll double the number of sentries. Woodsmen, fishermen, herders, and farmers outside the walls, they get protection. I am not too cautious?"

"You promised the men revenge for the murder. Might the rape and killing of one woman suffice?"

"No, no, that is different. We need to attack."

"But revenge, regardless of the victim? None but the small group from Nahanada's village is guilty. Not even Sabenoa."

"Unless he's responsible for the fire."

"Agreed."

"All right, all right, so you suggest we raid the group from Nahanada's village. Where are they?"

"Cousin, I do not know precisely. North, not far from Sabenoa. That is what I am told."

Gilbert pours more wine. "Seymour, we will put aside the retaliation question for now. I have another matter to bring up—and not for the first time. What I hear from Captain Davies, we are doing even better than the southern colony at Jamestown. They have suffered illness, starvation, and attacks. I hear our buildings are more substantial. I am heartened. Consider this, Cousin, both of us have little back home. We have talked of this. Now, by god, man, now we have a vast opportunity." Richard settles back into his chair, slightly chastened.

"Listen, I want you to sail back to England. I will ask you to deliver a letter to Gorges. It outlines our plan to establish a colony, a real one. It is our second stage after this beachhead. Seymour, I am asking for two hundred soldiers, settlers, enough to protect and fill a small town, an upriver one. Sabenoa is vulnerable. And they have different ways and a long-simmering feud with Nahanada's people. Would not Nahanada prefer our presence? Already we are his ally against the Micmacs. Nahanada, he can have guns."

Gilbert looks into his mug and tips it up to look at Richard. This appears to be a sly habit of his when making an offer.

Richard restates the proposition: "And you want me to sail and help explain your plans to the Plymouth Council?" The question is directed more to himself than Gilbert.

"For god's sake, man, yes—and the King—but not only my plans. You will be the commander of the Quabacook region, I think they call it. And with it you will be granted thousands of acres. Land allotted to settlers, to harvest lumber. It would be your domain. You, a third born, can become a baron—no, a duke—in the New World. An Englishman will be Lord of the Sagadahoc." Richard finds himself upright in the chair, not sure if he should laugh or plot.

"And you, Cousin?"

"And I will continue to be President of Northern Virginia. Others like you will occupy other lands east and west of the Sagadahoc. But for all this we need support. That will be your job, to motivate backers. I know of no one who knows better our plight or potential."

"It is kind, to place so much trust in me."

"We must act quickly. Settlers, soldiers—they must be here by late summer. This would give us time to rout Sabenoa."

"I see," is Richard's response. But he knows he doesn't.

CHAPTER 55

May 17, 1608, Fort St. George
Lilly's Wrath

Around ten in the evening, quite sated, Seymour leaves Gilbert's house and trudges up the small hill toward the chapel. During dinner of roasted cod and English potatoes, it dawns on him that his willingness to be Gilbert's ambassador is heavily influenced by his eagerness to hold Margaret in his arms, and more generally return to—or at least visit—home.

Life with Lilly has become unpredictable at best, and often quite draining. The dynamics he vaguely became aware of some weeks before. They both understood that her fear of abandonment grew after she gave up her sexual gaming, even though logic might have it otherwise.

Deep in her beliefs about herself was a sense of defectiveness. Why else would she have been shunted off to a filthy, perverted uncle? Why didn't those around her care? Something was wrong with her, so she had concluded years before. Lately, when these thoughts came vaguely percolating into her consciousness, they didn't make much sense. But that didn't change their implacable, corrosive existence. Maintaining an emotional distance from Richard, if only by a thin veil, had kept her safe from her overwhelming need. But now she felt exposed, her defenses down. Inevitably, Lilly imagined, he would leave her for somebody perfect—or at least, not damaged as she was. Why had she been such a fool? Some of this she tried to explain to Richard. Most she kept to herself.

Following one fiery argument, Lilly went to sleep in the sanctuary, leaving Richard at first totally confused. She sometimes kept her distance, barely seeing Richard during the day or night. At other times

319

she might enter his room and ask to be held. Late one night, she slipped between his covers. She began nibbling his arm, bringing him slowly to consciousness, and then a bite on the shoulder which both woke and startled him. Next, in a flash, she straddled his stomach and began pounding his chest. "Lilly, what on earth are you doing?"

To this she grabbed the hair above his ears and pounded his head into the pillow. She had moved herself up so her knees were spread wide, pinning Richard's upper arms, while his legs tangled in the heavy covers. His half-hearted attempt to dislodge her failed. "Stay," she ordered and then slid herself upward onto his mouth. "There," she ordered.

Confused and aroused, Richard at first obeyed, but she was becoming too wild with her thrusts. This time, with his arms freer, he grabbed a hand and yanked her sideways, allowing space to roll off the bed and onto his feet. She immediately turned on her back and pleaded, "Richard, for god's sake, finish me."

Her outrageous passion took charge. He joined it. He fell on her with more aggression and urgency than he, in hindsight, knew he had.

Afterwards the two had little to say. The event might have taken place with two strangers. They lay motionless, staring at the ceiling. Then they fell fast asleep in tandem.

That was before their trip to Pemaquid. Since then they have treated one another cordially. She has returned to his bed. Richard recalls this as he enters the chapel's main door. He notices a candle burning in the living area.

He enters his room to see Lilly sitting on the bed. At her feet, Margaret's letters lie ripped into tiny pieces and scattered.

"This," Lilly holds out her fist and opens it, revealing a tiny handkerchief. "Her perfect little present with her smell on it—her cunt smell. Charming."

"Lilly, those are private." Richard stands in front of her and subdues the urge to slap her.

"Not any more."

He can't do anything about the letters. He tells himself it doesn't matter really, he's read them all at least twice. He is heavy with food and drink and full of his own plans. Lilly has already receded subtly into his past. "Lilly," he says, sitting down beside her now. She watches him defiantly, her tears drying. "Lilly, Gilbert wants me to travel back to England. He wants me to be his spokesman. Actually, it is a command. The ships leave soon."

"I knew it. You will be with Margaret."

"Yes. We are still betrothed. You knew that." And then to change the subject, he adds, "Do you want to come, to go back?"

"Never! I am here. There is nothing for me there. And you can go to hell." Her tone suggests she would like to get up, storm out of the room and chapel and into the night, slamming doors behind. Rather, she sits, exhausted. He, on the other hand, feels lighter. The murkiness of their love—love, it had been love—now clears with a resolution. It is over. And in swift hindsight, that feels inevitable.

Richard raises his arm and gingerly settles it around her shoulders. At first she holds herself stiffly, head bowed. She snuffles every few seconds and wipes her nose on his sleeve. Then in their silence, she relaxes.

"I always knew you'd leave me," Lilly addresses her lap. "It's the way it is."

"Lilly," Richard says softly, trying to maintain the calm, "You know I've loved you. You do know that."

"Maybe, but I'm damaged property. And you know that. Your Margaret, she is whole."

"Lilly," Richard's voice now has an edge of protest, "that is not how I think."

In return Lilly scrunches up her shoulders, indicating she no longer wants his arm there. She rises and the arm slips off. With no more words, she leaves the room. A few minutes later he walks to the small anteroom off the sanctuary. The light of the candle reveals her head sticking out of the blanket roll. One accusing eye stares at him. He kneels to offer a kiss. "Goodnight," he says.

"Go away," is her quiet rebuttal.

CHAPTER 56

May 24, 1608, Fort St. George
Preparations to Sail

It took over a week to load over twenty masts and deposit a goodly amount of beaver, bear, deer, mink, and mountain lion pelts, the later with the heads attached. Bushels of sassafras were packed in baskets stolen from Sabenoa. In themselves, the baskets might be of interest. Gilbert had thought to include four canoes in his demands. Now he was directing the operations. No time to be wasted. They had only three months: June, July, and August. A return to England on the northern route would eliminate hundreds of miles. Running with the trade winds might reduce the length of the voyage to four weeks. Richard would have less than a month to drum up money, supplies, and men. Memories of the fishermen, Erasmus, and the native's murder faded. Gilbert restated his decision to defer retaliation until a time when the enemy had become better defined and the troops were reinforced and trained in the late summer or fall. Nonetheless, the fort continued in a state of readiness.

After leaving Lilly, Richard slept fitfully. In dreams Lilly's face merged into Margaret's and back again, as did the New World and the English countryside, blending the curvature and fine sands of the beach at the mouth of the Sagadahoc with a landscape parceled off by hedgerows and spotted white with grazing sheep. The dream left him uneasy. Awake, or at least conscious, he imagined the warm water of baths, the taste of roast beef, mutton, and porridge, of ale that didn't look and taste of piss. He felt the touch of the harpsichord keys, and then he fell back again into a deep sleep, emerging on the other side with the scent of pine and cedar and the taste of the morning's chilly air, awakening to the clarity of its actuality and to the fullness of expectation in his chest. They would embark in two days.

Richard wrote the following letter and left it for Lilly to give Skidwarres. Elliott agreed to take her to Nahanada's village where she would stay under Skidwarres' protection until Richard's return.

"Dear Skidwarres,

"Much has occurred since our recent meeting, and I would much prefer to speak than write. However, my new obligations, as well as my revelations—let me call them that—send me back to England with the ships and bounty.

"To begin, Gilbert is sending me to plead our case to Gorges and the Privy Council. Our backers are disgruntled. Without Sir John Popham, enthusiasm is waning. Our future—and here is part of my revelation— lies not with commerce but with exploration and colonization. Gilbert has persuaded me of this, though I must admit I needed little urging. The scale and future of Fort St. George has always been greater than a trading post. Furthermore, Gilbert believes he is now in a position to offer large tracts of land. President Popham before him focused his attention on commerce. Fear not, we are speaking of land west of the Sagadahoc, land more suitable for tilling. By looking west we respect the land of the Mawooshen. So part of my revelation is that I could become landed, something very unlikely to happen in England. Furthermore, I now come to believe I can live my life partly here in this land and not divorce myself from my homeland, which I have to admit lately I miss greatly. With Gilbert's encouragement, I see myself continuing and expanding my role as ambassador, both to your people and now to my own, thereby placing me with one foot on either side of the Atlantic. This has been my biggest revelation.

"My friend, do you think me grandiose? In any event, successful or not, I will return to Fort St. George by late summer. I will bring books for both of us.

"Two other matters. I have urged Gilbert to pay recompense for the murder of the native woman. I ask that you suggest to him what form that might take. Secondly, I am much worried about Lilly. As I told you in Pemaquid, our relationship has changed. With me gone, she worries for her safety. I don't think she is an alarmist. She thinks even Gilbert is not to be trusted. Therefore I ask, good friend, if you might harbor her in your village until my return. She asked me to write this after she refused my offer to leave with me.

"May good fortune shine on you until my return. Richard"

CHAPTER 57

June 10, 1608Fort St. George
Harassment

Twelve sentries walked the stone and dirt ramparts day and night, an increase of four. The nights shortened, though less so than in England, where in May light emerges as early as four and doesn't give up until after nine. But it wasn't winter—this they all reminded themselves as they marched in two groups of six past one another ten paces apart, one group going clockwise, the other counter-clockwise. By continually moving, they kept warmer and were able to communicate in short bursts as they passed.

A red-faced sergeant exhorted, "Be alert. Imagine your throat slit open ear to ear. Close your eyes, rest, and feel that blade. A ripped jugular and your pretty blond scalp hanging in some teenager's wigwam." Sergeants never lost their imaginations. "They'll roast your testicles, you know. Make you walk with your feet hacked off; a necklace of English ears for the savage's sweetheart. It is not an old wives' tale. They do skin prisoners alive." The sentries guffawed and took it lightly, but the tactic worked. The images were the stuff of nightmares. The soldiers stayed awake, most of the time.

When the diabolical high-pitched screeches began on the early June morning, more hawk and canine than human, the half-awake soldiers were at first curious, then alarmed. The sounds came from the hill within the trees off to the south and beyond the garden to the west, the half of the fort not separated by the bay and river moat. Trees within fifty yards of the fort had been felled, leaving a field of mutilated stumps, creating an unprotected open space, thereby allowing cannon and musket unimpeded aim.

The designated soldier rang the alarm bell. As cannoneers and riflemen scrambled to their positions, arrows began arching overhead and then dove like cormorants into and around the fort. They didn't come in great numbers or have a target other than the confines of the fort. They stuck in the ground or on roofs. As one soldier leaned slightly over to pull a white feathered arrow out of the ground, another plummeted into his exposed bottom and stuck. The embarrassed young man easily pulled it out, as others laughed and scrambled for cover or kneeled to spy over the wall and into the woods, some with their shields over their heads.

Cannoneers waited for orders. Riflemen couldn't find targets. Occasionally a brave at the edge of the clearing stepped out, exposing himself in order to take better aim and to prove his bravery. By the time anyone found him in their sights, he had vanished. Some fired anyway.

Gilbert conferred with Captain of the Fort Davis. "We've ammunition aplenty and the men want at it. Fire into the trees with grapeshot." The six cannon facing land erupted with a cheer from the men. They watched limbs and small trees fall. With the silence that followed came shouts and jeers from the woods. The large pine and oak beyond the stump-laden field and the garden offered even better protection than an open-air fort.

The sporadic shower of arrows included some tied with cloth, dipped with bear grease, and set aflame. The bucket brigade stood ready. Some were ordered to keep their eyes to the sky and alert others. The arrows coming from on high might be dodged. Others whistled lower over the wall. A few found a human target. One bounced off a man's helmet. Another caught an upper back and penetrated the breastplate, sinking an inch into flesh. Soon the arrows stopped coming. The cannon had accomplished their task.

From the waterside, the natives launched three canoes. They, too, had torched arrows, their target the *Virginia*. She bobbed in shallow water, as close to the fort as possible. The four men assigned to her were ready with muskets and a small, loaded three-pound cannon on her bow, but two larger ones stationed on the ramparts spoke first, one with a six-pound ball that carried over the canoes. Another bounced over the waters and sliced off a bow, throwing the four occupants into the air and cold water. The other three turned and headed back for shore, but not before another round of grapeshot from a third fort cannon tore a second canoe to pieces, injuring three of the four braves.

Then all was quiet again. The on-again off-again battle produced only one fatality. A brave taunted the English. He stood too long in front of the tree waving and screaming. A six-pound ball ripped through his stomach. He was dead by the time his friends pulled him away. Arrows caught only the one English bottom and punctured a breastplate. One thatched roof caught fire, but the brigade doused it before there was much damage. Cannon and rifle found their mark, blind as most of it was. Three braves from the canoe would need to have grapeshot dug out of their backs and legs. Many in the woods left with scratches from flying bark and twigs. Three had caught bullets, but only flesh wounds. All in all, both sides remained in high sprits. Weaponry on both sides proved imprecise. The English felt safe with their greater firepower, the natives jubilant with their intimidation.

The natives never intended to overrun the fort. The strategy, finally agreed upon by Woboz and Sabenoa, focused on harassment. Woboz argued for rushing the fort at its least protected area and engaging in hand-to-hand battle. Sabenoa was persuaded by Kasko, Woboz' father, and the few elders among the braves and the community that many lives would be lost. The elders had learned from Nahanada how the English deaths mattered little to their leaders. They were methodical, cold blooded, whereas the natives were devious but always mindful of their small communities where every life served a purpose. Nahanada had heard of these matters from Sipsis. He agreed that the growing tensions brought about by the fort over the past year needed to be released. Hence, he did not argue against attack, only that it be considered harassment. That was his word to Kasko, though he thought few cared to hear his voice.

Skidwarres continued to argue that a peaceful relationship with the English would make it less likely the Micmacs would launch serious attacks, as they had the past summer at the Saco. Nahanada made it clear that his village would not participate in the hostilities against the English, thereby allowing him to claim neutrality.

Woboz and his group of fifty or so braves, some of whom he had drawn from Sabenoa, others from villages on the Aponeg, were given permission to harass parties of Englishmen who ventured out of the fort to hunt, fish, explore, or harvest wood.

Again Nahanada declined to participate. Sagamores from the other villages on the Aponeg held various positions that changed from month to month.

Nahanada did not believe the English were strong or stupid enough to carry out a successful attack, though he wasn't sure. Information from Sipsis helped form this opinion. Nonetheless, they had frightened Sabenoa. Might they attack again or hit the smaller villages between

Pemaquid and the fort? He believed Gilbert knew such aggression would trigger wholesale warfare, for which the English had no more than fifty or so trained fighters against potentially hundreds of braves. If the policy of harassment forced the English to abandon the fort and sail back to England, then Nahanada could claim he sided with the aggressors. If the English increased their numbers and remained, as Seymour and Gilbert said they would, then Nahanada would have maintained his good name. The few muskets taken in trade would not be used against the English— at least not yet.

CHAPTER 58

June 14, 1608, North Atlantic
A Mission Begins

With summer near, the ship's stores half-full, and roomier accommodations on the *Mary and John*, Richard's sail on the North Atlantic was uneventful, if cold at night. Today he marveled at the mountainous, bluish green icebergs to the north. He'd read of these. The explorer Sir Martin Frobisher years before had attempted to find a Northwest Passage. His failure brought him fame, less for his rather inept adventures, more for the capture of an Inuit and his wife. Frobisher displayed the couple in London for some years, as if they were exotic animals.

This otherworldly landscape slipped by in accordance with Richard's mood. After nearly a year on the Sagadahoc, he had begun to acclimate, to consider it a home. Yet here he was heading to England on a preposterous mission, or so it seemed from a growing distance and among such a bizarre seascape. Ambition: the feeling resided in the stomach and probably needed to be constantly replenished. But in the North Atlantic, in this rather ethereal world, ambition felt ephemeral.

On deck, with little to do when he wasn't reading or composing letters for backers, he often thought of Margaret. She would not be expecting him. Should he post her a letter when he arrived or surprise her in the flesh? That was the expression that comes to mind, and indeed her flesh began to occupy his thoughts more each day. If the weather held, they would arrive in Plymouth in less than two weeks, a full three weeks shorter than his previous voyage.

Gilbert and Richard's strategy began with Ferdinando Gorges, Sir John's initial ally. He would know of the present tenor of the backers.

In each letter, Richard considered the proclivities and vanities of the recipient, as best he knew. Later he'd ask Gorges to edit them. Richard started with the Champernowne family, to whom both he and Gilbert were related. Unlike the southern colony at Jamestown, Fort St. George would continue for one more year as a military and commercial venture. Richard wrote Francis Bacon. He and Gorges knew Robert Cecil, the most influential member of the King's Privy Council and son of Queen Elizabeth's first and most trusted advisor, William Cecil. More important, Seymour and Gilbert's scheme needed trained soldiers and armaments, and needed them within a month. This Cecil could arrange better than anyone.

When occupied with these matters, Richard found himself full of a curious energy, part ambition and part—he couldn't quite identify. His ambition carried with it possessiveness, as if for a woman. Land, Richard mused, had a feminine aspect. At private moments he'd pull out Margaret's soft gift that he had wrested from Lilly. Soon the source of this scent would touch him. His ambition for land and wealth, the military nature of this ambition—amalgamated with his growing ardor for Margaret.

CHAPTER 59

June 28, 1608, Port Plymouth
Ferdinando Gorges

No icebergs on the horizon for days. According to the navigator's reckoning, the *Mary and John* would sail within sight of the Cornwall shore by nightfall. Richard stood by the rail in anticipation of the clay-red and chalk-white shore, porous and soft compared to the granite of Northern Virginia. He hoped Ferdinando Gorges would greet the ships. The distance between the New and Old Worlds appeared to shrink. But was not time essentially emotional rather than mathematical? This notion suited him, for he was now imagining a life residing in both worlds.

Beyond their two brief meetings, he knew little about Ferdinando Gorges, except what Gilbert passed on over glasses of Burgundy: "Crafty, full of avarice, dogged, sly." Gilbert offered up more details: "Born in 1558, the year the English defeated the Spanish Armada, his family prosperous. Gorges was well educated and then served in the military. The Earl of Essex, Robert Devereux, commanded Gorges' regiment. Due to his actions—whatever they were—the earl knighted Gorges—though the Earl of Essex never had Elizabeth's permission. As was expected, this annoyed the Queen immensely. But, as was the case with Her Highness, Devereux's charm nearly always greased his way. A few years later she awarded Gorges command of the fort at Plymouth. His main assignment involved defending the West Country from a Spanish invasion—which never occurred."

Gilbert continued, "I learned this from my uncle, Sir Walter Raleigh. The Earl of Essex is important to Gorges' story. The man learned to attach himself to prominent people, the most noteworthy being Robert

Devereux, the Queen's last heartthrob. You are aware, Richard, no doubt, that Robert Devereux, Earl of Essex, was the adopted son of Robert Dudley, the most favored man in the Queen's life. With Dudley's death, her attentions fell on the younger—considerably younger, given the Queen's age—Earl of Essex. Devereux, however, continued his rash ways—foolish really—and ended up losing his place on the Privy Council. Robert was a scoundrel, but one with the type of personality that attracted others, including Gorges. You are aware of Devereux's last stupid act? It involved an attempt to overthrow the Queen. His demotion from the Privy Council rattled him. He drew together a group of two hundred men, including Gorges. To bring the story full circle, the Queen asked Sir John Popham to intervene. Robert Devereux ended up charged with treason, much to the Queen's dismay—though she didn't lift a finger. So the Earl of Essex lost his head to the ax. Gorges, a key witness, testified against the earl. Popham sat as one of the three judges who pronounced the sentence.

"It was during this time Gorges began working with Popham. Both looked to the New World with a commercial eye. The fact he turned against the Earl of Essex created his reputation as a man to blow with the wind and added to the reported baselessness of his title. To his credit though, Gorges has many connections. He knows merchants, adventurers, many gentry, earls, barons, dukes, and members of the Privy Council. He and Popham were like-minded, men from solid families, not royalty. They aimed to amass wealth and prestige. I suppose we might have some sympathy."

Gilbert's offered Richard blunt advice: "Work with him, but hold him as you would a snake. Raleigh thinks him as essentially untrustworthy."

By next morning the *Mary and John* has slipped into harbor with the incoming tide and dropped anchor. As he is being rowed in a longboat to the docks, Richard recognizes Gorges standing, waiting.

After exchanging effusive handshakes, they amble and talk their way to a tavern for lunch. For Richard the ground continues to sway and swell, so he welcomes the steady bench and then the ale with poached eggs, plus his first slab of fresh bacon in over a year.

Gorges immediately wants to know the contents of the hold. His face clouds when he hears about what he considers to be a meager number of pelts. The large quantity of sassafras will only fetch a small price, given the now-flooded market for the popular herb. He agrees the straight, long pine masts are probably of the best quality. But small ships such as the *Mary and John* and the *Gift of God* could handle only so many. Rather than dampen enthusiasm, Gorges moves the conversation to a new topic.

The Plymouth Council has, of course, suffered greatly without Sir John's guidance. His wife and son Francis had added insult to injury. You heard, no doubt, how they brought suit against Robert Davies? A great mistake."

"We have, and so very disconcerting to hear of his death." Richard adds, "And strange to hear so long after the event, to realize for so many months during that bitter winter we relied on his stature and his enthusiasm to give us courage. And yet he died only days after our setting sail. Strange."

"Strange it was, sir." Gorges, in much the same manner as Sir John and his cousin, George swallows a large mouthful of ale as a preface to telling a story. "Strange that that his body was never found. That is the story. Some say he fell off his horse while riding alone, that he rolled off the road to be swallowed up in a swampy mire. There, it's rumored, he was sucked into hell. They say his ghost appears on the anniversary of his death and roams the countryside. Others say Raleigh poisoned him. Known for his concoctions, he is, made from Guianan, Cuban, Floridian plants. Perhaps both tales are true. Or neither. But you know how the common man speaks—their superstitions, especially for a powerful man, feared for his reputation as a hanging judge, feared for his connections."

"Incredible."

"Exactly, sir, probably not very credible," Gorges says with a chuckle, rather proud of himself for the slight play on words. "But the disappearing body—apparently true."

"If I might, Sir Ferdinando, what is the mood of the council here in Plymouth? The word from those who brought us news of Popham's death suggests discontent. But none could say with assurance."

"The mood has flagged greatly, I'm afraid to say. I hoped your cargo might brighten their spirits as it fattened their pockets. But perhaps we must approach backers with a different scenario."

Richard reached into his satchel, withdrew a stack of twenty letters, and handed them to Gorges. "Admiral Gilbert and I anticipated as much. These reports outline a shift in strategy." He hears himself say "we" and doesn't correct himself. After all, it was he who wrote the letters. "I ask that you read and alter them as you see fit. Could they then be delivered to the parties here in Plymouth and to those in Devon, Somerset, and Dorset? My father, I hope, will be of some help. I trust he remains well?

"He does indeed, if not a little older, as with us all."

"This last letter, Sir Ferdinando, is addressed to the Privy Council. Might you look at it and make arrangements for us to confer with Cecil or his representative? Might we meet at Middle Temple and with Bacon? I plan to visit my home and then my betrothed, Margaret Throckmorton. She, too, is in Dorset. I wish to be in London in a fortnight."

"You, sir, are a man on a mission."

Richard isn't sure whether Gorges' tone holds a hint of mockery. "I suppose I am. But it is to further the cause you and Sir John have championed, only the emphasis now, we believe, should focus on colonization, much as our counterpart in Jamestown. That will take time, I realize. First we need soldiers. We believe we have created the conditions for growth, but first we must expand our holdings. I am hoping to return within a month with one hundred, one hundred fifty soldiers and armaments. For that, the King's endorsement is crucial. You agree?"

"Yes, I'd say imperative. I will make the most of your bounty, and I will do my utmost to arrange for a new voyage."

After finishing a second helping of eggs and bacon, his stomach not entirely empty, Richard continues, "Then perhaps, if I may, I will immediately take my leave. Here is my itinerary so we may communicate by letter, if you see fit." Hearing his own confident presentation, he remembers his first days in the role of chaplain. In life, it turns out, we can slip in and out of character. Doing so with confidence helps others believe—and even more important, confirms one's own intentions.

Gorges nods, a little taken aback by Seymour's self-assurance "Indeed, then, we will meet in London. I will contact Cecil."

"Perfect, sir. Until we meet at Middle Temple, I bid you farewell." Richard rises. He is, in fact, aching to be in the saddle and heading through the countryside to his home in Dorset, and to Margaret.

CHAPTER 60

June 29th, 1608, Hanford, Dorset
Home

With a purchased three-year-old stallion under him, and at a steady, comfortable lope, Richard finds it difficult to believe a year has passed since he's ridden. The scent of lilac and roses periodically spills from farms. The countryside—sweet, soft grass dotted with fluffy sheep and their new lambs, the graceful line of hedgerows marking ownership, the undulation and curvature of hill and valley. Again, he thinks, feminine compared to the rock-hard, wild, unpredictable landscape of the New World, with its fast-running broad rivers and crisp, murderous winter air, the air that becomes so generously warm in summers—a landscape of great disruptive moods—whereas England again strikes him as mannered and domesticated.

This time of year, near the summer solstice, he might ride into an extended dusk. The eighty-mile trip to Exeter might be managed in six hours, if he didn't get too sore or his horse too fatigued. His mind wanders. He will aim for the Old Goat Inn, a favorite of his and other young men. He hankers for a pork pie and blood sausage. He remembers pubs in London he frequented while studying at Middle Temple. There they'd often sing. A portion of one ditty worms its way into his mind:

"Have you heard of Scratchy Bottom, Titington Mount or Lickers Lane?

They and others are English place names.

Cockermouth Green, Shittenton and a place called Pant,

And if you're on the go,

Happy Bottom, Sandyballs, and Titty Ho.

Giggleswick, Grope Lane, and believe it or not,

You'll even find a little place called Twat."

Mawooshen place names are more prosaic. From his knowledge, they nearly always described the character of a place. He would ask Skidwarres about this. Did place names ever involve humor?

At the Old Goat Inn, a very tired horse and rider are cordially received near nine o'clock. None of the patrons in the tavern look familiar, so Richard parks himself at a corner table and watches the conviviality grow loud with the sheen of alcohol. Tonight Richard relishes his own company.

After a meal of pot roast, boiled potatoes, and greens—everything on the menu looks tantalizing—the sweet, flirtatious barmaid, Lilly's age he guesses, serves up a third pint. He slugs it down and stands up at the same time. She shows him to his small room over the kitchen. The permeating aroma of onion and grease doesn't bother him in the least, not given the tight, moldy ship's quarters with long-saturated aromas of dung, brine, cooking oil, fish, rotted vegetables, and the unidentifiable. He would quickly fall asleep. "Would you wake me by daybreak? I have another piece of riding ahead, to Hanford, Dorset."

"Of course, sir," the young girl replies, with a tongue-in-cheek courtesy and a raised eyebrow. "And would you be needing anything else?" The friendly implication appears more hospitable than lustful. "Kind of you, but I must sleep."

The next afternoon, when Richard arrives at Hanford, Dorset, six hours northeast of Exeter, his thighs and hindquarters are aching. His depleted young stallion has earned the rest he'll receive.

Richard's arrival is entirely unexpected. Riding up the entrance road, he glances at its three trodden grooves, two made from the wheels of carriages, one from horses, unchanged from a year ago. Time, he thinks, has a way of embedding itself in landscapes. As he looks about, still undetected by anyone in the manor house or barn, all feels unchanged. He could be returning from a brief, exuberant ride. Two hours could have past instead of thirteen months. While the entire structure of his being has altered—or so it seems—these surroundings appear as static as a painting.

As Richard slides off his mount, his eldest brother, Robert, appears in the front doorway and calls out, half-believing his eyes, "Richard, that is you?"

"It is I, or some semblance."

Robert walks quickly and takes hold of the reins. "My god, man, why didn't we get word of your return?" Ten years older than Richard, Robert is not only the eldest of the four sons and five daughters of John and Agnes, he stands at least four inches taller than Richard. This, combined with his primogeniture, a reality known since childhood, has given Robert a slight aloofness, a reserve, though never pompous, nearly always kindly. Yet you were reminded of his position. In reference to his height, his three brothers held among themselves, "He was aloof because he was so aloft."

Robert unbuckles Richard's gear from the back of the saddle, slings it over one shoulder, and wraps his arm around Richard's shoulder. Richard has experienced this brotherly and only mildly condescending protection for his entire life. As they amble up the steps, Richard explains the urgency and brevity of his visit, while his parents, Robert's wife and six-year-old, three sisters, and various servants spill out of the door, all talking at once. Richard is home, a wonderment.

That evening family members fill nine chairs around the dining table. His parents, both in their mid-sixties, are healthy, but as Richard focuses on their faces, he notices how his father's eyelids droop like small awnings descending. His mother has lost, ever so little, the sprightliness in her step. His sister, Deborah, newly married, carries a watermelon-sized bulge under her petticoats and dress. His adolescent sisters have sprouted two inches, added soft curves, and new found coy vivacity. Three other sisters live with their husbands in Devon Country and two brothers are at Oxford. The serving girls, the cook, valet, gardener and stable hands, all in their twenties to fifties, apparently haven't changed at all. Robert and his wife live at the manor house, allowing him to assume many of his father's responsibilities, while also traveling to London where he serves as one of the Tellers of the Exchequer.

Richard, so barraged with questions, barely finds moments to put the delicious food in his mouth or shift the conversation to politics, other than to learn that James continues to maintain Elizabeth's moderate religious views and has not persecuted either Catholics or Puritans. From his frequent stays in London, Robert has become a repository of rumor and humor. He tells of King James writing that the monarchy is the most supreme thing upon the earth, "God's lieutenants who sit upon God's throne." Yet, how unlike Henry VIII and Queen Elizabeth—who thought the same—but, James, short, plump, who speaks with a lisp and stutter and with such a thick Scots accent, and who tends to prefer the company of beautiful young men. The lampoon catches Richard with a large mouthful of beef that nearly chokes him. How marvelous to be home.

Richard promises he'll be back in a week or so to spend more time. For now he'd stay two nights before heading to Margaret's estate. He also learns her father died three months ago, leaving the family in financial distress.

During the next day Richard can barely contain himself. Tomorrow he'd hold Margaret in his arms, and then in a few days be in London. Nothing could compare with the expansiveness of riding toward purpose, especially if part of that purpose wore a dress.

CHAPTER 61

July 2, 1608, Andover, Dorset
Reunion

Richard caressed Dancer's black withers, stroked his back as he came up behind, and finally wrapped his arm around the neck, rich with his dark sweat and hay scent. Richard placed his forehead against Dancer's and nuzzled. "Hello old friend. Put on a few pounds, you have. We'll soon work that off." Dancer turned, sniffed, then whinnied, stamping a front hoof, either in recognition or reproach for absence or both, or in confusion over the appearance and disappearance of humans.

He saddled Dancer with slow care. "We are on a mission, old friend." Around the table the previous night, he again answered every manner of question regarding everything from commerce to sea monsters and moose. When he allowed as he might be granted large tracts of land and spend months of the year in the New World, the family had responded with utter silence, a rare event around the Seymour dinner table.

When Dancer and his rider arrive at the stone pillars marking the entrance to a sun-baked road leading to Margaret's large manor, he notices the fields are ready to be hayed, but no evidence of work underway. The thatched roof shows signs of wear. No one sees him coming, and in the barn the equipment looks uncared for and misplaced, the stable boy nowhere to be seen. After removing Dancer's saddle, watering him, and finding oats, Richard opens the house's main front door and calls, "Hello, hello, Margaret, anyone at home?"

At first he hears only his echo and silence. He calls again. This time from deep in the house on the second floor, he hears his own name called out by Margaret and her hurried footsteps tapping along the hallway, then down the broad stairs from which, three steps from the bottom, she jumps into his arms.

"My god, Richard! Richard? Richard, are you really there? No, you can't be. I'm making this up. I'm dreaming." She wraps her arms tightly around his neck, her legs cling to his waist, her light dress hikes up above her knees, her face buries in his neck, his arms fold under her bottom providing a temporary seat.

Richard repeats her name softly in her ear.

"Don't let me down. Don't let me go. You might disappear again."

"Yes, my lady, whatever you say."

For at least half a minute they remain motionless. The emptiness of the house settles around them. They are a statue of impulsive, exuberant reunion in the large formal entranceway. Margaret finally unwraps her legs and slips down. She rearranges her floor-length dress. "I suppose I'm not very ladylike."

"Let's go for a walk," Richard suggests, their signature phrase which allows them to distance themselves from family or servants—though none are in sight.

Working out the stiffness in his legs from yet another long ride, Richard learns of the difficulties the household has undergone following her father's death, just two weeks after she posted her last letter. Landholdings that for years have provided the family with a comfortable income are now caught up in a legal suit. Margaret's elder brother has little knowledge of these matters. They are on the brink of losing a large portion of their holdings. The income has ceased. Though most servants live on the manorial property, as has been the case for generations, it is becoming more difficult to feed everyone, including the animals. Some of the farm hands have hired themselves out to other large land owners, leaving the Throckmorton estate a low priority. Margaret's brother would be selling his properties to the north and taking over the ancestral home, but arrangements are incomplete. Margaret's mother has fallen into a deep melancholic grief. She stays in bed in her darkened room for most of the day.

After some minutes recounting her family's trials, Margaret exclaims how sick she is of the whole matter, how eager to hear about Richard. "You've traveled to the other side of the world and back. You, Richard, an adventurer, another Francis Drake, and I talk of such dreary matters. Talk, Richard, talk."

"Francis Drake?" he chuckles. "No. But an adventurer, perhaps."

They walk hand and hand through the unkempt gardens and along the path that follows a small stream. Again he tells his tale, though as with his family, leaving out Lilly. By the time they return, Margaret knows of his role as spokesperson for Gilbert and his intention to return within less than a month. Her mood moves from fascination to amazement and finally, with the news he would sail back soon, dejection.

She sits down on a stone bench in front of the manor entrance, not leaving room for Richard to sit alongside. He hasn't quite anticipated this shift in mood, though now engulfed by it, he sees its inevitability. She sits staring at the ground. He stands, hands clasped behind his back, pacing back and forth in front of her as a general might in preparation for a campaign. But not for long. Margaret looks up and says flatly, "Marry me and take me with you."

Richard stops his pacing. He makes a quarter turn, hands still behind. On the *Mary and John* and on horseback, he thought of a future with Margaret. Multiple futures existed. Most likely he'd continue their present arrangement: betrothal followed by marriage in a year or so, when the Popham colony had secured more land and he a more definite position. Then she could join him. Or he would live six months in Northern Virginia—in the spring, summer, and early fall—returning to England for the five or six winter months. Margaret could reside at the Seymour estate or in London. Or maybe she would travel with him. Or maybe, he had thought, upon reacquainting themselves, they wouldn't be able to retrieve the love they had put aside. Maybe they'd find it untenable as a woolen jacket you've stored away, only to unearth it months later and find it riddled with moth holes. Hearts, he now better understood, calculate by their own devices. He had even considered calling off the engagement, saying too much was afoot. A scheming part of him suggested how unwise it was to close down future possibilities at age twenty-four. Every decision eliminated future possibilities. To decide: the word reminded him of suicide and homicide.

Margaret has delivered her salvo. Now, Richard must respond. The empty air stretches and quivers. The silence expands. Until he says, "Then we shall marry. Then we shall sail." His deliberateness, this tiny point in time, sets a course. He simply decides. It feels right—and as reckless as anything he's done in his life.

She rises deliberately, rather stately. He meets her sober mood in an embrace. For both, after hours upon months of pondering, hoping, worrying, yearning, they collapse into agreement. In the moment it doesn't feel like an act of love. It carries too much weight, too much obligation. Richard and Margaret, each in their own fashion, fill slowly with relief and joy, and yes, an unidentifiable sweet dread, the dread of finality.

The news kindles Margaret's mother's spirits. In the next two weeks, she and her daughter would impossibly, hastily, plan a simple wedding. Richard would send word to his brother, Robert, who would in turn assist Margaret's brother with his legal problems. Because of the present depleted circumstances of Margaret's household, the ceremony would take place at the Seymour estate. His sisters could be counted upon. It would be a family affair, after which the bride and groom would take a remarkable honeymoon, across the ocean and into the unknown.

By midnight plans are recorded on paper, with copies to be delivered to various family members. Richard will stay another day before continuing to London.

The second floor consists of a catacomb of hallways and doors. The two betrothed leave Margaret's mother with her maidservant. They remind the now-smiling widow how Margaret's brother and family would soon be residing with her. When they close the door and enter the hallway, Margaret's free hand finds Richard's. With the other holding the candle, they wend their way to her bedroom. With head of the family deceased and most servants temporarily working elsewhere, propriety is thrown out the window.

"Are you sure you still love me?" she asks, standing with the bed between them.

"Sure."

"Do I hear a wary tone?"

"You hear a man who has committed himself."

"And not to prison, I hope."

"If so, I have turned the key and thrown it out the window."

Margaret slips off her blouse, skirt, petticoat, and corset. She does so with great smoothness and agility and then scurries under the sheets. To him it appears a magic trick.

He proceeds to undress, much more clumsily; then he lifts the sheets and slides in on the other side of the bed toward her heat. She rolls over to him. Both lie on their sides, meeting one another covered, yet in their nakedness, exposed. His hand starts at the nape of her neck and runs slowly down her spine to settle on softness. They both sigh in unison and then laugh. With this laugh everything else disappears, everything but the expanded moment. Richard knows this feeling. It was the same and entirely different with Lilly. As before, his tactile self eclipses his thoughts. In hindsight he doesn't remember entering her. His mouth nestles against her ear. "Hello, Margaret," he offers, as he climbs a slow long rise, then releases. With his eyes closed, he looks far into the abyss.

CHAPTER 62

July 4, 1608, To London and Middle Temple
"We Quaff the Rich Juice Right Merrily."

On the trip from Margaret's home, ninety miles from London, Richard decides to set a leisurely pace on Dancer. He wants time to collect himself. On the second night with Margaret, he'd confessed his relationship with Lilly. He started by saying, "There was a woman at the fort," then went into considerable detail. Margaret held her tongue. They rested on her bed with a light sheet over their laps. He couldn't tell her mood in the slight light offered by a candle on the bed table. She stared at the ceiling.

Finally she said, "That is quite a story." Then she turned to him. "And did you love her?"

"I don't know. I don't think so. But I did have feelings. I adored her. That winter, it was unfathomably cold. And lonely. She offered herself up. It was strange. I was her protector—and lover."

"And then did you say she became too dependent."

"Not quite dependent. I'm sorry. I, too, have tried to find the correct words. She became desperate and wanting from me more, more than I could offer. My response—well, the more she craved love, the more I retreated."

They sit with their backs resting on pillows stacked up against the headboard. Richard takes her hand and rests it in the small space between them. "Perhaps I should have kept this to myself, except you will no doubt meet her. I thought it best to be clear with you now."

"Yes, I think it better you tell me now, yes. And if I love too much, will you run again?"

"No, Margaret, no. Please. It's difficult to explain. It was as if she stayed famished, no matter how much she ate. Something of that sort. And she was always looking to me to feed her. And by the way, you, Margaret, you didn't have suitors in my absence?" It is best to change the subject, Richard thinks.

"Richard, we were betrothed. Then she leans over and rests her forehead on his shoulder. "Well, a few came calling. You know, you English gentlemen are such cockerels."

"Of, course," answers Richard, kissing the top of her head.

"But, as they say,"—she lifts her head, offering up what in the semi-darkness he thinks is a wry smile—"I am a chaste woman. I will be a chaste bride—except for you, of course. I have chased all the others off." She gives his hand a squeeze, then lets go, only to place her hand on the sheet over his semi-aroused member. "And, by the way, I don't expect you to retreat from me."

As Richard and Dancer amble northeast on the dry road, he considers how he's managed to explain away his relationship with Lilly, at least temporarily. If he hadn't described the complexity of his feelings—and how could he? How can a love relationship be tied neatly in a bow—at least she heard a viable take on the facts. Or had he lied? Yes. No doubt, he had loved Lilly. But that's been stowed away. He imagines love doesn't disappear—or does it? Does any part of the past vanish, anything important? No, not what's important. Doesn't all significant experience accumulate, layer upon layer, more or less like a tree gathers yearly rings? Or perhaps, rather, doesn't each experience change the preceding ones, more like adding one color to another on a palate? Enough thinking. Enjoy the feel of Dancer, this very moment.

The easy pace and muggy air allow Richard to doze in the saddle and muse. With the smell of tilled soil, sheep dung, roses, and wisteria wafting and receding as he passes by farms and through woods, his thoughts fall back to London. A verse comes to mind: The Revels are held between December 12th and New Years Day, seventeen days of pageantry, gluttony, bawdiness, a nod to reverence—mostly, colossal merriment. More than the studying and fraternity, he remembers the Revels at Middle Temple.

"Bring hither the bowl,
The brimming brown bowl,
And quaff the rich juice right merrily.
Let the wine cup go round
Till the solid ground

Shall quake at the noise of our revelry.
Let wassail and wine
Their pleasures combine,
While we quaff the rich juice right merrily.
Let us drink till we die,
When the saints we rely
Will mingle their songs with our revelry."

Only blocks from Westminster Abbey, Middle Temple remained one among a number of buildings or inns in which the powerful of English society worked, trained, and resided. In the thirteenth century, the legal system fell within the church's purview. Ecclesiastical and civil law were one in the same. The separation of the two evolved, with a final break coming under the rule of Henry VIII. Before then, Middle Temple housed monks who were also judges. Neophytes also lodged at the Temple. Following the separation of the Church of England from Rome under Henry VIII, during the religious turbulence throughout Europe, and finally during Queen Elizabeth's reign, Middle Temple became a quasi-law school, though the curriculum included a wide range of humanitarian and scientific subjects.

By the beginning of the 1600s, members spent enormous amounts of time and expense preparing for the Revels. Knights Templar history melded with other English lore. The Revels became an extravagant pageant based on tradition and myth.

The Revels occupied Richard's memories on the warm summer ride in 1608. Middle Temple Hall represented the finest of Elizabethan architecture. Similar to, though more intimate than a cathedral, it ran one hundred and one feet long and forty-one feet wide. The span of double hammer-beams gave the effect of a huge carved candelabra dripping with varnished wax. Three twenty-nine-foot tables were cut from a single oak, a gift from Queen Elizabeth. Shields, in the form of family crests, hung from the walls. Temple Hall became the embodiment of Middle Temple, along with its gardens and dormitories, a university of sorts, an *alma mater* whose members acquired a sense of personal aggrandizement.

How could the Middle Temple, and especially the Revels, not impress a young man? Richard began his residency in 1602. Sir John Popham had donated the funds for the residence hall he and other West Country gentlemen called home.

Months after Richard arrived, cannon blasts rocked the building and announced the beginning of Revels. Richard and his associates spent hours learning how to comport themselves. With drums rattling in the background, they stood watching prominent personages, robed in knightly habits reminiscent of medieval times, walk through the main doors to the hall. Following them the Carver, Sewer, Cup-Bearer, Lord Steward, Treasurer, Keeper of the Seal of Pallas, Treasurer of the Household, Secretary, Prince, Sergeants at Law, Masters of the Revels, King of Arms, Dean of the Chapel, Lieutenant of the Tower with his Captains of Foot-Bands and Shot, Chief Butler, Panter (in charge of pants), Clerks of the Kitchen, Master Cook, four score Guards of the Prince of the Revels, and finally the Lord of Misrule.

When all had found their seats, trumpeters blasted, accompanied by drums and fife, heralding the high order of eating. On this first day, stewards delivered silver platters, held high for all to see. On them were boars' heads with their dead eyes and apples stuck in their jaws; on other trays roast beef, mutton, venison, and baked hens. The sweetness of violins, sackbuts, recorders, and cornets filled the hall.

On the evening of the fourth day, Revelers organized a grand parade, an event welcomed by Queen Elizabeth, who watched, feeble by 1602 but still enthusiastic.

At the front marched twenty footmen in scarlet livery with silver lace, each one carrying his sword by his side, a baton in one hand, and a lighted torch in the other. Next came the Marshall. He sat on a great high-stepping horse, saddled in leather and silver—horsemanship, of course, equated with gallantry. Besides him two lackeys carried torches. Following the Marshall rode one hundred gentleman from the Inns of Court, twenty-five chosen from each house, all proper and handsome young gentlemen, every one of them mounted on the best horses and livery. As Richard remembers that year, he and the other nine-nine had worn the richest of clothes, adorned with gold and silver lace. They strode five abreast. Lackeys on foot carried torches, hurrying to keep up.

Next came a gaggle of Anti-Masquers, some limping, many dazed, most drunk. The unseemly contrast, from elegant to freakish, delighted everyone including the Queen. A collection of cripples, paupers, idiots in rags, among them dwarfs juggling dead rats, giant men, a half-dressed woman bearing three breasts, all moved by, waving. Some hobbled. Others careened about. A few rode horses, lame, emaciated, near dead. When they fell off or the animals collapsed, either or both were pushed aside and eventually carted away. As with the gentlemen, the Anti-Masquers marched to music provided by a ragtag of men and women, like themselves plied with grog, beating on drums and whistling on fifes, making it clear how unskilled and extemporaneous they were, compared with the elegance of those ahead of them. Nonetheless, The Anti-Masquers were no less enthusiastic, even though many had been picked up off the streets, gathered from asylums and taverns. They'd all been offered some small change and free drink. Marching or riding a horse of any sort before the Queen, while illuminated by torch bearers— clearly they felt the honor.

As the clatter and banging passed by the Sovereign's ears, she would begin to hear the sweeter noise of skilled musicians playing pipes, imitating the chirps and songs of birds. A grown man wearing a great horned owl's costume and little boys dressed as magpies, sparrows, and doves flitted about and by her.

Next she'd hear the swoon of bagpipes. She'd see a little horse with a great bit in its mouth ridden by the King of Unfitness and Ridiculousness. On another small horse rode the Attorney of Annoyance.

Finally came grandly bedecked chariots, some filled with musicians, others with men and women dressed as heathen gods and goddesses. Four smaller chariots of silver and crimson contained the Grand Masquers, including a well-known playwright, William Shakespeare.

At Temple Hall, near the end of the festivities, the dinner tables had been removed, and the Master of the Game strode through the door followed by the Ranger of the Forest, both dressed in satin and bearing green bows and quivers. They blew from their hunting horns a succession of three staccato blasts, a rest and then repeats as they paced back and forth three times in front of the fireplace.

Next huntsman entered the hall with a fox and cat, each carried in a purse net at the end of a staff. Following them ten leashed hounds yelped and yanked. A horn blast announced the release of the fox and cat. Off leash went the slobbering dogs. Total pandemonium erupted. Dogs bayed, barked, and tore about. Benches were upended, spilling men to the hard wooden floor. Musicians blew, beat, and bowed raucous nonsense. Men reddened by food, drink, and heat shouted encouragement. Some, in their excitement, vomited on themselves.

The Master of the Games finally announced the inevitable finale by holding from an outstretched arm the bloodied carcasses of the fox and cat. The attendees cheered and lifted glasses. They sang:
"Let us drink till we die,
When the saints we rely
Will mingle their songs with our revelry."

On New Year's Day, breakfast and dinner arrived with the same solemnity as on Christmas Eve. After dinner all members of the Inns of the Court attended a play. In 1603, Richard had attended the premier of *Twelfth Night*. Afterward, men and women danced into the wee hours. Slowly, sanity returned.

Loping along on Dancer, Richard remembered that winter six years ago. During his travels to the New World, never had he witnessed anything so bizarre. Yet the Revels were his heritage, himself.

CHAPTER 63

July 6, 1608, London
Among Luminaries

Richard arrived at his old residency hall at Middle Temple a day and a half after his departure. Sir Ferdinando Gorges, who had preceded him by two days, arranged for his lodging and, more importantly, a meeting with Francis Bacon, who not only believed the New World a natural wonder—he the natural scientist—but also could vouch for Seymour's good character. "Remind Sir Francis," Richard had told Gorges during their dinner in Plymouth, "that I often wrote down his pithy remarks. Remind him, 'If a man looks sharply and attentively, he shall see fortune; for though she is blind, she is not invisible.' Tell him I am looking sharply and attentively."

Before dinner at a nearby tavern frequented by the influential, the two older men reminisced. Bacon, forty-seven, and Gorges, forty-three, had matured during the extraordinary expansive years of Elizabeth's reign. Her death in 1603 had coincided with Richard's second year at Middle Temple. He listened respectfully as both men explained how James possessed neither the wit nor the imagination of his predecessor. "Indeed," offered Bacon, "he is an affable man, his best quality and his worst. A king or queen must instill fear. James instills smiles."

"Yes," adds Gorges. "More and more in Parliament question whether the King speaks for God. Indeed, saying such a thing would have landed your head in your lap under Henry and Elizabeth."

"I agree," adds Bacon. "James, he writes of sovereignty with passion, but governs with tolerance leaning toward laxity."

"There is a story going about," Gorges says. "Is it true? I know the King hates crowds, unlike Elizabeth. But is it true that when he was told that a group had gathered to express love for him he said, 'Gadzooks! I will pull down my breeches and show them my arse!'"

"True, I do believe," answers Bacon.

They reminded Richard of what he already knew: the days of the adventurer were gone. And Bacon said rather whimsically, "Only Raleigh maintains the torch—and he found guilty of treason the year James ascended. And the judge was Sir John Popham, the charges mostly hearsay. Nonetheless, they relegated him to his present home, the Tower."

Gorges adds rather wistfully, "The days of stealing gold and silver from the Spanish and Portuguese are almost gone. Some say gold only grows where the sun shines all year. Fish is the north's gold, but it can only be maintained on a seasonal basis. The market for sassafras, bottomed out. Drake proved an Englishman can sail around the world, but to what end? The southern Jamestown outpost appears as doomed as its predecessor, Roanoke, and nothing but a rat hole for its financial backers. The return of the battered *Gift of God* and the ensuing attempt by Sir John's wife and son to file suit against Captain Davies—even though dismissed—only add to the King's assumption that one might just as well attempt settling on the moon as in the New World." So went the drift of the conversation.

As the convivial older men chatted, Richard's mood darkened. Had he traveled all this distance only to hear negativity? One never knew what Gorges actually thought. He always had this or that scheme in his back pocket. Yet he had convinced Seymour how important he thought Fort St. George to be. He had said, "It is my life's quest to move England to the Northern New World. Eventually England will listen, even without the weight of Sir John."

"Francis." Gorges decides to shift the conversation. "Perhaps now we can brighten Chaplain Seymour's mood. I have not told him about the Earl of Salisbury's joining us." Everyone knew of Robert Cecil, son of Lord Burghley, among the Queen's most trusted advisors, and like Bacon and Gorges, a man able to transition from the Tudor to the Stewart Court.

"Yes, indeed." Francis Bacon sits up in preparation for his small speech. "Cousin Robert is my first cousin. Indeed, the connection has helped over the years and continues so. I spoke with him only yesterday. I told him your visit to London is brief. He, unlike our sovereign, will have an ear for your colony. And, of course, he is aware of Ferdinando's good work. He will join us at any moment. But before he arrives, tell me, dear Richard, though I found your letter eloquent, I am not sure the extent of your requests."

"Sir..."

"No, Richard, you are no longer my student. I am Francis."

"Yes, Francis. Well, thank you. If you found my letter eloquent, you have none other than yourself, my teacher, to praise."

"Ah, good man, you hanker for a life as a diplomat?"

"Apparently I am already thrust into that position. But to return to our purpose, I do believe our request is modest and measured. We need but a few soldiers—say one hundred, though preferably more. This will provide for the protection of our expansion. We require more food and ammunition. We weathered one harsh winter. This coming season will find us better prepared, experienced. For the supplies I estimate fifty thousand pounds. At least three-quarters of this we intend to raise from backers." Richard looks to Gorges who nods his approval. "We hope the remainder might be approved by the Privy Council."

"Good," remarks Bacon. "I hear you are only in London through tomorrow. Cecil will hear firsthand. Afterwards rely on Gorges. And I'll do my best."

"Thank you." Richard quickly adds, "We sail within three weeks. Materials are already being purchased on credit. And the soldiers?"

Bacon continues. "A young man in a hurry—as you should be. If Cecil sees fit, no doubt he can muster a few companies—from somewhere. In any case, I believe that it is he just coming through the door. Like him, I'm sure I am eager to hear details of your past year—and your future."

After introductions the four men are escorted to a private room where they might dine and speak in private. Richard is both bemused and awestruck by the three luminaries. All wear identical mustaches and goatees, drawing attention to mouths made rather cavernous by their hairy doorways. Their ruddy cheeks settle on silk lace collars, typical of stylish men during the past thirty years. Bacon and Cecil, each brilliant in his field, Gorges steadfast with his foresight. Even given his years in Oxford and London, often in the presence of grand men, never had Richard sat in such company and been considered, if not of equal footing, at least breathing the same lofty, collegial air.

Both Cecil and Bacon begin a two-hour barrage of questions concerning the fort. Richard holds forth with his story, including his tutoring of Skidwarres, the fight between whale and swordfish, the hurricane, the fever-pitch building, the wild Eucharist; of Nahanada's people, the strife between different tribes, the impetuous Sabenoa, the bitter cold, the extraordinary river and woods, the death of George Popham, and Raleigh Gilbert's assumption of the presidency. In the telling he wishes to present the entire year with a force and momentum so its continuation would not be doubted. Richard ends by saying, "I used the word 'measured' in my letter, by which I meant we wish to grow thoughtfully. For this second stage, as perhaps it should be called, we will occupy land once tilled by natives; hence the enlarged army. But we also need men and women—it is important we begin importing women. It will improve morale."

To which Cecil offers with a smile, "And no doubt increase jealousy, fights, the murder rate, and disease, as well as stimulate rumors. But, of course, you're correct, Seymour."

Bacon intercedes, "If we're to have a civilization, women are indispensable—as well as vexing—and you need not write that down, Seymour."

Gorges has been quiet for some time. "I have already contacted a few religious groups, farmers mostly, wishing to escape England. And civil authorities who know men—and women—willing to start afresh nearly anywhere, and I assume anytime."

Cecil nods. "With the Queen we never had enough money. It is even worse with James. He loves to spend on lavish events, not unlike Elizabeth. Let me offer my best wishes, Ferdinando and Richard, for your undertaking. I will confer with a few on the council. Contact me, Ferdinando, in two days. And to you, Richard, congratulations upon your marriage. May the sun shine on you." Before anyone can say a word, Cecil rises, offers a "God be with you," and turns on his heel. He leaves the room with a purposeful stride.

The remaining three rise together in respect and remain standing.

"Ferdinando," Richard asks, perplexed by the other man's abrupt departure, "what do you make of Cecil?"

"Sit, sit. One never knows. He is burdened with many matters. But I do think him well disposed, basically supportive, though I'd guess we're not a priority."

"I concur," says Bacon. "You did your job well. A story well told. He will not easily forget."

"And Richard," Gorges shifts the conversation, "as you requested—and again with Cecil's intervention—I have spoken with officials at the Tower. You are granted an hour meeting with Walter Raleigh. They will see you at nine o'clock tomorrow morning."

Raleigh Gilbert had made Richard promise he would do everything in his power to gain access to Walter Raleigh, who by 1608 had already spent five years in his apartment on the second floor of the Bloody Tower, where below in the dungeon over the centuries had been meted out the most gruesome torture imaginable.

Sir Walter's trial for treason, presided over by Chief Justice Popham, had ended with Popham handing down a sentence of guilty. As punishment the poet, adventurer, and government official would be drawn and quartered. Most thought the trial an embarrassment, a setup, hearsay—that is, the evidence that Raleigh had plotted to overthrow the King by aiding the Spanish. Again Popham added to his reputation as a "hanging judge" and Raleigh as a brilliant orator in arguing his own defense.

Only due to Raleigh's long-standing connections to the court of Elizabeth, and especially Robert Cecil—who had at one time counted him a close friend and who also disdained the proceedings—did King James commute the death sentence to imprisonment.

CHAPTER 64

The next morning a thick layer of yellow mist hangs on the Thames and encircles the ancient Tower. Richard arrives by launch from Middle Temple. He follows the guards to the second floor, where he is first greeted by Raleigh's Orinoco manservant. Walter Raleigh then appears from the anteroom and offers Richard an enthusiastic embrace, though the two have never met. Once again Richard finds himself in the company of an illustrious representative of the previous generation.

Raleigh sweeps his arm in a gesture to introduce his guest to the two rooms of his apartment. A desk piled with books and papers occupies the middle of the main room, a comfortable looking bed up against one wall, two windows above eye level admitting a modicum of dirty light. A lit candle on his desk provides additional light for working.

"You are sailing back soon, I hear. So you can tell Gilbert I am well, indeed, more productive than I would be had I more options and distractions. People like yourself visit. My wife stays here at times. But tell him I am losing myself writing the history of the world. Tell him if one lives in the mind, it does not matter where your arse is."

Richard is offered one of the two chairs in sight. As with the night before, the younger man is pumped for information. When told of George Popham's death, Raleigh decides to talk. "I knew George, of course. We both sailed up the Orinoco in search of El Dorado. Sea dogs we were, and not so long ago. As I'm sure they told you at Middle Temple, many thought me a fool and a braggart. They chided me for Roanoke. But wouldn't you say, you who walk the New World, that success and failure cannot be assessed by small minds over short periods of time? I think about that while I write."

"I would say so, Sir Walter."

"Anyway, George, he was a good companion. And brave. It was no fault of his he had that snake John for a cousin. And you probably know, nobody hates him—John that is—more than Raleigh, my nephew. It is I who nearly had my heart snatched from my chest and my privates thrown in the fire by the Chief Justice, but it is Raleigh who steeps in hate."

"Of this I have heard from his mouth."

"Yes, and how the world sometimes turns topsy-turvy. You may not be aware, but a few years after I took up residency here, I hired John Popham as my lawyer. My estate, you see, was in danger of being snatched from under my wife. Most thought it queer I'd hire the man who condemned me to death. But scoundrel that he was, no better— or more well-connected—counselor existed. Besides, I wished to rub elbows with him."

"Yes?" Richard could tell Sir Walter wasn't finished.

"I am telling you this so you can report it to Raleigh. In the end his counsel did no good. That he knows. But I'd also hoped for some kind of recognition, recognition that he thought me not guilty of treason. He never said so, but by his demeanor—well, I don't know, he seemed forgetful. He found it difficult to keep eye contact, mentioned more than once how the trial was the most perplexing of his entire life. That's as far as he'd go."

Raleigh realized little time remained for their visit. "So, you will tell my nephew, I continue to busy myself with my writing and also with my medicinal concocting, many specimens originating from the Orinoco—so you see again, where is the failure? I've become something of a recognized expert. Tell him how even John Popham complained of joint pain and asked me for a cure. Tell Raleigh, 'a cure, most conclusive.' He'll know what I'm talking about. Write that down, those exact words." Richard sits at the desk, pushes aside various papers, and applies quill to parchment. Raleigh repeats himself. When Richard finishes, the older man writes a few additional notes, then folds the parchment, places it in an envelope and embosses it with wax from the lighted candle. "Tell him I miss his company. Tell him to hold fast. Tell him his father watches from heaven. No don't say that, heaven is for the superstitious. Tell him I am proud."

Richard doesn't think about the contents of the letter until a day later while once again on Dancer heading west toward Dorset. His brother,

Robert, had spoken about the stories surrounding Popham's death—how his ghost lived in a large oak tree, how when they removed the tree with a team of oxen, so spooked were the locals, some said they could hear the crying of a voice in despair. The first year after his death, the ghost reappeared, how its head bobbed to the side, the result a broken neck from the fall. There also came the rumor of his having been drugged, as his behavior during his last weeks was reported to be disorganized.

"A cure, most conclusive." Was he letting his imagination run loose? "Rumors, more than facts, live long lives." A quote from Bacon or Montaigne? Or his own thoughts?

CHAPTER 65

July 31, 1608, The North Atlantic
Optimism Abounds

Richard and Margaret stand at the rail watching England recede, the sunset reflecting off the sharp white and reddish-brown clay cliffs, dark green countryside beyond, while to their backs, their destination, the orange globe grows larger as it slides into the water.

"Without a splash," comments Margaret, "and I prefer the subtle reflected sunset to the east, off those cliffs, to the dramatic gaudy sunset to the west."

Richard nods in agreement. After the near month of strategizing, planning, traveling, cajoling—and marrying, his life—their lives—would now pass with the vagaries of the wind that is, for this languid moment in mid-summer, moving at an easy five knots. His arms wrap around her. They both love the four-inch height differential, allowing Richard to lower his head and Margaret lift hers just so, to look into one another's eyes. She feels protected on her "rash" journey—that is the word her mother used, though the excitement of the wedding lifted her grief and replaced it with optimism. The honeymooners converse quietly, their mouths no further than six inches away, when not leaning in more for a kiss or a tiny pleasurable nip.

"Your family was wonderful. I must say that again. And Robert—I didn't know he had such wit. How did it go, Richard?"

"Well, my dear brother, Robert, allowed me a copy of his little speech. He can surprise you. He isn't always so staid." Richard reaches into his pocket and unfolds a small piece of paper and reads:

"Oh those Seymours, they do work to get ahead.

Consider Queen Jane's power, her promise of bed.

Then with birth, her death; then King Henry's demise,
Leaving Edward, Royal Protectorate, so he did devise.
But soon, his reputation as a pig-headed nave
Landed him in the Tower, then finally the grave.
But not before brother, Thomas, through nepotism and craft,
Became Lord of the Admiralty
And Governor of the daft (in reference to the Scilly Isles)
There, with pirates he did wrangle and plot,
Until charged with treason, then the Tower to rot.
His warrant signed by Edward, with familial indignation,
Ordering Thomas to precede Sir Edward's own decapitation.
Cousins lost heads, and Jane's fate so unkind,
Where you, Richard, adventurer, romantic,
Meet Margaret and lose your mind.

Given the haste and Margaret's family's financial distress, only a few attended the wedding, thirty or so in all. Emily, the matron of honor, had married a few months after Richard and Skidwarres departed. The groom, a baron from Somerset, was a man in his forties. Her sixth-month pregnancy bulged under her frilly rose-colored poplin dress. In a year she had transformed herself from a coquettish intellectual to a matron. Richard commented to Margaret how something in her appeared to have burned itself out. But when he held Emily dancing, she clamped her eyes to his. "Make her happy, my darling." It had always been impossible to converse with Emily for long, before her sexual impishness appeared. So he returned her stare.

"Keep your flame alive," he said to her over the music. Her quizzical expression quickly became a blush. Did she think Skidwarres had told him the details?

Early into the post-reception morning, with the light creeping into the eastern sky, Richard and Margaret fell exhausted onto his boyhood bed after hurriedly peeling off their clothes. Richard rested his hand on her soft tummy, she hers on his hairy chest. Yet again he marveled at the female anatomy, how so many locations were designed for a hand. Her jawbone and cheek so perfectly rested in his hand, the back of her head, her rounded shoulder, her breasts, of course, all made for a hand; and the way his hand perfectly fit the curve of her hip and her back, perfect, his palm resting on her mons pubis, an exact fit.

When the couple arrived in Plymouth, they found Gorges busily overseeing the loading of the *Mary and John's* hold. The soldiers were billeted and waiting. Each had been promised fifty acres, if they were willing to stay beyond one year. Few had ever owned even the small piece of land their families and ancestors had tilled for generations. This promise appeared worth the fight, whatever that was to be. The savages, so they had been told, were no match for English prowess and firepower. Richard, in his urgency to recruit, had made this point again and again— and he had more or less persuaded himself of it.

The captain would navigate a northerly course, much the same as the last crossing. The weather in mid-summer might be rough, but the crossing was much shorter than a southerly route. Indeed, that night it began to blow off the Irish coast, and Margaret fell into a bout of seasickness. For the first two days and nights they remained on deck to escape the fetid air below, his lap serving as her pillow.

Finally her malady abated, and they began musing about their own prospects on the Sagadahoc. Richard explained how Gilbert had promised to build an addition to the chapel. The ship carried four Elizabethan stained glass windows which Richard had ordered for the spacious new room. The more constant light would awaken them in the morning and warm them in the winter. Her three trunks carried much wool clothing and bedding, plus furs. Both Margaret's cello and Richard's harpsichord, plus a newly- purchased lute, were also stowed away. Books filled another box.

They now talked of how they would fill the long dark hours of winter with music, reading and love. Richard let a comment slip, that if she were to become pregnant, the newly recruited fort's doctor would help her.

"Richard," Margaret replied with a mild condescending tone and a smile, "I am not quite ready. Do you not know there are ways to guard against conception?" He did know of such a thing, but it had not crossed his mind.

"Oh," he offered back, dumbfounded at Margaret's calculation.

" Just a small piece of cotton. Very simple," she asserted, her smile impish.

Richard thought Lilly would adjust to the circumstances. She might even learn to enjoy Margaret's company. Plus, among the women on board, certainly some would be companionable. It only made sense. Margaret raised a wry eyelid. "Let's see. For female company, I might first expect a few jolly whores, a boy who turned into your female lover, native women who speak no English, and perhaps some gentle lady in the crowd below, none of whom has two shillings to rub together."

Richard stood with a dumb grin on his face.

She wanted to know more about the natives. He realized, in his telling, how ideal it all sounded: with the additional thirty soldiers and their advanced weaponry, along with the support of Nahanada and the Mawooshen, the English would oust Sabenoa from the Quabacook. His people could move north upriver or west, where tillable land might be found or created, leaving acres at the confluence of the Sagadahoc and Androscoggin for the English to build a second fort and begin substantial planting in the spring—when boatloads of colonists would arrive. Optimistic to be sure, but how else might ambition be realized if ideal goals weren't believed and pursued? That was Richard's stated position. As for Nahanada and Skidwarres and their people, why could they not live in harmony with the English? As Richard explained, the natives had enemies and alliances in much the same way as the English. The English and Mawooshen would be allies. Had not he and Skidwarres been successful so far?

Richard had also insisted on bringing Dancer and Breeze. They would introduce Northern Virginia to horses and, with luck, their offspring. He imagined how astonished the native population would be at the sight of horses. Skidwarres would receive the first colt as a gift.

The only shadow that appeared in Seymour's path came in the form of a letter delivered to him the day the *Mary and John* departed. It arrived with the explanation from Gorges that Admiral Gilbert's eldest brother had died two weeks earlier, leaving Raleigh the heir to Compton Castle in Devon, the ancestral estate near Exeter. Gorges knew this would require Gilbert's attention. In an effort to waylay fears, Gorges wrote in an accompanying letter that he would await the admiral's written instruction, that he would make himself available to members of the Gilbert family.

From Richard's perspective, even if Raleigh Gilbert returned to England to settle personal matters, transoceanic voyages were becoming commonplace. Indeed, the idea of a future in both worlds appeared even more plausible than when he had first imagined it.

As they neared the Gulf of St. Lawrence, the winds pushed the *Mary and John* south of the icebergs and into warmer, foggy stretches of ocean. There they passed a Basque whaler, too busy on the hunt to chase an English ship. Nonetheless, the possibility of a fight enlivened the soldiers, the majority of whom, along with some of the women passengers, had shared Margaret's initial sickness, so that at one point a dozen soldiers, six women, and a lone gentlewoman were hanging their heads over the rail and retching together. Then, after a week at sea, the men began daily to march on deck; they oiled their weapons, slept, played cards, and acquired a taste for harpsichord and cello duets, played on deck when the weather permitted. Apart from the horses that were off their feed and looking quite emaciated, all went well. The passengers experienced only a few uncomfortable squalls, and then, nearing the end, disorienting fog.

Finally, after two days of it, the sun showed itself as a small disk with a dull shine, hardly sun at all. The glow grew into a gigantic, veiled beacon. The outer islands of Northern Virginia, the sparking granite and beyond the endless green hills, all arrived in sharp relief, as if a gossamer curtain had lifted. Margaret and Richard stood at the rail, their chosen station. "My god," she whispered. Look at it!"

"Yes," answered Richard. In the fog Captain Davies' navigation had been miraculous. He notified the couple at breakfast that he expected to arrive at the fort by evening.

And so they did. The *Mary and John* anchored a mile from the Sagadahoc to await a favorable morning tide. All passengers, except a skeleton crew, clambered onto the longboats which rowed out from the fort to fetch them.

By dinnertime the next day, Richard, Margaret, Davies, and various other members of the council were seated around the large table in Raleigh's house, the admiral their host. The general mood among the council had turned from enthusiastic and optimistic to perplexed.

CHAPTER 66

September 1, 1608, Fort St. George
Change of Fortune

Raleigh Gilbert had quickly gained control of the fort after Popham's death. His spirits during the spring and summer grew upbeat and pugnacious, despite—or rather because of—the periodic raids against the fort. The possibility of attacks put many on edge, but for Gilbert, moderate danger acted as an elixir. Gilbert did not wait for the natives to attack. Daily, platoons of fifteen patrolled the woody perimeter and more than a few times flushed out small groups of braves. For both parties the harassment became as much game as warfare. Still, muskets were fired, arrows released, and injuries sustained. One soldier remained in sick bay after undergoing primitive surgery to remove an arrowhead from his stomach. The real ordeal, the infection that followed, held him at death's door. But he recuperated. However, after three months of tension, many men were beginning to grumble.

Gilbert strategized about how best to employ another fifty to a hundred soldiers, the number he hoped would arrive with Richard. He had also requisitioned ten small, easily portable, three-pound cannon. It would be a fearsome army in the eyes of the natives.

A frustrated Gilbert had not seen Sipsis in months. Dorothy, one of the six who'd arrived in the spring, became her replacement. She happily took on the domestic chores of his house. Raleigh welcomed the cheerful chatter of an English woman, as she puttered about cleaning, cooking, washing clothes. Typically, in the evening, Gilbert would pace back and forth gesticulating. He prattled on about plans for the next days and weeks, and fantasized a glorious future where thousands of English men and women occupied the lands between the Sagadahoc and the

Saco—with himself the appointed governor, the one in position to tax, sell, and rule. Before long, Dorothy would arise from her chair where she been knitting or simply trying to keep herself awake. Rather than endure his verbiage, she'd pull herself against the president. This small encouragement would turn his grand enthusiasm into lust.

The threat of attack did not squelch the good cheer brought about by the summer weather and new supplies of grog, victuals, and letters— especially letters. The air warmed by nine in the morning. Often they enjoyed days in the seventies and eighties, with breezes with enough strength to push the mosquitoes upriver. Compared with the previous fall, the men labored in moderation. As plans shifted from commerce to colonization, Gilbert no longer searched for sassafras or led wild goose chases for gold, silver, or passages to the Orient. They erected a few new buildings for the anticipated additional population and created the bedroom off Seymour's study. The men felled large straight pine for masts; oak, hemlock, and pine for lumber; and hardwood, especially maple and birch, for firewood. They fished and hunted under armed protection and even earned time to sit on the beach. They'd strip and run into the ice-cold water which, on the hottest days and given favorable currents, might turn tolerable. On some sweltering evenings, the women joined them, wearing flimsy petticoats, though they remained yards away. The armed guards standing on the dunes watched them and needed reminders to be alert for an attack. None ever did arrive during the mid-summer.

All had been offered free land by Gilbert. Most were patient. It was their lot to wait and trust. Where mud puddles had once covered the fort's ground, grass now grew. "Do you remember when we piled twenty feet of snow here? Is that possible?" For the land to turn from white to green, from frigid to humid-hot in so short a time, most men agreed, was impossible. But there you were. Where before they had believed the Virginia Company profits were the sole purpose of their work, now their own well-being appeared to be part of the calculation. This attitude grew out of Gilbert's hopes. They awaited the *Mary and John*, bringing yet more supplies, letters, more soldiers, more power. More women might arrive, so rumor went.

With this optimism abounding, Richard and Margaret stepped onto the gravel shore. Minutes later Richard handed the admiral the letter sealed with the waxed Compton Castle crest.

"Do you know of its contents, Cousin?"

"I do, Raleigh."

"It is not good?"

"Sad, I am afraid."

Gilbert stepped a few feet away to read. His arm dropped. He held the letter alongside his thigh and stared up the river, as if an answer might be heading his way. Richard and Margaret stood together, hand in hand. "Do you want some time to yourself, Cousin?" Richard asked.

"Yes—I mean, no. No. Why don't you go inside? Ask Dorothy for some tea. Let me think just a minute. His voice didn't convey any emotion, no grief or surprise or the edge of excitement, though all such reactions seemed possible. Raleigh Gilbert was calculating.

Three hours later, the principals of the fort were assembled around Gilbert's table. All by now knew the dilemma their leader was facing. Beyond whatever grief he might feel for his dead brother, the rewards were obvious. Compton Castle and its thousands of acres, occupied by tenant farmers, represented a fortune. Maintaining such wealth and position, however, took time and skill. All wondered whether he would be able to do so while commanding Fort St. George. In spite of his hatred of Sir John Popham, Gilbert had become the very leader Popham would have wished for: bold, ambitious, able to combine his youthful energy with a willingness to learn.

After lobster and blueberry cobbler chased by Champagne, Gilbert stands and pushes his chair back. He is apparently unaware of the bits of lobster meat and a few blue stains on his white shirt. "Gentlemen— and lady"—he had invited Margaret to join the council meeting—"I am sure you all know of my recent news, of my good brother John's demise, leaving me heir to my family's estate." The party is groggy and Gilbert himself too bubbly with Champagne for such seriousness. It takes a few moments for the gravity to reestablish itself. "I have not yet been able to assimilate this news. I am now pulled by two obligations. I am in the throes of indecision."

The attendees around the table sit quietly, struggling for sobriety.

"At the moment, it appears to me imperative that I travel home and settle my affairs. Yet our plans here are about to hatch. We are on the verge of making history. I feel this in my bones—I do, indeed."

"Here, here," many of the men offer in a low, guttural mumble.

"For the next few days, I will be conferring with you separately and as a group. We are stronger than we've ever been, well-provisioned, and armed. Not as many men as I'd hoped for, but more than we've ever had. And more cannon. Whatever winter deals us, we're prepared. The natives, if they dare seriously attack, will taste English fortitude. In any case, we will visit the Lord of the Sagadahoc. And lord it over us, he will no more."

The "Here, here!" comes in a higher register and with chuckles.

"Perhaps some of you have questions." Gilbert has changed his style since taking on the presidency. In the beginning he tended to pontificate and dismiss others' suggestions. Later he began asking in private how he might be most effective. Richard and others carefully suggested he spend more time listening. To everyone's surprise, Gilbert did just that.

But tonight, late as it is and dulled by dinner, the room falls silent. When finally Gilbert sits, the captain of the fort, Davis, stands up.

"Admiral, Mr. President, it will take me no more than two weeks, maybe less, to bring the old and new troops together. As you know, many are tired of the intermittent harassment. They wish to fight. They have for months. Might we then attack in a fortnight? After we have established our ground, you will sail and an interim president will be elected. I then might take command of the forces. As you have planned, a second fort would be constructed. We have enough men and cannon to defend two forts. Just a suggestion, before we all retire." The captain sits and the admiral rises again.

"I appreciate your readiness and dedication. I must admit, at this day and hour, it appears the best option. So, let us rest on that."

Margaret and Richard, with lantern in hand, open the door off the chapel study and walk into the newly constructed bedroom. His old bed is now the only furniture. Three gaping holes are ready for the many diamond-paneled stained glass windows, now crated somewhere in the hold, along with all their belongings. Tomorrow they will oversee the hoisting of the horses onto the barge. It will be a joy to see them eating fresh grass and gaining weight. They wouldn't have lasted much longer at sea. At Richard's request, Dorothy has draped silk over the four-poster bed, protection from the mosquitoes and hated greenflies. They strip and fall into their soft cage, lie back, and hold hands.

"We're not moving. And it doesn't smell of brine and sweat and god knows what else. It's warm but not stuffy," comments Margaret.

They watch the moon slide by one of the openings, providing its hypnotic allure through the silk. He looks over to see Margaret breathing softly, eyes closed, apparently asleep. Her strawberry blond hair tumbles over her pillow, sheet, and breasts that, along with her cheeks, nose, and forehead, reflect moon light. The rest of her lies in shades of shadow. She smells of herself, sweet-earthy, with a hint of jasmine cologne. He has never been in the presence of anything so beautiful. Touching her would be a sacrilege. Perhaps, he thinks, that is why women are so desirable. Impossibly, they are created to be worshipped and craved simultaneously. He leans over to kiss one nipple, hardened by the light breeze. He rests there momentarily and then brings the sheet up to her chin. He lies on his side gazing at her and relishing the desire flowing through his body. Restraint in love and music is best honored—sometimes—he thinks. His adoration and lust ebb, and then like a breeze, diminish to not quite nothing. His mind wanders, no longer focused on the object of his desire. He had noticed at the meeting, with the suggestion of an interim president, a few eyes briefly turned his way. Would he not be a logical choice? Was he qualified for such an undertaking? And with this question, his hand rests on her belly. They both sleep.

CHAPTER 67

September 3, 1608, Fort St. George
Raleigh Gilbert's Dilemma

For the next three days, Gilbert said little of his personal dilemma. Out of respect, no one else in his presence did either. Richard and Margaret busied themselves unpacking, arranging the new and old quarters in the chapel proper, and tending to the skittish, hobbled, and hungry horses, which were grazing just outside the fort wall. Might the braves, if they came upon them, take them for a type of moose?.

That second night they dined with Gilbert and a few others. Afterwards, Richard and Margaret played duets, well-practiced during the ocean voyage. The next day they conferred with Gilbert about taking a stroll on the beach. For the past few weeks the patrols had found no evidence of the native braves. Besides, both Gilbert and Seymour agreed, the natives would be unlikely to expose themselves on an open beach.

Margaret packs a picnic and wears one of her favorite dresses, one she might have donned for tea. They walk to the Sagadahoc's mouth and settle there on the sand. They nibble at sausages and cheese and sip red wine. Formations of cormorants, fifteen or so to the flock, beat their way, only a few feet above the river. "They seem to work so hard," Margaret comments, "as if when they relaxed, they might fall into the water."

"That's true," offers Richard. "I'm told they have an oily substance that allows them to swim under water more efficiently. But as a result, flight is more difficult, because they're heavier. Not so for the osprey and eagle. They catch updrafts." He points a few hundred yards upriver. "Almost weightless. Do you see up there, circling? Or over there in the dead pine? An osprey waiting to dive." The ever-present scavenging gulls cry like savages, squawk, laugh, and coo at one another. Finished, groggy, hot, the two lie back in the sand, close their eyes, and take it all in by nose, ear, and the feel of hot sand. Later they rouse themselves, and under the protection of a patrol of soldiers on the other side of the dunes, the couple walks the mile to the tidal river. "Soon," Richard suggests, "we'll come back and swim. When it's the right tide."

"Yes, marvelous." Margaret takes in her surrounding as a child might gifts.

That evening Gilbert invites Richard to talk. The president has recently bathed and shaved. He wears a clean white shirt of the type worn by the soldiers, and britches that just cover his knees, stockings below that. It is casual attire.

"Sit down, sit down, Seymour. Some tea?"

"Yes, thank you. That would be perfect."

Without taking his eyes off Richard, Gilbert calls out, "Dorothy, tea for the two of us."

A muffled "Yes, sir," comes from the next bay, the kitchen.

"I don't have to tell you, I've been thinking a good deal about what I must do." Gilbert ushers Richard to a seat at the council table. "About the future of this fort, of the plan we discussed before your mission, your voyage."

"Yes, I've imagined so."

"Well, let me begin by being forthright. I'm sure you and Gorges did as well as anybody could. I have no doubt of this. But I hoped for a total of a hundred soldiers. Maybe that was unrealistic, but only fifty? Fifty! It's exasperating. With two hundred, even a hundred and twenty-five, we could overwhelm Sabenoa and easily hold ground up there and down here. But fifty? Really, how many are needed to defend the fort? Then a second fort, the two held by—I don't know—twenty-five at each? I don't know, Seymour."

"Yes, but I believe Cecil did his best."

Dorothy arrives with a steaming pot of tea. She curtsies with more assurance than Richard remembers. "Good afternoon, Chaplain." Inadvertently Richard rises and bows, and then feels silly. She seems to have taken on a curious role, part maid, part mistress, and part wife.

After Dorothy leaves, Gilbert continues, "We could wait for reinforcements, just occupy the fort, but that wouldn't be until next spring. I would go back, tend to my affairs, put the case to our backers." Gilbert pours more tea and stares at Richard. "Your thoughts?"

"Again, I have considered that option. It seems a natural one, except..."

"Yes, except?"

"Except, I am not sure there is the will either in the Privy Council or among the present backers. They are looking for results. Gorges is working to find those who will colonize. Perhaps, you can rally more troops. But the continued troubles at Jamestown have dampened the enthusiasm for funding exploration and colonization. You know this already. And what of the men here, the ones who endured last winter? Their patience is threadbare, no? I sense this is more the case since I've returned. The increase in supplies has helped, for the meantime at least."

"Yes, I, too, expect the recent good cheer will fade. And do you know what is most uncanny? I feel this myself. It is not the occasional arrow that that flies into camp, even the ones aflame. They haven't done any serious damage. It's their infernal yelling. No, not yelling. It is more animal than human, high-pitched like an eagle. It curdles the blood. I think that bothers the men more than anything. Many feel trapped; even with our patrols, they feel cornered. We take the fight to the natives, but they hide behind trees or disappear. I'm concluding I need to act more like my father. With forty or so men—the remainder to guard the fort—and especially those small cannon, small but versatile, by god. We attack and kill many of Sabenoa's men. Devastate them. We've played the Popham diplomacy game too long. Too long! We have our fort. We've done our trading. Now it's time to expand. Are we cowards?" Gilbert rises, slugs down his tea, and walks to the one small window in the room. He looks out at the overcast day, one of the few in the past two weeks. The fog is rolling up the river, a long grey ghost of a snake. "It's time to raise hell. What do you say, Chaplain Seymour?"

Seymour remains seated and listens. That's his newfound occupation, if not his natural bent. He takes in Gilbert's perspective before establishing his own. "I see the logic. Eliminate Sabenoa. That has been your plan. The survivors move on. If we devastate them, the chances of counterattack dwindle. It's all been sliding in this direction." Richard mouths these words, but with no enthusiasm. They were not his views. Not yet, anyway.

"Exactly. Then you become interim president for half a year—or so."

The two fall into a silence. Gilbert takes in a long breath that puffs up his chest He lets out an equally long sigh. "It now seems obvious to me, now that I've stated it out loud."

Richard stands up and fills his cup. "Raleigh." Using his first name underscores their growing familiarity. "I understand. You're a military man. I have come to appreciate your position over the year. But I think

I need to place myself in my own shoes. Am I not a chaplain, perhaps a diplomat?"

"That is so."

"So I must consider your ideas."

"Good, good. Can I press the matter?"

"Does not bloodshed cause more bloodshed?"

"Bloodshed wins battles. Power depends on the possibility of bloodshed—and inevitably bloodshed. You've read history."

"Yes, the possibility of bloodshed. Might we achieve the same objective by threat? Your previous bombardment of his village must have made an impression. Skidwarres has said as much."

"That's possible. Possible. You suggest sailing up there and giving that crazy savage an ultimatum? And if he doesn't abandon the site, blow him to hell?"

"Something along those lines, yes."

"I think killing him and a bunch of his braves would be much more effective. A quick devastating attack, that's the impression I like making. Talking is for women, that is what my father said."

"For women and chaplains, I suppose."

"Yes, well...no, I did not mean to imply that. You are here because I asked your opinion."

"Indeed. As I said, I've come to appreciate your responsibility."

Both men recognize they've reached a temporary impasse. Again Gilbert stares out the window. The expanded fog now settles over the mouth of the river, obscuring the other side. "It's uncanny how the weather can change and with it my mood. Dorothy," Gilbert calls out, "bring us some port. It's that time."

The two return to the table with pewter goblets.

They sit sipping, their eyes avoiding the other, each occupied with his own thoughts.

Richard speaks first. "Raleigh, I wish to sail in the *Virginia* to Pemaquid to retrieve Lilly. While I am there, I might confer with Skidwarres. It has been nearly four months. When I left we were not under attack, if 'attack' is the correct term. Might I learn something from him to help with our dilemma?"

"You have my permission. But dilemma? I feel only one dilemma, and this I have not expressed to anyone, hardly to myself."

Richard looks hard at Gilbert. The tone sounds like a prelude to a confession. Richard raises his eye brows in expectation. Both sip.

"Tell me, Cousin, how was it back home? I mean to say, I envied your returning. And there is something else." Gilbert isn't interested in Richard's answer. "Growing up as a second born. You know this. I envied my brother. He would get nearly everything. I knew this as a strapping boy. Simply by birth, he was all-important. I had to make my mark as a military man, while he could go to Oxford, Middle Temple, and inherit a life. I had to make mine. Now that he's gone, I can take his place. I could find myself a fine woman, one who adds to my wealth. I could represent Devon in Parliament, while away my time in London, instead of freezing here and swatting mosquitoes and killing savages—if it comes to that. That's my dilemma."

"Yes, when I found myself on English soil, I had to admit what I had missed: taverns, mutton, Exeter, galloping on roads, London."

"But then, Cousin, you had that little scoundrel Lilly to occupy you last winter, and now Margaret."

"And you Sipsis, and now Dorothy, no? But I have returned bringing some of England with me. Those windows—wonderful. The horses. Could you, could we, not live in both worlds?"

"I don't know. I don't know if I can imagine it, or if I want to." The admission is more than Gilbert expected to divulge or was aware he thought. For Richard, it is a disturbing revelation. Gilbert clears his throat, as if expunging his last words. "Ah, I sound like an old woman with such musings. Hell, we've got much to do. You go to Pemaquid. Learn what you can without divulging our plans, and we'll continue to train our new troops. Seymour, you're a bad influence on me. You bring out my weaknesses."

Both men rise from the table at the same time and shake hands vigorously, their coolness toward one another partially melted by their shared burden, heritage, and future.

CHAPTER 68

September 8, 2012, Pemaquid
Futures

Richard had sailed the Virginia during her brief shakedown cruise late in the spring. Now with her augmented sail capacity, including adjustments to the rigging and increased ballast, she heads briskly down east under a beam reach. He and Margaret stand holding firmly to the rail, with Davies at the helm. The fifty-foot pinnace heels under the twenty-knot blow. Gilbert insisted three small cannon be installed, manned by six soldiers. Whoever the attackers had been for the past months, they appeared to be coming downriver, hiding canoes, and then setting up camp a few miles from the fort. One camp had been found a month ago, abandoned not long before the English patrol arrived. The likelihood of an attack by sea or by natives in the Pemaquid area he considered remote. Nonetheless, Gilbert remained cautious.

Richard is effusive. "Nothing compares," he shouts over the whistle of the wind and the banging about of blocks and tackle, "to standing on a deck you helped build. Margaret it's magical, fashioning boards cut from the forest here, together with iron nails produced in our own forge. Now look—wood, once alive, now resurrected into something heavenly—an angel flying."

Margaret looks at him and rolls her eyes. "And if we sink, I will blame you personally." Growing up, her father had often chided her impertinence. Richard relishes it.

More than once Margaret told Richard, "Pinch me. Tell me I'm not dreaming." A few weeks before while she stood alone at the rail of the *Mary and John*, staring out to sea, a whale emerged only feet away. It lollygagged along with the ship for a few minutes. "Our eyes locked. I swear, Richard, it was the most uncanny thing. I swear we communicated." Now she is once again at a rail, standing on the first English ship built in this strange place, winging their way to a native village to meet Skidwarres and her husband's former lover. "Pinch me again," she orders, and he does, but this time on her bottom. She smacks his hand and looks at Davies. By the smirk on his face, he'd seen.

Soon the *Virginia* lies at anchor. Four canoes bump up against her sides. Skidwarres, and close behind him Lilly, are the first to scramble on deck. He and Richard greet one another with their hands grasping the other's upper arms. Their eyes meet. Both smile, but neither can find words. Much has happened during their four-month separation. Their eyes appear to confirm their friendship, but what of circumstances? Each feels the ground has shifted under him.

Margaret's words break their embrace, "Skidwarres! How wonderful to see you." On her tiptoes she kisses his cheek, and he bends, and in good English form, kisses hers. "Margaret, how beautiful you look." The three laugh. It all sounds so polite. Richard holds up her left hand and points to the wedding band. "My wife, Mrs. Seymour."

"Ah!" answers Skidwarres. He's pleased, but not surprised.

Lilly stands a few feet behind. She wears a traditional Native American deerskin vest and moccasins. Her black, curly hair is fashioned into a braid. They all turn her way. Richard stares and finally gains some composure.

"Lilly?" The word comes with a slight question. "Lilly—this is Margaret. The small smile Lilly's been holding broadens. Richard and Margaret have wondered what reception they might receive. The answer appears to be a wholeheartedly pleasant one. Lilly takes a few, quick small steps and embraces Margaret. "Welcome, I really am glad to see you." She then looks at Richard. "And hello to you too," she offers with a kiss close to his lips.

They all back up to form into a small circle, and there is more laughter. Each, in their own way, had imagined the meeting would be awkward. Instead it feels rather easy.

Lilly, out of nervousness and eagerness, breaks her news, "I'm Skidwarres' second wife." The four stand wordless, then break into laughter once again, though this time less certain.

Richard manages a few words to normalize what feels strange, "Well, Skid, when I asked you about taking another wife—what, less than two years ago?—you told me that was the province of prosperous, important men. So, Sir Skidwarres." He is halfway through this small accolade, when all including Richard listen for an edge of jealousy in his voice over Lilly. And to everyone's relief, no one hears it.

Richard then turns to Lilly. "And you, Lilly, you were one of the reasons for our visit, to return you to the fort. Might I assume this will not happen?"

"Richard," Lilly moves a step closer to Skidwarres. She holds his bare forearm with two hands. "Richard, I have never felt safer, not in my whole life." Her words shift their mood to the serious. "His first wife, Sokw, is kind to me. We've become friends. Before, I had never learned to share. It's just different. I help doing many things, but I have time to read. I'm teaching some to speak English, even to read, the children anyway. Skidwarres and Sokw and Nahnibssat, they are teaching me their tongue. And Skidwarres likes to speak English with me and talk about the books you gave him." Her presentation comes hurriedly and breathily.

"In the beginning," adds Skidwarres, wishing to lend credence, "many in the village stared at her, and they talked behind our backs. Remember how your neighbors and those in the cities stared at me. It was much the same, but now, not so much."

Margaret decides to add her voice; otherwise, she feels, it would be impolite. "I do so want to hear more. I think it sounds extraordinary. You look very happy. Congratulations." The group has reached another point of completion. All laugh in unison again.

"Let us go ashore." Skidwarres redirects the conversation. "You will stay a few nights?"

"Tonight, if you will have us. There are, as you can see, the two of us, Captain Davies, three crew members, and six soldiers. No doubt the crew members and a couple of soldiers will remain on board tonight. But I can assure you, they are hungry." The soldiers, who are listening at a distance, raise their voices in approval, "Aye, sir!"

Ashore, Skidwarres suggests to Richard that they confer. Lilly can take a walk with Margaret to see the village buildings and enlarged gardens. Arrangements for sleeping and eating were already underway. Young sentries had identified the *Virginia* long before she dropped anchor.

Once again Englishman and native sit on a comfortable rock overlooking Monhegan Island ten miles away. Skidwarres asks about Richard's trip. He begins with pleasantries over the health of his parents and siblings. Skidwarres nods his head and turns away to stare out to sea when he hears of Emily's marriage and pregnancy.

Inevitably the conversation turns to the Privy Council and to the particulars of the fort. At this point Richard begins dissimulating, ever so slightly. The purpose of this conversation is to leave the impression that Fort St. George is growing stronger with more soldiers—the number Richard offers is, "...now around one hundred. More soldiers and hundreds of colonists will be coming nine months hence." Skidwarres looks expressionlessly at Richard. Because Seymour is confident that the gist of his report rings true, the delivery feels natural and trustworthy. "But before I continue..." Richard stops himself. "I am, of course, eager to hear your explanation for the attacks that began soon after I departed."

"Richard, it is not much different from when we spoke before. It is a very difficult matter for Nahanada. Do you remember Lilly's friend, Moskwas, the boy who gave her a lacrosse stick? When she began living in my hut, he became angry and soon after joined Woboz in the north. Other young braves from here and from the village on the Aponeg, the village of the murdered woman, they, too, have joined."

"Do you know their numbers?" Richard interrupts.

Skidwarres had anticipated this question. He planned to be less than honest. In fact, he did not know. There were rumors of two hundred braves living on an island in the Androscoggin. They relied on Sabenoa for some of their food. "I do not know. I have heard different numbers. I guess more than two hundred. It is popular to be a brave. Stories are told about the English, how they cook and eat children. They say no women are in the fort because the English soldiers prefer goats and one another."

"Yes, well, women have arrived."

"If Nahanada or I try to stop this ignorance, we are looked at with distrusting eyes. Richard, we wish for peace. To the east, Bessabez continues to face raids from the Micmac. Your muskets—some fire, others make no noise. Most have returned to the bow and arrow or the spear."

"And I say again, we want peace with the Mawooshen. We do not want to settle on your land." At this point Richard decides to say more than he and Gilbert had discussed. The tone between Skidwarres and Richard has an edge. He wishes to smooth things, but he also wants Skidwarres to know what is transpiring. "The English will expand up the Sagadahoc. We are capable of eliminating Sabenoa. I think this would not be a terrible blow to your people."

"Richard, you think Sabenoa is not 'my people?'"

This was a question Richard had not anticipated. The quizzical look on the Englishman's face spurs Skidwarres on. "As I said, many of our young braves, Mawooshen, have banded together, including some of

Sabenoa's men. Richard, if the English and the French were attacked by the Spanish, would the English and French not fight together?"

"Yes, sometimes they have, yes, Professor."

They both shake their heads. It brings them quickly if briefly, back to their old camaraderie.

"Skid, up to now little bloodshed has come to pass—excepting the murdered fishermen."

"That is true. And the murdered woman."

"Yes, the day I left. Yet now matters have worsened. Do you or I, do we have any power—as diplomats?"

"Again, my friend, you say the English will expand, use their cannon, eliminate Sabenoa. As you told me months ago, this is inevitable."

"And your braves sharpen their arrows and tell stories. Yet Gilbert thinks they do not want to fight, not seriously."

"They will fight. The English have the cannon and the musket and the clock that gives you the exact time of day. But we, the savages, have the time. We can wait. Wait for the best time."

Richard rises. As before, he picks up stones and throws them beyond the foamy surf while it piles over the seaweed- and kelp-covered rocks, recedes, rises again and again, as it will long past the Englishman's and the native's lifespan. That is what Seymour thinks. He begins talking more to the ocean than to Skidwarres. "Try to imagine. Ten years from now. A hundred and fifty English soldiers occupy the fort. Up on the Quabacook, an English village surrounded by farms. There a smaller fort protects the inhabitants, but there have been no attacks for five years. The Mawooshen and English remain on friendly terms. Your children and mine speak the other's language. They ride horses and fish together. Some of your children are half-English, my grandchildren part Mawooshan."

Skidwarres remains seated, his arms folded across his chest. They both stare in the same direction. Richard stops and looks at his friend, who nods his head, indicating he's listening. Richard continues, "You will be pleased to know Dancer and Margaret's horse, Breeze, accompanied us. You wish to ride again?"

"Yes, I do. Yes."

Richard smiles and continues. "We will learn and prosper from one another. The baskets your women make, we will buy. Some will be sent to London and become popular. Your people will receive money or bartered goods—including horses, cattle, and sheep. We will help protect the Mawooshen from the French, if necessary, or the Micmac. You will be a sagamore and I the appointed—I don't know what the word would be—the baron of that section of the Quabacook. Other villages lie to the west, but not to the east. East and north of the Sagadahoc would be Mawooshen Land, recognized by a treaty."

Richard turns. He has planned this speech. He returns to the rock where Skidwarres remains staring out to Monhegan. The native speaks without making eye contact. "Your imagination, it is what I admire most—and what I fear. You, Richard, the English, you try to control the future. Not just tomorrow. You say ten years. Your time stretches in a straight line, and you English march down it and conquer. My people—I have explained this—time is not a straight line that goes over the horizon to the unknown, like your sailing over the horizon. Our future is our past. It is a circle. What you say sounds—what is the word—promising?"

It is Richard's time to nod agreement.

"I have seen your cities. You might persuade me with your imagination. But my people wish to live as our ancestors lived. They know nothing else. They don't imagine other futures."

Richard continues the thought with a recollection. "Do you remember? We are looking at the sea now. Do you remember a favorite quote of mine from my teacher, Bacon? It goes something like, 'They are ill discoverers that think there is no land, when they can see nothing but sea.' That is what you tell me. Your people can see only sea."

"I speak for myself. Your imagination, I fear, and your future—little by little, it will eat my people. No. I do not think that we—diplomats, you say—can change my people or yours. Either Gilbert attacks with more and more English and you banish or kill Sabenoa, and your imagination wins. Or our young braves make your lives a hell. And you, as you English say, 'raise anchor' and sail away."

"And you, Skidwarres?" asks Richard. Their eye contact is only fleeting. "What do you want?"

"Richard, I do not have your imagination. I do not see harmony between our people. It would be a friendship between the fisher and the otter. I have no wish beyond my village. You show me how man can live apart from his village. Your Montaigne and Bacon, I can begin to understand what they write. Lilly helps me be bigger—or is there a better word? She helps me expand. But I cannot be beyond my village. I was dragged away. But I have returned."

In the long silence they hear the ocean breathing with long rollers that crash against the rocks and fall away. Way offshore a storm must be brewing. The earth is always creating unpredictable undulations, a subconscious, no different from what moves human desire. Richard wonders, is that a thought of Montaigne's or mine?

"Where is our friendship?" Skidwarres hears Richard's question, as it is meant, devoid of artifice.

"It is here, my friend."

"I suppose, an impossible friendship? But a friendship."

"We will return to the village and eat together. Nahanada will ask you questions. He talks often of London, at least to me and Lilly. His experience there improves with time. We will hear from our wives and you will sail. That is our future. No?"

"Yes, soothsayer. We will sail and we, you and I, will wait for events."

CHAPTER 69

September 18, 1608, Fort St. George
Loosened Tongue

Lying in their bed in the new bedroom, Richard and Margaret watch the early sunlight filter through the multicolored and clear glass eastern windows. Margaret comments about the softness of the mattress, compared to the bearskin over pine bows in the hut offered to them by Nahanada the night before last. Early fall is approaching. Cool nights and mornings necessitate a wool blanket. Underneath the covers they have taken to wearing nightshirts. Face to face, stomach to stomach, Richard's hand massages the small of her back. The silence asks not to be broken.

When Richard and Skidwarres returned to the village, no longer did they mention the pending conflict. Nor did Nahanada inquire beyond personal aspects of Richard's voyage. The news of horses on their soil created great interest. Word traveled quickly. By the end of dinner the entire village insisted they hear from the English, as well as the sagamore and Skidwarres, about horses: how they pulled large loads, went into battle, ran faster than deer, and bonded with humans. Margaret did her best to paint a rough image of her Breeze with dyes the natives used for decorating objects and themselves. The children crowded around her. When finished, she held it up, a red and blue facsimile. They giggled and oohed. Finally, Richard invited all to visit to see for themselves the strange creatures. For entertainment, Lilly played her lute, accompanied by a teenager on the bugle, on which she had instructed him. Other natives joined with drums. The result was a curious mixture of English and Native American dance. The evening pastimes, as well as conversations the following morning, did not hint of larger hostilities.

The sail back required many tacks against the prevailing westerlies, thereby tripling the time. Seymour arrived at Gilbert's house at eight at night to offer his report: Nahanada did not control the hot young braves. Nor did he have sway over Sabenoa. The fighting force was four or five times larger than the English, if Sabenoa's braves were included. Gilbert had opened his second bottle of Bordeaux. He poured a glass for Richard and shrugged his shoulders. "So be it." He raised his hands as if to shove off the subject. He then launched into an unexpected short monologue.

"What do you think, Seymour? We've had our year of exploration. We can tell our grandchildren and lecture at the Temple and at the Merchant Hall in Exeter. Why bother to stick our necks out any longer? Since the news of my brother's death, sometimes—often—I think fondly of Compton Castle. Maybe that's my fate." The information appeared to be a tease, fueled by wine, from a man simply musing with possibilities.

Richard had grown to relish this Bordeaux. He sipped and sniffed his way through the glass. "I do not have a castle to return to."

"Hell, man, with your education and lineage, you will always prosper."

"Gilbert, have you grown weary?"

"Seymour, I have lived most of my life believing my fate led me to pick up my father's sword. I am a determined man. I have not wavered. Single-minded. It is your company I blame. You loosen my tongue as much as this wine." He lifts his empty glass as a toast, looks at it, and fills it again. "My fate is now divided. I have a choice."

Never before had Richard witnessed Gilbert being introspective. Richard viewed fate as a concept for those who wanted a simpler world, or who after making a decision did not want to hold reservations or regrets. In its worst form, the Puritans believed in "predestination." God had a plan for us all. "Perhaps," Bacon had told him, "but give me the evidence." In any case, Gilbert's small revelation simply showed the man to be human.

"Oh, Cousin, don't take me seriously. You will have your dominion."

"Ah, yes, the new Lord of the Sagadahoc."

"The men are nearly ready. We will attack in several days. I am waiting for a high tide at midday. Before I spoke more as a dreamer, and you the interpreter. No, we will attack. Kill Sabenoa and many of his ablest braves. I'll have their heads on stakes. My father, Sir Humphrey, would be proud."

"Well enough, sir. It is late."

"And that lovely bride is waiting, no doubt."

"Tomorrow," Richard says as he prepares to leave, "Margaret and I plan to ride the horses. They've regained much strength. Galloping on the beach seems a better idea than the trails, given how they're best suited for human traffic, and given the possibility of attack. Would you recommend guards? I gather there has been no sign of braves in the past weeks?"

"True enough. We've cut back on patrols. Apparently they've returned to their camp, wherever that is. Who is to make sense of their thinking? Besides they'd probably think the animals magical and run. When will you ride?"

"In the afternoon, just before high tide. I enjoy swimming up that small river, the one that divides the beach and meanders a mile or so north into a pond. If you time it right, you can float up with the incoming and out with outgoing tide. The water gets almost warm. It's surrounded by mud flats and sea grass. Nearly impossible to walk on."

"Not warm enough for me. I'll see there's a patrol out."

"Goodnight, Raleigh. Thank you for your honesty."

"For my dithering, you mean."

CHAPTER 70

September 19, 1608, Beach and Tidal Stream
Turn of Events

Richard continues to hold various responsibilities. Counseling the men usually occupies a couple of hours a day. On Sundays he conducts the Eucharist with fifty or so in attendance. Teaching and physical labor occupy his afternoons. Now that the Virginia is afloat, he cuts, splits, hauls, and stacks firewood. Margaret tends to the horses and helps in the garden during her first few weeks at the fort, and she tidies up the chapel. Richard sometimes feels obliged to eat with the men or with Gilbert and the council members. Mostly, he enjoys intimate dinners prepared by Margaret. In the evenings they read alone or to one another—much as he had with Lilly.

At two, an hour or so before high tide, they saddle Dancer and Breeze and walk them to the captain of the fort's building, where Gilbert usually is at this time of day, discussing military matters with Davis. Raleigh looks up and smiles at their arrival. "Fine looking steeds." His eyes stay on Margaret. "Don't wear them out. I'd welcome a ride myself soon." Richard assumes the possible sexual connotation is inadvertent. Gilbert has spent too many years either in male company, or lately with Dorothy.

"Of course, plan on it tomorrow," offers Richard. "What of protection for our beach ride?"

After the harassment began some three months ago, patrols had maintained a more or less one-mile perimeter to the west. A small strip of land between ocean and bay separated the few hundred acres of land on which the fort was constructed from the mainland. In effect the fort stood on a small peninsula within a larger peninsula. It was nearly an island. The ocean and the Sagadahoc provided protection from the north, south, and east. On the occasions when arrows had emerged from the woods, a few musket and cannon blasts ended the matter. Except for a few periodic engagements weeks before, the patrols had found no evidence of native activity. But Gilbert and James Davis agreed their adversary is unpredictable. "The patrol is out there now and will be until well after sundown. They've been instructed to secure the area behind the dunes," asserts Captain Davis.

"Safe as the beaches in Devon," adds Gilbert.

Richard helps Margaret into the stirrups and then mounts himself. "We should be back by dusk."

"Tally ho, newlyweds," chimes in Gilbert. He appears to be in a buoyant mood.

Soon they emerge from the woods on the broad path leading to the section of beach at the mouth of the Sagadahoc. Husband and wife, Dancer and Breeze, in tandem, gravitate to where water meets beach and wavelets advance. They need to rein the horses in after their long confinement on the ship. Richard has walked this way often and observed the tiny quarter-inch mountain ranges that cover this section of beach between the high and low tide, carved out by the advancing and receding surf. He imagines himself high in the sky, an eagle perhaps, looking down on a miniature landscape. The horses snort and strain, then gallop before they ease into a gentle lope.

When Richard sees the opening to the small river, he makes a clicking sound. Dancer throws himself into a gallop, Breeze right behind. Just before the sand drops off three feet into the little river, Richard reins up and swings off.

From a pouch attached to the rear of his saddle, he withdraws four hobbles.

"Best we swim now. That fog is rolling in. Wrap your clothes in these towels. We'll leave them here above high water. The horses can feed on the sea grass." Richard begins peeling off his shirt. Margaret seems uncertain.

"Well?" Richard said, hopping on one leg and pulling off a boot." "Once you're in, you'll love it."

Margaret is wearing a pair of Richard's pants she'd radically altered. She collects herself and strips. Then she, too, stands naked, her hands covering herself. They both laugh. The sensation of wind and sun, the enormous open space, leave them feeling exposed and absurd.

Richard begins wading in. Margaret follows. "Mary of God, it's cold." The water covers her calves.

"Yes, but it will warm." he yells.

Within fifty yards the estuary narrows and deepens. When they are up to their waists, Richard submerges and begins floating. Margaret follows his lead. The flow widens around a sculpted bend, then shallows. They begin walking, chest deep. Margaret puts out a hand to hold Richard's in order to steady herself against the current. They both lean backward against the push of the incoming tide. Uncanny how powerful, and yet gentle under the circumstances: the heat of the sun, the softness of the sandy banks, the clean hard-packed sand bottom, an uneven bottom that brings them up, knee-deep and naked, on a small underwater dune that then slopes down. The current lifts them off their feet. In order to keep heading straight, they revert to the breast stroke.

"You weren't lying. It does get warmer." They'd flipped to their backs, a bright china-cup-blue sky without a cloud overhead. Out to sea, fog waits.

Three quarters of a mile past the beach into the dunes and sea grass, the river spreads and shallows. Underfoot the bottom turns mucky. "Let's get out here," Richard points to a last section of flattish sandy bank. Their feet move out of the ooze to dry sand. "Naked sea creatures emerging," Margaret offers. "Really Richard, I never felt so at home in the water. It must be how fish feel when they travel the ocean currents."

They sit and stretch themselves on the hot sand. Across from them a mother duck hides in the grass with her ducklings. At first she quacks and collects her brood, but then settles down when the strange creatures are motionless, their eyes closed—each species in its protected warm enclave.

Richard awakes from his brief nap. Momentarily, he was on the banks of the stream that runs through his father's estate—the close sandy dampness, the intimacy, Margaret's hand in his? He must be, and then realizes as he bends to give Margaret's sun- painted pink belly a kiss, that they are not at home, but aliens. "Mmmm," was her reaction, one eye opening.

"I think it's slack tide or it's already turned. Ready to get wet again?" Richard throws in a small stick to confirm his hunch. Margaret sits up, and they both watch the stick slowly head downstream.

"It should be even warmer now, what with the shallowness and baked mud flats upstream."

Margaret dips in her toes. "Right again." This time, she wades in first. When the water covers her chest, she gives a little hop. The current pops her up so she is horizontal. Richard watches and smiles. "You're an albino otter." He isn't far behind.

They lie on their backs, this time making no effort to face in one direction. The exiting current turns them slowly. Above the fog drifts in, silky over the sun. Margaret yips in surprise and then laughs when her bottom rubs on a sand bar. She stands up on it, almost entirely out of the water and watches Richard drift and turn yards away. She dives in. Within minutes they are close to the mouth where the outgoing tide meets the cold, stolid sea.

"Are you warm enough?" Richard calls out to Margaret a few yards behind.

"Yes."

"Then let's keep walking." Instead of dropping off to deeper ocean, the mouth of the river formed five small channels, two to six feet deep. They were separated by sandy deltas, underwater at high tide. As the tide receded, some sandy sections became exposed. Richard knows this from his previous exploration.

"This way," he points. Three-inch waves begin breaking over their knees.

"There, I think that's it."

The fog has rolled in and thrown wispy strands over the beach. The sun is a bright grey blob. Richard points to a round spit of sand just barely visible. He can tell by the wavelets breaking on it. This section four or five feet in diameter provides them a miniature, sandy island.

He puts his arms around Margaret, still warm, though the water at this point—some fifty yards from the beach where their clothes and horses wait—must have been at least twenty degrees colder than their recent place of rest. The fog has thickened.

The muffling fog makes it impossible to see land. The breaking of waves becomes multi-directional. They face the shore line, at least they think they do, yet the light and surf are so diffuse they can not be sure. They decide to sit, holding their knees up to their bare chests. The receding tide expands their island inch by minute.

"Before, a year ago, it was all sun."

"Richard?" Margaret begins to shiver. "I'm getting cold, but this is enchanting. It reminds me of the fog during the journey, though I think it even stranger now. I had the boat to trust then. Here it feels we're the only ones in the world. Does it seem like that to you?"

"It does feel, well mysterious."

"Yes, mysterious but eerie, too."

They sit silently encompassed in the sound of surf.

"What was that?" asks Margaret. Richard hears it too.

"It sounds like Dancer or Breeze whinnying. But hard to decipher." They hear it again. Then nothing.

"Let's go back, Richard. I'm cold. I'm sorry. It feels too strange. Which way?"

"This way." He takes Margaret's hand. He's worried she might get pulled off her feet and disappear into the grey fog. And with that thought arises a moment of panic. She could so easily disappear, be lost forever. The water right off their little oasis is up to their thighs and then their calves, proof they're headed in the right direction. His surprising fear vanishes as quickly as it appeared. They don't hear from the horses again, but the surf is now clearly in front of them breaking on the sand. Forty yards or so later they stand with the water lapping at their ankles.

"If we go left, we'll come to the river. And if we find our clothes, we won't have to ride back naked."

"You will. I will remain here naked in the saddle until you fetch other ones."

In a few steps they arrive at the river's mouth. They look around in the thickening mist. "Over here, I think," says Richard

"Are you sure?"

Both are looking down when out of the fog appear two figures, then three more behind them: natives. Three hold half-drawn bows, one a spear, another a large bloodied knife. The native with the knife wears Richard's pants. Margaret's shirt hangs around the spear holder's neck. All stop and stare at one another. The knife holder finally points at Margaret's nakedness and says something. The one with the spear offers up a lascivious laugh. The three with arrows at the ready remain stone-faced. The five approach a few more steps.

"Richard?" Margaret's voice quivers.

"Be calm. I don't know what they want."

The one with the knife takes two strides and reached out to grab Margaret's crotch with a bloody hand. Instinctively, but ineffectively, she backhands him. In the same instant Richard, three feet away, takes a quick step. "No, stop!" Margaret's assailant, with his one hand on Margaret's tuft of hair, directs his knife so it meets Richard's thigh, penetrating half an inch. Margaret looks down and screams. Then he switches his hand from her crotch to cup her mouth, blood smearing one cheek. She stares at Richard's thigh trickling more blood. The three archers drop their weapons and rush Richard. They bring him down hard on to the sand.

One produces rawhide and binds his arms. Another does the

same with Margaret. He, unlike the knife wielder, appears curious but embarrassed by her. He simply cautiously touches her shoulders in wonderment. Both are then gagged with pieces of Margaret's chemise and pushed in the direction of the river.

Four birch bark canoes are pulled up on the sand. To Richard and Margaret's horror, three other braves come out from the mist lugging hacked apart pieces of Dancer and Breeze. These are thrown in two of the canoes. Margaret gapes at Breeze's severed head lying in a pool of blood. Her legs give way as she collapses with a moan.

The brave with the knife quietly commands Richard into the bottom of a canoe. Margaret is lifted into another. The natives hurry efficiently. Due to lack of space, one of Dancer's hind quarters is left on shore. Richard sees the saddles in another canoe.

The braves push off and they float to the mouth of the river. There they turn west, away from the fort. As far as Richard can tell, they are paddling close to shore. When he raises his head, he sees another canoe thirty feet away. At one point Margaret's face rises above the sides. For a second their eyes meet, hers wide in shock. He takes stock of himself. A damp chill has set in. The bleeding has coagulated. The two in his canoe don't say a word. He knows enough Algonquin to ask questions, but that is impossible with the gag. The sound of the waves on the sand change to what he thinks must be rocks. An interminable amount of time passes. Foggy dusk turns to night. Exhaustion takes over.

Richard awakes from a semi-conscious daze. A cool wind has blown the fog out to sea. A three-quarter moon offers some light. He calculates they are paddling in a bay. He can see land not too far off to his left and right. Last spring Gilbert explored this section beyond the beach and rocky outcropping. He had sailed in the *Virginia* until it got too shallow, then they'd turned around.

To escape his chill, Richard focuses his mind. He chooses a day at Middle Temple Hall. He loved the building's openness and intimacy. He keeps concentrating. He is sitting at the end of a hug oak table. He is alone. He tries to remember how it sounds, sitting alone in this, his favorite of all spaces. He hears the scraping sound of the canoe bottom against sand. Two braves pull him to his feet. Everything aches. Margaret is likewise removed from her canoe. Their gags are removed.

"Are you all right?" he speaks in a low voice, imagining he might receive a blow to the head. None comes.

"Yes. My shoulder hurts. Richard, what is happening?"

"I don't know." They will either die, or not. It seems that simple.

Each receives a shove toward the trees. Single file, over a well-traveled path of pine needle under bare feet, they arrive in a clearing. Twelve or so men surround a fire. Some get to their feet as they approach.

Many surround Margaret in amazement. One runs his hand over her frizzled hair. Another strokes a breast. She is too tired and scared to respond this time. From the fire they hear a reprimanding voice. The young braves back away. An older man presents himself authoritatively. He, too, stares at the English. His grunt holds the possibility of disapproval. He looks at Richard, then steps to the side for a profile view.

"Skidwarres?" The one name comes with a gesture, two hands held together indicating friendship.

Richard repeats, "Skidwarres—friends." The older one turns to the brave who had brandished the knife some hours ago, and says something short and harsh. Then the older one issues orders to another brave. That one scampers away into a hut and returns with two bear pelts. Meanwhile another unties the rawhide, first from Richard, then Margaret. They rub their wrists and stretch their arms. Richard takes one of the pelts and wraps it around Margaret.

The robe offers a sense of security and modesty. Margaret begins weeping.

The older brave points to the fire and says, "*Kzab da*" (warm).

Richard believes he's met this native at Pemaquid. The knife wielder, too, now looks familiar. Others do not. Their hair is shaved on the sides and spiked. But the older one and a few others he's sure come from Pemaquid. They wear their hair long. Probably all were part of the renegade group. Luckily, the older brave appears to be in charge.

Kasko, the elder, and his son, Woboz, confer, while the English warm themselves. By tone their voices indicate disagreement. Two braves come out of the dark carrying a horse's front quarters. They throw it on one end of the fire. Immediately it spatters and sizzles. The odor is that of charred hair and flesh. The two English feel their stomachs churn with disgust. The smoke rises and wafts in their direction. Margaret buries her nose under Richard's chin as he stares into the fire. To his chagrin, he begins salivating. They've had only a light lunch. That was over twelve hours ago—before horseback riding, swimming, the shock, the cold and pain. A baser part of his anatomy craves a portion of horsemeat.

Kasko and Woboz end their conversation and approach the fire. The younger brave puts a hand on Richard's shoulder and gives him a push, then guides him with Margaret under Richard's arm. The brave points to the opening of a hut and says something Richard understands to mean, "Go." With the deerskin flap drawn back, the two duck through the opening. They stand huddled together in total darkness.

"Richard, are we going to die?"

"I don't think so. Not now anyway. The only thing we can do now is rest. We need strength for whatever happens tomorrow." Richard unwraps his own pelt and places it on the earthen floor, covered with pine needles. He guides Margaret to lie on it, then settles himself next to her. He draws her pelt over them. They lie on their sides. He pulls her against him for their mutual warmth and begins to hum softly. It turns out to be the ditty sung at the Middle Temple.

"Bring hither the bowl,
The brimming brown bowl,
And quaff the rich juice right merrily.
Let the wine cup go round
Till the solid ground
Shall quake at the noise of our revelry.
Let wassail and wine
Their pleasures combine,
While we quaff the rich juice right merrily.
Let us drink till we die,
When the saints we rely
Will mingle their songs with our revelry."

Halfway through, he realizes he'd best hum the last the last three lines.

Sometime later a young brave carries in a basket and a small pouch of water. He says something and leaves, replacing the flap.

Neither moves. Finally Richard sighs and sits up.

"Are you going to eat it? How can you?" Margaret asks.

"Because I have to. We have to. Who knows what today will bring. These lads are on a military operation. Who knows when or what they eat. Margaret, you have to eat." He smells the contents of the jug, then tastes it. "Water, fresh."

She sits up. He adjusts the blanket around her shoulders. She sips. He brings a piece of meat to his mouth. He smells it, then nibbles. Then he takes off a larger piece and chews. "Eat, Margaret."

"I'll be sick."

"No, your stomach has a mind of its own. It needs food."

"I'll try." They eat in small bites. Neither admits to the other that it tastes good. When they finish, Margaret announces in a mock little girl voice, "I have to water."

"Just go near the side. I already eliminated in the canoe. The bottom was so wet."

"I did too. But..." She gets up and squats, then titters. When she returns to the warmth of blanket and Richard's arms, he whispers in her ear. "I love you."

CHAPTER 71

September 20, 1608, On the Androscoggin
Sipsis

When the English awake again, a pile of clothes lies inside the entrance. They sort out two deerskin tunics, two pair of leggings, and flaps, as well as an assortment of deer hide straps. The adjustments turn out marginally successful, the choices being too small for Richard and too big for Margaret.

Richard steps outside. A guard stares at him and calls out something three times. Richard hears fear in the voice. For a moment the two look at one another, expressionless. When Richard gives a slight smile, the brave reciprocates, mirroring him reflexively.

Around the corner of the hut stride the elder, Kasko, and three others, including Woboz. All four break out in laughter at the Englishman in his leggings and flap made for a much smaller brave. When Margaret pokes her head out of the hut and steps into the sunlight, they stare; no laughter for her. She elicits a different chord. Rather than an erotic oddity in the dark, a beautiful woman stands before them, transformed. Her deerskins make her familiar.

After a small meal of berries and bitter, root tea, the entire party of eighteen heads up the bay. It turns out they are on the west side, no doubt because it offers better protection from any English patrols. Richard and Margaret are allowed to travel in the same large canoe with six paddlers. They watch the expansive bay quickly turn into a river. The paddlers put impressive effort against the outgoing tide. This is not the majestic and quick-moving Sagadahoc. The outcroppings of granite are smaller, the temperature warmer, the vistas modest by comparison.

Within two hours they arrive at a small elongated lake. They cross this in a few minutes and slip into a stream only yards wide. Fresh water. Soon they run aground. Both English are ordered to help portage the heavy canoe.

From Richard's reckoning, they are heading due north, just as the Sagadahoc does. If they continue, he judges they'll reach the Androscoggin. That suggests Sabenoa's village might be their destination. But logic might not have much bearing. These thoughts he passes on to Margaret.

As predicted, they soon reach the banks of a large river, most likely the Androscoggin. The party reenters the water and heads upstream, away from Sabenoa's village at Quabacook. Before Richard has time to consider this turn of events, they land on the muddy beach of an island.

Young braves, plus a few women and children—sixty or so in total— line the shore. Many have never seen a white person, at least not at arm's reach and certainly not a female—and dressed like them. Two braves immediately stick the horse heads on sharpened poles for all to see. "Not a *moz*," Kasko informs the gawking crowd. "They ride the beasts." The saddles are thrown from the canoes for everyone to touch.

To Richard and Margaret's relief, Kasko remains at their side. Many curious natives come to touch and smell the couple. A few dare to look under their flaps, though Kasko quickly discourages this with a loud barking command.

They are again ushered into another hut with four braves stationed around it. Kasko tries to explain by gesticulating, talking, bringing his hands closer and closer together, herding something invisible. Richard nods his head and smiles. "I think he is going to meet with others."

Again in the hut they lie on bear pelts. When the flap opens, an adolescent girl hands them corn, squash, and a jug of water. "*Olioni*," Richard says, thank you. The girl blushes and smiles, then giggles.

"The elder brave is from Nahanada's village. I believe his name is Kasko. Let's hope he's persuasive. The one who captured us is Woboz. I overheard his name. He's Kasko's son. He is trouble."

The couple's fate hangs in the balance between generations. During the winter under Woboz' leadership, less than thirty braves had forged a hatred for the English. Some came from the Pemaquid tribe, others from Sabenoa's village, a scattering from other Mawooshen locations. Woboz exuded daring, intelligence, and courage. Besides, he provoked fear and had a reputation for impulsiveness. They knew of the English murders. His father provided a counterbalancing presence. Kasko had decided to join partly because he shared some of his son's views of the English. He believed they could not be trusted. The father also mistrusted his son's judgment, but in a protective, familial way. Besides, he wanted to keep his family together, so he persuaded cousins and a brother to join them.

With the spring, the small band had left the more northern section of the Sagadahoc, where they'd spent the winter hunting. Sabenoa advised them to occupy the island where the Lord of the Sagadahoc could help feed them. By doing so, he'd gain stature and reinforcements, if needed. They would also be within striking distance of the fort. Rumors began to filter west and south. What in April began as a village for dedicated fighters had by August grown into a motley group of nearly two hundred, with perhaps a hundred and twenty-five fighting-age braves.

When the sporadic attacks on the fort began in June, all became merry with excitement. The most dedicated among them tried to encourage Woboz' ferocity. But many who had come to the island expected the light-hearted warfare typical to their culture. When introduced to lethal cannon blasts and musket fire, enthusiasm took a hard knock. A brave from the Sakohki region received a cannonball through his stomach, nearly severing his chest from his hips. When his remains arrived at the bottom of a canoe, all filed by on the beach. A spent cannonball retrieved by a brave became another exhibit.

Woboz agreed to the decision to harass instead of attack, but not happily. Again his father, this time privately, held sway. Finally Woboz came to believe it was a smart tactic. Wearing down the enemy might be just as potent as killing them. It also allowed for dancing, music, story telling, feasting, fishing, frolicking, and love making to continue during the summer. Woboz might be occasionally agitated with the lax atmosphere, but he, too, enjoyed a good time. It remained unclear if it would become a year-round village, inhabited mostly by young people, dedicated to the eliminating the aliens. When Sipsis appeared with two other young Mawooshen, including Moskwas, Lilly's friend, it did not take her long to rekindle his ardor and dismiss the English she visited: "Very smelly with a tiny *askoks*" (penis), she insisted.

During July and August, the raids were discontinued, though periodically small bands traveled to observe activity in the fort from a hill a mile upriver. They could not decide what to do next. Woboz persuaded his father that kidnapping a few English might be an interesting alternative. Besides, the risky skirmishes apparently were inconsequential. Kasko had not anticipated catching such an important English, much less a woman.

Fifteen men presided over the foreigners' fate. Usually Kasko said little or nothing. He tended to confer in private with Woboz, thereby allowing the younger man to save face. Such was the case this evening. Woboz began with a display of anger. What of the tribes way to the west and north, the Mohawk and Iroquois? They fought heroically. They used torture–it stirred the passions. He insisted the Englishman be brought to the center of the village and flayed to death. Then take his scalp and place his head on a post next to the beasts he loved to fornicate. And the woman, let her be our slave. She would be shared for various purposes.

The group listened with interest. The possibility of torture fascinated some of the younger braves. And a white slave woman? It had never occurred to them before. One of the more confident men voiced his disapproval of torture. It was not the way of his forefathers. Another pointed out that the English had not yet left their camp to engage in warfare, with the exception of last fall when they sailed to Sabenoa's village for food. If the man and woman did not return, might they not seek revenge? Yes, but their island village could not be reached by the English boats, excepting their small ones they paddled backward.

Finally, as Woboz and his father had planned, the elder spoke. "I know of this man, the English. A brother of mine, Skidwarres, is his friend. I would not like him killed or tortured. My honor would be diminished."

Woboz nodded in approval. "We should send them to Sabenoa. Let him manage. He, like his father and grandfather, is sagamore in this region with many braves. He has experience with these English warriors. I am not naive. This friend of a friend may also be our enemy. Let Sabenoa decide. We have shown the English how at peril they are on our land. We can also show them we have large hearts."

The men in the circle eyed one another. Most nodded their approval. Around the inner circle of representatives sat an outer circle of braves, women and children. They listened quietly. At the end they together offered their approval, "*Oligo, oligo*" (good, good).

Sipsis sits among the observers. She rises to leave with the others, then goes to the guarded hut where the English wait. Many know of her chameleon-like migration from Admiral Gilbert's bed to Woboz' hut. Her fairer skin and green eyes have been a curiosity since childhood. Many kept their distance when she first arrived. In her support, a few of Sipsis' friends insist she had left the white man disgusted and repentant. After some weeks, she won acceptance. Woboz could not believe his luck. Her return, her willingness to finally give herself to him proved his importance. He had been enamored since childhood. Beautiful, impertinent, and his first woman years ago. His ardor was stoked even more after she pulled away. And now at the camp on the island, she spoke of her hatred of the English. She even suggested she might become a spy. Woboz thinks it a good idea if she queries the two, to learn what she can. This is exactly what Sipsis had devised.

Ducking through the entrance, she smiles. Richard sits while Margaret lightly sleeps. When she senses another's presence, she grabs Richard's arm.

"It's all right, Margaret. I know this woman. Her name is Sipsis."

"Chaplain Seymour." The two had often been in the same room together but had never carried on a conversation. Sipsis sits. She crosses her legs and stares at the couple, not sure herself what it was she entertained. "Who?" she asks, pointing at Margaret.

"My wife, Margaret."

"Margaret," she says slowly. "Margaret, English. I speak with Skidwarres, Gilbert. Know words."

"Your English is impressive." Margaret realizes "impressive" is too advanced. "Good."

"Thank you. You pretty." Sipsis reaches to touch Margaret's hair that for lack of combing is a snarl of curls "First English woman. Pretty hair."

"Sipsis?" Richard now speaks. "What are they going to do with us? You are a friend?"

"Friend, yes, friend."

"Good." Richard decides to take her declaration at face value. "What will they do with us?"

"Give to Sabenoa. No want here. Not good here, say Kasko."

"When?" asked Richard.

"Next sun...tomorrow?"

"Tomorrow?" asks Margaret. "Richard, Sabenoa, he's the one Gilbert stole food from, the crazy one?"

"Yes, maybe crazy."

"He not good," offers Sipsis. Margaret calms herself enough to look at her. She wears a band of eagle feathers laced with tiny shells that trails down her back over her deerskin tunic. Margaret realizes her beauty is not just physical. Her keenness appears to shine through her skin and eyes. Sipsis watches Margaret as she stares. "I help English friend."

All are silent.

"Richard," Margaret says, not sure she is making any sense. "Can Skidwarres help us?" Richard has wondered about this, but can't imagine how they might contact him, except that Gilbert, he might do so.

Richard asks the obvious before his mind settles on possible action. "Sipsis, can you tell Skidwarres? Can you, can you send word?" He speaks the last sentence slowly. "To Pemaquid?"

Sipsis brightens. She is half calculation, half impulse. Sipsis is with Woboz because Nahanada wished it. She, as the woman of the leading brave, has gained stature. Yet Gilbert had promised to take her to his land, the land where her grandparents may still be living. It is this destiny she feels most keenly. If she earns Gilbert's respect by helping, it is less likely Gilbert may change his mind. "Yes, I help. Moskwas, he go Skidwarres." She rises. "*Bamegizegak*" (today, right away).

She prepares to exit the hut. "Food? More?"

"Oh," Margaret, stands showing Sipsis how her vest and leggings hang so loosely on her. "Big."

"Yes, yes, Sipsis points to Margaret and then herself.

"Yes," smiles Margaret, "Same size."

Sipsis' excitement propels her out the opening.

True to her word, she runs to Moskwas. "Skidwarres must know the English are here. Go. Do this for Lilly and Skidwarres. You will be honored." Moskwas over the months has lost some of his resentment of Skidwarres for taking Lilly as his wife. He is also tiring of his life among the braves, many of them so full of ignorance and hatred for a people they know nothing about. He, Moskwas, knows better.

Sipsis recommends that another brave join Moskwas. "Do not worry about Woboz. He told me to do this." This is a lie. Later she will concoct a story. Besides, with the English in the hands of Sabenoa, Woboz can be easily distracted.

The second time she visits the captives, Sipsis brings clothes and good news.

"Perfect," Margaret exclaims. Her well-fitting leggings usher in a happiness that surprises her.

"Perfect?"

"Yes, it means...good, very good."

Sipsis repeats, "Perfect."

Later Sipsis reports to Woboz how she'd delegated Moskwas to tell Nahanada the news. At first Woboz scowls, so she puts in play her well-honed impertinence. She takes his hand and nibbles on his fingers, smiling. "You are my brave, but he is my sagamore. He would want to know." She offers an extra nip. They both laugh before she skitters away.

CHAPTER 72

The Day Before, September 19th, 1608, Fort St. George
Plan of Attack

When night fell at the fort the day before, it dawned on Gilbert that he had not heard from the couple. Not particularly troubled, as they often kept to themselves, he wandered over to the newly constructed horse shed: empty. One of the new boys, whose welcome job it was to tend to Dancer and Breeze, sat on a fence looking worried.

"They have not returned?"

"No, sir."

"If they do, find me immediately."

"Yes, sir."

Gilbert didn't often run—it seemed to him unbecoming—but he did then, straight to the captain of the fort's lodgings. No, the patrol had returned only minutes ago. Nothing unusual reported. No, they did not walk the beach; instead they had watched the perimeter of the dunes from the land side.

"I want fifteen men to search that beach. Torches, obviously. Have them ready in ten minutes. I'll join you."

Half an hour later, all stood looking at the bloody horse torso and offal. The disturbance of the sand indicated sections of the horse had been dragged to the river. A man and woman's footprints, as well as many moccasin prints, told the story Gilbert had feared.

An hour later the council sat around the large table in Gilbert's quarters. The president asked for suggestions. Since the news of his brother's death, Gilbert had grown more compelled to act in two ways.

Compton Castle awaited him; it was now his. Yet a world away, troops prepared to take action against Sabenoa. This he must do soon, right away. Nights fell sooner. The temperature was dropping. He was determined to sail before the worst of the storms. One of the possible substitute leaders was either in the hands of the natives or dead.

Listening with one ear, he heard James Davis claim, "Probably Sabenoa."

"All the more reason to blow them to hell," Gilbert heard himself say.

"We don't know this," offered Robert Davies.

"We don't know, but act we must." Gilbert's voice rose. "We lose nothing by continuing our plans. If Sabenoa is holding him, then we must face that."

This time Robert Davies asked, "Might we query Skidwarres or Nahanada?"

Gilbert found the suggestion irksome, partly because he hadn't raised it. "I don't know. I never trusted them, even Skidwarres. I don't believe what he tells Seymour."

Captain Davies spoke. "They might help, Admiral. If nothing else, sir, translation. We could take him with us."

"All right then." Gilbert's quick endorsement might lessen the fact it wasn't his idea. "We'll send the *Virginia* to Pemaquid in the morning. Bring him as soon as possible. All in favor?" All were. "Second, we prepare for battle in three days, Skidwarres or no Skidwarres. If Seymour and his bride are alive, well...well, we'll face that. We hope we'll face that."

Gilbert knew how in warfare and politics the unsolvable matters often got shunted aside and faced only when more information arrived— or when no other options remained.

CHAPTER 73

September 21, 1608, Sabenoa's Village
Hostages

S oon after sunrise, Kasko orders Richard and Margaret out of the
hut. With no conversation, they march between two lines of staring,
silent, half-awake natives. Margaret thinks she sees a few women
sharing her apprehension; even a smile shows from the girl who brought
them food. By the time they reach the same canoe they had arrived in
the day before, the men and boys are delivering laughs ranging from
light-hearted to derisive and sinister. Four paddlers are waiting. Kasko
tells the English to sit on the bottom; then he adjusts himself on a woven
seat in the middle.

The trip takes less than an hour, down the gentle river with earthen
banks on both sides. It appears the entire village is waiting at the shore.
First they hear the drums, then a guttural humming to the beat. It is
similar to a greeting Richard heard from Nahanada's village, though in
this case wild screeching erupts, dies, and erupts again.

Their canoe slides up on the sand and rests only yards from Sabenoa.
He perches on his velvet red cushion and throne, the gift from President
Popham, his feet not quite touching the ground. His right hand holds
a staff with four scalps hanging from leather straps. Behind the throne
stand four large braves, their chests and faces painted blue and black,
their hair cut short, dyed green, and applied with grease, so it stands up
porcupine style. On his left side, his three wives stare and whisper to one
another.

Kasko escorts his prisoners so they stand in front of Sabenoa. The
Lord of the Sagadahoc pounds his staff into the pebble beach, jiggling the
scalps together. He points to the ground and says, "*Wkedokw*" (knees).

But Richard doesn't understand. To make the point, a nearby brave pushes down hard on Richard's shoulders. On his knees he receives a foot to his neck that pushes his face into the stony beach. Margaret quickly goes to her knees. She looks over at Richard's bleeding nose.

Sabenoa slips off his throne and places his staff not so gently between Richard's shoulder blades. He speaks in a loud, high-pitched voice. Richard understands none of it, but the audience is amused. Over the oration they become a chorus. He gets the gist of the words: "The English are under the spell of the great Lord of the Sagadahoc. His sons, grandsons, and their grandsons will rule till the sun disappears." Rule till the sun disappears is the refrain.

The king moves over to Margaret. She is bent over, forehead on the ground. Sabenoa pokes the staff into her shoulder blades and slides it down her back, so eventually the staff lies in the crevice of her buttocks. Onlookers continue their refrain: "Rule till the sun disappears." Their mood is jovial. Seymour, with his forehead resting on the beach, sees none of this.

The chanting ends. The two are yanked to their feet. Richard's view of Margaret's wide-eyed fear and Margaret of Richard's bloodstained face lasts only seconds. From behind, both are blindfolded and led in separate directions. Two women, one on each arm, direct Margaret down the beach. Other women, young and old, follow. Margaret hears no reply when she cries out for Richard. Everyone in the village is talking, shouting, or laughing. Some continue the refrain, "Rule till the sun disappears."

The night before, Richard had expressed optimism. Their lives would be spared. They'd be used as pawns, to be negotiated away. Warfare among villages rarely ended in death or torture—though enslavement, yes. This viewpoint now felt overly optimistic. With the blindfold removed, he was able to take in his destination: a small pen one might use for domesticated animals, though the tribe kept no such animals. Birch saplings have been bent and tied together a few feet over his head. It's about three paces in diameter. A few men busy themselves tying the poles with leather straps.

The men who'd escorted him now strip off his clothing and push him through a small opening. Richard stands naked. He turns slowly and sees faces peering at him, as if he were an exotic animal. In defense he sits cross-legged, arms across his lap. Throughout the morning natives file by and watch him. Some sit and attempt to carry on a conversation. They give up, some in disgust. A group of teenage boys stick their heads through the openings and taunt. Richard looks up and stares. It is his only weapon. He wonders whether, if he just keeps looking at them as if he had special powers, they might leave him alone. He thinks of Skidwarres spooking the wayward highwaymen. It seems to work. Their insults peter out and they straggle off. He remains seated, eyes focused on the ground. His mind wanders enough to find humor in his peril.

In the afternoon a boy shoves a basket of maize, cooked wild rice, and dried fish under the doorway. Richard huddles over it, pushing the food into his mouth with his fingers. He remembers a not-so-different cage in London with monkeys from Africa and the Southern New World. They'd scamper about, sit, swing, eat, and have sex. They, too, ate by stuffing food into their months, and, as he had to eventually, squatted to defecate.

Sabenoa's grinning face appears at dusk. Richard, who has curled up, attempting as much modesty as possible, decides to get up and approach. None in the village speak English. Nor can Richard grasp much from the sagamore's rapid-fire, apparently mocking gibberish. While trying to comprehend, a brave hands Richard a blanket. Sabenoa points to it and then says something, laughing. Richard can not imagine acclimating to his nakedness. He'd grown accustomed to the cold last winter and the rocking of the *Gift of God*. But not this ignominy. Stupidly, he thanks the boy for the dirty covering. Then sitting again, he wraps his submissive self. On the corner of the blanket he notices a small label: "Made in Tiverton, Devon, England"—another gift from Popham. He falls asleep, wakes in the dark and sleeps again, with images of three locations mingling: his cage, a small castle he'd visited in Devon, and Margaret, naked, tied to a stake, a fire licking at her feet.

Margaret's first day's ordeal involves other forms of intrusive indignities. Humiliation, they were both learning, discourages and weakens more than physical discomfort.

In a large hut, three women attend to her. Their ages, she guesses, range from mid-forties to mid-teens. With her blindfold and her native leggings, flap, and shirt off, Margaret feels like a meal in preparation. Prone on a reed mat, at first she imagines being boiled or roasted. Fleeting thoughts of her mother fretting over a side of beef come to her. They weren't being hostile; rather, they seemed to consider her less than human, though, while inspecting through probing and commenting, they apparently approved. What appears at one moment as survival humor—herself as beef or a chicken being plucked—settles into fear. It grows from her groin and spreads up under her ribs to flush her chest and face. Then to her dismay, she wets herself, just enough so the women laugh and quickly sponge it up with moss.

For what seems a long time, they attend to Margaret with scented water. Then she is left alone with the youngest, a pretty, moon-faced, shy girl. Like Richard, Margaret is lying curled on her side, naked. The others have gone off to eat, Margaret guesses.

Some time later, while in a doze, she is startled by a soft touch and quickly turns to see her young guard blanch at her awaking. They look at one another, green eye to chocolate brown. The girl says something kind and then touches Margaret's arm. The native girl's hands glide gently over her forearm with pleasant smelling grease. Margaret knows the smell. Richard had shown her seal oil, a gift from Skidwarres, and then applied it on her arms and legs on their honeymoon. Hungry for human response, Margaret smiles. At first the girl is stony-faced, but then she cannot resist. A smile, then a giggle. Margaret relaxes. She finds herself appreciating the girl's touch. She, the English woman, imagines herself thousands of miles away, attended by her lady-in-waiting.

Margaret, too, relishes food in a basket. Afterwards, still naked, escorted by the teenage wife past staring natives, they relieve themselves in the woods. Finally at dusk she receives a bear pelt blanket. A few hours later it becomes clear why she has been so groomed.

The three wives enter Margaret's hut, the eldest taking charge. She gestures for Margaret to get up and follow her outside, this time with her robe wrapped around her shoulders. Margaret hopes to be reunited with Richard. She clings to his optimism that they would remain alive as ransom. With a little push through the door of a hut, larger than the one she just left, or so it appears in the dark, she faces Sabenoa sitting on the ground, cross-legged on his throne's cushion. A small fire in the center overheats the space that smells of smoke, pine, and sweat. Behind him, an ominous shadow of the man falls so that the head on the domed ceiling looms down on her. She stands, the fire between them, he talking to her in a soothing tone. He continues long enough for her to shift her weight from one foot to another. Her eyes cautiously roam the hut's contents: a basket of food and a jug of something that he picks up twice and sips. To his right on the ground is a huge bear pelt, to his left weaponry: knives, bow, arrows, and spears. Near the entrance, within her peripheral vision, a black-haired skull with shrunken yellow skin glowers at her.

Finally he stops talking and points to the pelt in front of him. Margaret understands. She does as she is told. She moves next to it. Next, with two index fingers held together, he points to her robe. She holds the pelt together with both hands. Sabenoa widens his finger, indicating for her to open the robe. She continues to hold fast. At this, he rises from his cushion with a couple of grunts. The man is in his fifties. His physique once must have been impressive, if small. Now his biceps and thighs sag. She hasn't been sure, what with his position and the shadows, but now clearly he wears no groin flap. Under a belly grown round hangs his inert, preposterous member.

Both stand. He opens her robe. It drops to the ground. He begins moving his hands over her, from her shoulders down over her breasts. He rubs her belly and says something and laughs; one prominent finger finds its way between her legs. Before she can decide what to do, he withdraws and holds her shoulders. Then one hand caresses her back. His face comes closer. His breath is strange but not entirely unpleasant, an odor of nuts and tobacco. He faces her. Both hands rest on her buttocks. He gently squeezes them and then, with a short breathy, appreciative laugh, pinches. Margaret's entire body stiffens even more.

The Lord of the Sagadahoc steps back. He takes her hand and places it on his still limp member. When she doesn't respond, he wraps his hand around hers and himself and jiggles. Margaret begins to shake, then moans. The knives in the corner catch her eye. She might be faster than he, but to what purpose? To fend him off? To stab, even kill him? But the repercussions? Instead, she simply collapses on the pelt—more a response than a strategy—complete nonresistant helplessness. He would have to make the next move, one probably worse than what she'd already endured. At least up to now he hasn't been brutal. Waves of emotion ripple through her, none of it very identifiable, even if she had the wherewith all to try: fear, guilt—why guilt?—then guilt's close neighbor, shame—exposed, powerless. Anger, alive for just that brief moment, allowing her to conjure the possibility of a knife, is at first extinguished by reason, then replaced by the anguishing emotions of childhood helplessness.

Sabenoa looks down at her, still curled up. He thinks she's a beautiful white flower curled up at night. She is not the first woman he's forced into his hut. His second wife he captured years ago in a skirmish with a Mawooshen village. In revenge, they stole one of his village girls, and the matter ended. He took the woman as a wife, so young and beautiful. He learned to be patient with her fear. A sagamore does not always have to demonstrate his power. Mercy has its rewards. He instructed his first wife with kindness. Within two months, the young one welcomed his ardor with more enthusiasm than he'd expected.

So it shall be with this English. He has time. To Margaret's great surprise and relief, he lets her lie there. After a while his three wives arrive. The two eldest lead Margaret back to her hut and let her sleep for the night. The youngest wife remains with Sabenoa, to continue where Margaret had refused to proceed.

Before falling fully asleep, Margaret relives her feelings. With some surprise, she feels gratitude for the queer savage. The sensation settles around her heart. How curious. She must remember to tell Richard. Then Margaret sleeps.

CHAPTER 74

September 22, 1608, Sabenoa's Village
Play

A pattern begins for the English captives. Richard's old loincloth is returned to him, along with the tattered shirt and moccasins. Instead of being a source of entertainment, he is given a crude wooden hoe to till with, always under the watchful guard of at least two braves armed with bows, arrows, and spears. Replacements arrive every few hours. Richard gathers by their staring and conversation that the braves vie for this responsibility.

Rather than fear for the moment, both English have the luxury of worrying about the next day, or in Margaret's case, the next night. Two of Sabenoa's wives remain close by throughout the day. With them, she takes part in their chores, helping to build and maintain the fire, preparing food, harvesting berries, and mashing maize. The youngest wife patiently instructs Margaret how to weave baskets. All speak loudly to her, as if volume might help her understand. The abducted middle wife, the least patient, occasionally swats Margaret atop her head when she fails to understand instructions. When they are alone, the kinder, younger one whispers—pointing to herself—"Mosbas" (mink). Margaret repeats it and says her own name.

When night falls, Margaret again finds herself alone and naked, sitting across from Sabenoa on the pelt. He gazes at her. He converses softly, as if she understands. To make a point, he reaches over and strokes her hair or the inside of her thigh, or pulls on her ear. He is trying to seduce me, she thinks. In fact, within a larger state of tense, fearful anticipation, she does find herself less on guard, if for only moments.

Again she is ushered back to her hut without being assaulted. Again she lies with two of the three wives. This night the middle wife is the chosen one.

Richard occupies a hut with two guards, one inside, one out. The village contains some one hundred and fifty huts—Richard had heard this figure from Gilbert—circled around a large meeting hall structure. Deep into the night, Richard signals to his guard he wants to urinate. Two of them escort their captive to the outskirts. He relieves himself, gazing up at a full harvest moon. The surrounding light is as might be in London under torchlight. He remains looking up, long after his bladder has emptied. A great longing wells up in him. Where is Margaret? Surely she has not been killed. But what might they have done to her? He doesn't want to think about it but must think about it. What comes to him next feels primeval. He cries out her name, long and plaintive, "Margaret!" as loud and as elongated as he can. Might she hear me? How far away is she? Might she awake? Taken by surprise, the guards grab his arms. But he stands firm, listening. And yes, he is sure he hears her muffled response, his name, not that far off. Off in another direction comes the high-pitched howl of a wolf, probably domesticated. Then another howl elsewhere, each species evidently expressing a similar yearning.

The next day Richard again works in the fields, while Margaret occupies herself with domestic tasks. The routine brings with it a modest calming effect. Both eat and remain clothed. The natives still stare. Girls giggle. A few young males continue to taunt Richard and make obscene gestures toward Margaret, but no one abuses them physically. Most have acclimated themselves to their presence.

Surely, Richard calculates, by now Gilbert has realized they have either been killed or captured. The president must have contacted Skidwarres. Or Sipsis' emissary found him. No doubt the English could offer bounty more attractive than two white slaves—bounty plus threats. Their abduction occurred four days ago. If Gilbert had waited a day or two and then sent for Skidwarres, he should have arrived at the fort by now—if he could be reached. Or perhaps Moskwas found him first. That being the case, within a day or so they might expect Skidwarres' arrival. The possibility—logical, the more he thinks about it—provides comfort. He wishes he might pass this on to Margaret, who might not be making the same deductions.

That evening, as with the two previous, Margaret finds herself in Sabenoa's hut. Again lavender-scented grease is applied by the youngest wife, Mosbas. The girl is gentle and, like Sabenoa, speaks at length. With

Mosbas, Margaret has learned to close her eyes and enjoy the sensation.

Again Sabenoa sits on his cushion, nibbling berries from a small reed basket. This time the two other wives are in attendance, also sitting cross-legged a few feet away. Margaret stands next to the pelt, wrapped in a light blanket tied at her waist and around her neck with a leather strap. The fire in the middle is blazing. The night has turned crisp.

Margaret's curiosity doesn't last long. Native male voices approach the tent and someone pulls the door flap aside. Stooped over, Richard enters through the opening alone, head down. When he stands, Margaret rushes to him. "Richard, oh my god, Richard, you are all right?" She is in his arms while he is still surveying the small smoky room.

"Margaret?" His bearing is off-kilter and he aches from stooping to work the fields.

"Richard, you're all right?"

"Yes, yes, I am all right." he holds her and looks at Sabenoa, then his wives. Even under the strange and hostile circumstances, Margaret's scent of bear grease stimulates an erotic response. An indecipherable smile appears on Sabenoa's face. Does he, Richard wonders, enjoy this reunion?

"Margaret, have you been....hurt?" The word carries with it many possibilities.

"No. I have not been hurt."

The two then release one another and stand facing Sabenoa, the fire pit to their side. His smile flickers into something less beneficent, a tiny darkening. His head nods. His tongue travels across his lower lip and disappears, as a snake's head might. He stares at the couple and then speaks. By the cadence and tone, he appears to be explaining something. Richard catches a few words. They are being asked to do something for him. Sabenoa looks over to his wives. They nod in agreement. Richard understands the verb "*cowaldam*" (want and desire). But what does he want?

When Sabenoa realizes their ignorance, he rises, his loincloth his only clothing. He walks slowly to where they stand. This night they, too, wear loincloths under their robes. He places his hands on their shoulders, and while uttering something unintelligible, slides them down over their buttocks. This time in English, "English fuck." He nods his head, purses his lips, keeps nodding as if he's given them a present.

"What do they want?" She is quite sure she knows.

"I think they want us to show them how English...make love."

"Oh." Her voice is flat.

Sabenoa's hands remain on Margaret's bottom. Richard puts his hands on Sabenoa's chest and pushes, but not hard. The sagamore regains his balance and avoids falling into the fire. The youngest wife giggles but then shuts herself up quickly when the elder wife slaps her on the ear.

The man has not lost his light, sinister demeanor or his purpose. He stands in front of the couple, his tone quite reasonable. He points to the bear pelt and tells them to lie on it.

"No!" Richard's voice hides his growing anger and panic.

Margaret holds his arm. "He's crazy."

Sabenoa stares at them, his eyes now beady. He gives another short command to lie down, pointing with his finger. The two English don't move.

Sabenoa looks over at his wives and says something quickly. The two elder ones get up and move to Margaret's side. Sabenoa reaches over and wrenches her hand away from Richard's arm. Richard's fist swings into the portly belly. Sabenoa crumples. All three wives scream. Three braves burst through the small door single file, the last knocking over the middle one. In any other circumstance it would have been comical. The one on the ground tackles Richard. The other two fall on top of him. The two wives grab Margaret. The pandemonium stops. For a few seconds heavy breathing fills the hut.

Sabenoa gets to his knees, remains there to catch more breath, and then pushes himself up. Another command tells the braves to hoist Richard to his feet. Sabenoa, still reviving from the punch, turns around, stoops and picks up a spear. He points it at Margaret's bare stomach, visible from her parted robe. He looks at Richard and begins saying something slowly. Again a translation isn't necessary. He inches the head of the spear up against to her belly below the navel. He tells the braves to let Richard go.

Richard stares. The tip has created a pink indentation.

"Richard?" asks Margaret, staring at the tip of the spear.

"Sabenoa," Richard says, "please, no."

"Ah, please." He turns to his wives and repeats, "Please, please." Then he chuckles and backs the spear off just enough to make the puckered skin fill.

Then the sagamore barks another order and the braves file out slowly, each turning to take in the scene before they exit.

He points the spear at Margaret's loincloth, a signal for the eldest wife to remove her robe and untie the straps. Sabenoa backs off a couple of steps and points his spear at Richard. Richard hesitates. Might he rush the middle aged man? Useless. The distance established would allow for a thrust, probably at his stomach. Even if he overwhelmed Sabenoa, the guards would be on him. He drops his robe and unties the leather string of the loincloth. This he tosses a few feet away, a puny attempt at defiance that the eldest wife finds amusing. The other two join her snickering. He and Margaret face one another, two feet separating them.

Sabenoa says something soft and then, "Please." The eldest wife chuckles. No doubt she's witnessed the man's humor for years.

Richard looks into Margaret's saddened face. The end of the spear he now feels pushing against his left buttock. He moves closer to her.

"Kiss me. Just kiss me."

So he does, softly, beginning with her left cheek, her nose, her right cheek, and finally her mouth.

Sabenoa repeats, "Please." Softly. Sweetly.

Richard's left arm wraps around Margaret's shoulder, his right her waist.

"What do you want me to do?" He asks into her ear.

"We have no choice." Her head rests against his shoulder. "Can you forget they are here?"

"For god's sake, no."

"Try." She takes him by the hand then drops to her knees. It is in this position that Margaret takes charge. She stops after a little while. "I love you. Someday we will look back on this—and not be scared."

Richard's hands caress her hair that lies unusually flat and heavy with grease.

When he is ready, she lies on her back. Sabenoa joins his wives and comments about what takes place in front of them. By now the English have achieved a mutual remove. It doesn't matter what occurs outside their expanded and private universe. They don't even hurry.

And so when they recover, both lying on the pelt, it takes a few moments to acknowledge the grunting occurring on the other side of the smoldering fire. The Lord of the Sagadahoc is evidently mimicking their choice of coitus. He is on top, the younger one prone, the eldest standing over and rubbing his back. The middle wife straddles the younger wife's face and kisses the husband.

The English couple watch, quite fascinated.

CHAPTER 75

September 24, 1607, Fort St. George
Action

Aperturbed President Gilbert stands in front of his silent council members. His emissary to Pemaquid has returned empty-handed. From what Robert Davies could understand from an elder, Skidwarres, Nahanada, even Lilly have traveled to the Penobscot to confer with Bessabez. Their return, he asked? He could not decipher the answer. From the old native's face and raised shoulders Davies read, "I don't know." Whether he knew of Richard and Margaret's whereabouts, Davies couldn't tell.

Gilbert feels both stymied and energized. His troops, Captain Davis reports, are pulling at their confinement. Every day is a reminder of the approaching fall. If he is ever to establish dominance of the Sagadahoc, it must be now. Richard's disappearance troubles Gilbert on two accounts. The man was the likely interim leader. His year's experience, his good judgment, his relationship with Skidwarres, and not incidentally, his family connection were all valuable. And as different as they were in character, a friendship had grown between them.

"It is now—or maybe never. We must attack."

"Here, here!" Those around the table tapped enthusiastically.

"We will sail tomorrow. The tide will be fortuitous early in the morning. Twenty soldiers will remain at the fort, along with trained men—some, as we know, are more accurate with the musket than the troops. Most of the cannon will remain. The four larger cannon on the *Mary and John*, plus the smaller ones on the *Virginia*, provide twice the firepower we had on our last caper. We make no offers. This time we fire away. We land. We destroy."

"What of Seymour and his bride. What if Sabenoa has them?"

"Yes, yes. We've discussed this."

"Yes, sir," interjects Robert Davies, "but as for a plan, we have none—sir."

"Yes, damn it to hell! I repeat myself. They have either been killed or captured. Beyond that, we know nothing. What I do know is that we will not hide behind stone and mud. We will take the fight to them. We will give them a taste of English warfare. If we are lucky, we will face the dilemma over a living Seymour. Are there any final questions, objections?"

All around the table are silent. In fact, the plan, discussed over and over again, seems the best course. One suggestion was that a small search party should precede the ships by one day. But who would lead this? Gilbert trusted nobody with this ticklish tactic, except himself. At best, they would hide out around the perimeter of the village and gather information. What were the chances they could rescue one or both, if they were held separately? If they were there at all? Besides, an advance party would have a high probability of being captured. Gilbert knows he himself must direct operations from the ship and then on the ground.

On the chance Seymour and his wife are prisoners, Gilbert orders ten troops be trained for a rescue, once they had enough information.

Negotiations for Seymour's release might arise, if Sabenoa was holding them. Gilbert would face that prospect when and if it occurred.

"All right, gentlemen, prepare for tomorrow."

CHAPTER 76

September 28, 1608, Sabenoa's Village
Reunion

Before sunrise a spent Sabenoa finds the energy to sit up on his rug. The youngest wife offers him a robe and drink from his jug. He looks over at the two English.

Over the past few hours, Richard remained awake while Margaret slept lightly. He conjured up conversations he'd had in London over ale and wine. Friends spoke of the Romans and their debaucheries, their vomitoriums and orgies. And, of course, the French. His comrades assured him it was commonplace for the French to entertain themselves by watching others fornicate, including beasts—they being the French. Even in London such entertainment existed, outlandish sex apparently as universal as facial expressions. What next, Richard wondered.

Sabenoa called for the guards to escort the English back to their respective huts, but not until the couple had kissed and said a proper goodnight.

With the sun well over the horizon, Richard sat alone eating wild rice and fresh fish. On previous mornings at this time, he has found himself in the fields. Was he being rewarded for a job well done? Would he see Margaret today? What did Sabenoa plan? What of Skidwarres, Gilbert?

The two guards outside began talking, but not just to each other. Before it dawns on him who it is, Skidwarres is in the hut.

Richard grabs his friend around the shoulders and shakes. "My God, man, it's good to see you. It's about time."

"It is you, Richard, who worships time." It is Skidwarres turn to hold Richard by the shoulders. "Are you injured? Margaret?"

"My backside ran into a spear last night and my sense of propriety has been dashed—for other reasons. Margaret is nearby. I can't say that for Dancer and Breeze."

"Yes, I hear. I am sorry. Woboz is a fool. Richard, Sabenoa has allowed me to see you and Margaret. I am camped across the bay. Nahanada is here, and Lilly is with us. But I am not the only one who has come. Two ships have been sighted. Sabenoa is making preparations. Guards will take you where you will be safe. I will attempt to speak to Gilbert. But I must be quick."

Skidwarres continues, "I will inform Margaret." But as he turns to leave, three guards enter and grab him. They force his arms behind his back and tie them. A complaint and an attempt at an explanation result in a blow to the head with a large bow. Skidwarres goes to one knee, dazed.

CHAPTER 77

September 28, 1608, Sabenoa's Village
Engagement

By midday the Mary and John and the Virginia have passed through the narrow entrance to the Quabacook. Gilbert assumes his arrival is no secret. In fact, sentinels watched as far as five miles down the Sagadahoc from the village. From a chain of shouted alarms, Sabenoa knew of the impending attack two hours before the ship's arrival. This allowed him time to send a messenger with instructions to the young warriors on the Androscoggin island and to evacuate the women and children to a hill overlooking the village and bay.

Sabenoa and the elder, Kasko, developed a plan. The bulk of the young warriors from the island would take to fifteen canoes and congregate close to his village, but remain out of sight, up a creek, ready to attack when and if commanded. Sabenoa's braves would be positioned in two locations. Twenty were to hide in a small ravine covered by bayberry. The ships then might be in range of their larger bows. Forty would wait close to the beach, behind the tree line. They'd be well positioned to slaughter any English who might attempt a landing.

A third party of twenty from the island, led by Woboz, was immediately ordered to head south, reversing the trip taken with the abducted English. The same tide the English ships rode upriver on the Sagadahoc, they would conveniently take down on the smaller river. They would arrive at the beach near the fort by nightfall. This time fewer English would be defending it.

Sabenoa, Kasko, even Nahanada, who had eventually been consulted, hoped the plan would create a trap. Skidwarres could not be entirely trusted, but he, too, was informed, and when the ships were in sight, he would visit them under a white flag. His message: an attack would assure his English prisoners' death or torture. Skidwarres should also promise Gilbert that if he didn't leave, he, the Lord of the Sagadahoc would attack the fort with many, many braves. All the English would die.

Gilbert spoke again to his men on the deck of the *Mary and John*, the *Virginia* just yards away. All could hear his authoritative voice. "It is not complicated, men. We overwhelm them with cannon. We make them shit with fear. Then we eliminate what's left with musket fire. And finally the sword. Our purpose is simple: we destroy. We let them know this river belongs to the English."

If they held Seymour captive, he expected they would let him know. He was sure of this. The chances Seymour and his wife might be hit—he'd just have to take those odds—he thought them low. Gilbert would use his wit to finesse any negotiations, if it came to that. What else might he do? If he landed a party to ask about Seymour, they might be killed— the natives didn't play by the rules. Waiting gave the advantage to the savages. Commanders make difficult decisions under pressure. That's what he would do.

"Do your job, men."

The two ships move slowly to within two hundred yards of shore. The *Mary and John* drops the fore anchor, waits for the ship to adjust so her starboard side faces land, making a broadside possible, and then drops an aft anchor. A shallow draft and a critical breeze, but one typical of fall, allows the *Virginia* to sail in closer. With her smaller cannon from this position, she could pound the village, as well as help provide cover for the landing. No native emissary is in sight.

While the various native groups find their positions, Sabenoa, Kasko, and Nahanada wait outside the ceremonial hut for Skidwarres' return. He has been told to make his visits brief. Now all three consider it a mistake that they conceded to Skidwarres' request; rather he should have immediately launched a canoe in order to approach the ships. The English have arrived sooner than expected. Already they are positioning themselves to attack.

"Nahanada," Sabenoa orders and then points to one of the braves who is guarding the sagamore. "Go with him, Nahanada. Find Skidwarres. What trick is he playing?"

It takes longer than expected to locate Skidwarres, Richard, and

Margaret, who are all shackled and being led slowly to safety. The Mawooshen is untied and returns with Nahanada, while the two English are led in the opposite direction.

Sabenoa stares at the purple lump. Had the guard who cracked Skidwarres misunderstood instructions, or was he part of a faction within his village that did not trust anyone from the Pemaquid? This vocal group wished to fight and not talk. In either case the delay turns crucial.

"Skidwarres," Nahanada instructs, "make for the beach, quickly."

Minutes later the first fuselage thunders.

The cannoneers have discussed their position and feel confident they can calibrate based on previous success. They are correct. Volley after volley rip into the light structures. Within twenty minutes, dozens of huts lie in a heap of bark and rawhide. Some are burning after falling on hot embers.

The *Virginia* adjusts her position with a second anchor. Because they are closer to the village, they can take aim at the large meeting house. It represents the community and so carries more psychological weight. Those on the *Virginia* initially notice a few men standing and talking, but after the first firing, they have disappeared.

Intent and enthusiastic over their effective marksmanship, the crew and artillery men of the *Virginia* at first do not see the flotilla of canoes advancing from their hiding place. The elders insisted these braves, so ready to purify their land, not announce their attack with war cries. As a result, forty-five arrows take to the air, shot from the three archers standing in each of the fifteen boats. They sail high and then plummet nearly straight down, silent until too late. Most fall in the water. A few stick to the deck or poke holes in sails. Two find their mark: one penetrates deep into a crew member's shoulder. Another cannoneer, on his stomach trying to free a small cannon wheel, is pinned to the deck by an arrow that punctures his stomach.

Since her christening, Robert Davies has felt partial toward this first ship ever built by the English in the New World. She points well, is quick at the helm and seaworthy for such a modest craft. In every regard her construction shows the expertise put into her. And she is comely. For these reasons, he'd insisted on being the *Virginia*'s skipper.

Now, in an instant, Davies realizes that what had been an uncontested offensive maneuver has become, in a blink of the eye, a defensive matter. With his unsheathed sword, he rushes to the stern and cuts the anchor.

The *Virginia* swings into the breeze. In so doing she allows the cannon a shot at the oncoming canoes. Because the *Virginia* is anchored between the canoes' attack and the *Mary and John*, Gilbert decides it is more important to maintain his position. The *Virginia* must defend herself.

Davies orders ten men to quickly retrieve their loaded weapons; ten muskets against forty-five archers approximately a hundred yards off, and advancing quickly. With the exception of one volley that topples a standing brave into the water, the shots land short.

The next onslaught of arrows aimed at the *Virginia* arrives with less of an arch. This time all seek cover behind the railing or the mast; a few duck down to the hold. All remain untouched. A few strays follow and then more every second or so.

The second round of musket fire from the *Virginia* proves more effective. One canoe overturns. A paddler in another slumps over. Yet the arrows keep coming.

The canoes narrow the gap. Davies assumes they plan to board for hand-to-hand combat. He commands the three three-pound cannon to hold their fire until the canoes are within fifty yards. The men are told to stay in place. Two soldiers take arrows, both flesh wounds. One with an arrow lodged in his shoulder readies to light one cannon with a ball, another with an arrow in his backside loads grapeshot.

Davies bellows, "Fire!" The four small cannon roar. One skipping ball upends two canoes. The occupants are thrown helter-skelter into the water and the air. Grapeshot tears into another two, injuring or killing three and sinking both craft. The remaining canoes slow their advance. The smaller bark of musket fire continues; then the four small cannon erupt again. Two more canoes splinter. Men on the *Virginia* can see one archer's head explode from grapeshot. The men on the *Virginia*, as well as those on the *Mary and John*, watch the braves fish their comrades out of the water, then reverse course. "Fire again," orders Davies. A ball slices another canoe in half, this one, unlike the others, had not yet turned tail. From the beach a soldier sees a single brave begin pushing a canoe from the beach to the water's edge. "Devil take him," he says and fires. The native disappears in the bush.

Aboard the *Mary and John*, men wait in breastplates and helmets, muskets in hands, swords at their sides. Sabenoa, Kasko, and Nahanada watch from a strategic position behind a granite outcropping. The English scramble over the railing and down into three waiting longboats.

Sabenoa gives out a wild screech. Instantly braves rush from the tree cover to the open beach. They release their arrows, turn, and retreat. Others pop up from behind rocks. Because of their closer range, their arrows reach the *Mary and John* with more accuracy.

The English are barely established in the boats when the arrows rain down. Gilbert had not counted on Sabenoa being so prepared, though of course some resistance was inevitable. Shields save most soldiers from injury, and most arrows land in the water. The *Virginia* has yet to fully reposition herself to ward off the attack. The *Mary and John's* own cannon are late to respond. The natives' attack takes only seconds. By the time the balls and grapeshot plow into the trees, the braves have vanished.

After this first cannonade directed at the woods, a few emboldened braves rush to the beach and take more careful aim. The English find themselves in disarray. Three soldiers fall wounded; another grips an arrow which has penetrated his throat. He sits on the seat of the boat, both hands holding the shaft, coughing blood.

The five six-pounders on the *Mary and John* send a second volley into the woods, more from frustration than battle savvy. One shot offers up a soggy thud when it lands in a bog. Two braves are immediately killed from grapeshot wounds. Others pull out splinters from the splattered oak and pine. The group closest to the ship vanishes beyond the rocks. Gilbert commands the longboats to return to the protection of the *Mary and John*. The initial plan to surprise and overwhelm has failed.

Out of the line of fire, Richard, Margaret, Sabenoa's third wife, and four guards are watching. After attempting to launch a canoe and watching a musket ball land three feet away, Skidwarres joins them.

"Richard," Margaret says with her typical wry observation, "Your cousin must place great value on our lives."

"Yes, well, in his defense, he isn't sure we're here. I don't know. He's been pushed, the murdered fishermen, fire, us. Perhaps you will get a chance to give him your appraisal."

"He should hope not. Cannonade first. Seek information later."

Smoke from the cannon rises, spreads, and dissipates in the light breeze. Both sides take stock. Each has used its favored tactic to some effect. The English cannon have destroyed much of the village. Obviously some savages were injured, others killed, Gilbert surmised. It was impossible to tell how many. On the other side of the ledger, the natives' scouting allowed the women and children to evacuate. The surprise counterattacks checked the English—at least temporarily. Their arrows also found targets, one likely fatal.

Gilbert leans over the rail to his longboats filled with soldiers, now on the bayside of the ship and so protected from stray arrows. "Remain there," he commands, "until further ordered." The next move seems obvious. He sends a messenger to Davies in one of the longboats. A few arrows sail out of the woods to splash feet away in the water. They are answered by muskets fire, equally useless. The messenger arrives safely. Soon the *Virginia* pulls anchor and begins to move closer to the *Mary and John*, where she will be in better position to fire into the woods and support a second landing attempt. The proximity of the two ships will allow Gilbert and Davies to communicate by shouting.

Sabenoa watches and remains uncharacteristically close-mouthed. Then he grunts and begins giving orders. The women, children, and elderly must move further inland. The men from the Androscoggin island should join his own braves. They will continue to conceal themselves behind trees and fight when the English land, or retreat if the cannon fire becomes too strong. Then advance again. If the soldiers land, all the better. Cannon fire would have to stop for fear of hitting the enemy's own men.

"Get me Skidwarres," Sabenoa commands of one brave. He looks to Nahanada. "Your Skidwarres, bring him here. He will paddle again to the English, no?"

The first mate alerts Gilbert. They squint. The glare off the water in the early afternoon makes it difficult to be sure, but it looks like a lone native standing in a canoe, waving something white. Yes, Gilbert is sure: "Skidwarres."

"That son of a whore! He's here. Not at the Penobscot," Gilbert mumbles to no one in particular.

Those on ship who'd weathered the winter know Skidwarres. A few others hurl insults. "The savage is flying good English linen, fancy that." That was correct. A bartered English shirt substitutes as a flag.

Skidwarres pulls himself over the rail and stands facing a red-faced Gilbert. "Greetings, Admiral." Skidwarres offers his hand.

"Greetings?" Gilbert keeps his hands on his hips. "You here. Might have guessed you'd be involved. Never trusted you."

"I am here because Richard sent a message. He needed my help."

"Is that right? He is here?" Gilbert tone remains belligerent.

"Yes, captured by a group wishing you ill. They were persuaded not to kill them. Sabenoa is keeping them prisoner."

"Then I want them on this ship immediately—or I'll blow the village and your crazy friend Sabenoa to hell."

"Admiral, I speak for the man. I believe he can be reasonable."

"Then speak."

"Sabenoa will return Richard and Margaret. Then you will sail back to the fort. You will make no more attacks."

"You tell him to go to hell. You tell him no more attacks because he will move his village miles to the west. If not, I'll land and eliminate him. I will do it now. If he returns, I will attack again. Tell him to move, far away. This river, this bay, and this land are now English." As soon as he has spoken, Gilbert realizes his demands are preposterous, under the circumstances.

"Admiral, Richard and Margaret are there." Skidwarres points to two figures walking out of the woods, onto the beach, clad in native loincloths and deerskin shirts—light brown skin, Richard's brown hair and Margaret's strawberry curls.

"Admiral, Seymour is my friend. I say this only because Sabenoa says it. If the ships do not leave by sunset, he will kill them."

"Then I will take revenge by killing his women and children." Gilbert checks himself as frustration wells within him.

"Admiral, he also wants to inform you, in the woods wait more than two hundred braves."

"You tell him the English have thousands of braves. Tell him we piss on backward heathens. Wait here, right here!"

Gilbert breaks from the small group standing with Skidwarres, strides to his cabin, opens the door, and ducks through, slamming it. He heads straight to his wine cabinet and uncorks a bottle of Bordeaux, gulps a mouthful, then nearly smashes it against a bulkhead. He stops himself and looks at his crooked arm. He feels its tension and checks himself. He places the bottle carefully on the captain's table. Gilbert stands, hands on the tabletop, steadying and calming himself. He'd heard of his father's famous rages. After he was lost at sea, stories filtered down: frustration led to binges, followed by recklessness. Since becoming an officer, Raleigh Gilbert had sworn he'd never succumb to this character flaw. Yet here it was, an insidious inheritance pushing him.

Gilbert sits. He has to think. He'd told himself, hadn't he, that a commander had to make decisions on the fly. They shouldn't be stupid ones. Another swig, a small one would at least calm his nerves. What are the facts? That's what's important. The facts: his attack was at least temporarily halted. The savages held hostages, important ones. Would Sabenoa make good his threat to kill them? Probably. Seymour's death would bring an inquiry. He and his bride were gentry. How would he explain it? Already a few men were injured, the one with an arrow in the neck still alive, but probably not for long. How had it come to this blurred moment? Had he not won his rightful place, now the clear leader of the Northern New World—only to be stymied by savages with blue hair? And his brother's death, upending his single-minded mission, now leaving him imagining affluence, prominence, women, and a return to his beloved uncle. He the adventurer, he with his father's mantle, he with his Uncle Walter Raleigh's pride? He has to focus. Now, right now, he must collect himself.

Why not agree? Get Seymour and his wife safe on board. Why be bound to keep his word with a non-Christian savage? Isn't that the only decision, at least for the moment? Commanding is like a sword duel. Each thrust or parry creates an entirely new dynamic. Gilbert slams his hand on the table, pleased with himself. Why had this not been immediately clear? He congratulates himself with another small mouthful of that wonderful French Bordeaux. He adjusts his hat and readies himself to inform Skidwarres—the proposal agreed to, along with the promise on Sabenoa's part that harassment and kidnapping will cease. All empty words anyway. Seymour and Margaret on deck would be real.

When Gilbert pushes himself through the doorway, Skidwarres stands just outside waiting. "Admiral, a talk with you alone please?"

Gilbert agrees. "All right, I am prepared to talk." He reenters the cabin while beckoning Skidwarres to follow. Gilbert sits and point to the chair across the table with the uncorked bottle in the middle.

"A drink?"

Skidwarres shakes his head. "I have more to say. Sabenoa is not my friend. If you agree, Richard and Margaret will be returned, but he will hold Lilly and me hostage—at least for a while, until he is satisfied you will keep your word. I and she, we agree to this. He says if you attack, Lilly and I will die. I do not know how serious he is. But men in his village wish to kill. We might be—convenient."

"I don't give a damn..." Gilbert cuts himself short.

"She is my wife."

"Yes, I hear. Charming."

"And something else. Your friend, Sipsis, she wants to return to the fort with you. She tells me you have promised her she can travel to your lands."

Gilbert pushes his chair back. Sipsis? How long had it been since she left? What a mercurial woman. One never knew. "I did say that." He looks at Skidwarres, this time less belligerently. He has tired of Dorothy. Sipsis was always a wild challenge

"Skidwarres, if Sabenoa agrees to no more raids, I agree. But if he changes his mind, tell him I will blow his village—what's left of it—to hell. Tell him I want Seymour and his wife here immediately—and Sipsis." The thought of her activates another strand of motivation, though Gilbert is unaware of it at the time. "Otherwise I will begin more bombardment."

"Sabenoa will agree."

Gilbert rises and reaches across the table to shake Skidwarres' hand. The admiral feels his words have established a degree of authority, maybe even supremacy. Skidwarres hesitates. He stares the admiral in the eyes, just long enough to let the man know he feels disdain. Skidwarres then reaches out to reciprocate.

Skidwarres' canoe beaches some minutes before the longboat. He hasn't told Richard and Margaret the details of Sabenoa's demands. They stand silent and anxious—until they see Skidwarres' smile when he jumps out of the canoe into water up to his shins.

"It is good. Gilbert agrees. You will be safe—on ship. He—and Sabenoa—agree, no more attacks."

They have both been re-shackled, hands bound, but that does not stop Margaret from shuffling to meet Skidwarres, then throwing her body against his before he is out of the water. Skidwarres holds her lest she fall in. For the second time he cuts both of them free.

The two men embrace, then stand back to look at one another.

"Is Lilly safe?" Richard asks. "I notice they bound her."

"Sabenoa plays his games. If Gilbert doesn't keep his word, he says she dies. I too. I think not. He will not do this. She is my wife. He will not touch her. It would make for much hostility. Even he honors Bessabez— most of the time. But Richard, help Gilbert keep his word."

"Yes, of course."

The longboat's bow crunches against the sand. The six rowers and the first mate are waiting. Skidwarres urges them all, "You go now. Go before the Lord of the Sagadahoc changes his mind. We will meet again before winter. This year our garden will have much to offer."

Margaret is now able to hold Skidwarres. She rises on her tiptoes and kisses him on the cheek. "Thank you."

"We will meet again soon, my friend," Richard adds, helping Margaret over the longboat's gunwales. Richard realizes neither of them has thoroughly learned to negotiate modesty while wearing loincloths.

"One moment," adds Skidwarres. All turn to see Sipsis running from the tree line, down the beach toward them. She stops short in front of Skidwarres

"Skidwarres," Sipsis says breathlessly in her native tongue, "I am lucky. Woboz has gone to the fort now. If he were here, he would kill me. I must hurry. Who knows what Sabenoa thinks of me?"

"Then leave."

"Skidwarres," replies Sipsis, turning her head as she enters the water to board. She says in Algonquin, "Do I trust myself?"

"Speak to Richard. He is the one who knows of the future." He looks to Richard and changes to English. "Tell Sipsis about destiny, her destiny. She wants to know about the future."

As they pull away from shore, waving, Margaret is nearly overcome by a deep longing to sail home to England, not merely downriver to the fort. Fear remains, overlaid by a deeper humiliation. Now feeling the safety of the approaching ship, she wants to disappear. This she keeps to herself. Richard's arm around her helps.

The battle has brought its own rewards. It is no small matter that the combatants faced death. Many learned that purpose can override fear. The combat ended without any significant strategic outcome, but it was not meaningless. The men would carry the story to their deaths. Grandchildren would listen with their mouths open. Confirmation of manhood is no small matter. Such were the mostly unspoken sentiments on both sides, as they helped the wounded and prepared the dead—three English and six natives—for burial.

The English ships raise anchor and ride the last of the outgoing tide out of the bay and five miles downriver, before the tide reverses and the wind dies. They anchor and wait for the next turning, six hours and some minutes later.

With the ships out of sight, Sabenoa recalls the evacuees to survey the damage. Thirty huts ruined. It would take days to secure the bark and rebuild. Under the debris of the community hut, a teenager finds the splintered remains of the king's throne, putting its occupant in a foul mood. Of the six dead braves, one came from Nahanada's village, two from the west, and three from Sabenoa's. Relatives for generations to come would question the Lord of the Sagadahoc's wisdom.

Following the dying of the light, while sitting above deck eating and drinking, those on the *Mary and John* and the *Virginia* hear a blast. All agree it came from the direction of the fort, more than ten miles away. It isn't thunder or cannon fire. Gilbert's mood turns sour with worry.

When, early the next morning, the ships reach the fort, he learns the most consequential causality of the battle took place within the walls of the fort. This time, when the small group under Woboz' leadership let loose their fiery arrows, two landed on the roof of the ammunition warehouse. Reduced in manpower, the fire brigade could not keep up. The explosion blew the building to smithereens, thereby consuming half of the gunpowder in store. The natives had no clue what they had done, only that the monstrous explosion must have been caused by the wrath of some god or monster. They retreated to their canoes and departed as quickly as possible in the dark.

CHAPTER 78

September 29, 1608, Fort St. George
Aftermath

Gilbert and the other members of the council survey the remains of the demolished storehouse. Over fifty percent of the fort's gunpowder has gone up in smoke and noise. He isn't sure how to calculate the loss, except to say it is "critical." Members of the council request a meeting, but Gilbert insists they postpone it till later in the day. He needs time to think and to regain perspective through sleep.

Margaret lies on their bed, her face buried in a pillow, while Richard paces. Her strength, her pluck—as Richard describes her perpetual optimistic energy—seems to have been lost. Upon arriving on the ship, Richard asked Gilbert if they might repair to his cabin. "Of course," the admiral had said. He would be busy.

Within these confines, Margaret fell on the cabin's bunk and wept. Images kept plaguing her: Breeze's head on the stake, Sabenoa's oily finger. To no avail she kept telling herself to be thankful she hadn't been raped. On the cold wet bottom of the canoe, death had felt certain. For five days she had maintained her outward composure and sanity. Now both feel tenuous. Richard isn't at all sure how to help her. At first he sits on the bunk and strokes her hair. She says, "Thank you," but her breakdown apparently needs to take its course.

Now in their bedroom off the chapel, Margaret is silent.

Richard doesn't want to leave her alone. Besides, he, too, needs sleep. So rather than pace or struggle for words of consolation, he finally lies next to her on his back. His hand touches hers. Blue, green, and red light flows into the room through the stained glass window. Finally, both sleep.

In his dream he sits alone in the Middle Temple Hall. Colored light filters through the window to the floor, as if an artist had brushed the air. He had often been drawn to this space. It did not offer the grandeur of the cathedral at Essex, a space he knew well, and certainly not Westminster's immense authority. Middle Temple Hall conveyed something both intimate and substantial. The oak walls exuded warmth. The shields of so many long-ago knights, his family coat of arms among them, spoke of continuity and honor. There Richard felt a oneness with his surroundings that he found nowhere else, not even at his father's home, or on Dancer, or in Margaret's arms. It was different, though similar. The boundaries of his skin sometimes blurred with the walls and the colored air. It felt like a rendition of love, something perhaps spiritual. The dream conveyed remnants of these experiences—and something else. In the dream the space became eerie. Cracks in the wall multiplied. Pieces of ceiling plaster fell. He felt the building vibrate, then slowly slide toward and inevitably into the Thames, as a ship might be launched on her ways. As Temple Hall shivered and slid, a rafter crashed to the floor.

Richard wakes drenched in sweat. Margaret is stroking his brow with one of her linen handkerchiefs. In a state between sleep and wakefulness, Richard recounts his dream.

"Does it mean anything, do you think?" Margaret asks.

Richard waits to regain more consciousness. "If Plato, Bacon, and Montaigne are correct, yes. It feels like dissolution, something falling apart. I did so like that space." He sits up. "You shouldn't have come with me to this wild land. Look what I've put you through. I need to take you back."

"I chose to come. You didn't force me. But why did you say 'You did so like the space.' It sounds like it is no more. Gone."

Richard doesn't answer her question. "You didn't know what to expect. I did, should have."

"Richard, maybe it is you who wants to return. Maybe home is 'substantial.' Isn't that the word you used?"

"Yes, but I imagined myself living in both worlds. Do you suppose that is possible?"

"I don't know? Maybe?" Margaret rises. "I'll get you some tea. I started the fire while you slept."

While they sip tea in silence, there is an expected knock on the door. Richard goes into the study from their bedroom and returns within the minute. "Gilbert will meet with the council momentarily. We shall see." Richard put on the jacket given to him by Skidwarres. It's made of beaver, turned so the fur is its lining. The fog blowing in off the sea brings a damp chill.

"Richard?" Margaret sits on the edge of their bed. He joins her, steam still rising from his mug. "May I come? I will be all right. Already after sleeping I feel—I don't know. I'll be all right. You weren't rash to bring me. You saw—you see a future."

"I don't know what I see. I suppose I will listen. I don't know how much damage the fire caused. Yes, why don't you come?"

"No, on second thought, while you are conferring, I'll go to the mess and bring food back. I want to cook for you and be alone."

With his left hand, he brings the tea to his lips. His right holds Margaret's shoulder. He looked at the red shackle marks around her wrists. "Does it hurt?"

"No. I don't feel it." This is not true, but she does not want to dwell on it. They turn toward one another and touch their tea-warmed, moist lips together softly, and hold there, not pushing against one another, rather delicate as a butterfly might alight, fold its wings, briefly rest, then flutter off—an antidote to the carnal. Richard gets up. "It might be a long meeting."

CHAPTER 79

September 29, 1608, Evening
Fate of the Fort

A s with so many groups that meet periodically, each member of the council silently claimed a location around the table. The pattern had been established before the table existed. At first they sat in a circle on log stools, then in Gilbert's house around the long rectangular wood slab table on chairs. The pattern remained the same. Gilbert occupied one end, Popham the other. After Popham's death, his seat remained unoccupied, an unspoken memorial.

When Richard arrives, all are seated. Everyone has been discussing his ordeal, or at least the remnants of information they'd heard. With Gilbert's lead, all rise. In unison they offer their respect, "Here, here."

Gilbert points to the other end of the table, the Popham end. He says to Richard, "Sit, sit. Sit there, in the place of honor." Richard raises his hand to decline. Again Gilbert insists, "No, no." Captain Davis picks up Richard's chair and slides it against the wall.

"All right. Thank you, but just for now." All sit down again.

"Gentlemen," begins Gilbert, "we must decide the fate of the fort tonight. And Seymour, it is right and proper that you sit in Popham's place, for it is you who also must decide. We all must decide. Your decision, however, is crucial."

Richard—who less than half an hour earlier had lain between dreams and wakefulness—nods, his brain racing, trying to grasp the situation.

Gilbert continues, "I have spoken with most of you individually, if only briefly. I have asked for your judgment. Here are the facts. Our bombardment destroyed much of Sabenoa's village. We killed several of his braves. How many, we don't know. With no abduction, we would have routed them, killed many more." As Richard hears this, the implication seems to be he is at fault. "They are now fully aware of our destructive power—and our intent to occupy the area. If the English were a worry before, we are now understood for what we are, fearsome."

From Seymour's vantage point, so far the assessment sounds possible but not probable. Gilbert appears still not to grasp the native's strategy of attack and retreat. It sounds as if Gilbert imagined a final battle on an open field, instead of an extended game of lethal hide-and-seek. Nonetheless, the cannon and musket spoke an impressive language. He had seen that first hand.

Gilbert continues, "The enemy's lucky shot destroyed a good deal of our powder. We have two other troves, but they eliminated about half. We have enough to defend ourselves. An assault is unlikely. But, in any event, we have enough to defend ourselves. Do you agree, Captain Davis?"

"Enough to defend ourselves? Probably, yes. The addition of the smaller cannon gives us an advantage we didn't have before. They are maneuverable. Six more cannon with grapeshot, very messy."

"And what of the morale of the troops? What is your assessment?" asks Gilbert.

"President Gilbert, gentlemen," Davis replies, "we have just returned from an engagement. Three dead, one seriously wounded, others with cuts and bruises. They are ready to fight again, those who remained at the fort, even more so."

Gilbert intervenes. "And what if asked to remain the winter without a fight? They were fighting in part for land. We cannot take the fight to them without more powder. Better yet more men. Those who wintered here—many, some are unwilling to repeat it?"

"A reasonable assessment," answers Davis.

"As you all know," Gilbert continues, "I must return to put my estate in order. I will also continue the hard work of finding financial support, to continue Seymour and Gorges' present efforts."

"What of the food supplies?" Davis asked.

"We are in better shape than last year," Gilbert replies, "depending on how many remain. But we have more provisions, and the Pemaquid village, they are able to barter some food. That is true, is it not Seymour?"

"I believe so."

"Gentlemen." Gilbert clears his throat. "In my absence, I recommend that Seymour take on presidential duties. Though, of course, Seymour himself has not decided." Gilbert, with a small flourish of the hand, directs all toward Seymour.

Perhaps it was inevitable. Richard's father, Francis Bacon, as well as Sir Ferdinando Gorges, and the other backers—all seemed to assume Seymour's personal commitment to the Northern Virginia Company. Margaret herself had caught his newfound passion, even in the face of Bacon and Cecil's assessment that King James had only negligible interest in exploration and settlement in the New World. Financial backers wanted short-term gains. The wedding and the optimism that followed had overshadowed his and Gorges' mere modest success. He had convinced himself that willpower was the essential ingredient. History was a matter of willpower. Then Dancer's head on a stake, Margaret's attempted—no, possible—defilement at the hands of Sabenoa. Richard was still not sure what really happened. And the bloodshed. His will, he had considered while working in the fields under the guard of natives, might only be applied to himself. Everything else appeared out of his control. Grubbing in the field with the wooden hoe, Richard had thought, "I can do only what I can do."

Before his travels to the New World, Richard had thought of himself as making decisions based essentially on facts and well-honed emotions. Now with solemn, critical eyes on him, he simply wants to turn and walk out the door. He wants to walk and think, then return with his thoughts organized. Instead he begins talking. Whatever he needs to say is still swirling about, but he has no choice. He isn't confident he knows how to express it. He isn't really sure what he will say; only that it would be honest and therefore make sense, and that he will do his best to live with the consequences.

He takes in a breath. "Gentlemen..." Then he lets a moment hang in the air. He decides to stand. It might give him extra strength. "Margaret and I will return with President Gilbert." He stops again and watches the others look about. Gilbert stares. "I speak from the heart as well as the mind. My mind says our country is not ready to stand behind us. King James has minimal interest. It is true the Jamestown colony is surviving, but only tenuously. Many lives have been lost. From what I hear, our buildings and fortifications are stronger. We are better organized, better armed, more wisely led." Seymour turns to Gilbert, to the captain of the fort, to Davis. "But we are here on the other side of the world, nearly alone. As we know, tides are crucial for sailing. Our tide is ebbing. It is a power beyond us. That is how I see it."

Gilbert has settled back in his seat, his chin in his hands. He doesn't look perturbed.

"I also have a wife. Her abduction frightened her greatly—to the core, I believe. I'm sure you can imagine. To remain here at the mercy of the winter, with reduced gunpowder, with relations gone sour with some of the natives, that is more than I can ask of her. I didn't anticipate such brutality. That was stupid of me. Brutality is a fact of life. I'm her husband. I must protect her." Two of the married members nod their heads, though they haven't seen their families in a year. "And I do not wish for her to leave without me."

"I must speak of a final reason," Richard continues. "It is pure and simple, and I think it speaks for many of us, from President Gilbert to the gunners and the cooks. We haven't spoken of this openly. It would undermine our mission, but it is undeniable. I miss my homeland. I miss it in essential and in tiny ways. Would I appreciate my position, my future, the fort's future, differently if our tide was rising? Could I be wrong? Perhaps, but I must decline Gilbert's offer to become interim president. I will sail with him. Besides, I may not be suited for such a job. I am sure others around this table are better qualified." Taking a standing position had indeed allowed him more authority—the body leading the mind—how interesting.

Gilbert looks around the table trying to ascertain the mood. For the moment all keep their appraisal of Seymour to themselves. Most have learned in their various professions to forestall any sign of emotion. "Captain Davis, your thoughts?"

"I appreciate Seymour's candor. But I am much less qualified than he for the presidency. I captain a fort. My abilities are circumscribed."

"Well..." Gilbert decides to rise. "We have come to a decision. We will all sail, but never will we forget. This fort will be a monument to English pride and power. We will return. We endured a winter. By god, we made ourselves known. We will return."

The tone of Gilbert's delivery suggests relief. Considering a return in the future provides balance. He had already worked out in his head another speech in support of those who would stay and await his return in the spring. In the process of composing two speeches, his actual wishes had tilted from one outcome to the other. "Inform the men tonight. I will spend tomorrow morning with them. We will meet tomorrow afternoon. We will plan to embark within a week. The weather will turn foul soon enough. Extra beer rations tonight for everyone."

Richard waits for all to depart, so as to say goodnight and to hear if Gilbert has anything personal to impart. He does.

"Richard, Cousin, from the beginning you have been our preacher. So you were tonight."

"Raleigh, I hope I haven't disappointed you greatly. I think I have myself. My speech, it was not a heroic one. I didn't sound like Sir Walter. No empire is built on wanting to protect your wife or wishing to listen to fine music and live in comfort."

"Cousin, these sentiments are not foreign. We will return, and, as you say, wait for the tide to turn. All of us are disappointed. But..."

"Yes, well said."

Sipsis appears in the doorway to Gilbert's private section. "Hello, Chaplain."

"Greetings, Sipsis. Once again, thank you. We remain so indebted."

"It appears, my dear," says Gilbert with a hand outstretched to her, "that we all will soon be practicing English in England."

Richard opens the door to his study to find a table set for two. Smells of sturgeon and onion fill the small room. Richard comes up behind Margaret while she is stirring the pot. He wraps his arms around her waist. He nuzzles and then kisses the back of her neck. "We sail soon." She doesn't turn, busy still with her work and not sure she wants to display the emotion filling her face. He holds her. She offers up a slight tremor, along with a sniffle of joy.

CHAPTER 80

October 1, 1608, Fort St. George
Tea Time

Soldiers and craftsmen receive the news with good cheer. The fort is bustling, the men thinking about the voyage, about England. At least it would be a change. A few of the new arrivals grumble how Gilbert must have his head up his ass, ordering them across the seas, only to send them back again weeks later. But even they tend to agree with the explanations provided personally by the admiral.

Quarters on the two ships will be cramped. Robert Davies chooses to captain the *Virginia* again. Even though her mere fifty-foot length made her more appropriate for offshore voyages than a transatlantic one, he has great faith in her. And due to Richard's fondness for Davies and the *Virginia*—which Richard felt pride in having a hand in building—he and Margaret found room below, where they began setting their hammocks within a rudimentary cabin, a cubby really, even smaller than the one shared with Skidwarres over fourteen months ago.

Disassembling the larger cannon and stowing them below decks on the *Mary and John* became the most time-consuming and cumbersome task. Haste led to carelessness, and one of the six-pounders toppled into the river. Meanwhile the smaller cannon would provide protection in case the natives became encouraged by what they might perceive as surrender.

In fact, Woboz and his small band never returned to their island in the Androscoggin after creating the earth-shaking boom. They camped on the high promenade a mile upriver, a station they'd occupied for some months. Four days after their imprisonment, Sabenoa had released Skidwarres and Lilly. Along with Nahanada and a few braves, they were camped across the river from the fort. They watched the fort's dismemberment. In the afternoon Skidwarres and Lilly paddle across alone.

The native and his English wife walk into the chapel and knock on the office door, the room Lilly knows so well. Margaret opens it amidst the bustle of packing. Richard hammers on a box designed for a cello. The lute, the one he purchased two months before, resides in the box in which it arrived. Margaret offers quick hugs. A dumbfounded Richard exclaims, "By God, man, I didn't think I was going to see you. That old bastard, he let you go?"

"He's mostly a trickster. Besides, Nahanada offered him another wife, young and pretty."

Lilly stands silently, considering the room she'd shared with Richard. Margaret realizes this fact. Lilly carries a large leather pouch slung across her shoulder. Its contents stir.

"Skidwarres and I, we have a gift for you. For both of you." She scoops out of the pouch a black, brown, and white ball of fur. "It's Stow's offspring with a small wolf. Richard, you saved Stow many months ago. Do you want him?" She hands the puppy to Margaret. She instinctively lifts the cross-breed up to her face and nuzzles it. The tail wags. Simultaneously her hearts warms, more so than in the past days.

"I think there's your answer." Richard nods to the tear sliding down Margaret's cheek.

Margaret wipes it away. "And you two. We can't take back much. Take what you want from the new room."

"No room for the bed." Lilly's tone goes quickly from sarcasm to genuine thankfulness. "But some pots, yes. Correct, Skidwarres?"

"Yes, pots."

"And pants?" Richard asks.

"And you, you still want me an Englishman?"

"A man of both worlds, no?" Richard means this to be taken seriously. "Are you sure you don't want to sail with us? And you, Lilly? Who knows when we will return?" Richard knows her answer.

"Richard, I am staying. He is my husband. Do I not look like a native?"

Richard is impressed. A small red triangular tattoo has been etched on her cheek. "I didn't mean to offend. You, too, are a woman of both worlds."

Lilly turns toward Margaret. "Are there any clothes you might want to leave? Warm ones."

"Yes, yes, by all means, let us look."

"Good," Richard says, "While you are looking, Skid and I will walk. I've been in here all morning. Only one more day to walk before we find ourselves cramped on board."

The two friends walk the well-worn path leading to the beach where the river meets the sea. Conversation does not come immediately. Except during Skidwarres' recent intervention, they have not spoken in weeks. Both are considering how much or how little needs to be said.

When they reach the beach, Richard breaks the silence. "Thank you, friend. Without your help, Margaret and I—we might still be Sabenoa's slaves—or killed by Gilbert."

Skidwarres nods. "Sabenoa is a strange man, but now happy, though his throne was destroyed by the cannon. He wanted Lilly to stay with him. He offered me two wives and Nahanada one. We promised him a young bride, soon."

"And now you have two wives..." Richard doesn't know how to finish this point.

"Yes, now Sokw and my daughter Nahnibssat and Lilly, we sit in the hut and speak English. Only in the hut. Others think us crazy. And I think of you."

"Because I am English or because I am crazy."

"Both." Their laughter has a familiar ring.

"Skidwarres, you are not unhappy we are sailing. Is that correct?"

They walk on the hard-packed sand, avoiding the light surf as it froths and is absorbed, leaving little bubbles. "No, I am happy for my people. Not for me. The young braves, they think you have been beaten. When you leave, they will celebrate their victory. Nahanada and I, we know you will come back. You Richard, maybe. Maybe Gilbert. If not, then others. You taught me a complicated word."

"Yes?"

"Inevitable."

"Ah, yes."

"Will you teach me something else."

"Yes?"

"The future...you speak about building a future. My people—you know, I said this before. The past is our future. But I, I see England. I think it is our future. Someday. But not your fort. Not now. That I think is good for my people."

"Yes. I'm sure."

"And now, I will tell you something I don't tell anybody. Not even Lilly."

Richard stops. "All right."

"If there was only me—no Sokw, no child, Lilly maybe— I would then ask you to take me with you. I want to see more. Maybe I could help build the future. But no, I will stay. I am that person who stays."

Richard and Skidwarres stand face to face. They become aware that the surf is crawling over their feet. "And I am that person who leaves."

"Richard." Skidwarres reaches into his small satchel with the periwinkle shells sewn on for decoration. He withdraws a necklace made of bird beaks, large Pileated Woodpecker beaks. "My father gave this to me. My grandfather gave it to him. You are aware of the great bird with his red top-feathers. There are many fine stories about this bird. In one a lonely, shy boys falls in love with a beautiful girl. He does not know what to say to her. A large woodpecker watches. The bird finds a hollowed-out stick. Through it he makes holes so the wind can create what the boy hears as magical music. He takes the flute and learns to play for his love, so without words, because of his playing, she falls in love. Now Richard, it is your necklace. So you will continue to play for your love."

"No Skid, I can't."

"You must. It is a gift."

In the distance they hear the four o'clock bell ring. It is tea time. This small nicety began soon after the ship arrived in late summer. Gilbert thought it preposterous. But soon all relished the fifteen-minute break. It felt familiar. Plus, the newly arrived women insisted on serving, as a way to get acquainted.

"All right, we will return to the chapel and have tea. And when we sail, we will leave you books, pots, and wool to indulge your English habits. And I will never forget your elegance, your generosity."

The shadow of fall darkens the fort. The natives will scavenge furniture, the remnants of the iron works, a trash heap of bottles, bones, broken pottery, empty barrels, a garden not entirely harvested, thirty structures. The shallop will go to Nahanada, along with a longboat. He, Skidwarres, and Lilly will remain camped across the river. Nahanada sends word to Kasko: there will be no hostilities, only the spectacle of ships setting sail, turning tail.

CHAPTER 81

October 5, 1608, On Board the Virginia
Mutual Goodbyes

After an early dinner, all board the two ships. The tide will take them out soon after sunrise. Many have toiled through the night preparing the hold.

With the new day and morning tea, the two ships continue to bustle. Soon the sails drop, lines are hauled and secured. Richard and Margaret stand on the *Virginia's* deck. They watch the lurid purple and orange sky and then the brilliant ball. It's too bright and overwhelming. They have to turn their heads away. Anchors crank.

The men and women on deck look straight ahead, as if England were in sight. Most are slow to realize that over a hundred natives are standing on the fort's walls, lined up single file. Some have wandered down to the beach, close enough to make out their facial expressions.

The sails fill with the light morning breeze. The tide is lazy. But it does send them seaward. A curtain of fog a few miles out to sea will burn off.

"Take heed, boys," yells one of the mates. The English turn around to face the fort's ramparts. Stationed on top the earthen rock walls, the braves as well as some women, all in a line, turn to address the ships with their backsides. Again, all together, they bend over and flip up their loincloths. A hundred or so ruddy asses—a salute. Those closer by at the shore's edge, do the same.

At first the English look on in wonderment. A few on the *Mary and John* stand on the railing, holding a shroud with one hand and with the other awkwardly lowering their pants to return the gesture. One soldier nearly loses his balance. Dorothy, Gilbert's former companion, never to be outdone, joins the men on the railing, bends over and whooshes up her dress, displaying a large white rump known and appreciated by a number of sailors and artisans. But it is a half-hearted reprisal. Most are too tired. Some feel the sting of insult. Smoke begins rising from the middle of the fort. Then flames flicker above the wall. The fort disappears behind the dune.

Richard and Margaret look on. "That's a sight—naked native asses and our work going up in smoke—we won't easily forget," says Richard.

"I think I'll try, though," Margaret ventures.

Behind them on the other bank comes a high-pitched scream, that of a woman, a war cry or a cry of mourning, it was difficult to tell. Standing on the bank next to Skidwarres, Lilly waves. She wears one of Margaret's hand-me-down dresses and a broad hat. She cups her hands to her mouth and offers up another high-pitched wail. Skidwarres stands next to her as the ships pass by. Between them, Stow sits, keenly watching.

As they ease out of the mouth of the river, Skidwarres raises a hand and keeps it aloft. Richard returns in kind. They stand like statues for long minutes.

A quiet sea widens between the *Virginia* and *The Mary and John*. "So much more agile in a light wind, she is, the *Virginia*," Richard comments.

"All your doing I'm sure, my dear. This may seem silly, but do you feel like playing, playing music? I haven't since...well, since the incident."

"They're packed, but if you wish. I can uncrate them. Better sooner than later."

A half hour later, Margaret is seated, cello resting between her thighs. Richard cradles his new lute. They are playing a William Byrd duet.

For the next seven weeks they will play as much as the weather permits. The *Virginia*, alone in the vast sea, heads south to avoid North Atlantic gales. Then she points northeast. She points to verdant, luxurious England.

POSTSCRIPT

In 1617 the non-fictional Richard Seymour (or Seymer) became the secretary to Sir Henry Wotton, the ambassador to Venice, a man known as a poet, wit, and diplomat. (It was Wotton who wrote, "An ambassador is an honest gentleman sent to lie abroad for the good of his country.") It is unknown when Seymour married his non-fictional wife, Jane Washington, though it was probably late in life, as his son Spencer was a minor when Richard wrote his will in 1641 at the age of fifty-seven. During his adulthood Richard Seymour apparently lived in London. He was also jailed in the first English Civil war for being on the Loyalist side. It is also unknown if his wife was an ancestor of the first President of the United States. It is possible he also married earlier. His death is apparently unrecorded.

Robert Seymour, Richard's elder brother, built a manor house that is now the home of the Hanford School in Dorset. He was knighted.

Not coincidentally, in 1937—the same year Charles Seymour was installed as Yale's President—the University honored Richard Seymour for using the ritual of the Church of England in New England some thirteen years before the Mayflower.

Many of the American Seymours, including myself, are descendants of another Richard Seymour, a Puritan from Sawbridgeworth, Hertfordshire. This Richard Seymour arrived in Cambridge in 1637 and soon after moved to Hartford, Connecticut, and then Norwalk.

Genealogy is often a murky matter. It is unclear what the relationship was between the ducal family's Queen Jane Seymour, Richard Seymour of the Popham Colony, and the Richard Seymour who arrived in New England twenty-nine years after Fort St. George was abandoned. However, all three families utilized the same family crest as the Seymours of Wolf Hall—that is Jane Seymour's father's—the conjoined wings of the phoenix rising. All descended from Norman St. Maurs of Penhow Castle in Wales. It has been speculated that the two Richard Seymours who traveled to the northern New World in the early part of the seventeenth century were cousins. It is also likely that this novel's Richard Seymour was cousin to Raleigh Gilbert.

It is also possible that Richard tutored Skidwarres and they became friends. Unfortunately, Robert Davies' account of the first three months has a dead ear for personal relations.

The Mawooshen living between what are now the Kennebec and the Penobscot Rivers were decimated by disease around 1617. Many survivors moved north to the St. Lawrence Valley. Bessabez was murdered by the Micmacs in 1615. There is some evidence that Skidwarres continued to live in the Maine coastal region until the English and French began populating it in the 1640s.

The "Mawooshen territory" later became occupied by the Abenaki, whose villages prior to the seventeenth century were located at the more northern regions of the Sagadahoc.

During early Maine history, its largest river had two names: the northern section was called the Kennebec, the southern section the Sagadahoc.

Admiral Raleigh Gilbert returned to Compton Castle in Marldon, Devon. There he married an Elizabeth Kelly. In ten years they had seven children. We do know that he became a member of Ferdinando Gorges' Council for New England. Beyond that little is known. Raleigh Gilbert died in 1634 at the age of fifty-one.

Compton Castle remains occupied by the Gilbert family, though the National Trust now owns and manages the property. Geoffrey and Angela Gilbert's three children, now young adults, make up the ninth generation since Raleigh Gilbert. In 2011 it was unclear whether any of them would continue to maintain the tradition. Geoffrey kindly spent two hours with me, my wife Rosie, and Douglas Rice. We toured the castle and the beautiful hilly grounds.

Sir Ferdinando Gorges became known as "the Father of English Colonization" in North America. In 1622 he received a land patent, along with John Mason, from the Plymouth Council of New England for the Province of Maine. The original boundaries were between the Merrimack and Kennebec Rivers. In 1629 he and Mason divided the colony, with Mason's portion south of the Piscataqua River becoming the Province of New Hampshire. The "founder" of Maine never set foot in the New World. Gorges died rather destitute in 1647. His grandson sold to Massachusetts all rights to Maine for approximately twenty-five hundred dollars.

The Virginia, *the first ship built in the New World leaving the Sagadahoc (Kennebec) River.*

NOTES

Introduction

It wasn't until 1612 that Robert Davies' "Relation of a Voyage to Sagadahoc" appeared in a report put together by William Strachey, "The historie of travaile into Virginia Britannia." Sir Francis Bacon received one of the three copies, but not until 1618. One might expect Raleigh Gilbert or Richard Seymour to put to paper something, or Davis himself—who did return in the summer of 1608 to Fort St. George, and later became a member of the Jamestown Colony. If so, nothing has been found. Even Sir Ferdinando Gorges apparently wrote little to clarify matters, assuming he knew.

The definitive story of the early colonization of New England can be found in *The New England Voyages* (1983) by David B. and Alison M. Quinn. They lace together original documents with many helpful footnotes. The Quinns tell us time and again how difficult verifying historical fact can be. How many occupied the fort? One hundred, or as many as one hundred and forty? Do we count the sailors? How many cannon, nine or twelve? Violence between native and Englishman, perhaps? Stories crop up. Were eleven English murdered by natives? So one story has it, according to a Frenchman who heard it from a native. Natives mistreated or killed—or perhaps threatened by Gilbert's Mastiffs? The minutiae of history, much less human motivation, are elusive.

In 1994 Jeffery Brain of the Peabody Museum in Salem, Massachusetts headed an archaeological investigation. Before then no absolute proof existed that the spit of land facing Atkins Bay contained remains of Fort St. George. Brain's 2007 publication provides a concise history, as well as a detailed account of the dig. We now know that the remarkable site drawings made by a John Hunt, a member of the Popham Colony, accurately depicted the locations of the storehouse, Raleigh Gilbert's house, and the chapel, as well as the moat and the stream that became the fort's main source of water. Hunt's rendering disappeared into the hands of the Spanish ambassador to England in October of 1607. Nearly three centuries later, it appeared in the Spanish archives at Simancas—suggesting, to some, a spy was at work.

Very concrete artifacts, as well as a copy of Hunt's drawing, are exhibited at the Maine State Museum. These include musket balls, gun parts, pieces of engraved copper, an iron helmet cheek piece, iron ship's building tools, nails, and many pieces of glass— once flasks and wine bottles found near the Admiral's house, proving how gentlemen did their best to transport the good life to the New World.

Chapter 19 of Douglas Rice's *The Life and Achievements of Sir John Popham, 1531-1607* provides the most comprehensive and unified published account of the Popham Colony.

Below I include a few more historical facts. Some chapters are omitted, as they are essentially fictional.

CHAPTER 1

***Douglas W. Rice's biography, *The Life and Achievement of Sir John Popham, 1531-1607*, helped me immensely—though I fear by turning his meticulous prose into slippery fiction, I might be doing him a disservice. Douglas and his wife, Allison, hosted my wife Rosie and me for five days in June of 2011. Sight unseen they fed, bedded, and then provided a four-day tour of the countryside, including John and Amy Popham's resting place in Wellington Church. The Pophams' colorful wooden effigies lie perpetually at state, hands pressed together in prayer, eyes open and feet hovering miraculously a few inches in the air, so not to mar their robes.

Sir John Popham was the substantial person I depict. He did boast of being a highwayman in his youth. He did manage the lethal delicacy of Elizabethan politics. His reputation as a "hanging judge" Rice tells us is well deserved. He did play many roles successfully. And we learned upon death his body vanished. The coffin below his effigy is empty.

The portrait of Sir John Popham hanging at the Harvard Law School Library, Rice believes, is a fake. Yet again, in death the man eludes us. I have tried to give the reader an accurate account of Sir John, though by necessity I have turned to the probable and possible. I have no way to prove he lusted into his old age. It certainly was not beyond his class—or any class, for that matter.

***Richard Seymour was born 1584 in Hanford, Dorset. He matriculated at Oxford in 1599, then studied at Middle Temple, where he may well have attended the first production of Shakespeare's Twelfth Night in 1602.

Richard's parents are as depicted: father, John Seymour, and mother, Agnes Rawles. They had nine daughters and four sons, the eldest Sir Robert Seymour.

***Skidwarres was among the five kidnapped and brought to England in 1605 by George Weymouth. The four others were Nahanada, sagamore or leader of the Pemaquid village, as well as Manida, Amoret, and Saffacomoit (These names have been spelled in various ways.) Nahanada returned to his home a year before Skidwarres in a voyage led by a well known captain of the time, Martin Pring. It is a fact that Sir John took interest in these natives, especially Skidwarres and Nahanada.

***Probably Sir John Popham selected the twenty-three year old Richard Seymour as the unordained chaplain. As Jeffrey Brain points out in *Fort St. George, Archaeological Investigation of the 1607-1608 Popham Colony*, the Seymours, the Gorges, the Gilberts, the Raleighs, and the Pophams were all related to the Champernowne family. The Popham colony relied upon nepotism—though this did not necessarily imply a diminished capacity. Brain, among others including John Bradford, who has studied the Popham Colony for years, concluded these were indeed qualified men.

***The description of being drawn and quartered can be found in Douglas Rice's biography of Popham.

***Michel de Montaigne lived in southwestern France between 1533 and 1592. His personal, philosophical essays had been translated to English by the beginning of the seventeenth century. As an Oxford and Middle Temple student, Seymour probably read him. The subject matter includes among others, "Of Friendship," "Of Cannibals," "Of Custom of Wearing Clothes," "How to Cry and Laugh for the Same Thing," "Of Smells," "Of Cruelty," and "How Our Minds Hinders Itself."

CHAPTER 2

***The Ship Inn remains around the corner from the Cathedral at Exeter.

***A replica of the Hind rests next to the Globe Theater on the Thames River.

***In John Popham's biography, Douglas Rice tells the story of Francis Drake and Sir John Popham's son-in-law, Richard Champernowne.

***Douglas Rice and John Bradford both confirm that George Popham was Sir John Popham's nephew, though it took some genealogical sleuthing to be sure. It is also likely he became a privateer as well as "Her Majesty's Customer of the Port of Bridgewater." Ferdinando refers to him as an "ould" man.

CHAPTER 3

The history of the Seymour family is drawn from the following sources: *The Puritan Migration to Connecticut: The Saga of the Seymour Family 1129-1746* by Malcolm Seymour; *The Last Days of Henry VIII* by Robert Hutchinson; *History of the Seymour Family—Appendix IV: Richard Seymer of the Popham Colony*, by Geo. Dudley Seymour; *A History of England From the Tudors to the Stuarts*, from the Great Courses Audio Series by Robert Buccholz.

As with John Seymour, Richard's father, I found it difficult to distinguish rumor from fact when it comes to the particulars of Edward and Thomas's slide to decapitation. The compelling Tudor era probably has spawned more books—and rumors—than any other in English history.

***I am unable to prove a connection between Richard's father and Queen Jane.

***Jane, on Henry's lap, appears in most historical accounts and as well as the HBO Series, *The Tudors*.

***Henry's quip, about it being easier to find a wife than a male heir, is a fine example of myth and history. The quote abounds, though I came across no proof. The best evidence suggests he held Jane in great esteem, in good part for her production of King Edward VI.

***In fact, Sir John Popham did provide funds for the building of a dorm at Middle Temple, inhabited mostly by young gentlemen from the West Country.

CHAPTER 4

***Historical record provides a number of names for Abenaki males, but little is known about female names. Dr. Bruce Bourque, archeologist for the Maine State Museum and an expert on native history and prehistory, suggested I consider names from nature. I've taken his advice.

***For a period of time Francis Bacon lived at Gray's Inn, one of the Inns at Court associated with Middle Temple. It is possible, if not probably, he and Seymour met.

CHAPTER 5

***I adopted the name Mawooshen from Ginn and Ginns' *The English New England Voyages, 1602-1608*. It describes the territory roughly between the Sagadahoc (Kennebec) River and the Penobscot River. I have no evidence the inhabitants referred to themselves as Mawooshen. It was an area from Mount Desert to Lake Megantic, so couldn't have been home to a single people. All natives in Maine are now considered Eastern Abenaki. Their language derives from the Protoalgonquian tongue, which was spoken in the Eastern Great Lakes between two and three thousand years ago. Of course, as with any long-term migration, groups developed their own dialect.

As Bourque points out, we rely upon Europeans for the written record, the French being more reliable than the English, at least when dealing with ethnic divisions. During the beginning of the Seventeenth Century, in what is now Nova Scotia, lived the Souriquois, called by the English the Tarrentines and later the Micmacs. These peoples established trading relationships, primarily with the French and Basques. They learned to sail small sailing vessels and use firearms. As a result they wielded some hostile advantage over their western neighbors

West, of the Souriquois regions, somewhere between the St. John River and the Sagadahoc, lived the Etchemins. This region included the Mawooshen People. Later on in the seventeenth century, the eastern Etchemins were named the Malicites; the western Etchemins, between the Penobscot and Kennebec (some of whom were Mawooshen), became known as the Canibas.

Still further West, beyond the Sagadahoc, now the Kennebec, lived the Almochiniquois, or at least that is what the Souriguois called them. Almochiniquois translates to "dog people," then more of an insult than it might be today. "This group's territory," as Bourque describes, "began at the Androscoggin River. They were linguistically and culturally distinct from the neighbors to the east, wearing different clothing and hairstyles, using some dugouts in addition to birch bark canoes, and practicing horticulture to a greater extent. This group extended west and south to the Massachusetts." In my story I consider Sabenoa a member of the Almochiniquois, though he holds the Mawooshen Bessabez in esteem.

Some fifty miles north on the Kennebec, above present day Augusta, lived the Abenaki. Their cultural and trading connections were more aligned with Quebec. In later years, after much disruption due to wars, English settlement, disease and migration, all natives in what is now Maine were referred to as Abenaki—or to make things even more convoluted, Wabenaki, Penobscot, and Passamaquoddy.

In short, establishing names for an aboriginal, hunting and gathering people is murky business. History is dynamic. Names change. I chose Mawooshen in part because historical record states Skidwarres and Nahanada used the term. Besides, I simply like the sound: Mawooshen.

Regarding native history, I recommend Dr. Bruce Bourque's Twelve Thousands Years, American Indians in Maine, especially chapters IV and V.

CHAPTER 6

***The social mores for Native Americans living at the time of early exploration and colonization are difficult to ascertain. Given what we know about other native cultures and Native Americans more generally, plus the spotty reports from early explorers such as Verrazano and Champlain, sex before marriage would be taken lightly and with humor by the Mawooshen, at least compared with the English.

In *Sex and Sexuality in Early America*, edited by Merrill Smith, we learn Verrazano in 1524 describes the women in what is now Maine as "beautiful...they go naked except for stag skins" and are more "elusive" compared with natives in Central and South America. It is also reported that native women would be traded for goods, and that they had forms of contraception. Skidwarres story of the depressed woman being "cured" by adolescents making love in her hut is also told in *Sex and Sexuality in Early America*.

Richard's comment about the "blind fury" of love derives from the writing of a Lescarbot, who traveled to Acadia in 1607.

Of course all reports of the New World come with a certain amount of cultural blindness and hyperbole—perhaps, fired by testosterone.

CHAPTER 11
*** The men at the table did in fact sail on May 31, 1607.

CHAPTER 12
***The description of the *Gift of God* is based on details drawn from the *Mayflower*, a similar ship.

CHAPTER 14
*** The quotes are from Sir Walter Raleigh's *Discovery of Guiana*. However, George Popham stretches the story. Popham did travel the Orinoco, only his and Raleigh's ships traveled a few months apart. After being released from prison Raleigh did return, but for the second time came back empty-handed. The king had him arrested for disobeying orders. Back again to the Tower, only this time to lose his head.

Some centuries later, gold was discovered in the Orinoco regions traveled by Popham and Raleigh.

CHAPTER 15
***During the encounter with the Dutch, Raleigh Gilbert was abducted for a short period. In Davies' journal, English sailors working under the Dutch flag come to his rescue. George Popham's escape did, in fact, irk Admiral Raleigh.

CHAPTER 18
*** "Swordfish Fights Whales" is drawn from *The New York Times,* Nov. 2, 1896.

CHAPTER 19
***As planned, the two ships did anchor off what is now Allen Island near Pemaquid, where earlier Captain Weymouth had constructed a cross and abducted five natives.

CHAPTER 20
***The English did trade with natives sailing an old Basque shallop. Though its likely young English boys were part of the crew and didn't know how to swim, the drowning is fictional.

***The return of Skidwarres to his village, the hospitality offered by the natives, followed by growing tensions, are described by Robert Davies in his journal. Skidwarres refused Gilbert's demand to sail with them but agreed to remain with the English for one more day.

CHAPTER 22
***Seymour delivered the first Anglican sermon in New England on Allen Island.

***When Skidwarres was returned, Davies' journal describes the natives as suspicious, at first not allowing more than a few English to land. After negotiations, more English came ashore, followed by the inexplicable disappearance of Nahanada's people.

***The two ships did encounter a storm near the Sagadahoc (Kennebec) River.

CHAPTER 24
*** The date of the landing and the reading of the Charter is historical fact.

CHAPTER 27
***Work did begin almost immediately. And "savages" —men, women and children—did arrive. A church service was held, though I can't vouch for the one described.

CHAPTER 28
***Though Sipsis is a fictitious character, it is possible someone of her generation could have had a French grandfather. French traders and clerics had for decades traded in the Mawooshen area.

CHAPTER 29
***There is no evidence that Popham or Gilbert traded for women. However, Davies' journal had a tin ear for personal relationships, nor would this type of

personal matter be included. Trading and kidnapping women was an accepted native practice at the turn of the seventeenth century.

CHAPTER 31

***Gilbert did explore the Sagadahoc. It is unclear to me if he reached the falls at what is now Augusta or, as others have suggested, at Brunswick. Most believe the description better suits the Augusta area.

***During this voyage, Gilbert encountered the Lord of the Sagadahoc. In Quinn's *New England Voyages*, he is called Sabenoa. The name Sabino appears as well. Probably these are one and the same, given how spellings varied so during Elizabethan times. The meeting did nearly come to violence. Davies' journal provides the outline for this chapter. Some details, such as Sabenoa jumping into the shallop and the native snatching the fire box, are recorded by Davies. The location of Sabenoa's village is unknown, though the area around what is now Bowdoinham on Merrymeeting Bay would have been ideal, due to its abundance of fish, fowl, sea rice, and cultivatable land. And there is some evidence he lived along the Androscoggin.

CHAPTER 33

***Stories crop up about murdered English. In one account, eleven are killed by surprise, though this story is just that, a story told by a native to a Frenchman years later.

CHAPTERS 35

***The *Mary and John* did set sail on October 8, 1607, taking with her an unknown number of men. Robert Davies, the author of the only recorded account of the Popham Colony, was on board.

CHAPTER 39

***Buildings, the storehouse, and Gilbert's quarters in particular, did burn—for this there is archeological evidence—though when and under what circumstances is unknown.

CHAPTER 40

***Skidwarres' captivity and acculturation to things English are recorded facts, while all details of his whirlwind education and his psychological state upon return are imagined. As is, of course, his relationship with Seymour.

CHAPTER 44

***Lack of food is a known fact. The story that a fire destroyed some food is one that has been handed down. It is also likely that Sabenoa's village grew more crops than the villages to the east of the Kennebec. Also, as has been stated, hostilities, even warfare between natives groups was common.

CHAPTER 45

***The *Gift of God* did sail back, taking approximately half the men. George Popham's flamboyantly optimistic letter to King James has been slightly edited. The story of the rough passage, of having to sell much of the cargo to pay for repairs, and the failed lawsuit brought against the captain by John Popham's wife and son, all this is true and documented.

CHAPTER 48

***The winter of 1607–1608 in both England and Northern Virginia was extremely cold. Apparently no English died of disease or malnutrition.

CHAPTER 50

***The cause of George Popham's death is unknown. It must be assumed he was buried in or near the fort when the ground thawed.

CHAPTER 54

***May 12, 1608 did see the return of the two ships carrying provisions and some extra men—women, perhaps not. The specifics are not known. Of course the ship came with the first news of Sir John Popham's death, though it had occurred nearly a year before.

CHAPTER 59

***There is nothing written about the return of these ships. If Richard was on board to further Gilbert's cause, nothing has been written of it.

CHAPTER 61

***The Seymours did reside in Hanford, though "Ram's Head" is fiction.

***The ditty about English place names is of my own doing. The names are real.

CHAPTER 63

***The material about the Revels, including the song "Bring hither the bowl..." is drawn from historical documents. Richard probably took part in these activities and may have rubbed elbows with William Shakespeare.

CHAPTER 64

***Sirs Gorges, Bacon, and Cecil knew one another well and demonstrated a mutual interest in exploration and colonization. Their meeting with Seymour is fiction. The scuttlebutt about King James is drawn from historical documents.

CHAPTER 65

***The business relationship between Walter Raleigh and John Popham is described in Douglas Rice's biography of Popham. The possible poisoning of Popham cannot be entirely discounted. His death remains a mystery.

CHAPTER 66

***The number of people who returned in the summer, the nature of the contents of the ship, and the amount of money raised are unknown.

CHAPTER 67

***Raleigh Gilbert's brother's death is a fact, and no doubt had great bearing on the colony's abandonment.

CHAPTERS 71

***The tidal stream bisecting Popham Beach State Park and the Bates–Morse Mountain Conservation Area no doubt existed in some form four hundred years ago. It meanders and splits. One section loops, shallows and finally disappears into the sea grass. The other section becomes Spirit Pond, which is nearly all mud flat at low tide.

CHAPTER 81

***The decision to leave remains a mystery. The oncoming cold winter and the death of both Pophams and Raleigh Gilbert's brother were no doubt major factors; so were the political and commercial realities. In 1608 the survival of Jamestown was not at all certain.

CHAPTER 82

***As mentioned, archeological evidence proves at least sections of the storehouse and Gilbert's quarters were burned, but there is no telling when or by whom. One story has a few solders tricking a few natives. As a result, a large quantity of gun powder exploded, killing or injuring some. Another story has a few or even as many as fifty occupants of the fort remaining in the New World, either on Monhegan Island or near the natives at Pemaquid. Again this is mostly conjecture. The next year-round English settlement of the Sagadahoc probably didn't occur until after 1616, and then only in the form of small villages or isolated farms.

***The presentation of the native's backsides does have historical record. Giovanni da Verrazano, in 1524, describes a similar display. He is the first European explorer on record to visit Maine.

***The *Virginia* did cross to England under the command of Robert Davies. He then sailed her back to Jamestown. A replica of the *Virginia* is under construction in Bath, Maine. For further information contact Maine's First Ship: **www.mfship.org**

REFERENCES

Bradford, John W, Excerpt from a Manuscript in Process Entitled "The Popham Colony in Context," 2003

Bradford, John W, *The 1607 Popham Colony's Pinnace Virginia: an In-Context Design of Maine's First Ship*, Maine Authors Publishing, 2011

Bourque, Bruce J, *Twelve Thousand Years: American Indians in Maine,* University of Nebraska Press, 2001

Brain, Jeffrey Phipps, *Fort St. George, Archaeological Investigation of the 1607_1608 Popham Colony,* Occasional Publications in *Maine Archaeology* Number 12, 2007

Bucholz, Robert, *History of England from Tudors to the Stuart,* from the Great Courses Audio Series

Hardy, Kerry, *Notes on a Lost Flute: A Field Guide to the Wabanaki,* Down East Publications, 2009

Hutchinson, Robert, *The Last Days of Henry VIII: Conspiracy, Treason and Heresy at the Court of the Dying Tyrant,* Phoenix Press, 2006

Masta, Henry Lorne, *Abenaki Indian Legends, Grammar and Place Names,* Global Language Press, 1932

Montaigne, Michel de, *The Essays: A Selection*, Penguin Classics, 2004

Parker, Philip, *Webster's Abenaki–English Thesaurus Dictionary*, ICON Group International, 2008

Quinn, David and Quinn, Alison, *The English New England Voyages: 1602–1608*, The Hakluyt Society, London, 1983

Raleigh, Walter, *The Discovery of Guiana*

Rice, Douglas Walthew, *The Life and Achievement of Sir John Popham, 1531–1607*, Fairleigh Dickinson University Press, 2005

Seymour, George Dudley, *The History of the Seymour Family*, Yale University, 1939

Seymour, Malcolm, *Puritan Migration to Connecticut: the Saga of the Seymour Family 1129–1746*, 1982

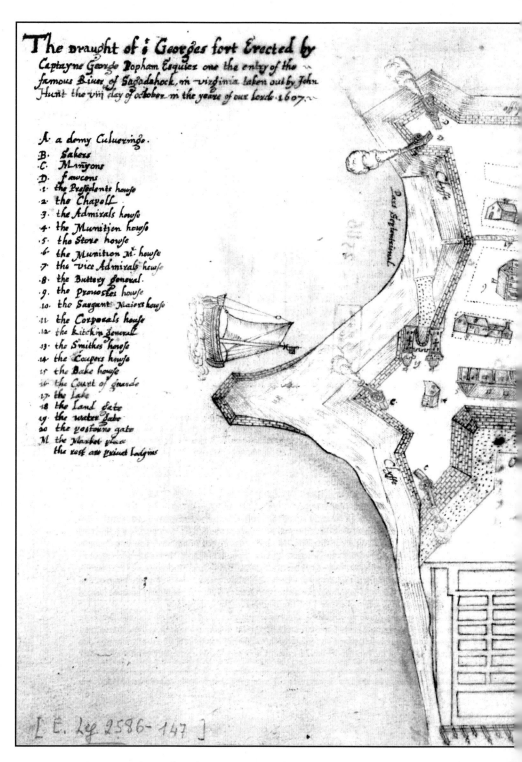

Fort St. George, as drawn by John Hunt on October, 1607, and acquired by the Spanish Ambassador to England. It was subsequently deposited in the Spanish archives at Simancas and rediscovered three centuries later.

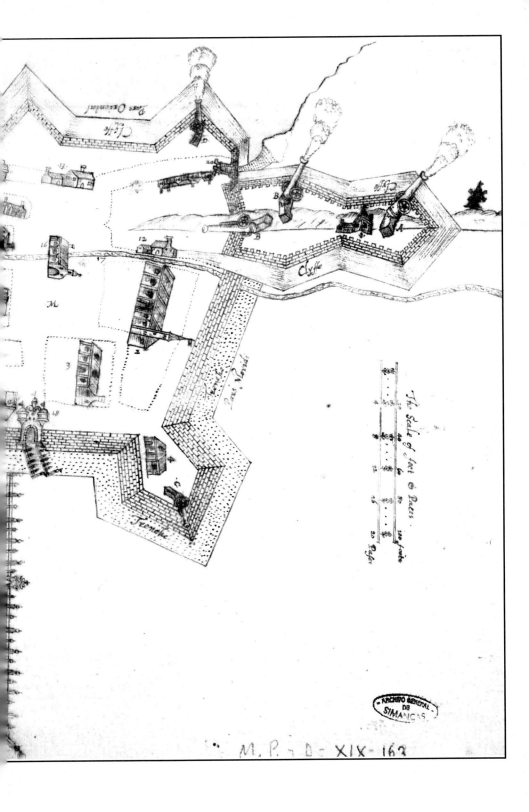

M. P. y D. XIX - 163